B

D0524521

Michelle Do... ... ... Boon since 2007, and ... ... world. She lives in a ... ... of ... ... Australia's east coast, with her own romantic hero, a house full of dust and books and an eclectic collection of sixties and seventies vinyl. She loves to hear from readers and can be contacted via her website: michelle-douglas.com.

Brenda Harlen is a former attorney who once had the privilege of appearing before the Supreme Court of Canada. The practice of law taught her a lot about the world and reinforced her determination to become a writer—because in fiction, she could promise a happy ending! Now she is an award-winning, RITA® Award–nominated national bestselling author of more than ... ...itles for Mills & Boon. You can keep up-to-date ... renda on Facebook and Twitter or through her ...ite, brendaharlen.com.

Also by **Michelle Douglas**

Snowbound Surprise for the Billionaire
The Millionaire and the Maid
Reunited by a Baby Secret
A Deal to Mend Their Marriage
An Unlikely Bride for the Billionaire
The Spanish Tycoon's Takeover
Sarah and the Secret Sheikh
A Baby in His In-Tray

The Wild Ones miniseries
Her Irresistible Protector
The Rebel and the Heiress

Also by **Brenda Harlen**

The Sheriff's Nine-Month Surprise
The Last Single Garrett
Baby Talk & Wedding Bells
Building the Perfect Daddy
Two Doctors & a Baby
The Maverick's Midnight Proposal
The More Mavericks, The Merrier!
Merry Christmas, Baby Maverick!

Discover more at millsandboon.co.uk

THE MILLION POUND MARRIAGE DEAL

MICHELLE DOUGLAS

SIX WEEKS TO CATCH A COWBOY

BRENDA HARLEN

MILLS & BOON

All rights reserved including the right of reproduction in whole or in part in any form. This edition is published by arrangement with Harlequin Books S.A. This is a work of fiction. Names, characters, places and incidents are either the product of the author's imagination or are used fictitiously and any resemblance to actual persons, living or dead, business establishments, events or locales is entirely coincidental.

This book is sold subject to the condition that it shall not, by way of trade or otherwise, be lent, resold, hired out or otherwise circulated without the prior consent of the publisher in any form of binding or cover other than that in which it is published and without a similar condition including this condition being imposed on the subsequent purchaser.

® and TM are trademarks owned and used by the trademark owner and/or its licensee. Trademarks marked with ® are registered with the United Kingdom Patent Office and/or the Office for Harmonisation in the Internal Market and in other countries.

First Published in Great Britain 2018
by Mills & Boon, an imprint of HarperCollinsPublishers,
1 London Bridge Street, London, SE1 9GF

The Million Pound Marriage Deal © 2018 Michelle Douglas
The Fortune Most Likely To... © 2018 Brenda Harlen

ISBN: 978-0-263-26525-5

0918

MIX
Paper from
responsible sources
FSC™ C007454

This book is produced from independently certified FSC™
paper to ensure responsible forest management.

For more information visit: www.harpercollins.co.uk/green

Printed and bound in Spain
by CPI, Barcelona

THE
MILLION POUND
MARRIAGE DEAL

MICHELLE DOUGLAS

ROTHERHAM LIBRARY SERVICE	
B53109253	
Bertrams	01/08/2018
AF	£5.99
SWI	ROM

In memory of James (Jim) Morris 23/4/51–21/11/17, who is sadly missed by all who knew and loved him.

CHAPTER ONE

A QUICK GLANCE around the Soho restaurant informed Sophie that she'd arrived first—which was unusual.

'And that's a gold star for me,' she murmured under her breath, before sending a smile to the approaching waiter. 'I believe there's a reservation in the name of Trent-Paterson.'

'Certainly, madam.'

He didn't even need to check the reservation book, but led her across the room to a table set in an alcove and screened from the rest of the room by palms. Knowing Will, it was probably the best table in the house. She wondered if this was one of the places where he normally brought his women.

Not that they were *his* women, of course. It was just that there was such a parade of them in and out of his life.

You can't talk.

She bit back a sigh.

The restaurant was upmarket, *of course*, and eschewed modern minimalist lines that were currently in vogue, celebrating instead a colonial décor popular over a century ago. It reminded her of Raffles in Singapore. Minus the heat and humidity. This wasn't the kind of establishment that needed to justify itself. She took a seat.

'Can I get you a drink, madam?'

'Yes, please. A sparkling mineral water would be lovely.'

He blinked before his face became a smooth mask again. Ah…so he recognised her too, huh? She resisted the urge to tease him. *New leaf, remember?*

She glanced through the screen of palms at the rest of the room and shook her head. 'Horrible,' she murmured. Normally she and Will met in the café at the Tate Modern. Where they could stare out at the vista spread before them rather than at each other.

And where occasionally their shoulders would bump. Accidentally, of course—Will would never purposely touch his best friend's little sister. Especially not now Peter was dead. But those accidental moments always made her feel less alone.

'Crazy,' she murmured. 'Also you have to stop talking to yourself like this or someone will overhear.' She thought about that for a moment and then shrugged. 'So what?'

It wasn't like a century ago, when they could've had her committed for such eccentricity. Besides, she'd been called far less savoury things than *crazy* by the press… and her father.

She watched the waiter return with both her mineral water and Will, and missed the Tate Modern's café with its view over a grey city. But today called for more salubrious surroundings. Today was Peter's birthday.

Maybe that was why she felt so claustrophobic amid all this airy, white-shuttered cane and palm expansiveness.

Will couldn't see her as well as she could see him, but she tried not to study him too intently anyway, though the temptation lurked at the edges of her consciousness. As usual her heart-rate picked up speed at the sight of those impossibly broad shoulders, long legs and lean hips. William Trent-Paterson was built along lines that made every woman in the room stand to attention, figuratively speaking. A woman had once told her that she ovulated every single time she clapped eyes on Will.

She tried to ignore all thoughts of ovulation, eggs and procreation. Regardless of what Will looked like she knew that, as usual, his lips would press into a thin line when he saw her.

'Such a shame,' she murmured, because, actually, she really liked him. Still, she'd love to see him run to fat. Just a little bit. Just one flaw—that was all she asked. Maybe then she'd feel on more of an even footing with him.

You might as well ask for the moon.

'Sophie,' he said when he reached her.

As predicted those lips pinched together. So did the skin around his eyes. It was a double shame because he had a nice smile, though she rarely saw it.

'Hello, Will.'

She rose and they gave each other perfunctory pecks on the cheeks, keeping the width of the table between them. A rush of lime and a darker musky note flooded her senses. She pulled back and planted herself in her chair again and tried to ignore the heavy thud-thud of the pulse in her throat.

It was like this *every single time*—the stilted distance and the heart thudding.

She suspected it was because there was no other person on the planet who had loved Peter as much as she had... except for Will.

And her father, but that was too difficult.

Since the viciousness of her parents' separation and subsequent divorce when she was eleven and Peter sixteen—when the only thing her parents were focused on was hurting each other—she and Peter had turned to each other. They'd seemed to realise they had no other family to rely on. She'd done her best to stop him from growing too grave and serious, while he'd done his best to stop her from feeling as if she didn't measure up. She'd looked up to him so much. Had depended on him.

And now he was gone...

She couldn't believe the hole it had left in her life.

It made her think that she and Will should hold each other tight on the occasions they did see each other, take comfort in each other. But it was never like that.

Because Will didn't really like her.

But some strange sense of honour kept them in touch, some respect for Peter they weren't prepared to surrender.

Would he be relieved if she hadn't shown up—if she just stopped turning up for their monthly coffee dates and occasional lunches? Would he feel he'd discharged some unspoken duty to Peter and was now off the hook? The thought made her heart ache. She couldn't stop coming. He was one of her last links to Peter. And Peter was the only person who had truly loved her for who she was.

She couldn't let that go. She couldn't let Peter go, which meant she couldn't let Will go. And she wanted to tell him she was sorry for that, sorry if that made things difficult for him.

But she didn't. Because it would make him uncomfortable…and she didn't want to do anything that would make him uncomfortable. She'd like to make him smile if she could.

'You look glum.'

That slammed her back to the present. 'Sorry, just feeling a bit wistful for…for what could've been.'

He closed his eyes and pinched the bridge of his nose, and she realised he'd thought she was referring to Peter. *Make things more cheerful.*

She waved to encompass the restaurant. 'I've not been here before.'

He straightened. 'Do you like it?'

'It's lovely,' she said, because she was always on her best behaviour with Will.

Amazingly he laughed. 'You hate it.'

'Well, the fact of the matter is I'm starved. So as long as the food is good, I don't care about anything else.'

Those lips pressed back into a tight line. 'Traditionally you barely touch any of your food.'

'Today I can promise you that I'll clean my plate.' *New leaf.*

He raised a sardonic eyebrow. 'You're planning on ordering the green salad and nothing else?'

She snapped her menu closed. 'I'm having the lamb.'

'Excellent choice, I'll have the same.' He handed the waiter his menu, his eyes not leaving hers. 'How's your father?'

Here began the ritual questions. She pushed down a sigh. Just once she'd like… She pushed that thought down too. 'Triumphant that I've been forced to toe the line and run all of his foreseeable charity events.'

For the moment. Beneath the table she twisted her watch around and around on her wrist. She needed a way to find a lot of money fast. Really fast. And she had no idea how she was going to do it. Her father paid her a generous allowance for acting as his event planner, but it was nowhere near enough to help Carla in any practical way…to make amends to the other woman. And she wasn't stupid enough to ask her father for a loan. He'd take too much delight in telling her that she was a carbon copy of her mother and to go to blazes.

Dark eyes surveyed her across the table. 'That's nobody's fault but your own.'

True, but… 'A more gallant man would've refrained from pointing that out.'

'I don't feel like being gallant today, Sophie. I feel like smashing something.'

Her ears perked up. Wow, that was out of character. *Interesting.*

But then he shook himself and asked, 'How's Carla?'

Her appetite fled at the mention of Peter's fiancée. She stared at the screen of palms rather than at him, pain throbbing in the back of her throat. She'd been toying with her bread knife, but she carefully set it back down, afraid that if she didn't she'd stab herself in the leg. Which was no more than she deserved, but *that* might get her committed. Besides it wouldn't help anyone. She couldn't abscond from responsibility. Not this time.

'That good, huh?'

Carla was in drug rehab—drug rehab Sophie had to try and find the money for—but Carla had sworn her to secrecy and Sophie owed her that much. At the very least. Self-loathing bloomed in her chest. How could she have let things get so out of hand? How could she have been so blind? How could she have let Carla—and Peter—down so spectacularly?

She pressed her hands together to stop them from shaking. 'She can't let the memory of Peter go.'

'And we can?'

The words burst from him, unexpected, and Sophie flinched, throwing up an arm as if to ward off the words.

Silence pounded between them.

Eventually Will cleared his throat. 'I'm sorry.'

She could feel the weight of his gaze, but she didn't want to meet it. She adjusted her cutlery instead. 'It's a valid point,' she squeezed out from a tight throat. 'But it's only been two years.' It was too soon for forgetting…for letting go.

From the corner of her eyes she saw him drag a hand back through dark auburn hair. 'I'm starting to think that us continuing to meet like this isn't doing anybody any good, and that—'

'No!'

Her gaze flew to his, snagged and held.

'Please,' she whispered. To her absolute horror tears slid down her cheeks and she wanted to close her eyes and will the floor to swallow her whole. She hadn't let him see her cry, not since the funeral. In the humiliation of the moment she wanted to get up and walk out of this horrible restaurant, but she had to stop what he was trying to do.

'Please, Will, I'm not ready to give this up.' The thought of it filled her with panic. 'Please don't bring an end to… this. I can't—' She swallowed down a sob. 'I know it's uncomfortable. And I know I'm a trial.'

She'd been a trial to every person in her life. Except Peter. She'd try harder not to be a trial to Will in the future. 'But, you see, you loved him. And I loved him. And remembering that, having proof—' *recognition* '—helps.'

His skin had gone grey and his jaw clenched so hard it made her feel sick.

She mopped at her cheeks. 'Will you excuse me while I go find the ladies'?'

He nodded.

'Will you be here when I get back?'

She held her breath until he gave another hard nod. Without another word she fled to the ladies' room, only giving herself enough time to splash some cold water onto overheated cheeks and to repair her eyeliner. Thank God for waterproof mascara!

'I'm sorry,' she said, sliding into her seat again. Their meal had arrived while she'd been away, and she spread her linen serviette across her lap and lifted her knife and fork. 'Today is always a tough day. I'm sorry that you bore the brunt of my dissatisfaction with it.'

'I'm sorry I wasn't more sensitive.'

He wanted to throttle her. She wasn't sure how she could tell—the hard set of his shoulders maybe combined with the deep burning in his eyes.

'How's Carol Ann?' she asked.

'Fully recovered from her surgery. She loved the set of DVDs you sent her. Though from all accounts the rest of the household are being driven insane.'

That made her grin. Carol Ann was Will's younger sister and the same age as Sophie, but she had Down's syndrome with all of the associated health issues that entailed. Sophie had only met her a few times, but she sent her birthday and Christmas cards…and gifts on the few occasions she'd been hospitalised. They spoke on the phone. Her last gift had been a DVD box set of musicals. 'I'm glad they've been such a hit. The world needs more *The King and I*.'

He almost smiled so she counted that as an almost win.

'How's your grandfather?'

All signs of humour drained from him and she winced. 'The grapevine informs me that he's been making another push to get you to settle down.'

'Good news travels fast. I supposed you were at Catriona McManus's thirtieth last weekend.'

Nope. She'd given up wild times and painting the town red. She was avoiding parties, other than the ones her father was forcing her to plan, organise and host on his behalf. It was all a part of her turning over a new leaf. But that didn't mean she could avoid the rumour mill completely. 'So it's true, then?'

'This time he's given me an ultimatum.'

A forkful of lamb halted halfway to her mouth. 'What kind of ultimatum?'

'Either I marry within the next twelve months and take over the reins of the estate or he's going to give everything to Harold.'

Harold was Will's weasel of a cousin. Her mind raced. Will didn't need the money—he was a squillionaire in his own right. He'd never shown the least interest in inheriting the estate, but… She lowered her cutlery. 'What about Carol Ann?'

'If Harold inherits there'll be no place for Carol Ann at Ashbarrow Castle.'

But…that was Carol Ann's home! Sophie might not

know much about Will's life beyond what Peter had told her, and the odd snippet Will occasionally let slip, but she knew he took his responsibility for Carol Ann seriously. She knew how much he loved her. And she knew Carol Ann's entire sense of security was tied to Ashbarrow Castle. She knew because Will had tried moving her to London to live with him and it had been an absolute disaster. Carol Ann had grieved so hard for her home that she'd fallen ill.

Talk about being in a bind. 'What are you going to do?'

He shook his head, remaining silent.

His earlier out-of-character snark made sudden sense. 'Maybe he's bluffing.'

'Not this time.'

Her stomach clenched. Will's parents' marriage had been fraught, ugly…and in the end they'd destroyed each other. All in the glare of the public spotlight. She'd figured that was why he'd sworn never to marry. *Ever.* She'd never met anyone so against the institution. She rubbed a hand across her chest. No wonder he looked so haunted.

Keep things light, she counselled, because he looked ready to snap and she was one of the burdens weighing him down. She lifted a bite of food to her lips, chewed and swallowed. And then she sent him a grin that made him blink. 'I'd marry you for a million pounds, Will.'

He stared at her for a long moment. 'And what would you do with a million pounds?'

She could see in his eyes what he thought she'd do— fritter it away on clothes and parties. She gave up being polite and leaned her elbows on the table. 'Create a new life for myself. A million pounds would let me turn everything around.' It would pay for Carla's treatment. It would let her get the stables up and running so that when Carla was better she'd have a job to come out to.

He leaned towards her, his eyes oddly intent. 'Specifics, please.'

* * *

It was the first time in two years that Will had seen anything approaching Sophie's old spark fire through her.

Every time he saw her she'd lost more weight, had grown paler, had become…less.

He'd taken one look at her today and had wanted to punch something.

But now…

She stared at him with those perfect blue eyes—the only part of her that hadn't faded—and blinked. 'Specifics?'

'How would you *specifically* turn your life around with this hypothetical million pounds?'

Her chin wavered between jutting up and angling down. He found himself holding his breath. Would she explain what she meant…or would she wave it all away with a laugh and descend into inanity as usual?

Her chin remained firmly at a midpoint, and he didn't know what that meant. Mind you, he'd never been brilliant at deciphering what went on in that puzzling head of hers. All he knew was that when Peter had died, he seemed to have taken a part of Sophie with him.

And it now seemed that she was incapable of reclaiming it. Or refused to reclaim it. He wasn't sure which.

He knew only what he'd promised Peter—that he'd keep an eye on Sophie—but today he'd had to face the fact that his and Sophie's lunch and coffee dates were doing her more harm than good.

A hand reached inside his chest and squeezed. He'd made her cry. *Well done!* He'd wanted to ease her pain, not add to it. But then, just for a moment, there'd been that spark. As if she'd had a vision of something better.

He wanted to see that spark again. He wanted to help her reclaim the part of herself she'd lost. He wanted to do it for Peter, because of the promise he'd made. But he wanted to do it for Sophie's sake too.

She speared a bean on the end of her fork—delicately because, whatever else you wanted to say about Sophie, she had an innate grace—and ate it. She'd eaten at least half of her meal so far. That in itself was cause for celebration.

'You really want to know?'

'I really want to know.' He knew he must be coming across as intense, but he couldn't help it.

'Well… The first thing I'd do is get out of the city.'

Why? Because of her father? 'I thought you loved London.'

'I do, but it's not exactly been good for me, has it? For the last two years I've thrown myself into the party scene trying to forget. It hasn't worked. All I've done is drunk too much champagne, had too many indiscreet photos snapped by the press and stumbled so late into my job so many times that they had no choice but *to let me go*.'

Until a month ago she'd worked at an art gallery in the West End.

Her fork made a circle in the air. 'Of course, the upside is all of that has annoyed my father no end, so…'

She and Lord Collingford had always had a fraught relationship. It was worse now that Peter was no longer around to play peacemaker.

'But it needs to stop.' She stabbed another bean. 'Enough is enough.'

Her self-awareness surprised him, though he wasn't sure why. She'd never been stupid just…wilful.

'Where would you go?'

'Cornwall.'

His jaw dropped and for the briefest moment she grinned, as if delighted by his surprise. That spark definitely lurked in the backs of her eyes. What had brought it back?

'My mother's mother left me a bit of land that borders

Bodmin Moor. It's not much…but it has a run-down stables and I thought…' She trailed off with a shrug.

He had to fight the urge to lean in towards her. 'You're riding again?' It had been her enduring passion since he'd met her as a pudgy eleven-year-old.

'I never stopped riding, Will.'

She hadn't?

'After Peter died I thought I should give it up. It felt wrong to still enjoy anything.'

He knew what she meant, but… 'He wouldn't have wanted you to.'

She stared down at her plate. *Please don't cry again.*

A moment later she lifted her chin and sent him a game smile. 'I haven't been riding as much these past couple of years as I normally would. Riding and hangovers don't mix.'

She was choosing riding over hangovers? Excellent choice!

'If I had a million pounds I'd turn those stables into a riding school—an equestrian centre. There are a few acres down there so perhaps I could offer agistment as well.'

'How many acres?'

'Seventeen and three quarters. There are fields and a stream but no house.'

Ah.

'My million pounds would buy me a modest cottage.'

It would buy more than that if she had a fancy for grander living, but before she could make any of that a reality, she'd need start-up funds.

She set about demolishing the rest of her lamb. When she was done—and true to her word she cleaned her plate—she set her cutlery onto the plate at a neat angle and dabbed her lips with her serviette. 'Will, for the last five minutes straight you've been staring at me without saying a word. I can't imagine that watching me eat is that fascinating. I really would prefer it if you simply said what was on your mind.'

Her words made him jerk back in his seat. 'Sorry, I didn't mean to be rude. I was thinking.'

'About?'

'I don't want you to take this the wrong way.' He pushed his plate away and folded his arms on the table in front of him.

She grimaced, but her chin didn't drop. 'Okay.'

'But what makes you think you could stick to this hypothetical plan of yours? I mean, running a stables and riding school isn't precisely glamorous. It's hard work and…'

'And hard work isn't something I've been known for these past couple of years.'

She nodded, evidently not the least offended. And that was what got to him about Sophie. She never reacted the way he expected. She could take criticism on the chin.

Unless it came from her father.

She stared up at the ceiling and wrinkled her nose. 'Needs must, Will. I'm losing myself. Playing the party girl isn't the answer—it's left me feeling hollow…ashamed.'

Whoa! He chose his words carefully. 'I think you're being a little too harsh on yourself.'

'No, you don't.'

He blinked.

'And being my father's hostess with the mostest is shredding what little self-respect I have left.'

He could see that was true, even though he didn't understand it.

She pushed her hair back from her face, pulled it momentarily into a tight ponytail that highlighted the exhausted lines fanning from her eyes, and Will's gut gave a sick kick. Hell, he'd be happy to just give her a million pounds, though he knew her pride would forbid her from accepting it.

'Of course, the million pounds is a pipe dream.' She let her hair go and it fell back down around her shoulders in a blonde cloud. 'But my plan is to get a job in Cornwall and save madly until I can do something with my little property.'

'What kind of job are you looking for?' Was she hoping to land another gallery job? He didn't like her chances.

'Events management. I know to the outside gaze it'd look like I'm just continuing with my party-girl ways. But running an event is very different from attending as a guest. I used to run all the gallery's events. And, even if I say it myself, I have a knack for pulling together a halfway decent party, ball, charity luncheon or any other kind of get-together you'd like to name.'

He sat up straighter. She'd be perfect at it. Lord Collingford demanded the best when he entertained. She not only had a name and experience, she had connections. 'You've really thought about this.'

'Doh!' But she smiled as she said it to soften the sting.

'If you were really willing to marry me for a million pounds, Sophie, how would you see that marriage working?'

It was his turn to have the satisfaction of seeing her jaw drop. The waiter chose that moment to clear their plates. 'Would you like to order dessert or coffee?'

'Chocolate cake,' Sophie said, not taking her eyes off Will. 'Please.'

'And champagne,' Will said, holding her gaze. 'A bottle of your best.'

'I wasn't serious when I said I'd marry you for a million pounds,' she whispered, when the waiter had melted into the background again.

'I know. You were being flippant. But if we were to speak *hypothetically*…' He let the rest of the sentence dangle and watched her mind race behind the perfect blue of

her eyes. 'I'd put a million pounds into your bank account…
What would I get in return?'

'A million pounds…?'

Her eyes glazed over and he could feel his lips start to
lift. 'I believe that was the price you put on it.' A million
pounds…and then she could live the life she'd just outlined
to him.

She shook herself. 'We're playing hypotheticals?'

He nodded.

'Well, if that were to ever happen…it'd have to be a
strictly business arrangement. A paper marriage—no sex,
no children, no complications.'

He nodded. So far so good.

'You've never wanted to marry.'

The ugliness of his parents' marriage had cured him of
ever wanting to trade in his bachelorhood for the vagaries
of matrimony. He wasn't inviting that kind of acrimony
and spite into his life. The very thought made him break
out into a cold sweat.

'But you'll do just about anything to keep Carol Ann
healthy and happy,' she continued.

She knew him better than the women he dated. He
should find that reassuring considering the conversation
they were having, but he didn't. It took a force of will not
to run a finger around the collar of his shirt.

She smiled at the waiter as he brought their champagne
and slid her chocolate cake in front of her. 'Thank you.'

The waiter's lips lifted and his eyes lit up. 'You're very
welcome, madam.'

That was one of the things Will had always liked about
Sophie. She didn't just have impeccable manners, but *gen-
uine* manners. She made people feel valued.

'You'd be in London most of the time and I'd be in
Cornwall most of the time, so I don't see any reason why
we should even have to live together.'

Better and better.

'If you needed me to host the odd dinner party or event I could certainly do that.'

He didn't entertain often but every now and again business demanded it. And he could see how having a 'wife' at those events could be an advantage. Sophie had a talent for ruffling the waters when she had a mind to, but she had an even greater ability for smoothing them.

'Though I'd expect notice. You couldn't just spring events on me at the last minute.'

That was reasonable. 'And if you want me to attend anything you need only let my PA know and—?'

She shook her head. 'In this hypothetical situation you're giving me a million pounds, Will. Nothing more will be asked of you.'

He frowned. That didn't seem fair somehow.

She ate a huge piece of chocolate cake and then nodded and pointed her dessert fork at him, her tongue sweeping out to check for crumbs, leaving a shine on her bottom lip that made something inside him clench tight.

No! Don't do that. Don't look at Peter's little sister like she's a woman, for God's sake.

'I know how much you value your…*independence.*'

Her words hauled him back, and he glanced at her to find her staring at him expectantly. A frown built through him. It wasn't like her to mince her words. 'What are you driving at?'

She shrugged, almost reluctantly…and as if in resignation. 'I know the thought of being monogamous to one woman fills your little bachelor heart with fear and loathing.'

He stiffened. 'It's not fear. It's just… Why the hell would anyone want to do that?'

Her eyebrows lifted. 'Whatever. What I'm trying to say is that I'm not expecting you to abstain sexually during this hypothetical paper marriage of ours. You could continue to have as many lovers as you wanted. But...'

His heart started to thump. 'But...?'

'You might want to consider being discreet.'

Ah. 'I'd have no intention of making you look like a fool or a stooge, Sophie.'

She dabbed at her lips with a napkin. 'While that's a relief, it's not really what I was getting at. I'm assuming we'd have to put on a convincing show for your grandfather.'

'Only until we were married. I'd have legally binding contracts drawn up. He could do whatever the hell he wants with his title and money, but the deeds to Ashbarrow Castle would pass to me the moment I married.'

'Well, in that case, once we're *hypothetically* married you can be as indiscreet as you want.'

Would it really not bother her? 'And you?'

'You can be assured of my discretion.'

Her answer left him unsatisfied, though he didn't know why.

'We would have to agree to a minimum duration for this paper marriage too,' she added. 'Eighteen months, perhaps?'

He nodded again.

'As for how we got married, that'd be entirely up to you—a quickie Vegas wedding, a big London society do, or something in between.'

His lip curled. There'd have to be a wedding. Nothing else would satisfy his grandfather, but he couldn't face the thought of some big society affair. 'Could you face a quiet family affair at Ashbarrow?'

She stared at him, and her soft laugh tripped down his backbone. 'The real question, Will, is can you?'

It didn't fill him with a shred of enthusiasm, but if it meant securing Carol Ann's future...

She folded her arms, her eyes narrowing. 'But I have

to ask, *hypothetically speaking*, of course. If you were to embark on this paper marriage for real, why would you choose me? There has to be someone more suitable.'

Sophie might have a certain reputation in the tabloids but... He knew a lot of women—all more than happy to keep him company whenever he wanted—but he wouldn't be able to rely on a single one of them to stick to an agreement like this.

Was he really considering this? His gut churned. Was he crazy? Or was this the answer he'd been searching so desperately for?

He drummed his fingers against the linen tablecloth. Beneath the table his foot began to bounce. 'You know me and you know that I don't want to give up either my freedom or my independence. I know you and what you want— money for a fresh start. We'd go into this arrangement with our eyes wide open. You wouldn't be expecting *a husband* in the real sense of the word. I know you wouldn't ever misconstrue our situation. Besides, you're Peter's little sister and, regardless of anything else, I don't believe you'd try and take advantage of being married to me.'

She folded her arms, her chin angling up. 'Are you sure about that?'

Positive. 'You haven't tried putting your price up to two million pounds, have you? Even though you know I'm considering a more than hypothetical arrangement here.'

She shrugged. 'I don't need two million pounds.'

Exactly.

If he married Sophie, it would secure Carol Ann's future. He recalled those few weeks he'd brought her to London to live with him and acid burned his throat. He'd had such high hopes, but she'd become so distraught. *She'd become so ill.* And he'd been helpless to ease her homesickness and her grief at being torn from her home.

Peter had always felt responsible for Sophie in the same

way Will felt responsible for Carol Ann. And if anything were to happen to Carol Ann…

His hands clenched. He couldn't bear the thought, but it reminded him of all the unspoken promises he'd made to Peter when he'd sworn to keep an eye on Sophie—promises to help her wherever and whenever he could. And here was the perfect opportunity to do exactly that.

'I trust you, Sophie.' And there weren't too many people he did trust.

She pursed her lips. 'I've been in the papers a lot recently—always linked with a different guy. I know how much you hate any kind of tabloid attention.'

'Do you mean to continue appearing in the gossip pages?'

'God no!'

He believed her. 'Which makes it a non-issue.'

She stared at him for a long moment. 'If you were serious about this, we'd need lawyers to draw up pre-nup agreements. I couldn't take you for anything more than that million pounds.' The blue in her eyes started to dance. 'And you couldn't take my little property in Cornwall.'

'Every word is music to my ears, Sophie.'

He poured out two glasses of champagne, and handed her one before raising the other in the air. 'I'm game if you are.'

CHAPTER TWO

'READY?'

Sophie swung from where she stood in front of a gently crackling fire that was more for show than warmth, and nodded across the room to an unsmiling Will. 'Absolutely.'

It was only four days since their crazy lunch in Soho, four days in which they'd signed their names to a contract to seal this crazy deal. Four days in which to consider pulling out.

She pushed her shoulders back. It might be crazy but she wasn't pulling out. All she needed to do to send determination rippling out to every near and far-flung part of her being was to think of Carla. They *would* make this work.

She glanced at Will again. He made no move to lead her downstairs.

They'd been given a suite at the castle—two bedrooms with a shared sitting room and bathroom. It had taken her less time to freshen up than it had him. Which indicated his enthusiasm for the task at hand. She clapped her hands together and tried to look not terrified. 'Ready whenever you are.'

The housekeeper had ushered them to these rooms when they'd arrived. Lord Bramley had not greeted his grandson at the door. Nor had Carol Ann.

If either event had disconcerted or disappointed Will, he'd not betrayed the fact by so much as a flicker of an eyelash.

He ran a critical eye over her now, raising gooseflesh on her arms. 'You look perfect.'

Her lips twisted. She did.

His eyes narrowed. 'What?'

'If there's one thing I *can* do right it's to wear the appropriate clothes whatever the occasion.' And when one got right down to it, it was an utterly pointless talent—so trivial.

She wore black three-quarter-length capris, a silk vest top in cream and a cashmere blend long-line cardigan in a shade of dusky pink. Complementing the outfit was a pair of pink and rose-gold sandals, light make-up and a loose ponytail. She didn't need to glance into the mirror above the mantelpiece to know she looked the epitome of casual country chic.

'What are you afraid you *can't* do? Pull this charade of ours off?'

He wore a pair of navy chinos, loafers and a lighter blue button-down shirt that moulded itself to his chest in such a way that it took an enormous amount of effort on her part to not notice. Or, at least, to appear not to notice.

'You look perfect too. We look perfect together.'

'You didn't answer the question.'

No wonder his start-up company was so successful— he was dogged, persistent when he sensed a problem, and, she suspected, ruthless. Not that she had any intention of hiding her current concerns from him. For heaven's sake, the man had promised her a million pounds! She had to do her absolute best here for him. She had no intention of letting him down—for his sake, for her own sake, but mostly for Carla's sake.

And Peter's.

'Sophie?'

'We *look* perfect.' She twisted the ring on the third finger of her left hand, before holding that hand up. 'We have the ring to prove it. But we need to *act* perfect too.'

He lowered himself to the edge of the sofa. 'Explain.'

She remained right where she was, too keyed-up to take a seat. 'Look, everyone is going to assume we're lovers, right? There are certain…intimacies we need to—'

'We're not having sex! We agreed.'

He remained seated, but it felt as if he'd leapt to his feet and stabbed a finger at her. Her heart gave a sick thud. 'Wow! I don't know whether to be offended that you're so repulsed at the thought of sleeping with me or not.'

This time he did shoot to his feet. 'That's not what I meant.'

'Well, it's by the by and totally unimportant for the current conversation. Sex is not the only kind of intimacy couples in love share.' She planted her hands to her hips to hide how awkward she felt. 'Or has that fact passed you by?'

He dismissed that with a single wave of an imperious hand. 'We'll play it by ear—wing it. Make it up as we go along.'

Did he really think that'd work? An unwelcome thought shuffled through her. She wanted to swat it away, but… 'Are you hoping we succeed? Or that we'll fail?'

'What the hell are you talking about?'

She couldn't take his money. Not if this were a farce. She searched his face.

'I want this to work. It *has* to work.' His nostrils flared. 'What is your problem?'

Her *problem* was his absolute lack of enthusiasm for her company. On their flight to Inverness he'd buried himself in paperwork, barely exchanging two words with her. And at the moment it seemed he could barely stand being in the same room with her. It was some kind of Peter hang-up. She recognised it because she had a few of those of her own.

'My *problem* is that you can barely bring yourself to touch me.'

He scowled. 'You're being ridiculous.'

She held out her hand. 'Then hold my hand.'

His scowl deepened but he took her hand. She immediately felt less alone.

Oh, but that scowl!

She tugged him closer and turned him so they could survey their reflections in the mirror above the mantelpiece. 'Now there's a lover-like expression if I ever saw one.'

He tried to smooth his face out and she was seized with a sudden urge to giggle.

'This isn't funny.'

But his eyes lightened as he said it and her smile widened. 'It's hilarious. You're just too tense to admit it. You're always tense when you mention Scotland, so I suppose it only makes sense that you're tense now we're here.'

His eyebrows rose.

'It's true. It's always been true. There'll be reasons for it—good ones, I expect—but I think it'll help our cause somewhat if you pretend that I've helped you to un-tense a little on that front, don't you?'

He stared down at her and it made her aware of their unusual proximity. Her pulse started to race.

'You've really thought about this, haven't you?'

'Of course I have!' His surprise stung. 'You're paying me a ridiculous amount of money to help you pull this off. I mean to do my best.'

His mouth opened and then closed. He blinked, and then something in the line of his jaw softened. 'Thank you.'

She wanted to tug her hand from his. She wanted to bolt across to the other side of the room and put a sofa and coffee table between them. She forced herself to remain where she was. 'Let's save the gratitude for later...when we've managed to pull this off.'

He gave a hard nod. 'Right. So...any other tricks besides holding hands that I should know about?'

His smile eased the chafe in her soul. This was a tense, high-stakes game they were playing. It made sense there'd be nerves, and that her every sense would be on high alert.

Carefully she reclaimed her hand and gestured to the mirror. 'Pretend it's after dinner and we've all adjourned to the drawing room. For a brief moment the two young lovers edge across to the fireplace to exchange a few private lover-like words.'

He grinned, entering into the spirit of things. His head drew down to hers. 'Sophie?'

His breath stirred the hair at her temples and her heart leapt into her throat. 'Yes?'

'You have the most exquisite toenails I have ever seen. They rival every other toenail in the universe. You should've been a toenail model.'

She glanced down at her toenails, painted a jaunty pink, and wiggled them. 'I had them done with you in mind.'

Her voice shook as she said it, and they both burst into laughter.

'Did we just spoil the effect you were after?'

She shrugged, shaking her head. 'I have no idea, but I'm pretty certain laughter is good, right?'

He smiled down at her, brushed a tendril of hair from her face. 'It's nice to hear you laugh, Sophie.'

Her stomach clenched. She had no right to laugh. She didn't deserve to have fun. She had too much to make amends for. Once she'd made amends maybe then—and only then—would she have *maybe* earned the right to some happiness.

'Hey, where'd you just go?'

Heavens, she needed to keep on track. 'Sorry, I...' She shrugged. 'Sometimes it still seems wrong to be happy when Peter's not here.'

'He wouldn't want you to keep grieving the way you have been.'

Wasn't that the truth?

But it also wasn't what Will meant, and it was none of his concern. He was doing enough for her already. She had to play her part here to perfection, and if that included laughing then she'd laugh.

'Right, next scenario.'

He straightened. 'Okay, hit me with it.'

'We're at a dinner party. There's milling around before and afterwards. We're talking to another couple or maybe two other couples. How do we stand?'

He pursed his lips. 'You were smart to bring this up. If I think of you as Peter's little sister Sophie, then I stand like this.' He moved a step away. 'At a discreet distance where I'd be careful not to invade your personal space.'

He'd always been very careful not to do that.

'But when you're Sophie, my bride-to-be, then…' He was silent for a moment and then draped an arm across her shoulders. Staring at their reflection, he frowned. 'Now we just look like great mates.'

She waited for him to work it out. If she were the one doing all the cosying up it would look wrong. She'd look desperate too. Not that she cared what anyone here thought about her. But she did care about that million pounds, so she had to make sure Lord Bramley didn't get suspicious.

'Okay, this is better.'

Will pulled her in closer until she was plastered against his side. She swallowed. Too close. She rested a hand on his chest.

He frowned. 'That could be a bit much.'

She raised an eyebrow. 'You think?'

'I'm not appreciating your sarcasm.'

Yeah, well, maybe she wasn't appreciating how long this was taking for him to get right. It wasn't as if he hadn't had a lot of practice. It wasn't as if he hadn't had a girlfriend before. He'd had a lot of them.

An itch chafed through her, followed by a burn.

He squared them off, his eyes turned towards the mirror rather than her, until his arm rested across her shoulders, the weight of it solid and reassuring while their hips bumped against each other's lightly. 'That's good. And this could be good too.'

He moved her in front of him and wrapped arm about her upper chest, just above her breasts, pulling her back against him. She gritted her teeth.

'Smile, Sophie.'

She met his gaze in the mirror and forced a smile to uncooperative lips. But as she continued to stare at him a ripple of recognition ran though her. This was Will—Peter's best friend—and while he'd never really approved of her, she'd trust him with her life.

'That's better. This is…nice.'

He smiled back at her, but their gazes clung for a few seconds longer than they should have and Sophie found herself pulling free from Will's embrace when what she really wanted to do was snuggle closer.

'Or,' she said, trying to cover her sudden sense of awkwardness, 'we could simply stand close enough that we brush shoulders.' She gestured to the mirror and brushed her arm against his. 'We could link arms or—'

'Hold hands,' he said, enfolding hers in a warm grasp.

'Or link hands,' she added, desperately trying to ignore the warmth flooding her system as she interlocked their fingers.

'Nice,' he agreed before she broke away.

She could feel his gaze like a physical weight as she took a couple of steps away.

'Is everything okay?'

His voice was quiet, measured, concerned. She turned and sent him what she hoped was a smile. 'I've become a firm believer that what we do with our bodies affects us emotionally.'

He widened his stance. 'You're going to need to explain that.'

She moistened suddenly dry lips. 'All of this touching…it's nice.'

He leaned towards her, a frown in his eyes. 'And?'

'I just don't want either one of us getting the wrong idea and imagining that it means something more.'

He reared back as if she'd struck him. 'If you think I can't control myself—'

'I'm not just talking about sex,' she snapped at him. 'I know you think that we can just breeze in and play these parts and that nothing will change and everything will be hunky-dory and…and tickety-boo!'

He raised an eyebrow. 'Hunky-dory?' His voice grew even more incredulous. 'Tickety-boo?'

She glared at him. 'I don't appreciate your sarcasm.'

He paced away from her, paced back. 'Sorry.'

That didn't look like what he really wanted to say.

His lips thinned. 'So can I assume you don't think this is going to be easy?'

'In my experience nothing is ever as easy as we hope it'll be. And despite what you think, we're playing a dangerous game here. I don't want anyone to get hurt.'

His eyes throbbed into hers. 'You're talking about hearts and emotions now?'

She nodded.

He leaned down so they were eye to eye. 'I can assure you that my heart is in absolutely no danger. You should know me better than that.'

Yes, but she was Peter's little sister. And she didn't know how or why, but in his eyes that made her different from other women.

He straightened. 'Are you telling me your heart is in danger?'

'Absolutely not.' Not as long as she remained on her guard. And she had no intention whatsoever of letting her guard slip. 'But what about Carol Ann and your grandfather?' They could become invested in this fake marriage.

He stilled. 'You'll always be Carol Ann's friend, won't you? You're not going to dump her the moment we get our divorce.'

'Of course not!'

'Then I think she'll be fine. Thank you for considering her well-being. I appreciate it.'

But she noticed he made no mention of his grandfather's well-being. She didn't pursue it. 'Fine. That leads us to the next topic.'

Will stared at her. He wanted away from the cloying heat of the room. Mind you, it had only become cloying in the last few minutes.

'You're supposed to ask me what topic?' she prompted.

'What topic?' he growled.

She sent him a falsely sweet smile that scraped through him like fingernails on a blackboard. 'Kissing.'

He rocked back on his heels. He couldn't help it. He was simply grateful he managed to stop himself from striding from the room altogether.

She glanced away, her lips pressed into a tight white line that still couldn't hide the luscious curve of her bottom lip. A fact he desperately didn't want to notice.

'Did you really think we'd manage to get through this weekend without the odd peck?'

He let the air out of his lungs, slowly. A peck? He could manage that. Her lips twisted as if she'd read that thought in his face and he knew what message he was sending her—that he found her unattractive. And he could tell

she was doing her best to try and not let that bother her…
hurt her.

Damn it! He needed this weekend to go smoothly. He
needed to convince his grandfather that he and Sophie
were serious. He tried to bring Carol Ann's face to mind,
but it was Sophie's wounded eyes that kept appearing there
instead.

Damn it! Letting her think that he didn't find her attractive provided him with a measure of protection, but
a real man wouldn't let her continue operating under the
misapprehension, wouldn't let her take the blame for his
own weakness. If it were any other woman…

But it wasn't any other woman. It was Sophie.

*Will you keep an eye on her? Be there for her if I can't
be?*

He'd promised Peter.

He slammed his hands to his hips. 'I don't find you unattractive, Sophie.'

She turned from surveying the fire. 'You don't need to
pander to my vanity and make excuses or apologise, Will.
These things can simply be a matter of taste or chemistry or—'

He held up a hand, holding her gaze. 'You're lovely…
beautiful.' His gut clenched as he said the words.

She pursed her lips, her eyes narrowing. 'But?'

Her chin didn't drop, the light in her eyes didn't fade,
and she suddenly appeared indomitable. Where he'd fancied he'd seen fragility, now there was only strength. It
made his mouth go dry though he couldn't fully explain
why. Except the realisation that what he thought of her
physically maybe didn't matter to her one jot. Which was
how it should be, of course. But it left him feeling at a distinct disadvantage.

Right, so that's new, is it?

He ignored the sarcastic voice as best he could, and

thrust out his jaw. 'But,' he ground out, 'you're different from the women I date. With them I…'

'Scratch an itch and then move on?' she offered when he hesitated.

It was crude but accurate, and everything inside him rebelled at it. 'We have fun, enjoy each other's company.'

'Yes.'

He shifted under the steadiness of her gaze, shoved his hands into his pockets. 'Are you saying it's different for you and the guys you date?'

'No.'

If he'd been hoping to put her on the defensive he'd have been sadly disappointed.

'The itch I've been scratching, though, is grief, and I finally figured out that the partying, the drinking, the dating an endless parade of guys—*having fun and enjoying their company*—hasn't helped.'

He pulled his hands from his pockets and then didn't know what to do with them. He moistened his lips. 'Has it made it worse?' How could he help?

She made an impatient movement. 'Not worse. It's just…pointless, and not how I want to spend the rest of my life.' She cocked her head to one side. 'I wonder what itch you're scratching? I think it's a big one.'

He realised then that she wasn't judging him. Lots of women did, and found him wanting. Not that he blamed them. He wasn't cut out for commitment and the long haul. But Sophie was simply trying to work him out. Some of the tension that had him wound up tight eased. When you had parents like his, when you watched them do their best to tear each other apart—and succeed—you promised to never let yourself fall into that same trap, to never get embroiled in the same predicament.

But he didn't want to talk about his parents. 'Is it really

so incomprehensible for a guy to simply want to keep his freedom, to not want to be tied down?'

One of her shoulders lifted in a graceful shrug.

'What I'm trying to say, Sophie, is that you're not like the women I usually date and that…' He bit back a curse. 'I can't treat you the way I would them.'

She nodded. 'Because I'm Peter's little sister.'

Exactly.

'And I can't treat you like the guys I've been dating.'

'Because I'm Peter's best friend.'

Very slowly she shook her head. 'Because I like you.' Her eyes grew shadowed. 'And because of who you were to Peter—yes, that too. It means I want you as a part of my life for…'

Things inside him clenched up tight. 'For?'

'Forever. Permanently. I know I'm a trial to you. I know you probably don't even like me all that much.'

What the hell…?

'But it means I don't want to mess things up between us.'

Where had she got that idea—that she thought he didn't like her?

'You're one of the few links I have left to Peter and I can't bear the thought of losing it.'

Her grief went so deep and he intended to do whatever he could to help her over it. 'That's not going to happen.'

'It will if we mess this up. If we lose our heads and forget ourselves…just once…then we're not going to want to see each other again.'

Her words were like a punch to the gut. Because they were true.

'It's what I meant when I said we were playing a dangerous game.' Her eyes flashed. 'If you found me unattractive that would be—' She broke off. 'But you don't.'

And he realised then what she'd made explicit but had

left unsaid. She didn't find him unattractive either. The knowledge made his blood roar.

Hell.

He ground his back molars together and counted to three, pulled in a breath. 'You have my word that I won't lose my head.'

He would not let her down.

'And you have my word.'

They had to be cautious, circumspect. He couldn't let himself feel too comfortable with her...and yet they both had to cultivate an appearance of tranquillity with each other for outside eyes. She was right. This could be trickier than he'd first envisaged. But not impossible.

Her lips lifted and she rolled her eyes.

'What?'

Before he knew what she was about she'd leaned in, stood on tiptoe and pressed a kiss to his cheek. 'Thank you.'

His heart crashed in his chest. His cheek burned where her lips had touched him.

She eased back, adjusted her cardigan. 'Right. Your turn.'

She was trying to make kissing him as natural as possible, and he had to do the same. 'Believe it or not,' he said, 'it's my pleasure.'

He pressed a kiss to her brow and tried not to notice how soft and warm and vibrant she felt beneath his lips.

She huffed out a laugh. 'Well, in that case I choose to believe it. Right, sit.'

She gestured to the sofa and he took a seat. She came from behind. Her arms slid around his shoulders, making him start.

'You do that downstairs and you'll give the game away.'

He nodded and gritted his teeth. 'Do it again.'

She eased back, walked away and then moved towards

him again and bent down to slide just one arm about his shoulders. He rested his hand on her forearm and felt a tiny tremor run through her. He pulled in a measured breath and her scent flooded his senses. 'You smell nice.'

Nice? That's the best you can manage?

She smelled sensational—fruity and warm, like Christmas. Though Christmas was months away.

'It's my body lotion. Frosted cherry. My favourite.'

They broke apart at exactly the same moment. This was exhausting, but he saw the wisdom of it. They needed to give the impression that they were physically comfortable with each other.

When nothing could be further from the truth.

'Your turn.' He waved her to the armchair.

She sat, leaned back, crossed her legs—for all the world as if she were completely at ease.

Time for them to get this over and done with.

Her eyes widened when he braced his hands on the arms of the chair and leant down towards her, effectively locking her in and leaving her nowhere to escape. 'Lips?'

She glanced at his lips and then back into his eyes and nodded. 'Dry lips,' she whispered. 'And we keep it brief.'

Every cell in his body burst to life. He recited, *Peter's sister, Peter's sister, Peter's sister*, over and over in his mind. 'I want to tell you something before we do this,' he murmured, his gaze not dropping from hers.

She swallowed. 'Okay.'

'You're wrong. I like you just fine, Sophie Mitchell.'

Her lips parted as if in shock. He couldn't resist the pull any longer. His mouth lowered to hers, lips brushing lips—light, teasing and nowhere near enough. She stiffened, but then he felt her force herself to relax. And then she leaned forward a fraction and pressed her lips more firmly against his and kissed him back.

Wind roared in his ears. It took all the strength he had

to not deepen the kiss, to not engage lips, mouths, tongues and hands.

Biting back a groan, he pulled back to stare into stunned blue eyes. They were a deeper shade of blue than he'd ever seen before.

She pushed him away and launched herself from the chair like a horse from a starter's gate. 'We better keep that to a minimum.'

She was darn right they were keeping that to a minimum!

He'd kiss her cheek, her brow, the top of her head, her hand, but he had every intention of staying as far away from those lips as possible. They were lethal!

CHAPTER THREE

THE MOMENT SOPHIE and Will entered the drawing room, they were greeted with a squeal and a woman with the same dark auburn hair as Will—Carol Ann—launched herself at her brother with a display of such unadulterated joy all Sophie could do was smile.

When had she lost that easy, unselfconscious joy? The answer came swiftly—when she was eleven years old. She glanced at Will and wondered when he'd lost his.

His current delight at seeing Carol Ann, however, was plain to see. He turned his sister towards Sophie. 'You remember Sophie, don't you?'

She'd prepared herself for any number of scenarios—from cluelessness as to who Sophie might be, suspicion, perhaps jealousy over Will…and even a studied politeness. What she got though was another whoop of joy and smothered by a hug.

'Sophie's my best friend.'

She was?

'We like the same movies.'

'We certainly do.' For one mischievous moment she was tempted to launch into a song from *South Pacific* or *Grease*, but she was aware of the other two people in the room…and she had a feeling they might not appreciate her musical prowess as much as Carol Ann and Will.

Not that Will would necessarily appreciate it either, but he'd appreciate the effort of making Carol Ann happy.

'She sends me the best presents.' She stared at Sophie expectantly now. 'Did you bring me a present?'

Will's head rocked back. 'Carol Ann, you can't—'

'Of course I did.' Sophie laughed at a thunderstruck Will. Digging into her pocket, she drew out a small velvet box. 'Here you go.'

Carol Ann opened the box and her eyes went wide. 'It's beautiful!'

It was a bracelet of pink and purple crystals, and she'd known Carol Ann would love it.

The other girl danced on the spot. 'Purple for me! Pink for you!' she shouted.

'Not so loud,' Will admonished, though he couldn't hide his smile.

'Put it on me,' Carol Ann demanded.

Will did and Carol Ann rushed to show it to Ms Grant and her grandfather.

'What did she mean about the colours?' Will asked, drawing her further into the room.

'Purple is Carol Ann's favourite colour and pink is mine.'

'How do you know that?'

'She told me.'

Carol Ann swung back to them. 'Because we talk lots and lots on the phone.'

His eyes widened, but he didn't say anything. She'd thought he knew. She'd thought Carol Ann would've told him. She'd never mentioned it to him herself because he'd never raised the topic. So rather than look at Will, Sophie grinned at Carol Ann. 'Because we're best friends.'

The pressure of his fingers on her arm informed her he'd be following this conversation up when they were alone. 'Do you remember Miss Grant?' He gestured to the other woman. 'She came to London with Carol Ann when they visited.'

She did. Esther Grant was Carol Ann's carer. The two

women smiled at each other. 'Of course I do. How's your father doing, Esther?'

'Coming along nicely, thank you, Sophie.'

'He had a hip replacement last month,' she explained to Will.

Will stared at her with narrowed eyes. 'And are you and my grandfather in regular correspondence too?'

She turned to the stocky man who surveyed her from the largest armchair she'd ever seen. 'I don't believe Lord Bramley and I have ever met.'

'Grandfather, I'd like you to meet Sophie Mitchell.'

For a moment she thought the older man wasn't going to rise from his chair, that he meant to snub her completely, but eventually he lumbered to his feet and briefly clasped her hand. 'Your reputation precedes you.'

Ouch! She refused to let her chin drop. 'As does yours.' She meant it in exactly the same way as he did, and had the satisfaction of seeing his eyes widen.

He briefly clasped Will's hand. He wasn't as tall as Will, but he was broader. Without another word he installed himself in his chair again. Flicking a glance at her left hand, he grimaced. 'I don't need to ask why you've decided to grace us with your presence.'

Carol Ann bustled up between them. 'You're here to visit me, aren't you, Will?'

'That's right,' he agreed.

He met Sophie's eyes over the top of Carol Ann's head and she sent him what she hoped was an encouraging smile. It was nice to see him with his sister, but there was no denying the tension that had him coiled up tight.

'And to tell you that Sophie and I are going to get married.'

Carol Ann's eyes widened.

'As long as that's all right with you,' Sophie added.

More squealing and jumping up and down ensued, especially when she realised Sophie wouldn't just be her best friend but also her sister, until Esther broke in and told Carol Ann that it was time for her Zumba dance class at the local community centre.

The room grew quiet when it was only the three of them left. Dark undercurrents she didn't understand swirled about the room.

'So you're not going to congratulate us?' Will finally said, though his tone implied he didn't care one way or the other if his grandfather approved of the match or not, was happy for him or not. It was all she could do not to wince.

The older man's gaze turned to her. 'I noticed you asked Carol Ann's permission, but you didn't ask mine.'

A myriad different retorts sprang to her lips, but she sensed hurt behind the belligerence so she swallowed them all back. She sensed similar retorts on the top of Will's tongue too, but she rested her hand on his arm to keep him from replying.

Will's grandfather glanced at that hand and then back into her face and pursed his lips.

'Carol Ann is a darling,' she said. 'But Will marrying has the potential to impact on her significantly. We didn't want her security to feel threatened.'

He thrust out his jaw. 'What about my security?'

The muscles under her fingers clenched and she tightened her grip. It took a ludicrous amount of willpower not to let her hand explore the intriguing line of that arm further—to test the solidity of the flesh that quivered beneath her touch. 'Forgive me, sir, but you're a man of the world and you don't need mollycoddling. May we sit?'

She needed to sit before her knees gave out. She didn't wait for an answer, but dragged Will to the sofa and all but fell down into it.

The older man grunted but for a moment she swore she detected a flash of humour in those eyes.

She glanced at Will in her peripheral vision. Why

didn't he say something? She gave a surreptitious nudge to his ribs.

He started. *Not* the reaction she'd been hoping for. It was all she could do not to roll her eyes.

'I take it, Grandfather, that you're in good health?'

That jaw jutted out. 'Fit as a fiddle.'

'In that case, as you're the one who demanded I marry, I'm at a loss to explain your appalling lack of enthusiasm at my announcement.'

Well, *that* was a no-brainer. He obviously had an objection to Will's choice of bride. But would Lord Bramley say as much in front of her?

She really hoped not because if he did she'd be forced to retaliate. But as the two men's gazes locked and clashed it occurred to her that maybe this had nothing to do with her at all.

What on earth was this pair's problem with each other?

She shuffled upright. 'We were hoping to be married here, at Ashbarrow Castle, if that's all right with you, sir.'

Her words broke through the silent battle and they both swung to stare at her. 'When are you planning to marry?' barked Will's grandfather. 'Spring?'

Spring was six months away.

One corner of Will's mouth lifted, but his eyes remained as cold as chips of ice. 'We're getting married in three weeks.'

'Three weeks!' The older man glared at them, his jaw working. 'That's impossible. There's too much to organise. People will talk!'

'People always talk,' Sophie broke in. 'But when there's no baby in nine months' time they'll realise they were wrong. I'm not pregnant, Lord Bramley.'

'Then why the rush?'

'I believe you're the one who set the timer, *sir.*'

If Will ever used that tone with her she might just shrivel on the spot!

'Then why don't you just go to some hole-and-corner register office?' he spat.

'Because that's not what I want,' Sophie inserted with a confidence she was far from feeling, her best hostess smile in place. She didn't actually know what a hole-and-corner register office might be, or if it even existed, but she caught the tone well enough. Will was going to give her a million pounds. She had to save the situation before Will blew it and told the old man precisely what he could do with his estate.

She refused to let her smile waver. 'I always swore that when I got married it'd be done right.' She'd just never envisaged a marriage like…this. 'I agree that three weeks isn't much time, but it's doable. Which is just as well as it's the timeframe Will has given me.'

Both men stared at her as if she'd grown a second head.

'Four generations of the Trent-Patersons have been married here at the village church. I happen to think it's important for Will to be married from here as well. It's a tradition that should be preserved.'

A different light came into Lord Bramley's eyes. He leaned back and folded his arms. Sophie held her breath.

'My grandson doesn't think so. He thinks tradition a waste of time.'

Will's hands clenched. 'When tradition is used as an excuse to force someone to do something unprincipled, when it's an excuse for bad behaviour and deceit, then it's empty, worthless and meaningless. And I refuse to have anything to do with it.'

Wow! Will vibrated with barely contained anger. *Damage control.* 'I think we might've just gone off track.'

Beside her, Will swore. She slipped her hand inside his

and he gripped it hard. 'The kind of tradition I'm talking about is a nice one. One that I'd be proud to be a part of.'

Will met her gaze and she sent him a smile. He stared at her for two beats and then shook his head and sent her a rueful smile in return.

Squaring his shoulders, he swung back to his grandfather. 'Sophie has her heart set on being married from Ashbarrow. And I want her to have the wedding of her dreams.'

'What does your father think about this?'

Her stomach clenched at Lord Bramley's sly question. 'As soon as I tell him I'll let you know.'

'He'll have his heart set on a London wedding.'

She bit back an inappropriate smile along with an even more inappropriate gurgle of laughter. 'Nonsense. What he has his heart set on is his daughter mending her wicked ways.'

Lord Bramley remained silent for several long moments. 'Very well, you can be married from here on two conditions.'

Will stiffened. 'If I don't like your—'

She dug her fingernails into the back of his hand. 'Which are?'

'That you delay your nuptials for another week. Give me a month to get the place ready.'

She glanced at Will. His lips thinned into a mutinous line. Lips that had touched hers and sent such a jolt through her she still hadn't recovered. *Don't think about that!* 'Will?' she murmured.

The anger in Will's eyes when he turned to her made her heart beat harder. This was more than just being forced to marry her. There was a whole history of anger that existed between the two men.

'It's only a week,' she whispered. 'It doesn't seem unreasonable. And Carol Ann will enjoy helping me with the preparations.'

At the reminder of what they were really doing here, some of the tension bled from his shoulders. Resignation replaced the anger in his eyes. 'Fine, we'll delay the wedding by one week but not a day more.'

She let out a pent-up breath. So far so good.

'My second condition is that your bride-to-be remains here to oversee the preparations.'

She swallowed. She hadn't foreseen that.

'That's out of the question!' Will shot to his feet. 'I want Sophie in London with me. Besides, she has her own life to lead and her own commitments to take care of, and doesn't have the time to be subjected to your whims.'

'She doesn't have the time to plan her own wedding?'

A million pounds...

'She can organise it from London.'

...in exchange for a month of her life.

'I believe Ms Mitchell can speak on her own behalf.'

'Sophie,' she said automatically. 'Please call me Sophie.' She turned to Will. 'I'd like to be personally involved in the preparations for the wedding, Will. I know I could do it all from London, but I'll be able to troubleshoot more effectively on the spot, make any split-second decisions that are needed.' And she didn't want Lord Bramley springing any nasty surprises on the day. 'But—' she glanced at the older man '—I need to tell my father the news in person, not over the phone.'

He made a few faces but eventually nodded. 'Yes, I can see how that's necessary.'

'He's out of the country at the moment. He returns on Friday, and we were planning on telling him then.'

She thought hard about the commitments she had for the next month. 'I could fly to London on Friday and stay overnight—we can tell my father that evening. I'll have a chance then to pack for a longer stay here and take care of a few bits and bobs at that end too. I'm also organising a charity ball my father is hosting two Saturdays from tomorrow. All the preparations are complete, except for a few finishing touches, which I can take care of from here, but I will need to return to London to host it.'

The older man looked as if he was going to argue.

The sofa cushion rocked as Will lowered himself back down beside her. 'You don't have to do this.'

Oh, she had the distinct feeling that she did. 'I want to.' She glanced at Lord Bramley again. 'It's the best I can manage, I'm afraid.'

He huffed out a breath.

'Also,' she added, 'I have a couple of conditions of my own.' A sly thought made her add, 'Though I expect Will can take care of those for me.'

The older man stiffened. 'I'm still the master of this establishment,' he thundered. 'I'm fully able to provide my guests with whatever amenities are needed.'

Guest or hostage? But she left that unsaid.

'Excellent! Then I'm going to need access to a car while I'm here.'

Shaggy brows lowered. 'What for?'

She raised an eyebrow. 'Have you ever tried to arrange an event like this before? I'm going to need to hire caterers, bar and wait staff, a photographer, as well as someone to do the cake. Not to mention a dress. At this late stage I can't expect all of the people I need to see to come to me personally.'

'We can use my people in London,' Will said.

'Nonsense! We have better people here in Scotland. I'll make sure there's a car available for whenever you need it, my dear.'

My dear? Heavens!

'What else do you need?'

'A horse.'

'What for?'

'To ride. It'll keep me sane.'

He thrust his jaw out. 'You think being exiled to the Highlands is going to be that much of an ordeal?'

'I want to look my best in a month's time, Lord Bramley. And that involves getting plenty of fresh air and exercise to balance out all of the sitting indoors and watching musicals that I plan on doing too.' A stiff canter every day would help her maintain her equilibrium and good humour in the face of Lord Bramley's disapproval. She crossed her fingers. At least, she hoped it would.

'He doesn't trust us.' It was the next morning—early—and not even the crisp clean air or the way the sun sparkled on the dew could lift the weight from Will's shoulders. Sophie had been right. This wasn't going to be easy.

'Of course he doesn't.'

Still, Sophie had somehow taken his grandfather from thinly veiled hostility to almost grudging acceptance. Almost, but not quite.

He scowled. 'And I don't trust him.'

'We can't discuss this in front of your grandfather's staff,' she murmured as they approached the stables. 'Too many people make the mistake of treating the staff as if they're invisible, but they're not. I bet the gardeners and stable hands have worked at Ashbarrow for a long time. Which means they'll be loyal to your grandfather.'

Not that he deserved such loyalty.

'We can't give anyone a reason to suspect anything we don't want them to.'

He glanced at her. She never treated staff as if they were invisible.

Did he?

A groom led out two beautiful-looking steeds and Sophie stilled and clasped her hands beneath her chin as she surveyed them. 'Oh!' Her face softened in awe and appreciation and his heart jerked about in his chest. A moment later she'd kicked herself forward to make friends with them, and the vice about his chest eased a fraction.

Magnus, his grandfather's huge grey gelding, had a reputation for being temperamental and he wanted to caution Sophie to be on her guard. But as he watched her with the horses he closed his mouth again. Both horses nuzzled her hands as she crooned to them.

She had a way with horses. She always had.

Not just horses but dogs too.

And last night it was her lap the household cat had decided to curl up on.

Okay, so she had a way with animals in general. He wondered why she didn't have a pet. Mind you, if she crooned to him like that she'd have him eating out of her hand too. He adjusted his stance. Hypothetically speaking, of course.

She sent him a self-conscious smile and he realised he'd been staring.

'You never told me your grandfather kept such a wonderful stable.'

He shrugged. 'You never told me you and Carol Ann were such regular chatterboxes on the phone.'

Idiot. Not in front of the staff.

But she laughed as if he'd amused her. 'It wasn't a secret. I thought you knew. Now I take it you're riding Magnus and I'm riding Annabelle.'

In all honesty she was the better rider, but he was stronger and Magnus needed a strong hand, so he nodded. And then did his best not to notice the finger-itching shape of her backside as he gave her a leg-up into the saddle.

The bay thoroughbred danced under Sophie's weight, but a few soft words and a pat to her neck quietened her again.

'She has a way with horses, sir,' the groom said with an approving smile.

What was the man's name? The face was familiar but... He shook his head and vaulted into the saddle. 'I'm in trouble if she challenges me to a race.'

'Magnus will see you right, sir,' the groom said with a grin and Will found himself smiling back. He'd initially suggested the ride for Sophie's benefit, but he found himself looking forward to a long canter.

'Which way?' she asked, and the eagerness in her eyes lightened his heart.

He pointed to the top of a low hill. 'We're going up there.'

'I'm dying for a canter.'

Every atom of her suddenly seemed on the boil, and just for a moment it held him spellbound. He moistened dry lips. 'Meet you at the top, then.'

She didn't need any further permission. She turned Annabelle's head in the direction of the hill, moved into a smooth trot until they'd cleared the yard and then broke into a canter.

Magnus immediately chafed to be after them and it was all Will could do to contain the giant horse until they were free of the yard too. He held him back for a few moments longer before letting him have his head. Only pulling him back again when they'd almost drawn level with Sophie and Annabelle.

Sophie moved as one with her steed, as if she were made of air and water and magic. Her hair streamed behind her, wild and free, and his mouth dried as desire pure and fierce speared into him.

Hell!

He could never act on it. He knew that much, but it would take an act of God for him to drag his gaze from that slim form at the moment—when it was filled with so much life and strength and purpose.

For the last two years he'd been taking her for coffee and/or lunch. He should've been taking her riding!

When they reached the top of the hill, all four of them were breathing hard. With one hand, she lifted her hair from her neck and stared at the vista spread before them. 'Just… Wow. It's stunning.'

It was. He used to love tramping across these hills and fields. Once. The jewel in the estate's crown was the loch that glinted blue and silver in the sunlight below them. The hill on the far side rose steeply, but on this side all was green and gentle and rolling. In another two months, though, this could all be deep under snow.

But it would still be beautiful.

'I had no idea that your grandfather's estate was so… *lovely.*'

She turned to him and her eyes narrowed when they settled on his face. 'Why should that make you frown?' she demanded.

It wasn't the view, but the heat stampeding through his blood that made him frown. 'What was the name of the groom?'

'Colin. Why?'

'I couldn't remember and it was bugging me. Felt like poor form.'

She sucked her bottom lip into her mouth and chewed on it. *Dear God.* 'I wasn't having some sort of passive-aggressive potshot at you when I said people often treat staff as if they're invisible.'

Which only made it worse because he had the sudden uncomfortable feeling that the criticism should've been aimed at him. 'You knew Miss Grant's name was Esther,' he couldn't help pointing out.

Sophie shrugged. 'She might be an employee, but she's practically a member of the family.'

His gut tightened. 'What's the housekeeper's name?'

'Ruby, but—'

'And the cook's?'

'Alice.'

She'd been here one night! He'd spent his childhood here and yet he couldn't remember Colin's name. He'd let his resentment at his grandfather spill over to innocent parties. It wasn't good enough.

'Hey.'

He turned at her soft admonishment.

'My father's household staff became my surrogate family. They looked after me during my parents' divorce. At a time when I most needed it. Since then it's become a habit to…' She trailed off with a shrug. 'What are the names of your development team at Pyxis Tech?'

Pyxis Tech was the name of his company. They developed supercharged wireless equipment. He blew out a breath. 'Jason, Daniel, Grace, Graham and Phillip.'

'There you go. You know the names of the staff in your own sphere.'

Her words eased some of the burning in his chest. But it did nothing to ease the heat collecting in his veins. He did his best to ignore it. If he did nothing about it—gave it nothing to feed on—then eventually it would dissipate. He gestured towards the loch. 'Would you like to go down?'

'Yes, please.'

'Can we walk and talk or do you need to canter some more?'

Her gaze sharpened as she glanced into his face. 'We'll walk. What's bothering you?'

He loved that she wasted no time getting to the heart of the matter. 'That you're stuck here for a month.' It wasn't fair on her. It might be true that she needed to tone down the partying and drinking, but that didn't mean she should be cut off completely from all entertainment and social interactions. 'I don't trust my grandfather. He's up to something.'

She grimaced. 'I think you're right. Do you have any idea what, though?'

Not yet, but he'd find out. His hands clenched. Magnus tossed his head in disapproval at the sudden tightening of the reins and he forced his grip to relax once again. 'I'm doing what he's asked. Why can't he just be…satisfied?'

'You're doing what he's asked *literally*, but you've not entered into the spirit of the thing.'

That was asking the impossible.

'And you had to know that when he said he wanted you to settle down he had one of the Strachan girls in mind or Gloria Campbell or Davina McNally.'

His lip curled. 'Never going to happen.' They were all nice women, but…*no way*. He liked his women footloose and fancy-free. He stayed away from women who'd turned their minds to settling down and making babies.

Annabelle took several dancing steps away as if she suddenly wanted to gallop, but Sophie brought her back under control in an instant. 'Instead you presented him with me. And in his eyes I'm not ideal granddaughter-in-law material.'

Why? Because she'd appeared in the society pages a little too often? Because the papers made her sound wild and out of control? He thrust out his jaw. 'You come from good aristocratic stock. I'm told that's important.'

She huffed out a breath. 'That depends on your definition of *good*, now, doesn't it?'

'I suspect he's going to do his best to make you toss in the towel and give up.' Something ugly shuffled through him. 'He might offer you a bribe to not marry me.'

Blue eyes speared to his. That chin came up. 'I will

not accept any bribe from your grandfather. You have my word on it. I can take whatever he dishes out. It's only for a month. But if you doubt that…'

As if by silent accord they pulled the horses to a halt. He stared at her and for the first time that morning he felt like smiling. 'When you look like that it's impossible to doubt you.'

Her shoulders unhitched a fraction. 'Good.'

For the last two years she'd seemed so fragile, but he could see now that she had an underlying strength he'd not recognised before.

Just as you haven't noticed your grandfather's staff.

'I think there's something else at play here.'

She moved off and he had to trot to catch up with her. 'What?'

She shot him a veiled glance and bit her lip as she turned to the front again. 'I think your grandfather is using me as bait.'

'For?'

'You.'

He stared at her, at a temporary loss.

'I think he's hoping that, if he keeps me hostage here, you'll be spending a significant portion of the next month at Ashbarrow too.'

'Of course that's what's going to happen,' he exploded, spooking Magnus. It took a concerted effort to get his excited steed back under control. 'I can't leave you stranded out here on your own.'

Her mouth dropped open. 'Of course you can. One million pounds, Will.'

It still wouldn't be fair.

'And I won't be alone. I'll have Carol Ann and Esther to keep me company. I can ride when I want.'

He'd make certain she could at least do that.

'And I have a wedding to organise. The month will fly.'

'Staying away won't seem very lover-like.'

'No, you can't stay away completely. You'll need to come up for weekends. But you have a company to run. That's a more than valid excuse for spending most of your time in London.'

It still didn't seem fair.

'And speaking of money…'

His ears pricked up. Had they been? And then he shook himself. 'I'll take care of all your expenses while you're here.'

She nodded and bit her lip. He watched the bob of her throat as she swallowed and imagined what it would be like to explore that throat with his lips.

'May I have a portion of my money up front?'

His gut clenched. 'Why?' What would she need money for while she was stuck at Ashbarrow?

Her eyes flashed. 'You don't get the right to ask how I spend the money, Will. I refuse to be answerable to you on the topic. I'm not a child.'

Ice tripped down his spine. 'Sophie, are you in some kind of trouble?'

Would she even tell him if she was?

'Absolutely not.'

'How much of an advance are you asking for?'

'A hundred thousand pounds.'

Acid burned in his stomach. 'Is someone blackmailing you—the press?' Was there some photograph that—?

'Oh, for heaven's sake, Will, I just want to get things started on the place in Cornwall. It'll be my…*carrot*, my reward, for doing a good job here. It'll remind me what I'm working towards if things get tough here.'

It all sounded perfectly reasonable, but some sixth sense told him she was lying. It also told him not to challenge her. Besides, it would be easy enough to check.

And, whatever else he might think, he'd lay ten times that amount on the bet that she wouldn't take the money and run.

'I'll have the money transferred into your account on Monday.'

CHAPTER FOUR

'IT'S GOING TO start raining again any moment. Go back inside.'

It was Sunday night and she and Will were waiting for the car to be brought around to take him to the airport. It would be both warmer and safer inside the house.

But warm and safe weren't the impressions they were after. They were striving for convincing and believable.

She leaned her shoulder into his. 'But that wouldn't be lover-like, now, would it? And we're being watched.'

He stiffened, but she only noticed because they were touching. She silently blessed him for not glancing in the direction of the great hall's front windows. 'What would you like me to do?'

He said it through gritted teeth. If they'd not had that conversation on Friday night she'd have wanted the ground to swallow her whole. But now she knew where that tension came from, and what it indicated. And in some ways that was worse.

And yet in others…

She refused to finish that thought.

'Sophie?'

What they should do, for the purposes of being convincing, was kiss—deeply, desperately, passionately. But that was too dangerous.

'I want you to drag me into the shrubbery there, out of sight of the windows,' she murmured, rising up on tiptoe to wind her arms about his neck.

One of his arms went about her waist, drawing her

close to his lean, hard lines, and it was as if he'd knocked the breath from her body. His other hand slid down to caress her backside. Points of light burst behind her eyelids and it was all she could do to contain a whimper of pure, unadulterated need. Those wicked fingers and the press of his palm made her shift restlessly against him. Heat and need surged through her as he lifted her off her feet and whirled her several feet to the right where they were shielded by a rhododendron.

He loosened his grip immediately, but didn't let her go. In the gathering dusk his eyes looked darker than usual and they throbbed with a primal beat she had a feeling it would be best not to decipher.

'What now?' he ground out.

Her breath came hard and sharp. 'We wait until the car comes.'

She sucked her bottom lip into her mouth and sank her teeth into it, chafed it. She did the same to her top lip, before starting on the bottom one again.

His Adam's apple bobbed up and down. Twice. 'What are you doing?'

'I need to look kissed to within an inch of my life.'

She hadn't known his eyes could go any darker. And she could see him thinking the same thing she'd considered earlier—that the real thing would be far more pleasant. But… 'I don't think kissing for real is a good idea.'

That gaze, heavy and persistent, pulled at something low down in her belly. The lids of his eyes had grown heavy—heavy with thoughts it was definitely in her best interests not to translate—and his lips turned sultry. A man shouldn't look sultry. That was a woman's job! And yet her breath jammed in her throat all the same.

He shuffled in closer. 'If we kiss often enough it's possible that we could get used to it. Inoculate ourselves to its effects.'

She snatched her hands from where they rested on his shoulders, and set about pinching colour into her cheeks with her fingers, pretending his words had no effect on her. 'Or it could simply lead to other things. No complications, remember? We agreed.'

Kissing Will made things inside her...churn. Not physically, but emotionally. It was possible to have sex—satisfying sex too—without one's emotions being engaged. But instinct told her that'd be impossible with Will.

This was aside from Peter, and aside from Carla. It was about self-preservation because falling in love with Will would be an exercise in masochism. She'd done some stupid things in the last two years, but she wasn't doing that.

She rifled her fingers through her hair, ruffling it first one way and then the other. 'Mess up your hair,' she ordered.

He did as she said.

She refused to focus on how divinely rumpled he suddenly looked. 'I can hear the car coming now.'

The scent of musk and citrus invaded her lungs as he leant in closer. 'We'll video conference every night.'

His hands descended to her shoulders squeezing them in a show of solidarity. She really, *really* wished that touch felt brotherly. 'Okay, just send me an email each day, letting me know what time you'll be free.'

'Sophie...'

She glanced up, mouth open to ask him what other instructions he had for her, when his lips swooped down to hers. One big hand cradled the back of her head to prevent her from drawing away as, with deliberate slowness, his tongue explored the outline of her inner lips with a slow deliberation that had her gripping the lapels of his jacket to keep her upright. This was no pretend kiss! It was hard and hot and demanding.

It was madness!

But he didn't stop.

And she gave herself over to it fully. Winding her arms around his neck, she pressed aching breasts against his chest, seeking relief, but it only inflamed her further. She told herself she was simply playing the game, not that she was powerless to control the rush of desire that pulsed into her every atom and tossed her every which way.

She sank her teeth into his lower lip. She should draw blood, remind him they were playing with fire, but she didn't. She lathed the point with her tongue until he pressed her back, taking control of the kiss again as droplets from the disturbed leaves of the rhododendron bush rained on their heads. He kissed her with such disturbing thoroughness it felt as if she'd never been kissed before, and she clung to him, mindless to everything except the sensations pouring into her.

His hand slid upward from her waist, up towards her breasts, as if he meant to take the weight of one breast in his hand, to test and caress it, fondle it, until she'd started to scale greater heights of pleasure. She wanted that. *Desperately.* She pressed against him, silently urging him on, when they were momentarily spotlighted in car headlights.

They both froze.

Slowly, Will eased away, keeping an arm about her until she found her balance. 'I'm sorry. That was stupid.'

She nodded, unable to speak.

'It won't happen again. I promise.'

She nodded again, wishing it were relief rather than disappointment that was her primary emotion.

It will be later, she told herself. She'd work on it until it was.

They walked back to the path.

He lifted her hand and pressed a kiss to her palm, before striding to the car. He chose to sit in the front rather than the back and she suddenly realised the driver was Colin. She sent him a weak smile and a wave.

The car started to move but then skidded to a halt. What on earth…?

Will's door opened and he leapt out and raced back to her. Good God! He wasn't going to kiss her again, was he?

He took her head in his hands when he reached her and lowered his brow to hers. 'You take care of yourself, Sophie. You hear me?'

'I… Yes, of course.'

'The old man is up to something and I don't want…'

'You don't want what?' she prompted when he hesitated.

He eased back to stare into her eyes. 'I don't want you getting hurt.'

The concern in his eyes melted things inside her that had been frozen for far too long, and she found herself absurdly close to tears. 'I'll be careful,' she whispered. 'I'll stay on my guard.'

'Promise me you'll look after yourself.'

He stared down at her as if he really cared.

Of course he cares. You're Peter's little sister.

But she had a feeling that he no longer saw Peter when he looked at her.

Her heart started to pound.

He drew back, a frown furrowing his brow, and she shook herself. 'You need to go. You're going to miss your flight. And, yes, I promise to look after myself.' She crossed her heart.

His gaze lowered to her chest. His gaze darkened and her breath hitched. But then he simply leaned forward and pressed a kiss to her brow and was gone.

Sophie watched the headlights disappear down the drive and only then did she turn back to the castle, enter the great hall and quietly close the door behind her, shutting out the night and the stars. If only she could shut out the confusion and the desire that continued to burn through her.

'A touching farewell.'

She started, pressing a hand to her chest and locating Lord Bramley a third of the way up the grand staircase. 'I wasn't aware we had an audience.'

He hadn't uttered the words with sarcasm, thank heavens, but it didn't leave her any the wiser to what he was thinking.

'Luckily my grandson was aware of the possibility and absconded with you into the shrubbery to take his leave.'

Heat flamed in her face. She must look a mess! She tried to smooth her hair down, even though *looking a mess* was exactly the effect she'd been aiming for.

She just hadn't realised they'd achieve the result so spectacularly. Or that it would leave her so discombobulated.

The old man stared at her intently and she found herself moving up the stairs, returning that stare. 'Do you always spy on your grandson?'

'Yes.'

She blinked at his frankness. *Wow!* Why?

It wasn't the question she asked. 'Why don't you like me?'

It was his turn to blink. 'It's nothing personal.'

'It feels personal.'

'I'm not convinced you're good for the lad.'

She chewed that over. 'You're referring to my party-girl reputation. You think I'll be a bad influence on Will.'

'I saw what that kind of lifestyle did to his parents.'

Will's parents had been drug-addled rock stars. 'I don't take drugs!' She released a pent-up breath and tried to moderate her voice. 'Only time will convince you that I've changed. I can't imagine anything I say at the moment will carry any weight with you.'

His eyes narrowed, not in suspicion but more…as if he were assessing her. 'You're more forthright than I expected.'

He approved of that at least. That much was evident.

'But I know who you are. I know you and Will have been meeting regularly ever since your brother died.'

She glanced away to stare at the shadows in the hall below.

'I'm sorry. I understand you must still miss him terribly.'

She couldn't look at him. It still hurt so much to talk about Peter in the past tense. 'You have a problem with us finding comfort in each other?'

'Comfort would be grand, but it seems to me there's little comfort to be had there. It seems more about keeping the wound fresh and open. That does Will no good. He deserves to be allowed to move forward with his life. You do too.'

She couldn't move forward until Carla was well again. But...

'You're still haunted, Ms Mitchell.'

She met his gaze then, and her chest clenched when she saw an almost identical reflection of her own pain in the depths of his eyes. His son, Will's father, had died of a drug overdose when Will was only twelve. He'd been a hard-drinking, out-of-control hellraiser. But she bet none of that had stopped Lord Bramley from loving his son, or from feeling he'd somehow failed him.

'It's late,' he said, swinging away. 'Goodnight, Ms Mitchell.'

She bit back a sigh. She'd work on getting him to call her Sophie again in the morning. In the meantime she'd ring Carla's rehab facility and tell them to expect the next instalment of money for Carla's treatment this coming week.

'So you survived your first day alone at Ashbarrow?'

That familiar sardonic eyebrow lifted and the thing that had felt missing and out of sync since he'd driven away yesterday fell into place now, and she instantly felt more at ease. 'I'm not alone. There's Carol Ann, a household of staff, not to mention your grandfather.'

She adjusted the screen of her laptop. 'Who, it probably won't surprise you to learn, was waiting for me when I came inside after we'd said our…farewells last night.'

All was quiet. It was after eleven o'clock and Sophie sat on the sofa in her private sitting room, elbows on knees and chin in hand, as she contemplated Will's image on her laptop where it was perched on the coffee table before her.

He was still heart-stoppingly gorgeous, even though her screen was in desperate need of a clean, but his potency was muted, thank heavens. It was the distance, the knowledge he was hundreds of miles away, and the fact that he appeared so much smaller on her laptop's screen than he was in real life. The fact she couldn't just reach out and touch him. It contained her temptation while at the same time allowing her to indulge in idle games of *What if?* She didn't need to be so careful of inflaming him…or on her guard for him inflaming her.

He straightened, his eyes shifting into that high-alert expression he often wore whenever he spoke about his grandfather. 'What happened?'

'He's worried I'm going to be a bad influence on you.'

The shock on his face made her laugh, and she set about recounting the conversation.

'You think he's still grieving for my father?'

'I'm sure of it.'

'But…' He frowned. 'That was twenty years ago.'

A weight pressed down on her shoulders. 'I don't think grieving has a timeframe. I can't imagine a time when I'll ever stop missing Peter.'

But she had to make sure her grief stopped hurting other people. Like Carla and Will.

He stared at her for a long moment. 'That's what I am to you, isn't it—just Peter's best friend?'

She lifted her chin from her hands, shifted back. 'You're not *just* anything, Will. You're your own person.'

He didn't look convinced.

She found herself fighting the urge to lean in closer again. 'Do you care what I think of you?'

'I…' He closed his mouth and shrugged.

She wanted desperately to lighten the mood. 'Sure, a part of me continues to see you as Peter's best friend. But there's a big part of me that's increasingly seeing you as a cash cow.'

Her frank irreverence made him throw his head back and laugh, and she called herself an idiot for thinking anything could mute this man's charisma. It reached out now and wrapped itself about her in ever tighter coils. It made her want things. Things she'd forgotten about.

Things she'd forgotten to want in her grief for Peter.

Things she no longer deserved.

She squared her shoulders. 'And you must still see me as Peter's little sister.' It was what their relationship had been established on.

'Is that what you believe?' He shook his head, sobering. 'The thing is, Sophie, I never did see Peter when I looked at you. I only ever saw you for yourself alone.'

'But…' She picked up the laptop and then didn't know what to do with it.

Dark eyes surveyed her steadily. 'But what?'

'Is that true?'

'It is.'

Then…then that meant he truly did like her—for *herself*. She didn't know what to say.

All she knew was that it left her feeling…golden.

For a moment Will barely recognised the face that stared back at him from his tablet. It was as if something had shifted inside Sophie, and it made his lungs cramp, making it impossible to breathe. He'd always thought her pretty, but now she looked…irresistible.

Maybe it was a trick of the light—maybe his screen needed a good clean. Whatever it was, he was glad they were over five hundred miles apart, and that he couldn't act on the impulses raging through his body.

'Now here's something you will probably be interested in knowing.'

She slid from the sofa to the floor as if to draw closer to him, hugging a cushion to her middle. He'd never been jealous of a cushion before. He swallowed. He had to get a grip before he saw her on Friday night. 'What's that?' he managed to get out.

'Your grandfather is planning to announce our upcoming nuptials in some newspaper I've never heard of.'

Announcement? An announcement hadn't even occurred to him! 'What's this newspaper called?'

He choked when she said its name. 'But that's… It's one of those sensationalist tabloids with zero credibility. You know the ones—*I was abducted by aliens… My canary is possessed… Here's a picture of Jesus's face in a piece of toast.* It's the kind of newspaper he'd call a scurrilous rag.'

Her new-found radiance drained out of her and he wanted to punch something.

'I guess he's making no secret about his lack of faith in our marriage, then…in his disapproval of your choice of bride.'

She bit her lip and he noticed how tightly she clutched the cushion to her chest. 'What?' he barked.

'If we can't get him to buy into the validity of our marriage then how are you going to get him to sign Ashbarrow over to you?'

It was a tricky situation, there was no denying that, but he'd been in trickier ones. And he wasn't sure what it said about him, but at the moment he was more interested in seeing her smile than he was in his grandfather. And it occurred to him exactly how to make that happen.

'What?' She shot forward, her eyes wide. 'Tell me what you're planning.'

She had beautiful lips. He'd been an idiot to kiss her last night, but that ridiculous temptation had seized him with a recklessness he'd thought he'd left behind at fourteen years of age. He'd used the excuse of their situation to kiss her deeply and completely. He'd wanted to experience it just once.

And it was all he'd been able to think about since. He burned to do it again.

You can't. This is Sophie. He'd promised no complications. And sex would be a complication. She'd made it clear she didn't want to be one of the parade of women who shared his bed. While he...? He'd give a lot to be one of the men to share her bed.

As long as he kept the thought of those other men out of his mind.

Keep sex and Sophie out of your mind.

Excellent advice. If only he could follow it.

'Oh, my God, Will. You're killing me here. Tell me your plan!'

Those lips... They were a dusky plum and perfectly shaped to fit his and, just from looking, he'd have never known that. But he did now. It made him realise the power of the mythical forbidden fruit.

He had to keep his head. For Sophie's sake. She deserved better from him.

'Will!' She groaned and disappeared, presumably fell on her side in a fever of impatience, and he suddenly found himself laughing. 'Give,' she ordered, popping back into view.

'Tomorrow I'm going to have our engagement announced in every major newspaper in the UK.'

She stared at him, her eyes widened, and then she

clapped her hands and threw her head back on a laugh. 'That's…inspired!'

Whatever else it was, it had made her smile, and that was all that mattered. Something inside him lifted.

'So…what's the deal with you and your grandfather?'

He crashed back to earth. It was all he could do not to scowl. 'You know how these things are.' He tried to shrug it off. 'Families.' He uttered the word as if it explained everything. 'Given your relationship with your father, I expect you can empathise.'

She shook her head. '"Every unhappy family is unhappy in its own way."'

The line sounded vaguely familiar and she said it as if quoting from a book. She'd always been a big reader. Him not so much.

'My father and I are unhappy because I look a lot like my mother and he can't see past that.'

Whoa! He knew they had a troublesome relationship, but he'd never realised that. Peter had shrugged off their clashes with the excuse that they were too alike. And he'd believed it.

'There's no need to look like that,' she reprimanded. 'It's not your fault.'

He wanted to make it better. Fix it.

He knew to his own detriment, though, that some things weren't fixable.

'How old were you when your mother left?'

'Eleven,' she replied.

'And she left your father for another man?'

'She did. And my father still hasn't got over it.'

Which was exactly why Will was never marrying. He was never opening his heart to that kind of damage.

Ahem, never marrying for real.

'Did she utterly abandon you and Peter?'

Sophie glanced down at her hands, and he found his

own hands clenching to fists. 'Father made it difficult for her to see us.'

She should've tried harder!

'And seeing her tore him up every single time.' Her eyes grew shadowed. 'It was awful.' She lifted her chin and sent him a smile that made his heart ache. 'But it's ancient history. So tell me the deal with you and Lord Bramley.'

After her disclosure, it would be churlish to refuse to answer. He rolled his shoulders and tried not to scowl. 'From the age of fourteen he's tried to control every aspect of my life—where I went to school, what friends I had, all of my extra-curricular activities. I was never permitted to go camping with friends, or even on day trips with anyone he deemed unsuitable. And what was considered unsuitable was as changeable as the wind.' In the school holidays he'd basically been cut off from all of his peers. 'My only freedom was spending those few weeks in London with Peter. He liked Peter.'

For the first time since Peter's death, she smiled at the mention of his name. 'Everyone liked Peter.'

That was true.

'At least he chose good schools and good friends for you,' she offered.

He dragged both hands back through his hair, pulled air into suddenly cramped lungs. 'Look, I know I should be grateful to him for taking Carol Ann and me in when my parents died. And I am. But I'm now a grown man. I've earned the right to make my own decisions.'

She nodded. He could see her mind racing behind the perfect blue of her eyes and it occurred to him that she'd like to try and fix things for him the way he'd like to for her. It wasn't possible, unfortunately, and she'd come to see that in time too.

'Forcing me to marry is just the latest in a string of attempts to control my life. He sabotaged my university applications, which is why I spent my first year at St Andrews rather than the university in London I'd chosen. It took me a year before I could transfer.'

Her jaw dropped. 'That's… It's outrageous!'

He'd been furious at the time.

'That's messing with your whole…future! Your hopes and dreams and…and *everything*.'

Her outrage helped pour balm on the old wound.

He glanced at his watch.

'Yes, it's getting late,' she agreed.

Maybe he'd try and make their video conference earlier tomorrow. 'Is there anything else I should know?'

She shook her head.

'Before I forget, I had an account set up for you and the money transferred into it today. I'll email you the details.'

She swallowed and sent him a smile that wasn't really a smile. 'Thank you. I appreciate it.'

There was a mystery there. And he meant to get to the bottom of it.

Will tried to dam the shuffle of excitement that squirmed through him when he logged onto his laptop to dial in with Sophie the next evening—half an hour earlier than the previous evening.

She sent him a cheery wave from where she was nestled into one corner of the sofa, legs tucked beneath her. 'How was your day, dear?' she drawled in a Hollywood voice that made him laugh, even as it drew his skin tight.

'Busy. Filled with meetings. Yours?'

'Full of wedding prep.'

He grimaced, but she just shrugged. 'It hasn't been too bad, but your grandfather did give me a guest list of all the people he wanted to invite.'

Dear God. 'Did you agree to it?'

She rolled her eyes. 'Give me some credit, Will. I said I'd

run it by you first. I'm trying to keep it small and contained—which I figured is what you'd prefer—but he's trying to blow it out into some kind of circus.'

He should be there fighting this battle with her.

She frowned. 'But maybe you'd prefer the circus.'

She couldn't be serious?

She took one look at his face and nodded. 'Right, scrap that. Just thought I'd check.'

'Who's on this guest list of his?'

'Well, we have two guest lists.'

Two?

'The apparently non-negotiable must-haves and the negotiable maybes.'

Great.

She stretched forward and just for a moment he thought he'd be gifted an unintentional eyeful of cleavage, but at the last minute she pressed her hand to the neckline of her blouse and all he was left with was an ache and the pounding in his veins. She settled back on the sofa with two sheets of paper and waved them at him. He grimaced. 'Hit me with the must-haves.'

She started reading them out. First came family—not that there was much of the Trent-Paterson line left. 'Okay.' He'd suck it up and endure them with as much grace as he could manage. 'That's not too bad.'

'Even counting Cousin Harold the potential usurper?'

He grinned at her mock ominous tones. He'd forgotten how playful she could be.

'Especially Harold. He'll be gnashing his teeth through the entire ceremony.' And he'd get his kicks where he could at the moment.

She laughed and that gave him a kick too.

'Next comes old family friends and neighbours,' she said, reciting the names.

He pursed his lips. 'We could cull half a dozen of those names, but…'

'What's the point?'

Exactly. 'Who's left?'

She wrinkled her nose. 'Dignitaries, local and otherwise.'

She rattled off the names and then a name came up that made him grimace. 'No way.'

She glanced up from the list.

'He's a local politician who's tried to model himself as some kind of philanthropist. Whenever he sees me—*every single time*—he tries to pump me for money…and then badgers me about improvements he believes are necessary to my grandfather's estate. It drives me crazy!'

She wrinkled her nose.

'And *every single time* he reminds me how I beat up his son when we were fourteen, implying that I owe him because he never called in the local authorities.'

She bit her lip, but her eyes danced. 'You beat up his son?'

He scowled and nodded.

'What did he do to deserve that?'

He didn't want to tell her. 'It sounds juvenile now,' he muttered.

She leant forward, more intrigued. 'You were fourteen. You're supposed to be juvenile.'

He pulled in a breath and then let it out in a rush. 'He used to sing my father's band's songs at me to wind me up. I ignored it for as long as I could. Eventually I told him to give it a rest or I'd beat him to a pulp. He kept going so…'

She covered her mouth with her hand and he had a feeling she was holding back a wave of laughter. 'So you beat him to a pulp?'

'Not exactly. I just… I gave him a black eye.' And bloodied his nose.

She threw her head back and laughed. 'Good for you!

Right, so we scrap them. There's only one more family on the list.'

She read the name out and he went cold all over. 'No.'

Her eyebrows rose, and he knew his face must look like thunder. All amusement vanished from her face. 'What did they do?'

It took a moment to unclench his jaw. 'I refuse to repeat the exact words, but they said the most disgusting things about Carol Ann and what should be done with her.'

Her eyes flashed and her every line grew so rigid the lists in her hands began to shake. She slashed a line through the names and called them such a rude word a laugh burst from him.

'I didn't know you had such a potty mouth,' he teased.

She stuck her nose in the air. 'I only pull it out on special occasions.'

He grinned. Good for her.

She turned her attention back to the list in her hand. 'Okay, so that means from your grandfather's list so far we have twenty-four names. You need to get me a list of who you'd like to invite.'

The short answer was nobody, but he knew that wouldn't wash.

'I've whittled my own list down to fourteen. The ten people my father would never forgive me for not inviting, and four of my closest girlfriends who'd be hurt beyond measure if I didn't include them. I thought we could keep it super simple and just have one attendant each. What do you think?'

Her words brought home the reality of what they were doing. He'd never wanted to marry, but going through the motions of a sham wedding left a bad taste in his mouth.

The wedding isn't a sham.

The wedding would be legally binding.

Think of Carol Ann.

He pushed down a sigh. 'Who have you chosen?'

'Carol Ann.'

That made him smile. 'She'll be thrilled.'

'To bits,' she agreed.

If Peter were alive he'd have asked him to be his best man. But he wasn't. And in all honesty, he was far from certain that Peter would approve of this sham of a marriage. Especially given that Sophie was involved. But this arrangement was just as much to Sophie's benefit as to Will's. It would enable her to carve out the life for herself that she wanted. Surely Peter couldn't disapprove of that.

'Who is on my grandfather's other list—the wish list?' he asked, determined not to dwell on Peter in case Sophie guessed the direction of his thoughts.

She read them out. Half the names he didn't recognise, but luckily they came with additional descriptions like 'local publican' and 'chair of the golf club'.

'None of them,' he said. 'We're keeping this small.' Were they really going to go through with this?

'Excellent.' She crumpled the sheet into a ball and tossed it across the room.

He shook his head. Of course they were going to go through with it, but it didn't mean he had to enjoy it. 'Anything else I need to know?'

She shook her head.

'Then I'll sign off. Ring me if you need anything.'

CHAPTER FIVE

THE FOLLOWING NIGHT Will logged onto his main computer with its huge monitor. It would be more comfortable to use his laptop or tablet from the comfort of his living-room sofa, but he didn't want comfort. He wanted to keep this businesslike.

'How are things your end?' he asked when she came into view. And then gulped. He hadn't taken into account the effect of seeing Sophie on the big screen. He should've used his tablet after all. He made a mental note to use it the following night.

'Hello, Will, I'm fine. Thank you for asking. How are you?'

He closed his eyes and counted to three. 'I'm glad you're fine. I'm well, thank you. Now, how did my grandfather react to the decimation of his guest list?'

'Threw a tantrum.'

He grimaced. 'I'm sorry. It's not fair that you have to put up with all of this.'

She shrugged, her gaze sliding away.

He stared at her and pursed his lips. 'Sophie, what did you do?'

She stuck out her chin and glared at him. 'I told him he'd interfered enough in your life as it was and that I wasn't letting him interfere any more. And that he better get used to it.'

She dusted off her hands and sent him a grin. 'Actually, it felt really good…which, perhaps, doesn't reflect all that well on me.'

He started to laugh. 'I'd have paid good money to see that.'

She rolled her eyes. 'You *are* paying good money.' She bit her lip. 'Afterwards I did feel a bit mean, though. Like I'd kicked a puppy.'

'Do *not* allow that sulky, hard-done-by act to sway you. The man is a master manipulator.'

She winced. 'Well…I kinda fell for it, and kinda said he could have beat-up boy's dad on the guest list.'

She looked so contrite and hangdog he almost laughed.

'But I promise to run interference for you.'

He shook his head. 'I'm sure I'll survive.'

She sucked her bottom lip into her mouth and worried at it. Things inside him clenched up tight. 'Will, what's the worst thing he's done? Is the university thing his worst interference?'

A familiar anger—frighteningly cold—settled over him. 'Why?'

She lifted her arms and let them drop. 'I'm just trying to work out what else to expect.'

His every sense went on high alert.

'Your grandfather doesn't want you to marry me. He's going to do everything in his power to prevent it from happening. I've already corrected a few *mistakes* that have been made in relation to the dates with the caterers and the minister marrying us.'

And she was evidently up for the challenge. And while it was good to see her concentrating on something other than her grief, it didn't mean she needed to know his entire history.

He scratched both hands back through his hair. But there was a lot riding on this marriage. And knowledge was power. *Damn it!* He dragged in a breath and concentrated on his breathing rather than the icy rage pounding through him. 'You recall how distraught Carol Ann was when she came to live with me in London?'

She nodded.

'I found out later he'd filled her head with all sorts of horror stories about the bad things that could happen to her in London. He made it sound like a hotbed of all things dire and disgusting—she was convinced it must be the most hostile place on earth.' *That* was the worst thing he'd done.

Her hand flew to her mouth. 'But…'

He just nodded.

She leaned forward, a frown filling her eyes. 'But that makes no sense. He adores her, dotes on her.'

'Anyone who'd deliberately frighten Carol Ann like that *cannot* really care for her.'

That frown deepened. 'He spends hours every day with her. I mean *hours*. They play board games, watch movies, go for walks. He truly dotes on her, Will. I think he was bluffing when he said she'd not have a home here at Ashbarrow.'

'I can't risk it. I don't trust him.' He couldn't bear the thought of Carol Ann ever being that distressed again. 'Besides, you don't want to do yourself out of a million pounds, do you?'

'I don't want you forced into a marriage you don't want either.'

For some reason her words warmed him. 'While we're sharing private confidences… What's the worst thing your father ever did?'

She froze and he suddenly wished the question unsaid.

She eased away from the screen as if physically moving away from him. 'I promised to never tell.'

His gut started to churn. Dear God, had he hurt her physically? 'You promised your father?'

She shook her head. 'Peter,' she whispered. 'I promised Peter.'

He could tell from the expression in her eyes that it hadn't been a good promise to make.

'But it was all a long time ago now. It's ancient history. So stop looking so worried.'

She shot him a smile that pierced through the Teflon coating around his heart, and made his pulse pound.

'What we need to do is focus on the current problem— your grandfather.'

He bet it had something to do with her mother. He made a note to investigate the matter further—check the newspaper reports of the time.

She rolled onto her stomach and he suddenly realised that her laptop was perched on her bed. She was chatting to him from her bedroom. She was lying on her tummy… *on a big double bed.*

Erase that thought from your memory.

He swallowed. 'Do you have any thoughts?' She wore a tight vest top and it highlighted the gentle swell of her breasts, and it took all his concentration to keep his gaze on her face…though his peripheral vision refused to obey that command.

She wasn't wearing a scrap of make-up. Her hair was pulled up into some kind of messy bun. None of it should give her the appearance of a being a temptress. She wasn't trying to be a temptress, which only made it worse.

Tomorrow night he'd go back to talking to her on his tablet.

And then the night after that he'd be picking her up from the airport.

Hell!

'Will!'

He crashed back at the exasperation threading her voice. 'Sorry, I was miles away. Long day,' he lied.

It wasn't a lie. They were all long days.

'I was asking if there's something you could request or

demand or be unequivocal about in relation to this wedding that would give your grandfather pause.'

'What kind of pause?'

'Something that would convince him you're really serious about this marriage.'

He had no idea.

'If you were ever to get married for real, what would you want? What's something personal, sincere…quirkily yours somehow?'

He stared at her. He didn't have a clue.

She stared back, the corners of her lips drooping. 'Well, you might want to give it some thought.'

He nodded.

She rested her chin in her hands. Her posture highlighted her cleavage, and thirst welled through him—incessant and demanding. He forced himself to keep his gaze on her face.

'A long day, huh?'

It was all he could do to nod.

'What do you do at that office of yours?'

'Meetings. I have a daily round of endless meetings.'

'With whom?'

'My different departments—Marketing and PR, HR, Legal, the development team. Then there are the clients. It used to be that I had to chase their business, but they approach me these days.' He could pick and choose the projects he worked on now. 'I'm in charge of project design. On top of that I've been brokering deals into previously closed markets overseas. All the usual stuff.

'What?' he demanded when she stared at him for a beat too long, feeling unaccountably defensive though he couldn't have said why.

'Do you enjoy it?'

The question made him blink. 'I like making money.' Money gave him freedom, independence, control. And he was never relinquishing those things. He was never allowing his life to be tossed around and disrupted on the whims of people like his parents or his grandfather—two extremes of the same pole. He was in charge of his own destiny now.

'Surely you've made enough of that by now.'

Had he?

'I remember you used to spend hours with the inner workings of a computer spread all around you, devising ways to make it run more efficiently and more powerfully. I used to marvel at your concentration. Do you still get to do that?'

Not any more.

Why not?

She cocked her head to one side. 'You know, the castle could do with an updated security system. I know it's not precisely your area, but it's all electronics, right?'

'You want me to design a security system for Ashbarrow?'

'Why not? You know the castle just about better than anyone. You'd know all of its security strengths—' her eyes danced '—and weaknesses.'

She grinned as if she'd known he'd developed ways of sneaking out of the castle and its grounds unnoticed as a teenager. He found himself grinning back. 'This is true.'

He sobered. 'Are you feeling unsafe at Ashbarrow?'

'Heavens no! Your grandfather employs a host of burly gardeners. But since the news of our engagement broke there's been a succession of reporters trying to get interviews. It's not a threat, just a nuisance.'

And one he could solve for her. She didn't need to put up with that. 'I'll get onto it straight away.'

'So the announcements in the newspapers weren't a joke? You're getting married?'

Sophie tried not to shrivel under her father's stunned

glare. She forced her chin up, forced a smile to her lips, but she clung to Will's hand for dear life. 'Yes, at the end of the month. I spoke to your secretary and she's cleared your calendar.'

He drew himself up to his full imposing height of six feet four inches. 'Why so soon?' He glanced at her stomach.

'No, Father, I'm not pregnant. There's not going to be a surprise baby in six or seven months.'

'Then why this ungodly rush?'

He was as remote and unemotional as ever. The total opposite of Lord Bramley's thundering tantrums. 'Well,' she drawled. 'As I'm marrying Will for his money, I need to get him down the aisle as quickly as I can.'

She had the satisfaction of seeing a flash of fire whip through her father's eyes before they became studiously unemotional again.

'Sophie,' Will admonished, making her realise how childish she was being.

'I'm sorry, Will, you'll have to forgive my flippancy, but nothing I've ever done has met with my father's approval. Though I can't imagine how he can find fault with you.'

Her father's head rocked back. 'Of course I don't disapprove of William. He's a fine man. I just don't understand the urgency. Marriage is a serious undertaking…and people will talk at the ridiculous speed of your marriage.'

'And as we know, that's an argument that's always carried a lot of weight with me,' she drawled.

Will squeezed her hand. Oddly, it made her feel less alone. The way Peter used to make her feel less alone.

'Why will you never be serious, Sophie?' Her father sighed.

Because she was tired of always being found wanting, though she didn't say that out loud. She didn't want him to know his disapproval could still wound her. 'All that was required of you was to offer your congratulations and wish us well.' She paused to give him time to respond. When he didn't she rushed on. 'The venue's booked and the invitations have gone out this morning. It's all prepared. I'm not changing the date now. Besides, people will talk more if the wedding is cancelled or delayed.'

His nostrils flared, his lips thinned, but if he'd wanted to reprimand her further he managed to hold himself back. 'And will I have the honour of walking you down the aisle?'

'I suppose people *will* talk if you don't.'

Could she be any more ungracious if she tried? She smothered a wince. Could he?

'Sir, I care for your daughter. I want the very best for her.'

'That's reassuring.'

'But there's something I've been wanting to ask Sophie, and it might be best if we all deal with that issue now…together.'

What on earth…?

'Sophie—' Will turned to her '—do you want your mother to attend the wedding?'

Her heart started to pound. Had he spoken to her mother?

As an eleven-year-old, she'd promised Peter to never speak of their mother to their father again. A rock settled in the pit of her stomach. She'd promised to never choose their mother over their father. *She'd promised.* But… Her pulse started to race and she couldn't look at her father.

She was an adult now. She no longer wanted to be anyone's pawn. Did she dare…?

She gazed into Will's eyes and it gave her the courage to face the fact that it was a promise she should never have been asked to make. It was a promise she didn't want to keep.

Not even for Peter.

She swallowed, her palms growing clammy. Her father had made it nearly impossible for their mother to keep in contact with them. It had been cruel and unfair. Still, looked at in the cold, hard light of day, her mother had relinquished all custody rights in exchange for an advantageous financial settlement.

She glanced at her father and wondered if he remembered that afternoon fifteen years ago. She moistened dry lips. 'If you want to walk me down the aisle, you need to speak to Mother and tell her she's welcome to attend my wedding.'

The colour drained from her father's face. She gripped Will's hand and inched a fraction closer to him, her heart pounding like a caged thing. Will's hand tightened about hers. Without another word, her father turned and left the room.

A fist tightened about her ribcage until she could barely breathe. The last time she'd mentioned her mother to him...

'Sophie?'

She was dimly aware of Will pushing her into a chair and forcing her to take a sip of brandy.

She loved brandy, and it scorched a path down her throat now, burning off the shroud of mist that had her in its grip. Will crouched down in front of her, those dark eyes crinkling in concern as he scanned her face. 'Did I do the wrong thing in raising the topic of your mother?'

'No.' With an effort, she swallowed. 'You've spoken with her?'

He nodded. 'She cried when I told her why I was ringing.'

Really?

'She said nothing would give her more pleasure than to attend your wedding.'

So...she hadn't forgotten Sophie? Hadn't given up on her?

'She said she'd only be there, though, if she had both your and your father's blessings.'

Her throat thickened. She might not be eleven years old any more, but... 'I can't stay here tonight.'

He took one look at her face and didn't press her to explain or tell her she was being silly. 'You can come home with me unless you'd prefer a room at the Savoy.'

She'd prefer to be away from prying eyes. 'Your place will be perfect.'

'Wow!'

Sophie moved to the wall of glass in Will's converted warehouse apartment that overlooked the Thames. She'd been to his house in Chelsea, before he'd sold it—after Carol Ann's disastrous stay—but she'd never been here to his Canary Wharf penthouse.

The lights on the Thames glittered, turning the river into a fairyland. 'This is amazing.'

She turned with a smile. He'd been quiet ever since they'd left Knightsbridge and she wanted to lighten his mood. 'I definitely made the right choice. Your place has an even better view than a suite at the Savoy.'

He didn't so much as crack a smile. He took off his jacket and dropped it to the nearest chair. The broad lines of his shoulders made her pulse flutter up into her throat.

He moved across to stare down into her face. 'Sophie, has your father ever been violent towards you?'

His words momentarily froze her. Finally she managed to tip up her head to meet his gaze. She swallowed, the lie she'd started to form dissolving on her tongue. 'He's never slapped or hit me.'

'But?'

She swallowed again and nodded. 'He grabbed me once

in anger. The look in his eyes, Will…' It had chilled her to the bone. For several long seconds her father's fury had made her fear for her life. She still had nightmares about it.

She chafed her arms. 'I had a puppy—a little terrier—and it flew to my defence and bit him on the ankle, which made him let me go.' The puppy was gone the next day. She pulled in a breath. 'So he frightened me, but he didn't hurt me.'

And yet nothing had ever been the same again.

'Why did he grab you like that?'

She turned to stare out at the river, barely taking in the twinkling prettiness of it. 'I was being a brat. He was hauling me over the coals for my apparently disappointing school report…so I told him I missed my mother and wanted to see her. This was during their divorce. I knew it'd get a reaction out of him. I wanted to hurt him. I can't even remember now if I really wanted to see her or whether I just wanted to provoke him.'

'Sophie, you were eleven.'

And yet the memory was as vivid as if it had happened yesterday.

'You were frightened to stay in the house with him tonight.'

'Old ghosts,' she murmured. 'It reminded me of how ugly it all was when my mother first left. I didn't want to… revisit those memories.'

His eyes scanned her face and she prayed he'd let the matter drop. 'What memories, Sophie?'

A breath hissed out from between her teeth; she could probably deflect him, but she wasn't sure she wanted to. It felt strangely freeing to talk about it after all this time. She lifted her chin and met his gaze. 'That was the very last time I ever raised the topic of my mother in his presence, Will. Until this evening.'

His eyes widened, and his jaw slackened.

'You have to understand that my father really did terrify me that day. I'd never seen him so angry in all my life— not before and not since. My screams alerted the household staff…and Peter.'

The intensity of his gaze didn't waver. 'What happened afterwards?'

'I promised Peter I'd never mention my mother to Father again, that I'd never ask to see her or speak with her. I promised that if I had to appear in court I'd choose my father over my mother.'

Will stared at her, his face grey. He reached out and cupped her cheek. 'He should never have asked that of you.'

'No,' she whispered. 'I know he wanted to keep me safe, and that was part of it, but neither one of them should've asked that of me. I've been hiding from that fact all this time…until this evening.'

'When I put my foot in it.'

She pursed her lips, fear and exhilaration pounding through her in equal measure. 'It's time for me to take control of my life, Will. It's what I want to do. It's what I *need* to do. I want to get away from the party scene. And I no longer want to be a pawn in my father's ongoing game of revenge. It's time that all ended.' It was time for her to be an adult.

Lord Bramley stared at her. 'Your mother is coming to the wedding?'

'We're hoping so.' She glanced at Will, who stared out of the drawing-room window, his back to them. He didn't turn around.

'But…does this mean your father is going to boycott the wedding?'

She couldn't work out if the idea appalled or appealed to him. 'I've no idea.' He'd refused to take her calls. She'd thought she wouldn't care a jot about that, but it appeared she did.

Will turned and his grandfather waved a finger at him. 'And you organised this? Didn't you know the hornets' nest you'd be stirring up? The Mitchell divorce case was…it was notorious at the time! And you want to go and rake all that up?'

'Don't start bellowing,' Will snapped. 'I knew what Sophie wanted and I set about making it happen. Lord Collingford will just have to deal with it. I won't have him bullying Sophie. If he wants to act like a child, then that's his affair.'

But his gaze darted to Sophie and she saw the uncertainty there. Before she could allay it, he'd rounded on his grandfather again.

'And while we're on the subject I won't have you bullying her either. You'll start by not challenging her every decision about this blasted wedding.'

'Blasted wedding?' Lord Bramley bounced onto the balls of his feet, stabbing a finger at the ceiling. 'Ha! I knew you didn't want this wedding!'

'I never wanted a wedding,' Will hollered back. 'If I'd had my way we'd have eloped to Vegas. It's only due to Sophie that we didn't. But in three Saturdays' time, Sophie gets the wedding she wants. And I'm not going to let anyone stop her from having it!'

Wow! He looked as if he meant every word.

He straightened. 'And, while we're on the subject of the wedding, I want Grandmother's wedding ring. I'd like Sophie to wear it.'

Double wow. For a moment the room went totally still. All the temper drained from Lord Bramley's face, though it was still grim—and behind the grimness lurked weariness. A part of her that she wanted to remain hard softened.

'You're both making the right noises, playing the roles of loving fiancés to perfection, but I'm not convinced the two of you haven't done some deal to try and trick me.'

'And what if we have?' she found herself saying. Both men swung to her, Lord Bramley's jaw dropping, Will's eyes throbbing though his face remained totally impassive.

'Yes, I know about your ultimatum. Of course Will told me about it. He's an honourable man. But because of your ultimatum you'll never know for sure now whether he marries for love or not. You seem to think you can just put some kind of schedule on love. Well, it doesn't work like that!'

She found herself pacing back and forth across the room, flinging her arms out as she spoke. 'And you know what—what's the big deal about love anyway? It didn't do my father any good. It didn't do Will's parents any good. Seems to me they'd have all been better off without it.'

The older man lowered himself into his armchair, brushing a hand across his eyes.

She wanted to yell at him that forcing Will into marriage was reprehensible, but she had a feeling he'd only hear the criticism implicit in the words, not the truth. For some reason he was hell-bent on bringing his grandson to heel. And nothing she said would change that.

She stopped pacing to slam her hands to her hips. 'Well, you know what? I think a marriage between two friends who like each other and respect each other has a better chance of success than either my parents' marriage or Will's parents' marriage, don't you?'

She stopped, breathing hard. Had she said too much? Had she ruined everything? She glanced across. Dear God, had she disappointed Will?

Will walked across, took her face in his hands and pressed a brief hard kiss to her lips that sent the blood stampeding through her veins. 'You're magnificent, you know that?'

She was?

'But it won't work,' he continued. 'You won't be able to guilt him into doing the decent thing. He won't let me off the hook.'

She bit back a smile. 'I don't really want you off the hook.' She had a million pounds to collect at the end of all this. Still, she wished he weren't in a position where he had no choice.

She glanced back at the older man, who stared at them with a frown in his eyes. 'I know you don't like me, Lord Bramley, but, whatever else you want to think, know this— I care about your grandson.'

She laced her fingers through Will's and it felt like the most natural thing in the world. 'You better get me out of here before I say something I really regret.'

A laugh rumbled from his throat. 'Your wish is my command.'

The older man shot to his feet. 'You'll be back for dinner?'

The expression on Will's face made her leap into the breach. 'Is Carol Ann expected home by then?' Will's sister was on an outing with a group of friends.

'Yes.'

'Then, yes,' she said over her shoulder as Will towed her from the room.

He didn't release her when they were out of their sight. If anything his grip tightened, and he scowled. 'I hate how he tries to control our every hour while we're here. Does he do that to you when I'm not here?'

'I'm rushed off my feet organising a wedding. He can't commandeer my time as and when he likes. He does like to know if I'm going to be in for dinner. But that's reasonable as he needs to let the cook know.'

Will stopped and stared down at her. 'Have you ever not been in for dinner?'

He asked as if the thought hadn't occurred to him. She nodded. 'I had a supper appointment with a prospective caterer last week.' It had been a blessing to get out from beneath Lord Bramley's oppressive surveillance.

She found herself grinning as she urged Will forward again. 'I took Carol Ann with me, which meant your grandfather had to dine alone. He sulked about it the entire day.' She hadn't felt the slightest bit guilty about it either. He'd been particularly tiresome that day, and she'd wanted to let him know she wouldn't put up with it.

'Where are we going?' she asked as he towed her towards the car.

'It's a surprise,' he said with a cryptic smile that immediately piqued her interest.

They drove for fifteen minutes before Will turned the car onto a country lane lined with tall hedges of hawthorn before turning into a driveway and pulling the car to a halt in a small car park. She read the sign and straightened. 'Moreland Park Equestrian Centre.'

She glanced through the windscreen, trying to take it all in. 'You've brought me to the local stables!'

'I thought you might like to have a look around. I phoned ahead so they're expecting us. The manager is going to give us a tour, which will give you an opportunity to ask all the questions you want.'

This was…perfect! She swung to him and he grinned at whatever he saw in her face. 'When did you arrange this?' Surely there'd been no time this morning?

'Through the week.'

His thoughtfulness touched her. 'Oh, Will, this is perfect. I can't thank you enough.'

He grinned and it made heat stir in her blood. Her fingers curled into her palms. She had to get these wayward feelings for Will under control. She had to stop thinking about him so…*carnally*.

'It's not entirely altruistic. I wanted to reinforce your reasons for being stuck out here in Scotland, help shore up any flagging defences.'

And just like that he made her laugh, and everything was comfortable again. Or, if not precisely comfortable, then at least contained. 'I always said you were a smart man.'

His gaze lingered on her lips for a couple of beats too long, but then he pushed out of the car. 'Ready?'

And she told herself she'd imagined the hunger that had momentarily flared in his eyes. She scrambled out of the other side. 'Yes, please.'

'So, what did you think?'

They were sitting across from each other in the quaintest of quaint tearooms—all frilly curtains, white tablecloths and perfect date scones—after their two-hour tour of the equestrian centre.

She lifted the teapot and poured them both cups of steaming tea, inhaling the fragrant brew as she blew on it. 'It was wonderful, brilliant. I mean, Morelands functions on a much larger scale than anything I'm planning, but…' She'd learned so much and her mind was reeling with it all. 'Have I thanked you yet?'

His smile hooked up one side of his mouth. 'Several times.'

'Good.' She took a sip of tea, before setting her cup back to her saucer. 'It has me so eager to get started on my own place. I don't have the room to set up an eventing course like they have, but I could set up one of the fields with some small jumps.' And not so small jumps if she attracted clients who wanted them. 'Though I'd love to build an indoor arena like theirs.'

After Carla's treatment, hopefully there'd be enough money left to improve and update the current stables and outbuildings *and* stretch to an indoor arena as well. Apparently such facilities were in demand. And if she could attract expensive dressage horses to her establishment... Well, things could really take off!

Which might mean there wouldn't be enough money to stretch to a cottage initially, but she could have accommodation built into the stables. A flat with two bedrooms—one for her and one for Carla. Or maybe two flats. She'd need to look into prices, organise some quotes.

She suddenly became aware of how intently Will watched her and it made her skin prickle and her stomach tighten. Where earlier he'd watched her with a kind of pleased indulgence, now he'd turned almost grim.

She finished ladling strawberry jam onto a scone, but she didn't lift it to her lips. 'Did I totally screw up with your grandfather this morning?'

'No, you played it pitch perfect. It hadn't occurred to me to actually be honest with the old man. By mentioning the elephant in the room you...'

'I?'

'Deflated it. Robbed it of its power.'

She had? She could've sagged in relief. 'You know, if you hadn't told me about all the instances where he's interfered in your life, I'd have simply said he's all bluff and no bite.'

Except the expression in Will's eyes told her there was a lot of bite to the older man...and Will was just about fed up with it. And yet she couldn't dismiss from her mind how much time Lord Bramley spent with Carol Ann, how much he loved her.

'I think he's lonely.'

'I think he's scared that he's running out of people to lord it over,' Will countered.

'He hates London.'

Will's lips twisted. 'A fact he's made no secret of.'

She dragged her gaze from those lips. They had the ability to sidetrack her. And she didn't want to be sidetracked. She wanted to work Lord Bramley out. For Will's sake. After all, he was paying her a million pounds. She should do all she could to earn it. Working Lord Bramley out was the least she could do. 'I mean, he *really* hates it. It's more than a rural man's disdain for the big smoke. It's…' She'd almost describe it as pathological.

She glanced at Will and bit her lip, wondering how he'd take any mention of his father.

He hadn't touched his tea. He hadn't touched his scone. And his grim gaze hadn't left her face. 'Go on.'

'Well, I wonder if he hates London so much because it's where your father died.'

He stilled before shifting in his seat. She couldn't decipher the expression on his face.

'Your parents' antics were well publicised.' Sex, drugs and rock 'n' roll seemed like the ultimate in bright-lights excitement, but from all she'd read it hadn't brought his parents much happiness. 'Maybe he blames London for the lifestyle choices they made.'

'No city can be blamed for my parents' bad behaviour.'

She winced at the hardness in his voice.

'My parents were hell-bent on self-destruction, and they didn't care how many people they hurt in the process or took down with them. It wouldn't have mattered if they were in London, Stockholm, Sydney or Pitlochry. Where they lived was the least of it.'

'But that's not exactly true, is it?'

His gaze speared to hers.

'There are more opportunities in a big city, more temptations. I mean, drugs are easier to get in London than they are in rural Perthshire.' Just look how easy it had been for Carla to fall under their spell.

'Don't be naïve, Sophie. Drugs are easy to get any-where. With the right connections. And, believe me, my parents had the right connections.'

She prayed to God that Carla had no such connections in Surrey.

'Have you ever asked your grandfather why he's inter-fered so much?'

Will's jaw dropped. 'What for?' he demanded, snapping his jaw back into place. 'The man's a control freak. It's as simple as that. I'm not giving him the satisfaction of letting him list all of my so-called defects and character faults, or to reprimand me with all that I owe him.'

She lifted her cup and prayed her hand didn't shake. 'I think you should try talking to him.'

'Why?'

She set her cup down with a clatter. 'Because he took you and Carol Ann in when you were orphaned. Be-cause he fed, clothed and housed you...sent you to good schools.'

His head rocked back as if she'd slapped him.

'Because it's still you who he wants to inherit the title and the estate.' Because she was certain that beneath it all, and despite appearances to the contrary, Lord Bram-ley loved his grandson.

'It's out of the question. And this subject is no longer open for discussion. What I do or don't owe my grand-father is no concern of yours.'

Ouch! So that told her.

He dragged a hand down his face. 'And it's not what I brought you here to discuss.'

So he did have something on his mind? But if it wasn't his grandfather and their current situation...? 'What did you want to discuss?'

'I had the money I sent to you tracked. I know it didn't go towards work at your stables. I want to know what you did with that money, Sophie.'

CHAPTER SIX

SOPHIE STARED AT Will in growing horror. 'You've…you've been *spying* on me?'

She found herself half out of her seat, but forced herself to sit back down. At the back of her mind a little voice kept whispering: *a million pounds, a million pounds*.

She couldn't create a scene. It wasn't just the money. She might be furious with him, but that didn't mean she wanted to wreck things for him where Carol Ann was concerned.

'I trusted you!'

He paled at her words, but his gaze didn't drop. 'I know the money was transferred to a medical facility in Surrey.'

She pushed all visible signs of anger deep down until they couldn't be seen, making herself go completely blank. She'd had plenty of practice doing that with her father.

'It appears you've just answered your own question, then,' she said, reaching for her scone, forgoing the cream. She wasn't sure she could face a scone with just jam as it was. 'So I wonder at you bothering to ask the question at all.'

His eyes narrowed. 'Sophie, I—'

'What is it with you and your grandfather? Is it a genetic thing that makes you want to control everyone in your vicinity?'

He leaned towards her, eyes flashing. 'I am *nothing* like my grandfather.'

His voice was tight and hard, and she forced herself to give a tinkling laugh designed to set his teeth on edge. His jaw clenched and she tried to feel a measure of satisfaction. 'Darling, from where I'm sitting you could be one and the same person.'

She bit into her scone and watched his hands clench and unclench on the table.

'Why did you send a hundred thousand pounds to this medical facility?'

'A donation.'

'I don't believe you.'

'I don't care,' she flashed right back.

Damn! She was supposed to be channelling a glacial composure, not lashing out in anger…and hurt. 'I told you that you had no say in how I spent the money. I'm wondering what else you're now going to renege on. What else are you going to demand for your million pounds, Will?'

His mouth went tight. 'I want to know what kind of trouble you're in!'

'I'm in no trouble whatsoever.'

'I want to believe you.'

Her heart pounded so hard her chest started to ache. 'But you don't?' She shook her head, searching for that comforting blankness, finding herself absurdly close to tears. 'I suppose I shouldn't find that so surprising. Or disappointing.'

He swore, low and savage, and she dropped her scone to her plate and reached for a napkin. She pressed it to her lips, her stomach churning.

'There's too much at stake here, and I'm not talking about the money. I don't care about the money. Hell, Sophie, you think I enjoy asking you this? I'm caught between a rock and a hard place, and I'm going to be flattened whichever option I choose. Maybe you can provide me with some advice for this particular dilemma.'

She had no idea what he was talking about.

'Do I trust you and hope for the best? Or do I keep faith with the promise I made Peter?'

Her heart burned at the mention of her brother's name. She moistened suddenly dry lips. 'What did you promise Peter?'

He sat back, dragged a hand through his hair. 'To look out for you. To help you if you were ever in trouble. To be there for you when he couldn't.'

Her brother had died in Africa. He'd been a pilot for a charity organisation in charge of establishing hospitals in remote areas. He'd flown in building supplies and provisions. However, hostile rebel forces had surrounded one of the villages he'd flown into and there'd been no chance of escape. During the six-hour stand-off, he'd rung to tell her he loved her. The memory of that phone call made her temples throb. The authorities hadn't arrived in time to save them. The entire village had been slaughtered.

'When did you make that promise?'

'The day he died. He called you first and then your father…and then me.'

She hadn't known he'd called Will too. The two of them had never spoken about it.

Just for a moment her mother's face swam into vision and she had to close her eyes against a different pain. 'Would you keep a promise made to Peter, even if it were a bad promise?'

'Sophie, it was the last thing I ever promised him.' Pain made his voice hoarse. 'Don't ask me to break my word to him.'

For a moment she had to cover her face with her hands. 'Please…won't you confide in me?'

She heard the agony stretching behind those words and it dissolved her anger. He was trying to do his best by Peter. She couldn't blame him for that.

She lifted her head. 'To confide in you means I have to break a promise I've made to someone else.'

'Peter?'

Not Peter. To someone who hadn't been thinking clearly…who still wasn't thinking clearly. An unexpected surge of relief at the thought of sharing her burden momentarily blindsided her. But…

She lifted her chin. 'I'll make a deal with you, Will.' Not that she was in a position to make a deal, but… If something good could come from breaking her promise to Carla, she'd take it.

'What kind of deal?'

'I'll confide in you…'

'And in return…?'

'You speak to your grandfather—really talk to him. Try and find out why he's so insistent you marry, try and find out why he's interfered so much in your life.'

He didn't draw back as she expected. He gave a hard nod. 'Deal.'

Wow. She swallowed and glanced around the cosy tearoom. 'I can't break a promise in such civilised surroundings. Can we go somewhere…wild?'

Without a word he rose, tossed some money on their table and led her out to the car. Ten minutes later she found herself halfway up a mountain with a green windswept valley spread out below. Lochs glinted in the intermittent sun as low clouds scudded across the sky, and when she pushed out of the car the wind whipped her hair about her face.

'Is this wild enough?'

'It's perfect.' Pulling a hair tie from her pocket, she drew her hair back into a ponytail. She planted herself on a boulder and stared at the view. Will stood beside her, although there was room enough for him to sit on the rock too. He stuck his hands into his pockets and braced his legs against the wind and just waited. He didn't prompt or pressure her and she was grateful for it. In fact, she found his presence somehow reassuring.

Finally she moistened her lips and started to speak. 'I

sent the money to that medical facility in Surrey because Carla is currently in drug rehab there. It's the first instalment of money for treatment that we expect will cost three hundred thousand pounds. I paid twenty thousand pounds a month ago to hold her place, but that pretty much cleaned me out.'

She'd been too busy trying to escape from the harsh reality of Peter's death and hiding from her grief to save money. It made her sick to the stomach with shame now. How could she have been so frivolous? How could she have been so blind?'

From the corner of her eye she saw Will turn towards her, sensed he was about to speak. She held up a hand. 'Please don't say anything yet. Let me just…finish.' She swallowed. She couldn't look at him. 'And don't look at me—look at the view. I'm betraying Carla's confidence in telling you this, and I've let her down so much already that I don't think I can stand for you to watch while I…'

She couldn't finish the sentence. Will turned to stare back at the view. She wanted it to help. She wanted it to ease the burning in her chest, help her breathe more freely, but it didn't. She forced herself to continue. 'I needed to pay a significant proportion of the money by the end of this week. They were threatening to stop her treatment unless monies were received.'

She could hardly blame them. They deserved payment for all their hard work. They were providing Carla with the very best care.

She glanced down at her hands. 'I know there are cheaper treatment options available, but this particular programme has had outstanding results and came highly recommended. I want Carla to have the very best treatment available.' She wanted Carla to have every chance for a bright and happy future.

She sensed rather than saw Will nod.

'You see, I wasn't even aware that Carla was doing drugs. I was too wrapped up in my own little world—too busy dancing into the wee small hours, guzzling champagne, going home with whoever took my eye…all while trying to forget that Peter was no longer with us. I didn't know Carla had taken it to a whole other level with drugs—snorting cocaine at every available opportunity, apparently. Not until one of my old school friends told me about the rumours she'd been hearing.'

That conversation had been the first slap back to reality.

The second had been finding Carla with a needle in her arm.

'By the time I cottoned on to what was happening, Carla had moved to heroin.' A better friend would've noticed sooner.

Will swung back to her. 'Can I speak yet?'

His voice shook with emotion, and it was all she could do not to throw herself into his arms and sob her heart out. She blinked hard and nodded.

'How did you convince her to get treatment?'

That hadn't been easy. 'She flat out refused at first. We had the most dreadful row.' She stared at a cow grazing far below them and refused to take her eyes from it. 'It was awful. I think it shocked her into realisation—that she was killing herself, that she was in danger of losing everything, that she needed help…that the path she was on was not the one Peter would've wanted for her.'

'Do her parents know?'

She shook her head. 'She made me promise not to involve them. She made me promise not to tell anyone.' A promise she'd now broken. 'I'm not permitted to see her at the moment—it's part of her treatment.' She pulled in a deep breath. 'It's also part of her treatment to tell those closest to her about her condition. She doesn't know that yet.'

She had no idea how Carla would cope with it. She just

prayed her friend would find the courage and the resources she needed when the time came. 'Before I laid down any cold hard cash I had a long talk with one of the doctors in charge of the programme.' He'd explained the process to her. 'There're no easy fixes. She has a long road ahead of her.'

She moved her eyes from the grazing cow to stare at the way the light played across the surface of a loch, making it look blue one moment and silver the next. There was hope for Carla. That bright future was still there waiting for her to claim it. But she should never have fallen so far before Sophie had noticed.

Will crouched down in front of her, blocking out the loch and the cow and forcing her to meet his gaze. She expected to see censure—she deserved censure—but there was only concern…and warmth. Her throat thickened.

'Soph, have you been dealing with this all on your own?'

The affectionate shortening of her name made her eyes fill. She swallowed, hard. 'It was the least I could do.'

'And that's the reason you wanted a million pounds—for Carla's treatment.'

She blew out a breath. 'I really only needed three hundred thousand.'

'But?'

She bit back a sigh and tried to find a smile. 'But I want a place where Carla can come to once her treatment is finished. And, at the risk of sounding like your grandfather, I wanted that to be away from London with all its temptations and associations. She deserves a chance at a fresh start.'

'And, like you, she's a rider,' he said slowly.

She should've twigged that something was wrong when Carla had stopped riding with her.

'I'd have given you the money, no strings attached, if you'd told me.'

She knew that. 'I made her a promise. I wanted to keep it.'

'But I forced you to break it.'

She shrugged, surprised to discover she didn't feel guilty. Not about that, anyway. 'You invoked Peter's name.' It still had the power to trump everything else. 'And I knew that if I didn't tell you, you'd investigate further and discover the truth for yourself. Besides…' She hesitated.

'What?'

'I'm glad someone else knows. I'm glad someone else has her back if she needs it.'

Will stared into blue eyes cloudy with concern and remorse and had to fight the urge to haul her into his arms and hold her close. He had a feeling that offering Sophie physical comfort could lead all too easily to other things.

And he'd promised her no complications.

Her life evidently had enough of those already. It made him wonder if he'd ever truly known her.

A headache started up behind the backs of his eyes. He'd forced her to betray a confidence. It had been a despicable thing to do, and yet… 'I wish I'd known about this sooner. I'd have helped.'

He understood why she hadn't, of course. She'd handled everything extremely well from what he could tell. But it tore at him that she'd had to deal with it alone. He rose and took a step back before the sweet plum-jam scent of her addled his brain.

She shot to her feet and made as if to seize his arm, but obviously thought the better of it and let her hand drop to her side. 'Would you have done it differently?'

'No!' He didn't want her thinking that. 'I could've just been a support for you.'

'For me? I don't deserve anyone's support! I let Carla down. If it wasn't for me she wouldn't be in this mess at all.'

He stiffened. 'That's nonsense! You didn't buy her the drugs. You didn't urge her to take them.'

'Maybe not, but before Peter she hardly ever went out to nightclubs or wild parties. She'd have never run with a fast crowd if it weren't for me. That was my doing. She became my partying partner in crime.'

He could see now, so clearly, how both women had been trying to hide from their grief.

'I should've taken better care of her. I should've realised sooner what she was up to.'

'People with drug problems learn to hide it.' He hauled in a breath. 'People have to make their own choices. And holding yourself responsible for Carla's drug addiction won't help you get over your grief for Peter any more than partying for two years has.'

She flinched, and he wanted to swear. He reached out and grasped her shoulders. 'Why can't you focus on the positives? Why can't you acknowledge the good you're doing now?'

'The good?' She jerked out of his grip. 'What on earth can be positive about any of it?'

'That Carla *is* getting the help she needs, that you've been instrumental in getting her that help.'

'But—'

'No buts, Sophie.'

She stared at him, confusion and consternation chasing themselves across her face.

'I want you to know something else.'

She gripped her hands in front of her as if waiting for some kind of judgement or condemnation. A part of him started to weep for her. 'I want you to know that I do trust you. I'm sorry I asked you to break your word to Carla. I should've known better. I won't make that same mistake again.'

Her eyes widened.

'I made a promise to Peter, which means I'll still ask questions if I'm concerned about anything, but if you tell me to back off and mind my own business, I will.'

'I…' She snapped her mouth closed, evidently at a loss for what to say. She didn't have to say anything.

'You're not a child who needs checking up on, but a woman who knows her own mind—an adult who can look after herself and the people she cares about. My loyalty lies with the living.' He dragged in a breath and made himself continue. 'My loyalty lies with you now, rather than Peter.' And in his bones he felt that this was exactly what Peter would've wanted.

Will settled in front of his giant computer monitor half an hour earlier than his and Sophie's scheduled meeting time. For the last two evenings, though, she'd been ready a good twenty minutes early.

But as he sat there waiting, he realised she wasn't going to be early tonight.

He frowned. Had she mentioned that she had some meeting scheduled for the evening? A moment later he shook his head. It could simply be his grandfather commandeering as much of her time as she'd allow. While Sophie had won points for her forthrightness last Saturday, his grandfather had still monitored her every movement on Sunday…and that same suspicion continued to lurk in his eyes, even if it had become tempered with a dash of uncertainty.

He found himself scowling. Why didn't she just make some excuse and pop to her room to see if he was here yet or not?

He knew he wasn't being fair. She knew he'd had an

important dinner and drinks meeting this evening. She couldn't know he'd left early. She couldn't know that chatting to her every night had become the highlight of his day.

He rolled his shoulders, stretched his neck first one way then the other. Frowned. It wasn't so much a *highlight* as a relief that their charade had survived another day, and that she was still coping with being stuck in Ashbarrow.

He pulled a notepad towards him and spent the next thirty minutes sketching out ideas for a new security system for the castle.

He spent the following ten minutes drumming his fingers and wondering why Sophie was late.

Thirteen and a half minutes later, Sophie logged on. She smiled and waved when she saw him. She always started their meetings with a wave. It was kind of cute.

'You're home! I wasn't sure you'd make it back in time for a meeting tonight.'

He shrugged, trying to look nonchalant as every cell fired to life at the sight of her. She was lying on her back. Her laptop must be balanced on her stomach...or higher. Perspiration prickled his nape. 'We finished early.'

'Nice.'

'While you've been running overtime,' he couldn't resist pointing out. Common sense told him to drop it. It was only a few minutes. 'How's your day been?'

Her eyes narrowed as if she'd sensed his mood, but she didn't pursue it. 'Wedding prep is progressing nicely.'

'Have you rung your mother yet?' He'd given her the number.

She sat up and crossed her legs, placing the computer and him at a further distance. 'Have you talked with your grandfather yet?'

Touché. It was all he could do not to let loose with a rude word.

'Also, I spoke too soon when I said your grandfather

had dispensed with his fun and games. He's back to his old tricks.'

He fought the urge to drop his head to his arms. He had to hand it to the old man—he had staying power. 'What's he done now?'

'We have a new house guest.' She rolled her eyes. 'Christian Dubois.'

His jaw dropped. How the hell did his grandfather know the world's most in-demand male model?

'Apparently Christian's grandfather and Lord Bramley were at college together,' she said, as if she'd seen the question in his face. 'Christian has been in the Highlands shooting some aftershave advertisement. You know the kind—all manly trout streams and drinking whisky in front of a roaring fire.'

In a recent poll, Christian had been voted one of the world's most beautiful men. The pencil Will held snapped. 'Is he as good-looking in the flesh as they claim?'

'Physically the man is an absolute god.'

Pencil lead powdered his fingers. He stared at the fistful of crumbling shards and tossed them into the wastepaper basket beneath his desk.

'Unfortunately,' Sophie continued, 'the illusion is shattered the moment he opens his mouth.'

Her subtle assurance should've reassured him, but something ugly had started to press against his breastbone. He did his best to dispel it. 'Full of himself?'

She shook her head. 'It's not so much that. I…' She hesitated before stretching out on her front and moving closer to whisper, 'Dear God, Will, the man is so vain! He keeps trying to catch glimpses of himself in any available reflective surface—mirrors, windows…the silver teapot. He acts as if there's a camera trained on him at all times. Unfortunately, he also likes the sound of his own voice.'

Her grimace almost made him laugh.

'What *is* amusing, however, is that as your grandfather is the one who invited him here he's the one who has to entertain Christian and sit there and listen to him boast about his exploits.'

That picture did make him laugh. A moment later he sobered. 'I take it you think he's invited Christian in the hopes the two of you will…hit it off.'

'Seems the likeliest explanation, don't you think?' She shrugged. 'Though, who knows? I'm starting to think your grandfather could make the sanest person paranoid.'

Spots flashed in front of his eyes at the thought of Sophie with Christian. 'Are you tempted?' he found himself growling. Had she and Christian been…*getting to know each other better*? Was that why she'd been late?

Her eyes widened, and then they flashed with an unfamiliar fire. 'I seem to recall that I promised you discretion.'

He folded his arms and leaned back. 'Are you *discreetly* tempted? If any of this makes the papers…'

That damn chin came up and her eyes grew as hard as his must be. 'It's two weeks to our wedding. I'm in your grandfather's house. I'm not sure what your definition of discreet is, but I can assure you that's not mine.'

He couldn't stop himself. 'And yet I notice you haven't actually answered the question.'

'I've no intention of dignifying such a ridiculous question with an answer either!'

He was being an idiot. But the strength of the protest running through him had taken him completely off guard. He owed her an apology, but he couldn't force the words from his throat.

His hands balled to fists. 'I want you to stay away from Christian Dubois.'

'That's becoming increasingly evident,' she shot back, colour high on her cheeks. 'You took such pains to let me know how much you trusted me on Saturday, but words are cheap, Will. I've no intention of cuckolding you before the wedding. You know I've no intention of making you look a fool. And, I've told you, I can't bear the man!'

It was true. He knew that in his head. But at the moment he was operating with a different part of his anatomy. Not even his anatomy but some strange beast that lurked inside him.

'So what are you really scared of?'

'I'm not scared of anything,' he shot back, stung.

'Then why are you shouting?'

Both of their voices had risen, and then he heard Sophie's bedroom door bang against the wall as if it had been flung open. Christian? He actually growled.

Sophie's head rocked back to stare at a point beyond him and then he heard his grandfather shouting. 'I heard voices! I knew you had someone in here. I...'

The expression on Sophie's face made Will wince.

She swung her laptop around and the room swam and dipped, making his stomach reel with vertigo. And then his grandfather came into view.

Will didn't uncross his arms. He didn't say hello. His grandfather's gaze met his and the older man visibly swallowed.

'I thought...' The old man trailed off, looking suddenly old.

'Get out of my room.'

Sophie's voice shook with so much suppressed emotion Will wanted to punch something.

'My dear—' his grandfather's mouth worked '—I'm sorry. I—'

'Now!'

She shouted the word so loud it all but deafened him. Without another word the older man turned and hastened from the room. Sophie appeared in his monitor again and he found himself swallowing at the anger livid in her face. 'I don't like either one of you at the moment.'

She couldn't put him in the same category as his grand-father!

'Don't even think about coming up here.'

How did she know he was?

'Because I'm in absolutely no mood to see you.'

'But—'

And then she snapped the lid of her laptop closed and everything went dark. She hadn't even said goodnight! He swore and swore...and swore some more.

He tried her phone, but his call went to voicemail. He sent her an email. She didn't reply. He checked flights to Inverness, but it was too late to fly out tonight. What the hell was he thinking? He couldn't fly to Scotland now. He paced the wall of windows that overlooked the Thames. He had important meetings in the morning. He couldn't fly out tomorrow either.

He pulled in a deep breath. And then another. He'd call Sophie tomorrow, once she'd calmed down. He'd give her a chance to cool off tonight, and then he'd apologise so abjectly she'd have no choice but to forgive him.

Tomorrow.

And tomorrow he might look into who among his staff could adequately represent him at all of these blasted meetings. Sophie was right—he had more money than he knew what to do with. He should be enjoying life, not wasting it on some corporate treadmill.

Sophie refused to pick up Will's calls the next day, so he finally ventured to ring the house itself. The housekeeper passed the phone to his grandfather rather than Sophie. It took all his strength not to hang up, but any news of Sophie would be better than none at all.

'Will, my boy,' his grandfather started in a hearty tone that immediately set Will's teeth on edge.

'I don't want to talk to you. Put Sophie on.'

'She, uh… She's not here.'

Not there? 'Where is she?' He roared the words. He couldn't help it.

'I don't know!' his grandfather roared back. 'She left a message with the housekeeper that she'd be out all day. And she's not answering her phone.' There was a short pause. 'I understand why she's not taking my calls, but why isn't she taking yours?'

'Because I made an absolute cake of myself last night because of Christian—thanks for that, by the way. I acted like a jealous idiot!' He raked a hand through his hair. He hoped to God she'd not washed her hands of the lot of them.

'I'm sorry.'

He blinked. Had his grandfather just…apologised?

'Christian has gone, if that helps at all. I…I've evidently misjudged the lass.'

'You have.' But then so had he.

'I—'

His grandfather broke off. Will heard voices in the background, and then Carol Ann's excited voice burbled down the phone. 'Will, I got a new dress.'

He did what he could to inject enthusiasm into his voice. 'What colour?'

She laughed. 'Purple, of course, silly! It's for the wedding.'

He swallowed. 'You'll be the prettiest girl there.'

'Second prettiest. Sophie will be the prettiest. And I have *another* new dress too.'

'Two new dresses?'

She chortled at his mock shock. 'For Sophie's dad's party on Saturday.'

He straightened. 'You're coming to the ball?' Carol Ann

was coming to London? *And* she was excited about it? His heart started to pound.

'Sophie invited me. She said there'd be cake and dancing.'

Sophie had…

'And she said that when you're married I can come visit in London and that…and that you'll take me to musicals!'

His throat thickened. 'That sounds like fun.'

'And we can have afternoon tea at the Ritz, and walks in the park to feed the squirrels, and…and I can't remember all the things Sophie said we could do, but they were all fun! And I want to do them all. I can, can't I?'

'Sure you can. I can't wait!'

'Good, 'cause Sophie said I could stay in your big apartment when I come to London—that I can have my very own room there.'

He couldn't speak for the lump that lodged in his throat. Sophie had… All this time she'd been quietening Carol Ann's fears about London? And he'd repaid that by—

He choked back an oath. He slumped against the wall, sliding down until he sat on the carpet.

'But on Saturday night I'm having a slumber party in her room at her dad's house.'

'I want to have a slumber party with you and Sophie on Saturday night too.'

Carol Ann laughed as if that was the funniest thing she'd ever heard. 'You can't, silly! And you know what else, Will?'

'What?'

'She's going to teach me to ride too.'

He blinked. Horses had always intimidated Carol Ann.

'When I go stay with her in Cornwall she said I could choose my own pony just for me. And she said we could be best friends forever.'

His head spun. 'Who? You and Sophie or you and the pony?'

'The pony, silly! Me and Sophie are already BFFs.'

And Sophie had used that influence to turn Carol Ann's unreasonable fear of London on its head. She'd given his sister something tangible to love about London—things to look forward to. Her kindness and generosity blew his mind.

Acid burned his stomach at his behaviour the previous evening. 'I can't wait to see you in your purple dress, Carol Ann. Can you give Sophie a message for me when she gets back?'

'Uh huh.'

He had a vision of his little sister nodding earnestly.

'Can you tell her that I wish that I could kiss her?'

Carol Ann giggled but promised to pass the message along.

'I love you, Carol Ann.'

'I love you, Will.'

CHAPTER SEVEN

BLAST! THERE WASN'T a darn thing left to do—nothing left to fuss and tinker with, nothing left to turn her attention to.

Sophie prowled through the ballroom of one of London's premier hotels casting a critical eye over the round tables covered in crisp linen, set with sparkling crystal and gleaming cutlery, and topped with pink-and-cream peony centrepieces, which even she had to admit were rather fabulous. Pity the perfection couldn't ease the burning in her soul.

She glanced at the pink and gold balloon displays that marched down the length of the room between French doors that led out to the paved terrace and wondered what it would be like to feel that light and buoyant. She felt as if someone had dropped a stone weight on her shoulders.

Stop being a drama queen. Stop overreacting.

But no matter how often she told herself that, it did nothing to lessen the weight pressing down on her. If only she could work through this tangle of emotions and—

She slammed to a halt, her thoughts scattering when a familiar figure appeared at the far end of the ballroom.

Will.

She swallowed. For the last three days she'd refused to take his calls or to return them. She'd refused to answer his emails. She'd been strung tight at the thought of seeing him tonight, so it made no sense to feel suddenly…lighter.

She inclined her head towards the one set of French doors that were open. He reached them before she did and stood aside to let her pass first. She did her best not to breathe in the dark, spiced lime scent of him too greedily.

Wordlessly, she selected a bench in the sun. He chose the one opposite in the shade. Crossing her legs, she met his gaze. She saw what she expected to see—what his phone and email messages had been full of—worry, regret, contrition. She hadn't thought seeing those things would help. But somehow it did.

She saw too what she hadn't expected to see—anger... and resentment? Or was it frustration?

Whatever it was, it made her heart pound.

He leaned towards her. 'Are you okay? I've been worried sick!'

'I'm fine.'

'That's not what my grandfather has been saying.'

She raised an eyebrow. 'You've been speaking to your grandfather?'

He threw himself backwards and scowled at her. 'I had to speak to someone. You wouldn't!'

She shrugged. 'I didn't feel like talking to you.'

'You made that clear.'

He leapt to his feet and paced up and down in front of her, hands clenching and unclenching, spine stiff. She considered patting the bench beside her and then thought the better of it. It might be wise to keep all of that unchecked energy at one remove.

'I was offended—*really* offended—at what you implied when we last spoke.'

He stopped pacing to stare at her with hooded eyes. 'I acted like a jerk. Sophie, I'm sorry. I've wanted to apologise ever since it happened.'

'I know. I've listened to your messages...read your emails.'

'But you wanted me to stew?'

She shrugged. 'You don't get to act like a jerk and expect no consequences, Will. Not even for a million pounds.'

His jaw dropped.

'And I needed time to think.'

He sat back on the bench opposite, his face shaded by a tulip tree. 'My grandfather and I have treated you abominably. I wouldn't blame you if you wanted to pull the pin on the wedding.'

She'd love to. But she couldn't. 'I'm not going to do that,' she started slowly. 'But I do have some concerns.'

His gaze sharpened. 'Tell me.'

He wanted to fix it, make things right. It almost made her smile. But then her concerns pressed down on her again and any desire to smile fled. 'Why were you so jealous, Will? I mean, despite the fact it was a needless jealousy... why did you lose the plot so completely?'

He shook his head. 'Because I'm an idiot.'

'Not good enough,' she said softly.

His gaze speared to hers.

'You've said in all your messages that you trust me, that you know I'd not do anything to jeopardise our...arrangement.'

'I meant all of that.'

'But the thing is...you were jealous.' She moistened dry lips. 'Which would indicate that you've developed feelings for me.' And that frightened her out of her wits. Every atom of her being screamed that she needed Will in her life. Sex would ruin that.

And love was out of the question.

Will's head rocked back. 'I don't *do* the kind of feelings you're hinting at, Sophie.' He shot to his feet, raking both hands back through his hair. 'I mean, I have feelings for you. Of course I do. Our lives are entwined. You mean a lot to me. But I *don't* have romantic feelings for you.'

She let out a breath and waited for relief to wash over her. And kept waiting.

'It's true that my feelings have recently become more—' he swallowed '—carnal.'

Her every cell snapped to attention before her muscles grew languorous with need. *Oh, no, no!* They couldn't go there. They'd already spoken about it!

'But I promised our relationship wouldn't turn physical. And I mean to keep my word.'

He stared at her, his lips set, his eyes proud and angry, and Sophie suddenly realised where that resentment and frustration she'd sensed earlier originated. There was an answering surge of those same things firing through her blood now. She couldn't answer him. She could only nod.

'It'll pass,' he growled.

Good to know. She nodded again.

He jammed his hands into his pockets. 'I panicked on Wednesday night because the stakes of this game are so high. And so many of the variables are outside of my control. I…' He hesitated. 'I hate that I have to rely on you to help me secure Carol Ann's future.'

That might just be the most honest thing he'd ever said to her.

'I hate that you're stuck in the Highlands when that wasn't part of the original deal.'

She shrugged. 'That's no biggie.'

'I hate that you've had to put up with my grandfather's nonsense.'

The older man had overstepped the mark on Wednesday night, and he knew it. In his own way he was as contrite as Will. He'd been carefully polite and solicitous ever since. 'I think that's all going to change now.'

'You shouldn't have had to deal with any of it in the first place.'

'When are you going to talk to him?'

He glanced away and she smothered a sigh. But she understood. 'I spoke to my mother last night.'

He swung back. 'How did that go?'

She wasn't really sure. 'She said she'd love to come to the wedding, but she'd only be there if my father assured her she was welcome.'

Apparently her daughter's blessing wasn't enough.

Will's hands clenched to fists. 'And your father…?'

She shrugged, though it took an effort to maintain a semblance of nonchalance. 'I told him this morning what I expected of him. Now I just need to wait and see if he delivers.' Or not.

'And you're…?'

'Passing Adulting for Beginners with flying colours,' she said. He stared at her with unconvinced eyes and she folded her arms. 'I'm fine, Will. You've no need to worry about me.'

He tapped a fist against his chin. But finally straightened and nodded. 'There are a lot of things I hate about our current situation, but I can't tell you how much I appreciate all you've done for Carol Ann. Is she really coming to the ball tonight?'

'She and Esther are at my father's place as we speak.'

'I don't know how you managed to contrive such a miracle, but I can't thank you enough.'

That had been easy. She'd simply started peppering their conversations with all the fun things Carol Ann could do in London if she ever came to visit. The fact that Sophie loved London so much had inevitably rubbed off too.

She'd raved about *The Sound of Music* and *Mamma Mia!* theatre adaptations she'd seen, had described in exquisite detail what a high tea at the Ritz looked like. She'd just filtered a little bit of London into the conversation here and there every day, managing to pique Carol Ann's curiosity, interest…and eventual eagerness to sample such delights for herself. 'She deserves to not be afraid.'

She forced herself to her feet. 'Will, I don't actually want you to be forced into a marriage you don't want. If you decide to rethink this whole scheme, I'd certainly understand. I wanted there to be other options if things… fell through.'

She couldn't read the throbbing in his eyes as they stared into hers. 'You have to understand that wanting to visit London and wanting to live here are two very different things. I don't know if Carol Ann could ever adapt to that.'

'True, but a start has been made.' With time, and a lot of patience, Will could help Carol Ann make that transition.

'Our marriage is still the best way to secure my sister's future.'

She swiped her hands down her skirt and nodded again, tried to force a businesslike crispness to her voice. 'Right, we'll call that Plan A, then. You still need to speak to your grandfather before the wedding, and you still have to get him to sign your legal papers.'

He set his jaw. 'Next weekend.'

'Excellent. Now, are you still sure you want to attend tonight's ball? Everyone is talking about our engagement. There'll be questions and comments, some good-natured teasing—' who knew? maybe some not-so-good-natured teasing as well '—and the press.'

His lip curled. 'You make it sound so enticing.'

She was just giving him the unvarnished truth. 'I know how much you hate any kind of publicity or attention. On the plus side, however, there'll be a beautiful meal, and dancing with me and Carol Ann later.'

'What man could resist that?'

The smile didn't reach his eyes, and she found she couldn't smile either.

'You don't think I can handle this evening, do you—the press, the loaded comments...the gossip?'

She hesitated. 'It's not in your nature to live a lie, Will. And that's what you have to do tonight. In the spotlight, in front of people you know...in front of friends. I think you're going to hate every moment of it.'

'I'll be there. It's what's expected of me. I won't let Carol Ann down.'

So they'd get to play the happy couple. Yippee. She'd need a soak in a hot bath before she could face that. And an aspirin.

All around him London's rich and wealthy—all the beautiful people—milled beneath the glittering chandeliers, smiling, air-kissing, dancing. It was all Will could do to not scowl.

If he received one more good-natured dig about being hog-tied and lassoed with his bachelor days far behind him, he might throw something.

He seized a glass of champagne from a passing tray—wished it were something stronger—and knocked it back in one. Across the room Sophie caught his eye and mouthed *smile*.

He forced the corners of his mouth upwards. He couldn't be too careful. With the press out in numbers tonight, you couldn't be certain who was watching. He couldn't let his guard down for a single moment. He winked and then blew her a kiss, and her lips twitched at what he guessed was the unexpectedness of it. A real smile lit through him. He liked surprising Sophie, liked taking her off guard...liked making her smile.

Not that he liked it too much. He ran a finger beneath the starched collar of his shirt. Her earlier words about her fear he was developing feelings for her knotted beneath his ribcage. He wasn't. Not a bit of it.

But she was Sophie, and that fact put her somehow apart from other women. Which meant his usual constraints weren't in place when he was around her.

That doesn't explain why you became so possessive of her.

He rolled his shoulders. As he'd said, there was a lot at stake.

'Will! Will!'

He nearly spilled his fresh champagne as Carol Ann came racing up and tugged on his arm. 'This is the most beautiful party I've ever been to!'

Her eyes sparkled, colour lit her cheeks, and she could barely keep still. 'It's pretty spectacular,' he agreed. 'Sophie sure knows how to throw a party. Want another spin around the dance floor?'

She shook her head. 'I want to watch for a little bit.'

It was clear that Sophie had lined up several young men to dance with his sister, and it touched him that she'd taken such pains to ensure Carol Ann had fun.

While news of his engagement had spread far and wide, Will noticed it didn't prevent women from sending him come-hither glances. He deliberately ignored them and did his best to forget the hog-tied comments that had him chafing as if he were on a leash. He wasn't hog-tied. He wasn't losing his freedom and independence. After the wedding he'd have the opportunity to follow some of those invitations to their logical conclusion. Discreetly, of course.

'Hello, Will, darling.'

'Simone, you're looking lovely this evening.' He and Simone had hooked up for a short while about a year ago. She'd left him in little doubt that she'd be more than happy to hook up with him again whenever he said the word.

'And you're as charming as ever. Aren't you going to ask me to dance?'

'Go away!' Carol Ann interjected, pushing in between Will and the other woman.

'Carol Ann, that's rude! Apologise at once.'

His sister pushed her lip out mutinously. 'You're not allowed to dance with anyone but Sophie.'

He blinked. 'I…uh… That's not exactly true, Carol Ann.' He turned to Simone. 'I'm sorry about my sister, she—'

'I love Sophie,' Carol Ann announced, too loudly.

Carol Ann loved everyone. But her face had turned a blotchy red, and if he wasn't careful she'd create a god-awful scene.

'So does Will! Right, Will?'

His tie tightened about his neck, making it increasingly difficult to keep his breathing even. Simone raised an eyebrow and he wanted to flee. 'Of course I do.'

'How much?' Carol Ann demanded.

He searched his brain for a suitable answer. 'To the moon and back,' he finally growled.

His sister continued to glare at Simone. 'Then you shouldn't want to dance with anyone else!'

Instead of dissipating at his assurances, Carol Ann's distress seemed to grow. *Hell!* He didn't want the press getting pictures of Carol Ann blowing her top. It would be like reliving his childhood all over again. 'Carol Ann, you—'

'Hello, everyone, are you having a nice time?'

Sophie breezed up as if she hadn't a care in the world, and something inside him eased. And then at the realisation his every muscle stiffened again.

'Ooh, Simone, your dress is divine. Is it an Alexander McQueen?'

Simone preened. 'It is. Like?'

'I'm absolutely pea-green.'

Carol Ann glared. 'She wanted to dance with Will.'

Sophie laughed. 'All the girls want to dance with Will. He's rather accomplished on the…dance floor.'

Her eyes danced as she made the strategic pause and he could feel his lips curve upwards, could feel himself falling under her spell.

'But—' she grinned at Carol Ann with such mischief that Carol Ann giggled '—they're not allowed to until he's danced with me first.'

With that she tugged him onto the dance floor and he had no choice but to slip an arm about her waist and draw her near, their bodies bumping together as they swayed to the music.

'Danger averted,' she murmured in his ear.

'Which danger? Carol Ann or Simone?'

She drew back, her eyes alive with laughter. It occurred to him that she really was in her element here in this glittering ballroom. 'Carol Ann, of course.'

'You're very good with her.' He should be happier about that. 'When did you get to read her so well?'

Like him she kept the smile on her lips, but it faded from the brilliant blue of her eyes. 'I've spent a lot of time with her this last fortnight.'

I love Sophie! Carol Ann's words went around and around in his head.

'She's becoming very attached to you.'

'I've become rather attached to her too. I'm not going to dump her when all of this is done, you know? Give me some credit. We'll remain friends. I'll still spend time with her, do things with her.'

Without him. Not that *that* mattered.

She squeezed his hands. 'Smile. One of the tabloid photographers has his sights set on us.'

He could do better than that.

The blood rushed through him as he pulled her firmly against him, twirled her before dipping her. She followed his lead effortlessly, not missing a beat. A huge smile curved her lips when he lifted her upright again, exhilaration spiking through her eyes and just for a moment he let that same exhilaration rush through him, let it slip all of his concerns from his shoulders until he felt free and light…and young.

Her head arced back in a laugh. 'You really are a demon on the dance floor.'

'And you really are stunning.'

She wore a blue satin cocktail dress that fitted her to perfection. It sported an intriguing rectangular cut-out that ran beneath her collarbones and above her breasts, highlighting the creamy perfection of her skin. He had to fight the urge to bend her back over his arm and press his lips to the skin there and taste her. If she tasted half as good as she smelled he'd be lost.

'Will.'

It wasn't a remonstration, but a whispered breath filled with need. It had nothing to do with them being friends and having this *arrangement*, or with her being Peter's sister. It was a primal call between a man and a woman, and he found himself powerless against the forces battering him.

The music changed—turned slow and smoky. He released her hand to curve both hands about her waist to keep her so close their thighs and hips touched. Their eyes locked in a stunned and increasingly heated stare that should have steam rising in the air above them.

Everything else receded—the other couples on the dance floor, the band, the very room. With a boldness that felt just right, he pulled her hips in so close she couldn't mistake the effect she was having on him. Her breath hitched, and her lips parted as if she needed to drag air into oxygen-starved lungs.

Her hands rested against his chest, but one of them slid up around his shoulders to his nape and the contact fired every part of him that it touched with heat and life. He lowered his head until their breaths mingled.

This woman filled his senses—the look, feel and smell of her. He couldn't get enough.

He wanted her in his bed, naked. He wanted—

A flash went off, making them both jump.

Sophie recovered first. 'Enough,' she laughed with a wave of her hand to the photographer. 'Leave my fiancé and me in peace. Go and pick on someone else.'

Ice poured through him. Had she known all along that they were being photographed? Had she simply been playing it up for the cameras? Had she been faking…?

He dismissed that thought in the next moment when common sense caught up with him. She wanted him. He knew the signs and he saw how she tried to suppress that need. But it was clear she had more control of the situation than him.

He swore softly.

'Why are you upset?' she murmured. 'By the way, you're crushing my hand.'

He loosened his grip immediately with a terse apology.

'You played your part to perfection,' she added.

Her voice, though, wobbled, and he had to swallow. No, she wasn't unaffected by him, but she wanted to be. And he'd promised her no complications.

Had he really been about to forget that and ask her to leave the party early? Had he really been about to ask her to come home with him? Had he really been about to break his word?

Acid burned through him.

Sophie remained in his arms, but she avoided his gaze and a respectable distance now separated them. 'You now have permission to dance with Simone.'

Her laugh grated down his spine, and his jaw tightened. 'I don't need your permission to dance with anyone.'

'I wasn't talking about my permission.' Her eyes snapped with a sudden fire. 'I was talking about Carol Ann's. Not only will she tell me all the names of who she danced with, but I don't doubt she'll tell me who you dance with too.'

Damn it! Sophie and Carol Ann were having a slumber party tonight. She'd never have come home with him!

What the hell had he been thinking?

He was getting too wrapped up in this woman. Their lives were becoming more and more entwined. He had to be careful not to take any of this too seriously. He couldn't let himself believe in the magic they were creating for the benefit of his grandfather.

It was a lie.

And even if beneath it all ran a thread of truth, he couldn't afford to let that thread have its head. He was determined that his heart remain free. He wasn't tying himself to a life of misery and manipulation, of anguish and grief. He'd never let a woman try to tear him to pieces the way his mother had done with his father. He would never do that to another person the way his father had with his mother.

He still sometimes woke in the middle of the night in a lather of sweat, recalling the screams, the fights, the tears. He wanted no part of any of that. He wasn't committing himself to any woman. He wasn't giving anyone that kind of power over him. He wanted peace, he wanted privacy, he wanted control—and if that made him selfish and an undutiful grandson then so be it. It was better than becoming a shell of a person, someone so damaged and defeated that they just gave up and didn't care if they lived or died. That was what a bad marriage could do to a person.

He and Sophie had a business arrangement. Nothing more. An arrangement that would end in eighteen months. His teeth ground together. As long as he maintained control, all would be well. Which would be easier with Sophie out of his arms, but for appearances' sake they had to continue with this farce of a dance.

'Carol Ann and I are going shopping tomorrow before heading back to Ashbarrow. Would you like to join us for lunch?'

He shook his head. 'I'm busy.' He'd make sure of it.

She stared at a point beyond his shoulder. 'I've been thinking... I don't think it's necessary to video conference every day now, do you? Maybe we can make it every other day?'

An impenetrable coldness washed through him. Sophie's primary motivation for being a part of this charade was money. He'd be a fool to forget it. 'I don't see there's any need for video conferencing at all now. We have everything under control. You can email me if anything goes wrong.'

She didn't blink, she didn't stiffen, nothing in her expression changed. 'Sounds like a plan.'

Sophie might be attracted to him, but she wouldn't let an inconvenient attraction get in the way of a million pounds.

You're being unfair.

Maybe he was, but he suddenly felt like the world's biggest fool.

He released her the moment the song ended.

She immediately stepped away from him.

'I'll go and see if Simone is still interested in that dance.'

With a smile and a cheery wave she tossed a, 'Have fun,' over her shoulder before sauntering off, her high heels making the sway of her hips more pronounced. It was as if...as if she didn't have a care in the world.

A million pounds? His lips tightened. Maybe she didn't.

His jaw started to ache at how hard he clenched it. Well, he'd show her he hadn't a care in the world either. He'd prove it to the both of them.

* * *

'Hello, stranger.'

Will turned, a little unsteady on his legs, to find Simone leaning against one of the tall columns that marched down the steps of the hotel to the street. After his dance with Sophie, he hadn't hunted Simone down to see if she still wanted to dance. Instead he'd found a quiet corner and a waiter more than happy to keep his whisky glass filled.

He was going to have a hell of a head tomorrow. But for now he relished the warm hum that kept other unpleasantness at bay.

'Simone of the pretty dress!' If Sophie liked that dress so much it occurred to him now that he ought to buy her one.

He'd think about it tomorrow, because he'd promised himself to not think about Sophie for the rest of the evening.

Simone raised an eyebrow. She had pretty eyes but they were nothing to Sophie's.

'Don't tell me your fiancée has left you high and dry?'

He stumbled across to sit on the low wall beside her. 'She's thrown me over to have a slumber party with my little sister.'

Simone blinked. 'Well…that's nice.'

He nodded. And then he frowned. 'Yeah, it really is.' But then, Sophie was nice.

Simone stared at him and then gave a rueful laugh, though he didn't know why. 'Do you need a ride home, Will?'

'I do!' He rose to his feet, but everything spun so he sat again. 'That's what I came out for—to hail a cab.'

'My driver should be here any moment. Why don't I get him to give you a lift home?'

He thought about rising to his feet and trying to hail a

cab, or remaining sitting here for a little while longer, and
he chose the latter. 'You're a pal, Simone.'

'And here he is now. Come on, Will. On your feet.'

With a laugh he tossed an arm across her shoulders,
and then found himself leaning a little too heavily on her.
'Sorry, I seem to have hit the whisky a little too hard.'

'Really?'

'You always were a good sport, Simone-of-the-pretty-
dress.'

'Yay for me.' But she laughed as she said it. So Will
laughed too and fell into the back of the car with her.

'Miss?' The driver turned to look at them.

'It's okay, Roberts.'

The world spun for a moment and Will had to take
several deep breaths. 'Soph throws a damn fine party,
doesn't she?'

'Indeed she does.'

He frowned. 'She looked so happy tonight—in her element—don't you think?'

Simone sighed. 'Absolutely.'

'So why would she want to open an equestrian centre
when she'd be London's best party planner?'

Simone shook her head. 'And another one bites the
dust.'

He frowned. What did she mean?

'Where to, miss?'

'We're dropping Mr Trent-Paterson home.'

The driver glanced into the rear-view mirror and said,
'I think it might be best if I drop you home first, miss.'

She nodded. 'I think that's an excellent plan.'

The moment Sophie entered the breakfast room at Ashbarrow Castle on Monday morning she knew something
was wrong. She bit back a sigh. What was Lord Bramley
up to now?

'Come and take a seat, Sophie.'

He'd started calling her Sophie since last Wednesday night, after he'd burst into her room in the mistaken belief he'd find Christian there. Finally his actions had shamed him. He'd been trying to make amends ever since. She had every intention of forgiving him, but not too quickly. She wanted him to understand that she wouldn't put up with that kind of behaviour.

'You look a little…serious.' Actually, he looked downright grim. She took the seat to his left. 'Don't tell me we're scheduled for another visit from Christian?'

His jowls worked. 'No, nothing like that. It's—'

He broke off and reached across to pat her hand. 'Now, my dear, I don't want you to fly off the handle or to get upset.'

Ice trickled down her neck, lodging in a hard chill ball in her chest. What on earth had he done? 'You better just tell me whatever it is and get it over with.'

He turned grey.

She found herself suddenly clutching his hand. 'Dear God, it's Will, isn't it? Has he been hurt or—?'

'He's fighting fit.' The older man's lips twisted. 'Too fit, it seems.'

She dropped his hand as a different kind of chill settled over her. Without another word he turned the newspaper that was open in front of him towards her. She didn't want to look at it. She knew that with every cell of her body.

She held Lord Bramley's gaze until his dropped to the newspaper. Swallowing, she followed suit.

And flinched.

'Lass…'

She held up a hand and the older man fell silent as she took the paper and scanned the photographs. The first was of her and Will dancing, and she had to swallow at the raw sexuality that simmered between them—the intensity of their attraction evident for all to see. The second photograph was of Will with his arm about Simone, running down the front steps of the hotel towards a waiting car; they were both laughing.

He'd danced with her as he had, making every latent desire she'd ever had spring to life until it had been all she could do not to claw off his clothes and climb into his skin. She'd known he'd been doing it for the benefit of the cameras, but she'd also thought it had been true—that he'd felt as intensely as she had.

The edges of the newspaper crumpled as her fingers clenched. All of that *intensity*, it hadn't been for her alone. It was just *testosterone*. And it appeared that any available woman would do!

She shot to her feet. He was the one who'd reminded her how high the stakes were. How could he have done such a stupid thing? How could he have done this…to her?

The captions read: Paradise Lost and Paradise Regained. She dropped the newspaper to the table and pressed a hand to her mouth, afraid she might be sick.

'Lassie, you need to sit and take a moment.'

There was a lot at stake. Too much. She forced her eyes wide. Forced air into lungs that didn't want to cooperate. 'There'll be an explanation for this. A perfectly innocent explanation.'

'Aye.'

But scepticism stretched through his eyes. How could Will have done this to her? She'd thought they were friends!

'I'm going for a ride.'

She wheeled from the room, ignoring Lord Bramley's entreaties for her to return.

'Saddle up Magnus,' she told Colin the moment she entered the stables.

He visibly swallowed. 'I'm sorry, Miss Mitchell, but Mr Will told me I wasn't to let you ride Magnus.'

Today Mr Will could go to hell. 'Then I'll saddle him myself.'

Still, she didn't want to get the groom into trouble. 'If it'll make you feel any better, you can saddle Annabelle and follow me.'

As soon as she had the big grey saddled, she swung up onto his back and cantered out of the yard, setting off towards the largest hill at a gallop, leaving Colin and Annabelle far behind. They galloped so fast she blamed the tears coursing down her cheeks on nothing more than the stinging wind in her face.

CHAPTER EIGHT

IT WAS THE helicopter that made Magnus become shy, grip the bit between his teeth and finally bolt.

Vaguely Sophie was aware of the machine landing in the forecourt of the castle ground, but most of her attention was taken up with Magnus and all the power hunched beneath her. She considered trying to bring the giant horse under control, but in the end she gave that up as a bad joke and just hung on.

Realising that she wasn't going to fight him, the horse relaxed his mouth, if not his speed, and she knew she could bring him to a halt if she wanted.

But she didn't want. She spurred him on instead.

They'd already been for a hard ride, but it hadn't been enough for Magnus. And it hadn't been enough for her either. She pushed him on hard—she wanted him thoroughly worn out. She wanted him to think twice before ever bolting on her again. His sides were heaving with exertion when she finally cantered him into the stable yard.

A grim-faced Will met her. He reached out and caught hold of the bridle, holding Magnus still while she slipped from his back.

'You could've been killed!'

The words emerged from between clenched teeth and Sophie found herself tossing her head, much as Magus had earlier. 'The only one in danger of being murdered today, Will, is you.'

Those lips whitened further. He turned his head the

merest fraction to glare at Colin. 'I told you she wasn't to ride Magnus.'

'There wasn't a whole lot he could do about it when I snuck into the stable and saddled Magnus myself.'

He glared at her. 'I could…'

She raised an eyebrow when he didn't finish. Throttle her? Good. That made them even.

She took the reins from Will's clenched hands and walked towards the stables. 'I need to give Magnus a good rub-down.'

Colin stepped forward. 'I can do that.'

She hesitated before handing over the reins. 'I'm sorry,' she murmured.

He shook his head. 'Don't be. It's not often we get to see such expert horsemanship. It was a bit of a treat, to be honest.'

She could feel Will's glower from where she stood, and Colin made a hasty exit with Magnus. She watched them go and wondered if she could poach Colin for her equestrian centre.

The next moment her arm was gripped by unrelenting fingers and she found herself marched away from the castle, away from all the outbuildings, and in the direction of a copse of trees. She knew from previous exploration that a clear sweet stream flowed down there.

'You could've broken your neck!'

She pulled free from his grasp. 'So could you!' She pointed towards the helicopter.

'That is a safe mode of transportation!'

'While I was never in any danger!'

They were both breathing hard and her legs were shaking. It was delayed reaction from the wild ride. It had absolutely nothing to do with the bristling display of masculinity in front of her. At least that was what she told herself. 'You're such an idiot, Will.'

They both knew she no longer referred to horses or helicopters.

'I don't want to have this conversation where anyone can see us.'

He went to take her arm again but she wouldn't let him. She leaned forward to poke him in the chest. Beneath her finger his muscles were bunched tight and hard. 'You were the one who told me how high the stakes were on Saturday night.' She kept her voice low, making sure it carried no further than Will's ears. 'And yet you were the one who went home with another woman. At a ball your fiancée was hosting…and where said fiancée was taking such pains to ensure your sister enjoyed herself so much she couldn't wait to come back to London. So that she'd no longer fear London but would start to associate it with fun and joy. And you—'

She couldn't finish the sentence. She'd never expected his fidelity, but she'd thought he'd…

She thought he'd treat her with respect.

Evidently she'd been wrong.

He bent at the waist, bracing his hands on his knees. 'Sophie—'

She pushed against his shoulder, though it barely made an impression on him. Still, he turned his head to meet her gaze. 'Do you think Peter would pat you on the back for this…tell you what a good guy you are?' She shook her head and then flung an arm towards the hill she and Magnus had just climbed. 'He'd take you out there and beat the crap out of you.'

'And I'd let him.' He straightened, his face white and his breathing coming hard and sharp.

She wheeled away, heading for the trees and stream. 'You needn't think that makes a scrap of difference.'

In two strides he'd caught up with her, his hands on her shoulders pulling her to a halt. 'Nothing happened.'

'Let go of me.'

He dropped his hands immediately. 'Nothing happened,' he repeated.

'Wow!' She folded her arms. 'You've never lied to me before. You must be feeling *really* guilty.'

His nostrils flared. 'I'm not lying to you now.'

She went to turn away.

'I did not sleep with Simone.'

She halted.

'I got stupid drunk and she gave me a lift home. End of story. I rang her yesterday to apologise for the state I was in and for putting her driver to so much trouble.'

'Why didn't you ring me as well?'

'Because there was nothing to tell! I didn't know the papers were going to run with the stupid story.'

Given he was a successful businessman, he must have a great poker face, but…

She wanted to believe him. How much frightened her.

'For God's sake, Sophie, give me some credit! You know how much I hate a fuss or spectacle in the newspapers. If I'd had my sights set on Simone I'd have slipped out with her far more discreetly than that.'

He had a point, but…

'Simone is a good sport. She'd been considering a final fling with me.'

That didn't make her a good sport! It made her a—

'But not once she realised how drunk I was.' He grimaced. 'Apparently all I could talk about was you anyway. So she gave me up for a lost cause.'

'Me? You talked about me?'

He raked a hand back through his hair. 'According to her I extolled your many virtues.'

'Oh, now I really don't believe you.' But she did. And she could tell that, from her tone of voice, he knew it too.

'I'm going to be brutally honest now.' They'd reached

the shade of the trees and Will shoved his shoulders back. The sound of the stream splashed and burbled in the still air. 'I got so drunk on Saturday night because I was going out of my mind with lust for you. I want you like I can't remember wanting any woman.'

'No!' She took a step backwards when all she wanted to do was hurl herself into his arms.

He cocked an eyebrow. 'Denying it doesn't make it any the less true.'

She twisted her hands together. 'It's only because we've put…limits on our relationship. If they weren't there I wouldn't seem half so attractive to you.'

'I wish I could believe that.' He dragged in a breath that made him grow taller. 'But I made you a promise.'

Her heart raced and her stomach churned. 'And it's one that I'm going to hold you to.'

'Why?'

The single word cracked from between white lips. What did he mean, *why*?

He leaned forward and took her chin between gentle but inexorable fingers. 'I could make you feel so good, Sophie Mitchell. I'd work so hard at it, apply myself so assiduously, that I'd make you scream—' his voice lowered '—with pleasure…and then I'd make you purr. And I'd do it again and again and again.'

Her mouth went dry with longing. 'Stop it!' She pressed her fingers to his mouth and tried to fight the tempting breeze that shimmered across the surface of her skin, tightening her nipples to hard, aching buds.

'Why not, Sophie? We'd be good together and you know it.'

Because the stakes were too high—her heart, this strange friendship of theirs…their shared memories of Peter. Not to mention the far from simple matter that she'd sworn to turn over a new leaf. She wasn't risking all of that. 'Because you don't do love and commitment, and I no longer use sex as a tool to…to forget.'

He let go of her as if she'd burned him.

She gestured. 'Let's go down to the stream.'

Once down at the stream, Sophie sat on a rock and Will stood with his back to her and started skimming stones at a spot where the stream widened and formed a calm pool. Her heart throbbed and no amount of deep breathing or swallowing eased it. 'You could call the wedding off, you know, Will.'

He spun around. 'No! Why would you even suggest that?'

'Call it a stab in the dark, but… Because you don't want to be married?'

He dismissed that with a snort and a wave of his hand.

'And because with a little effort on your part I believe you could reconcile Carol Ann to living in London with you. I'd help.'

He raised an eyebrow. 'For a fee?'

'Don't be ridiculous! Are you trying to deliberately rile me? We wouldn't be fiancés, but we'd still be friends.' Wouldn't they? Her heart started to pound. It was why she couldn't sleep with him. It was why she had to transform the idea from an alluring temptation for him to a potential nightmare instead. 'You know I wouldn't do it for money.'

She'd do it because she cared about Will and Carol Ann. She'd do it because it was what Peter would've wanted her to do.

One thing Peter most certainly would've counselled her against was getting involved in a physical relationship with his best friend.

He dragged both hands back through his hair and nodded. 'I know. I'm sorry.'

He came and sat on the ground, his back resting against her rock. 'My feelings for this place—' he gestured out in

front of them '—are complicated, Sophie. After the life
Carol Ann and I had with our parents this was…a haven.'

Living with his parents had been a constant roller-
coaster ride of anxiety and insecurity. And all of it lived
in the glare of the public spotlight. No wonder he hated appearing in the society pages now. It made Saturday night's
exploits all the more extraordinary. Usually he was so
careful.

She stared out at the rolling deep green fields, the clear
brook and the blue of the sky. 'This must've seemed like
an idyll after London.'

'Some days it still does,' he admitted. 'If you can dis-
count my grandfather, which evidently I can't. But back
then… I don't know. I could walk, run, ride. I could go
for a swim.'

She imagined him in nothing but a pair of brief swim
trunks and heat flooded her cheeks. It was all she could
do not to fan herself.

'I could do all of those things—normal things—without
having reporters shoving microphones under my nose or
having to dodge camera flashes every time I left the house.
It was such a *relief*.'

Her heart went out to the boy who'd had to live his life
in such a public fishbowl.

'This place was freedom and security. I'd never had
those things before.'

And finally she saw what he refused to admit even
to himself. Ashbarrow Castle was the home of his heart.
Despite the successful and autonomous life he'd created
for himself in London, this was where his soul craved to
be. He wanted to keep it safe for Carol Ann, yes. But he
wanted to keep it safe for himself too. Her eyes started to
sting and she had to blink hard.

'Unfortunately, the moment I turned fourteen this place
became a prison.'

Which was all due to his grandfather's attempts to control him. Why was Lord Bramley so unbending, rigid... determined to force Will into a course of action that was such anathema to him? It was as if the older man wanted to punish him. And yet, that didn't make sense, didn't quite ring true.

'I believe you about Carol Ann—especially after seeing her having such a good time on Saturday night. I probably could help her make the transition to living in London, but...'

He frowned and all his shoulder muscles tightened. It took all the strength she possessed to stop from reaching out and running her hand through his dark, auburn-tinted hair. 'But?'

His gaze swung around to meet hers. 'Ashbarrow has always been a haven for her—never a prison. She loves it. It's her home, and it's not fair that she should be asked to give it up.'

She pulled in a breath and then let it out slowly, a weight pressing down on her. 'You're right. It wouldn't be fair.' Life wasn't fair, but Carol Ann had already had her share of unfairness. So had Will. After the trauma and upheaval of their early years, they deserved to keep their home. Both of them.

'Sophie, I'm sorry I was such a total idiot on Saturday night. I'm sorry I made it look as if I'd been unfaithful to you.' He rose to sit beside her. 'I'm sorry I hurt you.'

She tried to shrug away the warmth that wanted to wrap about her. 'Look, Will, you never promised me your fidelity. I don't expect it.'

'But I did promise you friendship and discretion.' He was silent for a moment. 'I should've been careful not to set tongues wagging. I should've been on my guard, and not allowed a fit of pique to jeopardise everything.'

Her eyebrows rose. What had he called it? 'A fit of pique?'

His face darkened. 'You and Carol Ann were having so much fun—you'd been shopping, you were having a slumber party and I felt like the third wheel. I was...*jealous*.'

'You big baby!'

'That's fair.' He nodded. 'And I've been called worse.' He sobered. 'I promise it won't happen again.'

Good.

He glanced at her from the corner of his eye. She stiffened. 'What?'

'I didn't realise you were promising me *your* fidelity.'

She swallowed. 'Who said I was?'

'I no longer use sex as a tool to forget.'

She shot to her feet and strode to the edge of the stream. 'I'm not promising it to you. I'm promising it to myself.' She was determined to leave the party lifestyle behind her.

'You're allowed to have sex just for fun, Sophie.'

His voice came from just behind her and it took all her strength not to turn. 'I've been having a bit too much fun these last couple of years. I want to focus on other things.' Like helping Carla. Like building up something that belonged just to her. 'I want to find some balance in my life.'

'Good for you.'

Which was odd when she was standing here feeling more unbalanced than she ever had in her life before.

'So...we're good?'

She turned. 'We're good.'

He stood too close and it made her throat hitch and her mouth go dry. He bent and pressed a warm kiss to her cheek, and her heart pounded so hard she thought he must hear it.

'Except,' she pushed out from an uncooperative throat.

He'd taken a step away, but he froze now and she could see how his every muscle bunched. 'Except?'

'I want you to talk to your grandfather. Today.'

* * *

Will's every muscle screamed a protest. He wanted to shout a resounding No! until the sound of it rang through the hills.

He still couldn't believe he'd been stupid enough, careless enough, to create a media brouhaha that had allowed the tabloids to make any number of impertinent and unsavoury claims about his relationship with Sophie. He who hated any kind of media acknowledgement—even plaudits for his business acumen and the success of Pyxis Tech.

Sophie deserved better from him. She sure as hell didn't deserve him yelling at her now.

He forced himself to turn and meet her gaze. Was she really willing to forgo her million pounds so he could avoid a marriage he didn't want? He had a feeling that the answer to that question was an unhesitating yes. *Damn it!* He nodded. 'Okay.'

Her shoulders loosened and she let out a shuddering breath, the beginnings of a smile playing across her lips. 'Good.'

He wanted her to have her million pounds. He wanted her to have the chance to follow her dreams. And he wanted her to know how much he appreciated her.

If he could, he'd like to wipe away all the hurt he'd caused her. She'd felt betrayed—not romantically, but that didn't make the betrayal any the less painful. He understood that.

'I couldn't do this with any other woman, Sophie. I want you to know I appreciate all you've taken on, all you're doing. You've earned your million pounds several times over.'

Her eyes narrowed. 'Don't even think of offering me any more money.'

Why the hell not?

'And I think you're underestimating some of the women you know.'

He shook his head. On this point at least he was certain. 'No other woman knows me as well as you do.'

Those eyes widened and he lost himself in the clearness of that blue for a moment. She shrugged. 'We've known each other a long time, Will.'

'I keep women at arm's length.'

She snorted and picked up a stone and tried to skim it across the stream, but her technique was all wrong and it sank like a…uh…stone. 'That's not what I hear.'

He winced. 'I mean emotionally. I keep them—'

'I knew what you meant.'

A hint of laughter lit her eyes, making them sparkle like this stream in the sun at midday. How had he never clocked the many expressions in her eyes before? They were utterly fascinating.

'Well, I don't do that with you.'

She stilled and then shook her head. 'You would if we slept together.'

Would he?

She turned so they faced each other fully, hands on her hips. 'It's the same for me, you know? I'm more emotionally vulnerable to you than I am to any other man.'

Emotionally vulnerable? Was that what he'd been describing? He supposed it was, but, rather than feeling emotionally exposed, with Sophie it felt comfortable… comforting even.

'Does it frighten you?'

His head rocked back. 'No! I trust you.' She'd never try to manipulate him. 'I value the person you are. I think you feel the same about me.'

She nodded.

A new thought—one that appalled him—rippled through him. 'Does it frighten you?'

She met his gaze, swallowed and nodded.

A vice tightened about his temples. 'Why?'

She turned and started back towards the castle. She stopped before they cleared the copse of trees. Shadows played across her face, making it difficult to read. 'Why?' he repeated. He hated the thought that anything about him frightened her.

'Because I'm attracted to you, Will. Because I want you.'

Roaring in his ears shut out every other sound. He had to swallow hard to quieten it to a manageable din. His mouth dried. 'But you said…'

'We're not going to sleep together. If we do you'll become more emotionally distant while I'd be in danger of become more—' her fingers grasped the air as if searching for the right word '—emotionally invested.'

He took a step back, shock rocketing through him when he finally realised what she'd been trying to tell him. Sometimes sex meant nothing, but sometimes it meant everything. And he knew that because he always ended his romantic liaisons before sex meant even a potential something. Sophie didn't have any of the usual barriers where he was concerned. If he slept with her, he'd be in danger of breaking her heart.

He couldn't do that!

He raked a hand back through his hair. 'Complicated,' he murmured, recalling her warning the first night they'd spent here at Ashbarrow.

She nodded. 'C'mon, it's time we returned to the house.'

Returning to face his grandfather suddenly didn't seem anywhere near as intimidating as it had a moment or two ago.

'You should—'

He took her hand. He wanted to squeeze it to tell her

how sorry he was that he'd been so obtuse earlier, that he'd forced her to spell it out for him in detail. 'I should?'

She laughed. 'Hold my hand for the benefit of all the noses currently pressed against the castle windows. But I can see you were ahead of me.'

To hell with watching eyes! 'Can I raise another topic in relation to Saturday night?'

She glanced at him. 'Go on.'

'You.'

'Me?'

'You were in your element hosting that party. You really seemed to enjoy yourself.'

'I was seeing off my last commitment to my father. It was…satisfying.'

Had he misread the situation? A moment later he shook his head. 'I think you enjoyed the party.'

She opened her mouth as if to deny his words, and then her shoulders sagged. 'I did,' she said, as if it were the worst thing in the world to confess. 'I'm the shallowest creature on the face of the planet—I love parties.'

He pulled her to a halt. 'That doesn't make you shallow. It makes you a people person. You did a brilliant job on Saturday night—you made sure everyone had a great time. You not only helped to raise a ridiculous sum of money for charity, but you were instrumental in encouraging the guests to open their wallets so widely. That isn't shallow.'

She stared at him, unconvinced.

He lifted their linked hands to point a finger at her. 'You did nothing to be ashamed of on Saturday night.' That'd been his domain. 'You think I didn't notice that while you were never without a flute of champagne in your hand, you never took so much as a sip?'

Her mouth dropped open.

'Do you think I didn't notice that the young men you

had lined up to dance with Carol Ann were the kind of young men who'd enjoy her company too?

'And you dealt with Lord Graham—' a notorious drunk '—without fuss or drawing attention to him.' She'd packed him off home in a cab before he'd managed to disgrace himself or his wife. 'You should be proud of yourself, Sophie.'

She moistened her lips, an unfamiliar vulnerability shining out from her eyes, and for a moment he felt unaccountably honoured that she didn't try to hide it from him. 'Do you really think so?'

'I know so.'

Before he thought of the wisdom of it, he bent down to press his lips gently to hers, telling her without words that he thought she was wonderful. Their lips held, clung, and then he forced himself upright.

'Believe me?'

'I...I guess.' With her free hand she tucked a stray strand of hair behind her ear.

He turned them back towards the castle. 'Which begs the question... If you love event planning so much, why aren't you pursuing a career in that? I know you want to look after Carla, but there are other ways to do it. You don't have to go to the trouble and expense of setting up an equestrian centre.'

She was silent for a long moment. 'I've pretty much squandered my entire trust fund and inheritance, other than that bit of property in Cornwall. I want to do something *good* with it, something worthwhile. And I think you'll understand it when I say I'd like to have something that's just mine. Something that I built and created.'

He did understand that.

'Something to fall back on if I ever need to.'

She could fall back on him whenever she needed.

'I don't want to manage an equestrian centre forever.

I'm hoping that, down the track, it's something Carla would like to do. But in the meantime I can't wait to get started on it. It excites me so much.'

The truth of that shone from her eyes.

'I wonder if maybe I couldn't find a way to do both things—run the equestrian centre *and* event plan.'

'Of course you could. You're smart, talented, energetic and amazing. I don't doubt for a single moment that you could achieve anything you set your mind to.'

With a laugh, she bumped his shoulder with hers. 'Careful or you'll be in danger of turning my head.'

He grinned. Flattery was not the way to her heart. He knew that. They were both safe. But it was good to hear her laugh again.

His grandfather was waiting for them the moment they crossed the threshold. 'I want to speak to you in my study, young man. *Now!*'

'Have fun,' Sophie murmured under her breath. 'Come find me on the terrace when you're done.'

He dropped a kiss to the top of her head and then turned to his grandfather. 'That's fortuitous because I want to talk to you too.'

Thirty minutes later Will slammed himself into the chair opposite Sophie's—one with a view of green fields and that babbling brook of a stream. She had a view of the castle, and she'd seen him coming—her gaze had felt like a physical presence on his flesh—but he hadn't meant to slam himself with quite so much force to the chair. She winced and he grimaced. 'Sorry.'

She shook her head, all that abundant blond hair fanning about her shoulders. 'It looks as if perhaps I should be the one apologising to you. I thought talking to your grandfather would help.'

He appreciated her optimism, but...

She leaned forward. 'I thought it would give you some answers.'

He held back a harsh laugh. 'Oh, it did that.'

She halted halfway through pouring him a cup of tea, her perfect lips forming a perfect O. With a shake of her head she continued pouring the tea, cut him a luscious slice of chocolate cake and set both in front of him. As delicious as the tea looked it was nothing to her lips.

Her lips are off-limits.

He took a sip of tea. He took a bite of cake. But neither eased the burn in his soul. 'You know, when I was little— before my parents died—my grandfather was my hero.'

The blue of her eyes deepened to the colour of the ocean. 'He was?'

'He'd sweep in during the holidays and bring me and Carol Ann up here for as long as he could get away with. It was a respite from the chaos of living with my parents.'

'I wonder that they didn't simply leave you both with him.' The moment the words left her, her hand flew to her mouth. 'Oh, I don't mean they didn't love you and Carol Ann, it's just…' She grimaced. 'I think I better quit before I dig myself a deeper hole.'

He laughed and took pity on her. 'My parents weren't interested in parenting. I think we can agree on that much.'

She nodded, her eyes shadowed.

'But they were interested in displaying the accessories of family life that would garner them as much media attention as possible. The tabloids lap up pictures of celebrities with their kids.' He could feel his lips twist, saw the way her gaze flicked to them, lingered, before she glanced away again, and it took a force of effort to keep his breathing even. 'And they love stories about celebrities behaving badly and having sordid affairs with nannies and pool boys even more.'

She rubbed her fingers across her forehead as if trying

to push back a headache. He sympathised. His parents had always been headache-inducing.

He bit into the cake, munched and pondered. 'I think my father enjoyed punishing my grandfather.'

She nodded as if his words made complete sense. Which shouldn't be surprising, he supposed, but as far as he was concerned his parents had never made any sense whatsoever.

'But here's what I never realised—my grandfather blames himself for my father's wild lifestyle. He says he wasn't strict enough when my father was growing up, that he spoiled him and went too easy on him, didn't keep him on a tight enough rein. He believes that's the reason my father went so completely off the rails. As a result he's determined not to make the same mistake with me.'

She clapped a hand to her head. 'Oh, that makes perfect sense!'

It did.

She frowned. 'Except…you're not fourteen years old any more but a grown man.'

His point exactly.

She seized her cup and took a gulp as if she needed the sustenance.

Will's insides twisted. 'He claims I'm a chip off the old block—that I'm as bad as my father.'

She'd started to choke as if her tea had gone down the wrong way and he went to slap her on the back, but she pointed behind him. He turned to find his grandfather standing there, all bristling aggression.

'You *will* learn to toe the line, William, and to curb your reprehensible behaviour and degraded way of life, *or* there will be consequences as you'll learn to your detriment.'

The table rattled and Will turned to find that Sophie had shot to her feet. Her hands had clenched to fists and she literally shook.

She looked magnificent!

'Lord Bramley, you're mistaken! And in danger of sounding like a fool because only a fool would consider Will and all he's achieved as bad, reprehensible or degraded. He's built an unbelievably successful business empire entirely through his own ingenuity and sheer hard work, but do you pat him on the back and tell him how proud you are of him? No! *What is wrong with you?*'

In her frustration she shouted the words so loud Will thought the entire valley would hear her.

His grandfather started rumbling something about duty and what Will owed his family name, but she wouldn't let him continue.

'He is not his father! Will doesn't do drugs. He doesn't lie, cheat or steal.'

'He's a womaniser!'

'He only has affairs with women who are willing! He doesn't have affairs with married women. He doesn't use his position as the boss to chat up junior members of staff. He doesn't sexually harass women. He rarely drinks to excess, he mostly stays out of the tabloids—even given who he is and his family history.'

'But—'

'No buts! He's a man who's doing something productive and useful with his life.'

'But—'

'And you should love him for who he is rather than trying to force him into a carbon copy of you.'

For a moment the only sound was the twittering of birds in the nearby hedge, and Sophie's ragged breathing.

'You want him to love this place, you want to bind him to it, but all you've done is turn the one place in this world that he considered home into a prison.'

Her voice had quietened, but it was all the more deadly for it. She lifted her chin. 'Given what happened to your

son, I can understand why you're a mass of insecurities.'
She blinked as if something startling had just occurred to
her. She moistened her lips, her mind racing behind the
blue of her eyes. With a shake, she set her shoulders again.
'But nobody else can shore up your insecurities for you,
except you. Asking and demanding that someone else do
that for you isn't just pointless, it...it's unfair.'

She stared at both men with stunned blue eyes. 'It isn't
fair,' she repeated. Before Will could say anything, she'd
taken off for the house and disappeared inside the depths
of the castle.

Will went to go after her, but his grandfather's hand on
his arm stayed him. 'Do you consider this place home?'

'I did. Once.'

And then he shook off the older man's hand and set off
after Sophie.

CHAPTER NINE

SOPHIE KNEW THE exact moment Will entered their shared sitting room, sensed that he stood in the doorway and watched her to try and decipher her mood.

But, for the moment, she couldn't control her pacing. The best she could manage was to toss an, 'I'm sorry,' over her shoulder to him.

Again, she sensed rather than saw him move a little farther into the room. 'You have nothing to apologise for. I…I loved what you said to my grandfather just now. Nobody has ever defended me like that before.'

That managed to still her. She turned, folding her hands at her waist. The warmth of his smile, the affection in his eyes increased the ache in her chest. 'Oh, Will, I'm not apologising about that.' It was well beyond time that somebody took Lord Bramley to task for his attitude to Will. For all the good it had done. She started to pace again.

'Then what are you apologising for?'

Another glance at him had her wanting to cover her face with her hands. 'Because, in my own way, I've been as bad as your grandfather.'

His face darkened and his stance widened as he pointed a finger at her. 'That's not true.'

Yes, it was. 'I've been using you to keep Peter's memory alive. I've forced you into a role that you've hated, all because… All because I've been afraid that everyone would forget him.' She pressed her palms to her eyes. 'Because I've been afraid that I'd forget him.' And because she'd felt guilty—guilty that she was alive when he wasn't. Guilty for enjoying all the things she'd once enjoyed—and for enjoying new things—when he wasn't here to enjoy them too.

She'd clutched her grief and her memories to her tightly so as to keep her brother's memory fresh and alive, refusing to move on—and refusing to let either Will or Carla move on either.

It had been spectacularly unfair.

She dragged her hands away. 'I'm sorry I've forced you into a role that you didn't want and that you didn't ask for. I'm sorry I tried to turn you into a substitute for Peter. I've been trying to shore up my own grief and fears, just like your grandfather. Only I didn't see that until I accused him of it just now.'

In three strides he was in front of her. He took her hands, making her pulse skitter and start. 'Sophie, you've not forced me into anything. Watching you grieve these past two years has been hard. I've wanted to do whatever I could to ease your pain, but I've had to face the fact that it's the one thing I couldn't do.'

'Oh! So I've made you feel like a failure too!'

She tried to tug her hands away, but he wouldn't let her go. 'Not a failure, Sophie, just…human. You've kept me human. Through all of this.'

Her heart stopped and then gave a gigantic kick, and she found herself clutching his hands in an effort to keep her balance. 'You—' She had to swallow the lump in her throat. 'You've always been human, Will. You're one of the kindest people I know.'

He shook his head. 'I've tried to be kind to you. Always. From that first day I met you I knew your parents had hurt you in some way…in a similar way that my parents had hurt me.'

Her throat thickened and her eyes stung.

His grip tightened. 'My parents, and to a certain extent my grandfather, have left me with a burning desire to succeed and to never be vulnerable to anyone again. Carol Ann, Peter and you are the only ones I've let myself care about. When Peter died I was in danger of closing myself off completely—of becoming a robot. But, Sophie, our monthly coffee dates wouldn't let me put my heart on ice. It's only just occurred to me but you made me keep feeling, and while a part of me resented it, another part of me realises it was a gift.

'So.' He lifted one of her hands and pressed his lips to her knuckles. 'Don't ever apologise to me for your grief or for the past two years, because you've helped me more than you've harmed me.'

She couldn't speak. All she could do was stare at him.

'Say something,' he finally begged.

She pulled her hands free from his and he let them go. She had to take a few steps away from him and his dark lime scent to gather her scattered thoughts. From the window she saw Lord Bramley and Carol Ann tramping across the fields.

She swung back to Will. 'Everything feels different now,' she blurted out.

He pursed those divine lips and leant towards her. A flush of heat shot through her. 'Good different or bad different?'

She considered that for a moment. 'I don't know.' She lifted a shoulder and then let it drop. The weight that had been pressing down on her had lifted. 'I feel…lighter, freer.'

'That's *good* different.'

She lifted her chin and stared at him, openly admired the broad sweep of his shoulders and the athletic strength of his legs. She took in the dark glint of his hair and the firm promise of his lips. 'When I look at you now I no longer see Peter.' A sense of loss accompanied that, but it was a good difference too. Will was his own man. He deserved better than to be defined by a ghost.

His eyes darkened and the pulse at the base of his throat pounded. 'What do you see?'

'I see all the things you are to me. I see *our* friendship now.'

He swallowed and nodded. She glanced at that pulse in his throat and knew he was fighting the same desire that flooded her.

'I see a man so potently attractive it's all I can do to not fling myself at him.'

The confession should frighten her, but it didn't.

Will's quick intake of breath and the way his nostrils flared were the only signs that betrayed her words had any effect on him. *'Sophie.'*

She ignored the warning in his voice.

'I've used Peter as an excuse to hide from the attraction I feel for you too...used it to keep you at arm's length. I've basically emotionally blackmailed you into not sleeping with me.'

'That's garbage! It's—'

'Is it?'

He broke off, his eyes burning into hers, and all she wanted to do was kiss him and feel those hands on her body.

'I let you think that if anything happened to our friendship, I wouldn't be able to cope. I let you think it'd be like losing Peter all over again.' She had to swallow. 'But finally I've realised that my love for Peter and the memories I have of him don't depend on you or Carla or anyone else. Peter lives on in my heart and there's nothing that can remove him. So whether we continue to fight our attraction or give into it, Will, it'll have no effect on how I feel about my brother.'

His eyes glittered and he held himself unnaturally still. 'Why are you telling me this?'

'And that's definitely a good change,' she added, not answering his question.

She moved across to where he stood, reached out and placed her hand over his heart. His warmth and the steady beat beneath her palm made her feel free. 'I'm tired of lying—to myself and to you. I don't want to fight what I feel for you any more. It's a long time since I did something I wanted just for me.'

The pounding beneath her palm grew harder and stronger.

'And just so we're clear on this, I'm not after love and commitment, white picket fences and children. I know you don't want to be tied down and I'd never try to do that to you.'

'So what are you after?'

She could feel her lips curve upwards and her eyes start to dance. She threw her head back provocatively to stare him full in the face. 'Pleasure,' she said boldly. 'Physical release and pleasure.'

His hands gripped her shoulders and while they were gentle against her flesh, she could feel their latent strength. They silently narrated the battle raging through him. He didn't know whether to hold her or shake her—whether to pull her to him or thrust her away.

'You said if we slept together it'd become complicated.'

And yet now it seemed incredibly simple. 'It'll only become complicated if we're not honest with each other. We're friends, yes?'

He gave a hard nod.

'This is just going to be a fling, right? We're not doing anything long-term. Eventually it'll burn itself out, and when it does we call it a day with no hard feelings. And we remain friends.'

He moved in closer until their chests touched. Heat spiked through her and her nipples hardened to tight aching buds. *Kiss me. Kiss me. Kiss me.* The plea sounded through her but she didn't utter it out loud. She had a feeling he could see it shining from her eyes.

'Can you do that?'

The words grated from him and she could tell he was holding on to his control by only a thread. 'I can. I have no unrealistic expectations of you or myself. Can you?'

Those firm lips lifted upwards into a hungry, wolfish smile. 'It's my speciality.'

And then his hands lowered to her hips and he pulled her hard up against him, leaving her in no doubt of his desire for her; she sucked in a breath and tried to keep her balance. His fingers curved into the flesh of her backside and stars burst behind her eyelids.

She gripped his waist to steady herself. 'This is all completely separate from our marriage arrangement. That's business and this is…'

He stilled. 'This is?'

'It's something completely different. It's just for us. Because we want to. And for no other reason.'

His hand curved about the back of her head to cradle it, to hold it still while he explored the shape of her jaw with his other hand, tracing the outline of her bottom lip with his thumb.

Her breathing grew ragged. 'Stop tormenting me, Will, and kiss me.'

His lips curved upwards. 'Whatever the lady wants.' And then his mouth lowered and his lips touched her, sparking heat and need. He kissed her with a thoroughness that made her tremble, that made her want to crawl inside him. She wanted more, so much more.

Her tongue tangled with his and she gave up wrestling with the buttons on his shirt to pull it free from the waistband of his trousers instead, her breath hissing out when she finally made skin-on-skin contact. He felt firm and silken beneath her palms and she gloried in the way he shivered when she raked her fingernails lightly across his bare skin.

In the next moment she found herself pressed firmly against the wall behind her and her hands captured and held above her head. Will pressed lazy kisses along her jaw to her neck, each and every one of them sparking sensation through her. She moved against him restlessly. 'What are you doing?' she panted.

Dark eyes met hers and the intent in them melted her bones. If he hadn't been holding her up she'd have fallen in a heap. 'I've waited a long time for this moment, Sophie, and I've no intention of rushing it.'

Her pulse went off the chart. 'Not even if I were to beg?'

Was that her voice? She swallowed. 'I mean for this fling to last beyond one encounter, Will.' She tugged and he released her hands. She fisted them in the front of his shirt and pulled his head down to hers. 'I want you *now*! Slow and leisurely can wait until later tonight.'

And then she kissed him with all the fire in her soul, and her soul could've sung when the final thread of his control snapped and he kissed her back with just as much hunger and just as much need.

Sophie turned her head from where it rested beside Will's on the pillow. She hadn't curled up against his side. He hadn't flung an arm across her waist. But their hands were clasped on the bed between them, their fingers interlaced. 'Just…wow!' she breathed.

He turned to meet her gaze, a grin stretching across his face. 'I couldn't have put it more eloquently myself.'

'This isn't feeling awkward for me. What about you?'

He shook his head. 'Regrets?'

'Uh huh.' She nodded. 'One huge one—that it took me so long to sort out how I really felt about everything. We could've been doing this for weeks!'

His rumble of laughter vibrated through her, warming her to the soles of her feet. And then, before she realised what he was about, he'd rolled her under him and every part of her quickened in response.

'There's nothing like making up for lost time,' he murmured, his teeth gently tugging on her earlobe.

Pleasure spiked through her and she arched beneath him, glorying in his weight and the sparks of heat that shot through her wherever they touched. 'Very true—making up for lost time could become my new mantra over the next couple of weeks.' She gasped, running her hands down his sides and relishing the way it made him quiver. 'Tell me you don't need to rush back to London today.'

'I may never go back to London again,' he murmured against her lips, before capturing them in a kiss that hurled them both back into a maelstrom of pleasure and desire.

Three days later, Sophie wondered if that grip would ever ease. She'd had good sex before, but what she shared with Will wasn't just good. It was *spectacular*. She hadn't known it could be like this.

Not that she said that to Will, of course. It smacked too much of a neediness that would send him running for the hills. She didn't want him running for the hills. Not yet.

Not that they spent all their time in bed. They spent hours on Magnus and Annabelle as he showed her all the places he'd loved when he was young. They explored the glens and the hills, traversed lochs and cantered through crystal-clear streams. They spent hours playing board games and watching musicals with Carol Ann.

But when they retired to their room each night—they made love as if they never wanted to stop. Not just once, but again and again. As if they couldn't get enough of each other. As if they were addicted.

It wasn't until Thursday, though, that Sophie finally realised how much trouble she was in. When Will told her he had to go back to London the next day. The depth of the protest that rose through her had her clutching the wedding folder she held to her chest. As casually as she could, she leant a shoulder against the bedroom doorframe to counter the sensation of falling, of dizziness. Loss, anguish and despair all pounded through her.

Will sat on the side of the bed, his back to her, pulling on his shoes, so she allowed herself precisely three seconds to close her eyes and drag in a breath, to pull herself together. 'No rest for the wicked?' she forced herself to ask, with award-winning composure.

He didn't move and she tried to paste what she hoped was a cheeky grin into place. 'I suppose I should be focusing on the wedding anyway. Nine days, Will. The month has flown!'

He turned, a frown in his eyes. 'Do you want to back out?'

'Of course not.' It was just… She hadn't known when she'd agreed to this paper marriage that she'd be marrying the man she *loved*. 'Do you?'

He shook his head. 'I'm determined to safeguard Carol Ann's future, but…'

'But?' she echoed from her spot in the doorway. She couldn't move, not a single muscle. Those ruthless eyes scanned her face and panic spiked through her. He couldn't tell that she was in love with him. *He couldn't!*

'You look…' He hesitated.

'Stressed?' she supplied, lying madly. 'The caterers have made a mix-up with the canapés and it's made me cross. Why must these things be so hard?'

He looked as if he wanted to challenge her, but she leapt

in with a question of her own. 'Has Lord Bramley signed your papers yet, the ones that will give you ownership of Ashbarrow?'

His lips twisted. 'Our estimable lord doesn't know about the papers yet. That's this coming weekend's work.'

She tried to hide the way her chest hitched. 'So you'll be back on Saturday?'

He gave a terse nod.

Will's stomach churned and he couldn't remember the last time he'd had to fight nausea with such vehemence. He stared at the beautiful lines of Sophie's face—all smooth and composed—and wanted to smash something. If he hadn't been admiring her reflection in the mirror when he'd told her he was returning to London tomorrow, he'd have never seen it—the stiffening of her muscles, the clutching of that folder to her chest as if to shield herself from some latent hurt, the dazed realisation that had leached the light from her eyes.

If he hadn't been admiring her reflection he'd be none the wiser. He wished to God he were none the wiser now!

His heart pounded so hard against his ribs it made it hard to breathe. 'Would you mind very much if I skipped our ride this morning? There's some work I need to get done before tomorrow's meeting.'

'Of course not.'

She moved across and dropped a kiss to the top of his head, tossing the folder to the bed they shared, for all the world as natural and normal as if her peace hadn't been shattered.

As if her heart hadn't been broken.

His heart burned for her.

She dropped to the other side of the bed to tug on a pair of socks. A wholly reprehensible part of him wanted to reach across, undress her and drag her beneath him to slake the lust that rose through him. He didn't. He controlled the twin beasts that roared through him—lust and anger. Anger that she'd broken the rules and had fallen in love with him.

She didn't mean to!

And anger that he wasn't able to return that love.

'Gosh! I sure as heck don't want to be the person you're about to drag over the coals.'

He snapped himself back. 'Sorry, I…' He rubbed his nape. 'Work,' he growled.

She leapt up. 'Well, don't work too hard.'

With that she was gone, but Will still couldn't catch his breath or ease the constriction in his chest. He strode into the sitting room and across to the window, waited until Sophie had cantered off on Annabelle and then reached for his phone. 'Get me on a plane for London asap,' he snapped to his PA. In his head he heard Sophie berating him. 'Please,' he added.

Closing his eyes, he drew in a breath but the constriction about his chest only tightened.

Will was no closer to finding a solution to the Sophie problem on Friday night.

She'd tell him there was no problem.

But it would be a lie.

And only a coward would hide behind the lie.

He tossed his uneaten microwave meal in the bin and collapsed to the sofa, head in his hands. For all his money and his fancy warehouse apartment, it seemed he couldn't keep the people he cared about safe—Peter, Carol Ann… Sophie. After a moment he added his grandfather to the list. The old man drove him crazy, but that didn't stop Will from caring about him.

Though both his grandfather's home and heart were safe.

He sagged back, staring at the lights that danced upon

the Thames, but they did nothing to lift his spirits. 'If you were here, Peter, you'd kick my butt.' Air whistled out between his teeth, filling the silence. But nothing seemed capable of filling the chasm that yawned through him. His hands clenched. 'But I swear to you I'd rather cut off my own arm than hurt Sophie.' She deserved so much better.

She deserved the world.

He stilled as that thought pierced through him. Dear God! That was the answer, though it made everything inside him quake.

He leapt up and paced the room, back and forth in front of the windows. He'd rather hurt himself than her. He didn't *have* to hurt her. Now that he saw it, it seemed so simple.

When Will arrived at Ashbarrow the next afternoon, he chafed to get Sophie alone, except she wasn't even there.

'Last-minute wedding preparations,' his grandfather told him.

So, instead, he presented his grandfather with the legal documents that would assign Ashbarrow Castle to Will upon his marriage. To his utter disbelief, his grandfather signed them without argument. And without hesitation.

'What?' he barked when he handed the signed document back to Will. 'It's what I'd have done in your place. There's a clause in there that states I'll have a home here until my death. That's good enough for me.'

He didn't know what to say, and then Sophie's voice sounded through him. He swallowed. 'Thank you.'

His grandfather clapped him on the shoulder. 'I only ever wanted to provide you with a home, lad. I'm sorry if I made it seem like a prison.'

He stared after the older man, had to plant his legs against the strange disorientation that battered him.

Lord Bramley turned in the doorway. 'I have no intention of interfering in your life any more, William. I'm sorry. For all of it. But you have my word from this day forward that I'll no longer try to force your hand in any way. Sophie's right, you're an adult. You've earned the right to make your own decisions.' He pulled in a breath before thrusting out his jaw. 'I'm proud of you. I always have been. I should've told you that more often.'

Will's mouth dried and he had to swallow down a lump. 'That means a lot,' he managed.

The older man's face darkened. 'But I will tell you this—you'll be a fool if you let that girl slip through your fingers.'

His jaw dropped. Luckily the older man was already striding away, a response evidently not expected of him.

Carol Ann then co-opted him to watch, not one, but two movies with her. He only agreed if she promised him the second movie wasn't a musical.

When she put on a soppy romantic comedy, he rethought his strategy, but it was too late. He watched the female lead's heart break and could feel his scowl deepen and a weight press down on his chest.

Sophie came in just as the movie ended.

'Hello, Will.'

She greeted him with a kiss, composed, casual, and with her usual smile—the one that could light up a room. She was good, he had to give her that.

'Miss me?'

Her grin was full of teasing merriment. If he didn't know better…

But he did know better.

He pulled her in for the kind of kiss that sent a fire rushing through his veins. *Keep a grip.* 'Can I steal you away from your wedding prep for an hour? There're a few things I want to discuss with you.'

She glanced at her watch and grimaced. 'Will forty-five

minutes do? I have the photographer coming to discuss—' she spread her hands wide '—things.'

'I'll take what I can get.'

Grabbing her hand, he raced her upstairs, slamming the door to their sitting room behind him. She gave a breathless laugh. 'You really *did* miss me.'

The come-hither blue of her eyes nearly undid him, threatened to weaken his resolve and have him tumbling them into the bedroom. Maybe this would seem more natural if they were naked and sated.

In the next moment he dismissed that idea. He'd discovered he was never more vulnerable than when he was naked and sated with Sophie.

He moved away from her. He needed space. He needed to breathe. He needed to ignore the metaphorical noose that had started to tighten about his neck.

Frown lines appeared on Sophie's brow. 'Will?'

'Something unexpected has happened.'

She perched on the edge of the sofa, those blue eyes not leaving his face. 'Your grandfather refused to sign your paperwork?'

He shook his head, still marvelling at that strange turn of events. 'Here's the thing—he signed them *without hesitation.*'

Her eyes widened and her lips parted. He ignored the hunger that roared through him when he stared at those lips.

'Not only that. He told me he was proud of me.'

Her mouth dropped open fully. She hauled it back into place a moment later. 'But that's…brilliant!'

'I know.'

'I knew he was a good guy beneath all of that bluster. I knew…'

She trailed off when he planted himself on the sofa beside her and took her hand. 'I didn't drag you up here to talk about my grandfather. Something has happened and I'm trying to find a way to tell you.'

She leaned in a little closer to stare up into his face. 'If you want to call this wedding off, Will, I'll be totally fine with that. I'll support you a hundred per cent.'

'I don't want to call off the wedding.' His heart thundered in his chest. 'In fact I find I now want this marriage to work on a whole new level.'

Her lips curved upwards. 'Sex on tap?'

He girded his loins and drew in a breath. 'I've fallen in love with you, Sophie. You've always been different from other women. I should've known what that meant.' It was easier to utter the lie than he'd thought it would be. 'I know I've always thought marriage was a…a…'

'Prison?' she offered with an arched brow.

'Exactly!' He warmed to his theme. 'I've always thought marriage would mean losing my freedom and independence, but that's not what this feels like. Not with you.'

She'd kept those blue eyes trained on his face the entire time, but now she snatched her hand from his and strode across to the window.

He moistened parched lips. 'I know it wasn't planned… that it's a shock, but… Aren't you going to say something?' He'd thought she'd have thrown herself into his arms by now, giddy with delight!

She half turned, pressing a hand to her forehead as if to keep a headache at bay. 'I'm just trying to work out how to react. Whether I ought to yell at you…'

Yell at him?

'Or whether to play along in the hope that…'

He found it suddenly hard to breathe.

'But I'll do neither.' She turned, both hands folded neatly at her waist. 'Several weeks ago I decided to turn over a new leaf—to stop hurting myself, to stop hurting others, and to become…useful. I'm not going back on that now.'

He rose, the blood pounding in his ears. 'What do you mean?'

'You've never lied to me before, Will. You don't love me. The only reason I can think for you to say you do is that you've discovered I have feelings for you.'

'Do you deny it?'

Her eyes suddenly flashed. 'No, I don't! I've no intention of lying to you the way you just lied to me. I'm not ashamed of the way I feel.'

'But—'

'I didn't mean for it to happen, but it has. You've always meant a lot to me. You did before Peter died…and you've come to mean more to me since.' She rolled her eyes. 'Evidently.'

'Then why not—?'

'I don't want to trap you into a marriage you don't want. That's not love! What kind of person do you think I am?' Her hands slammed to her hips. 'And I'm a little offended you think I can't cope with having a broken heart. I'll survive, you know? It'll mend in time.'

'But—'

'No.' She held up a hand. 'The original plan stands. We marry and you get to safeguard Carol Ann's future while I get a million pounds. We spend the wedding night here at Ashbarrow Castle and then the next day you're for London and I'm for Cornwall.'

'But—'

'No buts. And no more sex. It's obviously addled your brain.' She glanced at her watch. 'I'm sorry, you'll have to excuse me. I have to meet with the photographer now.'

He watched her go and wondered why, when she'd just let him off the hook, his world felt in ruins.

CHAPTER TEN

SOPHIE DIDN'T SEE Will all week. She hadn't minced her words when she'd told him that she hadn't wanted to see him—that if he really wanted to help rather than hurt her, he'd keep their contact to a minimum for the foreseeable future.

She didn't spend her nights sobbing into her pillow. She spent them staring up at the ceiling and calling herself every kind of fool she could think of for not getting with the programme and pretending to believe him when he'd told her he loved her.

But everything inside her rebelled at the thought of trapping him into a pretence of love and commitment. A fake marriage was one thing, but to pretend it was a true union— soul mates, hearts and flowers, promises of forever—was something else entirely.

In the darkness, she shook her head. She tried to find a measure of comfort in the fact that he'd not have attempted to make such a sacrifice if he didn't really care for her, that he'd not have made it for any other woman, but in reality it was a cold comfort. He might care for her, but he didn't love her.

She tried not to ache for the life she wanted with him, but it was impossible not to. All she could do to keep herself strong was remind herself how such a marriage would leave him feeling suffocated and trapped. How, in the end, he would come to hate her.

And *that* she couldn't bear.

She knew she had to stay strong because on Saturday—

the day of the wedding—she suspected Will would try again. He hadn't got to where he was by giving up.

The day of the wedding, a morning in early October, dawned clear with an invigorating chill in the air. Sophie slipped out of the castle and down to the stables to saddle Annabelle. Today of all days she needed to ride—needed to calm her nerves, to quieten the clamour of her mind, so she could present a picture of calm composure to the world in a few hours' time.

Will was waiting for her on her return. Her stomach softened at the sight of him, but she straightened her already straight spine. He'd stayed at the pub in the village last night...but he looked haggard, as if he hadn't slept a wink.

She swung down off Annabelle. 'I thought it was bad luck to see the bride on the day of the wedding.'

'I'm thinking it's only bad luck if she doesn't show up to the church.'

He tried to smile, but it didn't really work, and it was all she could do not to hug him. She handed Annabelle's reins to the stable hand who magically appeared. 'Is everything okay?'

'No. Everything is wrong.'

She led him to a bench in the kitchen garden bathed in early morning light and scented with rosemary and lemon balm. 'Tell me. I'm the party planner extraordinaire, which translates into me being an expert troubleshooter. Has the best man broken his leg? Have half the guests come down with food poisoning? Hit me with it, Will. I'm used to dealing with last-minute emergencies.'

He jutted out his chin and glared. 'I love you, and you refuse to believe me. *That's* what's wrong.'

She swallowed. She hadn't expected him to sound so... *sure*. He must've been practising.

'Last week when I told you I loved you I didn't realise it was true. I said it because—' he flung an arm out '—because I didn't want to hurt you, because you deserve to be happy, because you deserve the best. But my whole week has been grey and bleak and miserable.' He raked both hands back through his hair. 'I've felt as if I've been stumbling through a thick fog or…or trying to wade through quick-drying cement. I've been an idiot, Sophie, a grade-A fool.' He hauled in a breath, resting his elbows on his knees, looking so haggard her stomach started to churn. 'I told myself to pretend to love you because the truth scared the living daylights out of me. What good is my so-called independence and freedom if I don't have you? I love—'

'Stop it!' Her voice came out sharper than she meant it to, but his every word was a cold stab to her heart and she couldn't bear any more. 'That's enough. I know you feel guilty, but you've no right to toy with my affections like this.' She shot to her feet, trembling with the power of emotion coursing through her, from the strength it took to hold back from throwing herself into his arms. 'If you really respected me, *cared* for me, you'd stop this now.'

'But—'

'This is not the time for such a discussion!'

He shot to his feet too. 'It's the day of our wedding! What better time is there?'

'A wedding for a paper marriage, a fake marriage, Will. That's the arrangement and that's what's happening here today. You have no right to change the rules now.'

He took her shoulders in both his hands, his eyes blazing down into hers. 'Even if the real thing—a marriage based on love and respect—would add greatly to both our happiness?'

He looked so convincing she wanted to slap him. 'Maybe I have misjudged you. Maybe what you want is more important to you than what I want? Maybe easing your guilt is more important to you than my need for space?'

He took a step back, his face white. His hands dropped to his sides. 'I only want you to be happy. I only want what's best for you.'

'Fine! Then rather than forcing your version of happiness onto me, let me make the choice for myself.'

He stared at her for a long moment and then nodded. 'This isn't over.'

Whatever. She turned and started for the house. 'I'll see you at the church.'

Three hours later Sophie stared at her reflection in the full-length mirror that had been brought to her suite of rooms and gave a satisfied nod. She looked suitably bridal. She'd chosen a wedding gown in a nineteen-twenties style—a dress with a slim skirt, but overlaid with lace and intricate beadwork. Those who knew her well would smile when they realised the dress wasn't white or cream or ivory or dove grey, but the palest shade of pink.

Carol Ann stared at her from the other side of the room, where she was doing her best not to crumple her own gown. 'You're the beautifullest woman in the world, Sophie,' she breathed in awe.

'We're the most beautiful women in the world,' she corrected. Carol Ann looked a picture in her pale lilac dress. 'Okay, you better help me on with my veil.' A heavy Chantilly lace and chiffon number that would hopefully hide the strain in her face when she made her farcical vows to Will.

Once her veil was in place and she clutched her rather splendid bouquet of peonies, she sent Carol Ann a smile—if it trembled she doubted anyone would notice. 'Ready?'

Carol Ann nodded vigorously.

They made their way down the stairs to find Lord Bramley and her father waiting in the great hall. Both men turned to watch her descent. Lord Bramley grabbed a large handkerchief from his trouser pocket and blew his nose loudly. 'You look a picture, my dear, a perfect picture. Don't you agree, Collingford?'

'Lovely,' her father agreed, and for a moment she fancied she saw approbation in his eyes. 'I'd kiss you, but…' He made a vague gesture in the air.

She nodded. 'It's probably best that you don't muss me up.' Her heart started to pound and she feigned preoccupation with her skirt. 'It's nice to see you here, Father. I take it you spoke to Mother and that she's waiting at the church?'

He stiffened. 'Absolutely not! I thought I made myself more than clear on that front. I vowed to never speak to that woman again and I've no intention of ever going back on my word.'

She nodded, her heart burned but she refused to let her chin drop. 'Very well. I believe I also made myself clear on that particular point. Your assistance at this wedding will not be required. Lord Bramley—' she turned to the other man '—would you be so kind as to walk me down the aisle?'

Lord Bramley's mouth worked as he stared from one to the other. He snapped his mouth closed and gave a hard nod. 'I'd be honoured and delighted.'

'You can't do this,' her father roared at her. 'I'll be a laughing stock!' He paused to draw in a breath and the sudden silence pulsed with fifteen years of unspoken things. His hands clenched to fists. 'You promised to never choose her over me.' The words were quiet but deadly.

Sophie lifted her chin. 'It's a fine thing to hold your child to ransom over a promise made when she was eleven years old! When she had no real idea of its consequences. And, just for the record, I'm not choosing her over you. I've spoken to her, yes, but she said she'd only come if she had your blessing.'

He gave a harsh bark of laughter. 'Because otherwise she knows she'll lose the house in Spain and the money I settled on her as part of our divorce agreement. Rethink this decision, Sophie, or understand that I'll never forgive you.'

Neither one of them loved her enough. Had it always been that way? 'I've not chosen her over you,' she repeated. 'I'm asking you to choose me over your hate.'

He blinked.

'Your pride and desire for revenge are still more important to you than your daughter's happiness *on her wedding day*.' She frowned. 'Doesn't that shame you?'

He opened his mouth. He closed it again.

'I refuse to be a pawn in your nasty little game any longer. If you want to be a part of my life and the lives of any children I might have, then you need to change. I won't bar you from the church, and I won't throw you out of the reception, but until you contact Mother and build a bridge there, all contact between us stops.'

'But—'

'No buts. I'm tired of men trying to bully me and direct my life. I'll steer my own course, thank you very much.' She took Lord Bramley's arm and started for the door. She turned back just before they stepped through it. 'You've lost one of your children through no fault of your own. You have a choice with me. This time it's up to you.'

'Are you sure about this?' Lord Bramley said when the limousine pulled away from the castle grounds and towards the village abbey.

She turned to meet his gaze. 'About what? Not having my father walk me down the aisle? About marrying Will?'

'Your father.'

She nodded. 'Oh, yes, I'm sure about that. Sad but sure.'

He blew out a gusty breath. 'Your father always was a frightful prig. I hope he comes to see sense, my dear.'

So did she.

He sent her a calculating look. 'What would you have done if I'd refused to take his place?'

Her lips twisted. 'Don't take this the wrong way, Lord Bramley, but to be perfectly honest I'd prefer to walk down the aisle on my own and give myself away—I'm nobody's property or responsibility. But it'd cause a stir, and you know how much Will hates that kind of thing. So…'

He stared at her for several long moments. 'The boy loves you, you know.'

'So he says,' she said, grateful when they pulled up in front of the church.

She breathed in a cleansing breath as she stepped out of the suddenly cramped confines of the car, but Lord Bramley followed right behind her. 'But you don't believe him?' he persisted.

She bit her lip and took another breath, before turning to face him. 'How can I believe it when this is a marriage you've forced him into? He's marrying me because he must.' There seemed no harm in saying so now—not after he'd signed Will's papers.

Her conscience pricked her though when he seemed to age before her eyes. She forced a smile to frozen lips. 'But never mind. I expect we'll muddle along.'

'I wanted so much more for him. I'd like so much more for you too, lass.'

Tears blurred her vision, and she found herself gripping his hand hard. 'If that's the case then go in there and tell him he doesn't need to marry, that Ashbarrow is his and Carol Ann will always have a home there.' He had the power to stop them from going through with this awful farce of a wedding.

He patted her hand, his eyes damp. 'I would, my dear, except I promised the lad I'd no longer interfere. I gave him my word. Believe it or not, I've finally learned my lesson.'

She gave a shaky laugh. 'Finally the man develops a conscience.'

'I only ever meant well.'

'I know.' She squeezed his hand and kept her mouth shut about the road to hell being paved with good intentions. She wasn't going to hell. At the end of this day she'd be a million pounds richer. Well, actually, nine hundred thousand pounds richer, seeing as though she'd had that advance, but it was more than enough to build a new life for herself. And for Carla if the other woman wanted to be a part of it.

It was enough.

It would have to be enough.

The church was full. It seemed the entire village had turned out to watch Will marry. A sigh went up when Sophie appeared at the end of the aisle. A chorus of nose-blowing ensued, which normally would've made her smile. However, while she might present the picture of a perfect blushing bride, she couldn't smile. She could focus on nothing but the man waiting for her at the end of the aisle.

The man she loved with every atom of her being.

The man she was going to marry.

The man who was breaking her heart.

He looked stunning, which was no less than she deserved, she decided. If her heart had to be broken, she wanted it broken by the best.

Those dark, dark eyes matched the black of his tuxedo; the stark white of his dress shirt highlighted the colour mounted high on his cheekbones, softened only by the pale pink rose in his buttonhole. He stood tall and firm and solid. She stiffened her spine and pushed her shoulders back, determined to match him in every way, determined not to let him down.

They'd go through with this pretence of a wedding. And then tomorrow she'd let him go with courage and grace. When some time had passed she'd make sure they salvaged their friendship. And then everything could go back to being the way it had always been.

Liar. Nothing will ever be the same again.

Need, desire, possessiveness all roared through Will the moment Sophie appeared at the end of the aisle. But as she slowly made her way towards him, it was quickly followed by despair. He loved her. He loved her in a way he'd not realised it was possible to love another person. He loved her in a way that didn't frighten him. She'd never try and tear him apart the way his parents had tormented and persecuted each other. Having Sophie at his side wouldn't make him weaker. It would make him invincible!

But she didn't believe him. And he didn't know how to convince her that the vows he was about to make to her were vows he ached to make, that he'd mean them with every fibre of his being.

You have time. Not today, but tomorrow and the day after.

He had the rest of his life to convince her that he meant what he said—that he loved her. And he would convince her. Somehow.

It was only when the minister asked, 'Who gives this woman to be married to this man?' that he realised it was his grandfather and not Lord Collingford who had walked her down the aisle. The burning glare his grandfather sent him made him swallow.

'You look stunning,' he murmured to her as he took her hand. He wanted to pull her to one side and ask her if she was all right, to find out if her father had upset her.

He couldn't. It would be outrageous, would cause all sorts of gossip and speculation.

'Ready?' the minister said.

Sophie turned back to the front. 'Absolutely.'

That was when Will saw it—the silvery track of a single tear making its way down her cheek. He turned to face the minister too, his throat thickening.

'Dearly beloved…' The minister started the service.

What the hell was he asking her to do? This must be tearing her up inside.

Tomorrow. You can make this all up to her tomorrow.

Or better still, he could make it up to her tonight. Or, even better, right after the ceremony. He would prove to her that he was sincere.

Yeah, right, like you managed that so brilliantly this morning.

He closed his eyes as the minister droned through the introduction to the ceremony.

'If any of you can show just cause why they may not lawfully be married, speak now; or else for ever hold your peace.'

His eyes sprang open and he found himself holding his breath.

Sophie glanced at his grandfather, who refused to meet her gaze. Will's lungs started to burn, but his grandfather remained seated. Sophie's shoulders slumped as she turned back to the front, and Will couldn't stand it any longer. He opened his mouth. He snapped it shut again.

Deal with it later. Don't make a scene.

He glanced at Sophie. He wished he could see her face behind that damn veil better.

What if later is too late?

'Damn it!'

The minister's head rocked back at Will's curse. 'Mr Trent-Paterson?'

'Sorry,' he muttered, but, honestly, if there was ever a time to make a spectacle of himself it was now. Sophie was worth it. She was worth everything.

He released her hand. 'I have a reason why we shouldn't

marry. The bride doesn't believe I love her, and I can't have her marry me when she's operating under such a misapprehension.'

Sophie's gasp filled the hushed church. 'Will,' she whispered. 'The press are here.'

'I don't care.'

'You will tomorrow,' she whispered back.

'Come tomorrow I'll know whether I've won or lost you. Tomorrow nothing else will matter to me except that.'

Her mouth worked, but no sound came out. Eventually she turned to the minister. 'Reverend Todd, do you mind if Will and I retire to your vestry for a moment?'

'Not at all.'

For a moment Will was tempted, but then he planted his feet and remained firm.

'Will,' she groaned. 'You hate public scenes.'

'I do. But we're staying here. If it'll help you realise I'm serious then I'm willing to risk one.'

Her every muscle suddenly twanged with tension. She seemed to vibrate with it. 'Now I'm mad!' she ground out.

Mad was better than martyred. He pointed to her veil. 'You could be anything at all behind that thing and I wouldn't have a clue. I can barely see your face.'

Her hands clenched to fists and she swung back to the minister. 'Reverend Todd, would you be so kind as to give me a hand with my veil?'

'It's most improper. I—'

He broke off at whatever Sophie managed to convey to him beneath the folds of lace. Even Will saw the blue flash of her eyes and they weren't currently focused on him.

'Of course, my dear Ms Mitchell.'

When she swung back to him, her entire face was alive with fire and frustration. The breath caught in his throat even as a smile curved his lips. Now *this* was his Sophie.

She flung an arm out to encompass the congregation.

'How do you think this is going to convince me of anything?'

She'd been trying so hard to reform her image, to stay out of the papers, and here he was flinging her right back into the middle of all that again. He understood her anger.

But he knew exactly what he had to do. It should frighten him witless, but it didn't. The only thing that frightened him now was losing Sophie. He couldn't bear to think of his life without her in it.

'I love you, Sophie.'

She glanced away, lips pressed tightly together.

'And I think I've finally found the way to prove it to you.'

She glanced back, her chin tilted at a defiant angle while her eyes blazed blue outrage at him. It took all the strength he had not to pull her into his arms and kiss her. She wouldn't accept the physical as a symbol of the emotional. Not yet.

He wanted—needed—her to come to him instead.

Very slowly he drew out the document from the inside pocket of his morning suit. Unfolding it, he held it out for her to see what it was.

She glanced at him with suddenly unsteady eyes. 'That's the agreement between you and your grandfather.' She took it and scanned it, before handing it back with a shrug. 'There's nothing new here—no clauses I was unaware of.'

Without another word he tore it in half. Her eyes widened and she tried to grab it, but he evaded her to tear it in half again.

'Will, don't be an idiot!'

He tore it again and again...until it was nothing but black and white confetti. He flung the pieces into the air.

She watched them flutter to the ground, mouth agape. 'What are you doing?' She stared at him. 'Have you lost your mind?'

'Finally—*finally*—I'm seeing things clearly. I refuse to buy a home for me and Carol Ann at the expense of your happiness.'

She stared at him with uncertain eyes. 'This isn't necessary.'

'I think it is. If my grandfather makes good on his threats I'll find a way to cope with the fallout. You've shown me that's possible. You've shown me what I'm capable of. What I'm not capable of is living without you.'

She swallowed and he wondered if she realised that she'd edged a step closer to peer up into his face. The hope she tried to hide nearly tore him in two.

He'd made so many mistakes—mistakes that had hurt her—but he'd make them up to her a hundred times over if only she'd let him.

'You *never* wanted to marry.'

He nodded, but not in agreement. 'I never understood the power of love before. I didn't understand it until this week. And you know what?' It was his turn to thrust out his jaw.

'What?' she whispered.

'Not every marriage is as detrimental and destructive as my parents' marriage. Or your parents' marriage either.'

She nodded. '*I* know that.'

'I'm *not* my father.' He thumped a hand to his chest. 'And you're not my mother.'

Tears shimmered in her eyes, making them look like a bright summer morning filled with promise. 'You love me?'

He nodded. 'With all that I am, with everything I have, with my entire heart.'

He pulled forth another document—the contract he and she had signed. He held it out to her. 'Tear it up, Soph.'

She stared at it. She stared at him. She folded her arms. 'You need proof of my love?'

No! But this was in effect a pre-nuptial agreement, which entitled her to nothing other than that million pounds. He wanted to give her everything, not just a measly million pounds!

Her laugh suddenly rang around the church—merry and full of joy. He'd not known if he'd ever hear it again. Hope he'd barely dared to entertain threatened to lift him off his feet. 'Sophie?'

She took the contract and slid it back into his pocket. 'Not a chance, Will. I don't want your money. I don't need your money.'

'But—'

'Will, I only want you.'

And then she took his face in her hands and pressed her lips to his in a kiss so full of warmth and promise and love that it nearly knocked him off his feet, but then she pulled away to fling her arms about his neck, and holding her righted him again. It righted the whole world.

'I love you, Will. I'm not sure we have any right to be so happy after playing such foolish games, but I love you.'

He took her face in his hands. 'I want to marry you for real, Sophie. I want to love, honour and cherish you,' he murmured, his heart pounding in anticipation for what he planned to do with her the moment they were finally alone. 'Forsaking all others,' he added. He wanted them very clear on that.

She nodded. 'Yes, please.'

'So…' Reverend Todd broke in. 'Does this mean you wish me to continue with the service?'

'Oh, yes, please.' Sophie turned with shining eyes. 'We're definitely getting married today.'

Behind her the entire congregation cheered. Will was too happy to groan. 'From the top, if you please, Reverend.'

'Dearly beloved…'

EPILOGUE

'We have made so much money for Peter's charity!' Sophie said over the music, and Will smiled at the way her eyes danced, the way her excitement brought her entire face alive. She squeezed his hand. 'Isn't that the most wonderful news?'

He brushed his lips across her cheek. 'It is. And I'd be happy to donate more. I—'

She dropped his hand to point a finger at him, doing her best to look stern but failing miserably. 'You've given more than enough, thank you very much.'

'You've pulled off an amazing event.' He slid an arm about her shoulders and pulled her in close, burying his face in her hair for a moment to fill his lungs with the scent of her, relishing the way she pressed against him. *This*—having Sophie close—made everything right. *Everything*. The joy, the exhilaration, the contentment, none of it had waned in the sixteen months they'd been married. He delighted in making her happy. He delighted in her.

He glanced down into perfect blue eyes—giving thanks as he did every day—and then nodded across the glittering ballroom filled with smiling beautiful people towards her parents. 'Who'd have thought we'd live to see this day?'

Her mouth opened and closed and she gave a dazed shake of her head. 'I still can't believe that they're not only speaking, but also actually working together. I know you're behind this, you know?'

'Not true. It was your father's determination to make things right with you coupled with your mother's immediate acceptance of the olive branch he proffered that set this in motion.'

After Will and Sophie had returned from their honeymoon, Lord Collingford had contacted Will begging to know how he could make things right with his daughter. Will had merely suggested that he and Sophie's mother might consider working together to create a lasting memorial to Peter. The older man had immediately run with the idea. Hence, the establishment of the Peter Mitchell Foundation.

When her parents had presented the idea to Sophie she'd offered her services as an event planner immediately, and with a grace that had humbled Will. Her capacity for forgiveness and desire to make things better inspired him. The Peter Mitchell Foundation raised funds for medical supplies for Third World countries. It seemed a fitting memorial to a man who'd been so passionate about the cause.

'Now...' He turned Sophie to face him. 'What was Mildred Campbell talking to you about so earnestly?' He'd watched from the other side of the room, intrigued at the play of surprise, interest and delight that had flitted across Sophie's face at the time. Mildred was the owner of Moreland Park Equestrian Centre—the one he'd taken Sophie to see that first week she'd been stuck at Ashbarrow. He hadn't known Mildred would be here tonight.

'Oh, now this is exciting! She wants us to go into business together. She's been watching how well my equestrian holiday packages in Cornwall have been doing and wants me to create something along similar lines in Scotland. She's offered me a partnership.'

His jaw dropped. 'That's brilliant news!'

He shouldn't be surprised. Sophie deserved her success. She and Carla had been working tirelessly to get the stables in Cornwall up and running. In addition, Sophie had brought her event-planning skills to the fore in the holiday packages she'd started offering. In and of themselves such packages weren't unusual, but Sophie's mix of eclectic evening entertainments to complement the daytime riding—streamlined to meet each tour group's requirements—had proved a runaway hit.

She glanced up at him. 'You really think so?'

'Absolutely! Mildred's a tough cookie. Rumour has it she drives a hard bargain, and she doesn't suffer fools gladly.' He recognised a fellow entrepreneur when he saw one. 'The fact she's offered you a partnership—in her beloved equestrian centre, no less—is proof of her respect for what you've achieved. Heck, her hard-headed business acumen coupled with your creativity...' He shook his head. 'You'll have taken over the world before we know it.'

She leaned back to stare into his face, twisting a lock of hair about her finger as she surveyed him. 'Well, I'm glad to hear you're so supportive of the idea, because...'

'Because?'

He tried to look hard-headed and shrewd, but her smile told him she wasn't fooled. 'Because if I decide to take up the partnership it'd mean spending a lot of time in Scotland. Like, perhaps, six months of the year.'

Sophie could have whatever she wanted. He meant to make it his life's work to keep her happy. He'd move to the North Pole if it was what she wanted. As far as he could tell, there wasn't a single reason why they couldn't move to Scotland. Pyxis Tech didn't need him—he'd put a capable management team in place. He was free to go wherever he wanted.

He glanced around the room until he found Carla, who was talking with a group of other women. 'You think Carla is ready to take over Cornwall on her own?'

'More than ready.'

Something in her voice had him swinging back. 'Have there been problems?'

She shook her head. 'I just mean Carla's already in charge of the daily running of the stables. And I know she's grateful to me…'

'But?' he asked softly.

'It's time she started dating again.'

Ah. 'And you think that could be awkward for her with you around?'

She grimaced. 'Don't you?'

He chewed his lip for a moment. 'Will you be okay with it when she does meet someone?'

She nodded so eagerly her hair bounced. 'I can't wait for that to happen. I want her to be as happy as we are.'

He should've known that would be her answer.

'And I know she's grateful to me for everything, but I'm sure she must feel like I'm watching her—to make sure she doesn't slip up. I'm not, but…' She shrugged. 'It's just time to let her take over the reins in Cornwall completely.'

'While you conquer new horizons in Scotland?'

'Exactly.'

He pretended to scowl. 'Well, I'm not living in Ash-barrow Castle.'

Her mouth dropped open. 'Will! You and your grand-father are getting on great these days.'

They were, although the older man still liked to get a rise out of Will whenever he could. They still argued about everything from estate management to politics. He was here somewhere. Will scanned the room, and, while he spotted Carol Ann on the dance floor, he couldn't see his grandfather. He'd probably snuck out for a game of cards with a few other like-minded souls.

'True,' he allowed. 'But it doesn't mean I want to live with him. And I also love it when Carol Ann comes to stay with us in London or Cornwall, but…'

'But?'

He slipped his arms about her waist and drew her in

close, relishing the way her breath hitched as their bodies met. 'But I'm not ready to share you with anyone just yet. Not full-time.' He loved the freedom of kissing her whenever he wanted, of making love with her whenever they wanted. He wasn't ready to have their hours-long conversations interrupted or cut short by other people. He wasn't ready to relinquish their privacy. 'How does a little cottage somewhere not too far from Ashbarrow sound?'

She stood on tiptoe, her lips a breath's distance from his, and things inside him clenched up tight with need and heat. 'Will you be there, Will?'

He nodded.

'Then it sounds perfect.'

Before he could answer, she feathered a kiss across his lips in just the way she knew drove him insane. The heat in his blood spiked, his skin suddenly feeling too small for his body. He captured her face in his hands before she could draw away and deepened the kiss in the precise way he knew drove her insane, trailing his tongue along the inside seam of her lower lip with a slow precision until a ripple of desire shook through her body.

They were both breathing hard when they eased apart. Their love hadn't waned and nor had their desire. He revelled in that knowledge.

She smoothed down her hair and cleared her throat. 'By the way, did I mention I'd booked us a suite here for the night?'

Heat sped through his veins and he didn't bother trying to tamp down on the desire coursing through him. 'You didn't.' His London apartment was only fifteen minutes away, but... 'So, if you were to leave the party early?'

She glanced at her watch. 'Ooh, I think the event planner clocked off about two minutes ago.'

He needed no further encouragement. Taking her hand, he made straight for the exit. Sophie started to laugh, but she didn't resist. 'So there's nobody you want to say good-night to, then?'

'Only my wife. But I can assure you it won't be because I'm wishing her a good night's sleep.'

She arched an eyebrow at him, but he could see the pulse fluttering in her throat and he couldn't wait to place his lips there, to lathe it with his tongue. 'I do intend her, however, to have a good night. A *very* good night.'

Wordlessly, she collected their key.

They waited with another couple for the elevator. When the other couple exited at the third floor and they had the space to themselves Will wasted no time in backing Sophie up against the far wall, and beginning a sensual assault on her throat, pressing kisses there, grazing the skin lightly with his teeth until she clung to him.

'If you don't stop that,' she murmured, her voice gratifyingly breathy, 'you're going to have to carry me because my knees are in danger of giving way.'

The door to the elevator pinged open, and in answer he swept Sophie up in his arms and headed for the door at the end of the corridor.

'Will?'

He slowed at her softly whispered question, meeting her gaze.

'I love you,' she whispered, her eyes the bluest of blues.

His gut clenched up tight.

'I love you more than any equestrian centre, or event-planning business, or…or anything. If you'd rather not move to Scotland, I truly wouldn't mind. I just want you. If I have you then nothing else matters.'

He stared down at her and his heart grew so big he wondered how his chest could contain it. 'Sophie, I have everything I want right here in my arms. Where we live doesn't matter to me as long as you're there. I love you. I have no right to be this happy.'

Her smile was like his sun. 'You deserve every bit of happiness that comes your way,' she told him. 'And I promise that in about two minutes' time you're going to be even happier.'

With low laughs, and promises of love forever, they fell into their room and set about proving exactly how much they treasured each other.

* * * * *

SIX WEEKS
TO CATCH
A COWBOY

BRENDA HARLEN

For everyone who is looking for love—whether the first or forever—may you never lose heart in your quest for happily-ever-after. xo

Chapter One

Spencer Channing felt as if he'd been trampled by a bull.

To a cowboy who'd spent almost half a decade on the professional rodeo circuit, it was more than a figure of speech.

Not that he'd ever actually been trampled, but he'd been tossed up, thrown over, dragged across and stepped on. Even successful rides left their mark on a cowboy in the form of strains and sprains and bruises, and for more than half a decade, he'd loved every minute of it.

But now, he was battered to the depths of his soul.

He'd always prided himself on working hard and playing hard and doing the right thing. But he'd screwed up. In a big way.

So he'd decided to go home to lick his wounds. And work on rehabbing his dislocated shoulder, since licking wouldn't actually fix anything that was wrong.

Still, he was confident that the injury would heal. In fact, the doctor had assured him that he could be back on the circuit in time for the National Finals Rodeo in Vegas.

If that's what you want.

Six weeks earlier, there would have been no *if* about it. Of course, he wanted to be back on the circuit and competing for the biggest prize of the season. Being a cowboy was more than just a job—it was his identity. If he wasn't Spencer Channing, two-time PBR and PRCA bull riding champion, he was nobody.

He'd worked hard to get to the top and even harder to stay there. And then, it had taken only 6.2 seconds to change everything. Or maybe it was the unexpected meeting that happened before he went into the chute for the fateful ride that was to blame. A meeting he'd been confident he could put out of his mind for eight seconds.

He'd been doing pretty well, too, before his attention had shifted—for just a fraction of a second—away from the fifteen-hundred-pound beast bucking beneath him. That momentary inattention had been rewarded by a quick toss in the air and a bone-jarring thud on the dirt.

And another one bites the dust, the announcer had gleefully informed the crowd.

Coming back to Haven hadn't been an easy choice, but Spencer knew it was the right one. And yet, six weeks after that life-changing day, he still hadn't figured out what he was going to tell his parents when he walked through the front door. He'd driven eight hundred miles to get here, but his thoughts were as much a jumble now as when he'd started the journey.

It was almost 9:00 p.m. when he passed the town limits. Main Street was mostly quiet, as was usual for a Tuesday night, though there were several vehicles parked on the street near Diggers'. On impulse, Spencer steered his truck into an empty spot.

Stopping for a drink would only delay the inevitable, but he turned off the vehicle and stepped out onto the street, anyway. He walked through the main doors, then turned left, toward the bar section of the Bar & Grill. Only a few of the stools at the counter were occupied, and he straddled an empty one and studied the assortment of taps.

"Spencer?"

He lifted his head, his eyes skimming over the brunette working behind the bar. Pretty face with warm, dark chocolate–colored eyes, sweetly shaped lips, a tiny dent in her chin and long dark hair that tumbled over narrow shoulders. She wore a black vest over a white T-shirt tucked into slim-fitting jeans that showed off her feminine curves.

His gaze dropped automatically to her left hand, and he noted the huge diamond weighing down the third finger.

A glittering, princess-cut stop sign.

"Do I know you?" he asked, because that question seemed safer than *Did I sleep with you?*

Over the years, he'd learned that most females didn't appreciate being forgettable. Although he'd realized that the forgetting said more about him than it did about the companions he'd forgotten.

There had been a lot of women while he'd traveled the circuit. Too many women; too many one-night stands. A few hookups had lasted longer than that, but he'd had no long-term relationships. It was too hard to maintain a connection when he was constantly on the move to new rodeos in new towns—and when those new towns were filled with a whole new array of willing women. The longest relationship he'd had was with Emily Whittingham, as they'd traveled the same route for a few weeks, and the friendly parting of ways had certainly not prepared him for the chaos she would introduce into his life years later.

The pretty bartender shook her head, yanking his attention back to the present like a lassoed calf at a roping competition. "No," she said. "But you look so much like Jason, I knew you had to be his brother."

"And you are?" he prompted.

She reached across the counter. "Alyssa Cabrera—his fiancée."

As Spencer took her proffered hand, he looked her over again, this time attempting to picture her with his brother. Jay had always had a way with the ladies—a family trait—but he'd usually gone for long-legged blondes. Another family trait.

"I know," Alyssa said, following his train of thought. "I'm not his type."

"Not his *usual* type," Spencer agreed. "Obviously he raised the bar."

She laughed softly at that. "I see you have the same glib tongue as well as the same blue eyes."

Channing blue, his mother referred to the clear, deep shade that each of her children had inherited from their father.

He pushed the distracting thought aside.

"Jay said that you're a teacher," he noted.

"I am," she confirmed. "I also work here two nights a week. I originally took the job because I had too much time on my hands—but since we've started planning the wedding, I've got none. Now, I'm only working until Duke hires and trains a replacement.

"Or until he fires me," she suggested as an alternative. "Because I'm not doing a very good job, am I? Gabbing your ear off instead of asking what you want to drink."

He scanned the taps. "I'll take a pint of Icky."

She grabbed a glass and tipped it beneath the spout. "So when did you get into town?"

He glanced at his watch. "About ten minutes ago."

Her brows lifted. "This was your first stop?"

"As my brother's fiancée, I'm sure you've met my parents and can appreciate the need for a little fortification before facing them."

She gave him a stern look that probably worked well on her students, but he could see the ghost of a smile hovering at the corners of her mouth as she set the beer glass on a paper coaster in front of him.

Maybe he was surprised to discover that this was the woman his brother had chosen as his bride—and even more surprised that he was choosing to get married at all—but he instinctively sensed that Alyssa would be good for Jay. And though Spencer had never thought in terms of a wife and kids and happily-ever-after, he decided that his brother was a lucky guy.

"Does anyone know you're here?" she asked, after he'd sipped and nodded his approval of the draft.

"Sitting on this stool?"

"In Haven," she clarified.

"Nah. I talked to my mom yesterday and told her I was on my way home, but I didn't tell her when I'd be arriving."

"You didn't want her to slaughter the fatted calf in honor of your return?" she teased.

"All the calves at Crooked Creek Ranch were scrawny," he told her. "Which was probably just as well, because if one had been slaughtered, my mother might try to cook it."

"More likely she'd have Celeste do it," Alyssa noted, referring to the Channings' long-time cook. Then her expression grew serious. "How's the shoulder?"

"Healing," he said.

"How long are you planning to stay?"

He lifted his uninjured shoulder. "I'm not sure yet."

And while it was true that he wasn't working with a specific timeline—except maybe the end of season event in Vegas—this was the first time he'd returned to Haven since his freshman year at UNLV that he wasn't already counting the days until he could leave again. This time, it was entirely possible that he might decide to stay. For a while, anyway.

"Are you staying with your parents?" Alyssa asked, her question again bringing him back to the present.

"For now," he admitted. "Although I'm not sure I'll last even a week there."

"Well, if you decide you want to hang around longer than that and you want your own space, you could always stay at my place," she invited.

"I'm not sure how my brother would feel about me bunking with his fiancée," he said cautiously.

Her cheeks flushed prettily. "Not *with* me—just in my apartment," she clarified. "Most of my stuff has been moved to Jason's place already, so it wouldn't be a big deal to get the rest of it out of your way."

His surprise gave way to curiosity. "Is the apartment furnished?"

She nodded. "It's not fancy, but it's got all the essentials."

"Bed, shower and TV?" he guessed.

"And a fridge and stove in the kitchen, too."

He didn't tell her that he didn't cook, because he knew he was going to have to learn to do more than warm up canned beans to serve on toasted bread. Just one more adjustment to be made in a life he soon wouldn't recognize as his own.

"That could work," he agreed.

"Just let me know when you want to see the place," she offered.

He finished his beer and pushed the empty glass across the bar. "Would now be a good time?"

She laughed. "I'm working now. Plus, you were going to stay with your parents for at least a few days."

"Only because I didn't think I had any other options," he confided.

She smiled at that, then she touched a hand to his arm. "It's great to finally meet you, Spencer. And I know everyone will be thrilled that you're home."

He didn't know if it was the warmth of her touch or the sincerity of her tone, but with those words, the weight that he'd carried on his shoulders since he'd started this journey began to lift away.

For the past five years, he'd lived like a nomad, not always knowing when he woke up in the morning where he'd be laying his head that night. He hadn't had a home—just a series of hotel rooms that all started to look the same after a while.

But Alyssa was right—this was his home.

And it was good to be back.

Spencer Channing was coming home.

The town of Haven had been buzzing with the news all week—and it was only Wednesday!

Kenzie Atkins first heard about the rodeo cowboy's imminent return on Monday at The Daily Grind, where she stopped for a tall vanilla latte every morning on her way to work.

"He's coming home for his brother's wedding," Lacey Seagram told her.

It was a credible explanation for his return, except Kenzie knew that Jason and Alyssa weren't getting married until December and the nuptials were taking place in California.

"I heard he was suspended for fighting," Jerry Tate had reported to her the following afternoon.

He was a twice-weekly patient at Back in the Game—the local sports medicine clinic—who suffered from chronic lower back issues. Kenzie suspected he must be on some kind of pain medication that muddled his brain, because the idea of Spencer Channing ever doing anything that might jeopardize his career was completely outrageous.

The man she'd known seven years earlier had wanted nothing more than to be a rodeo cowboy and would let nothing get in the way of his goal.

Of course, seven years was a long time and people did change. And what did she know about his life now?

Less than nothing.

Because although she'd kept in touch with his sister after Brielle moved to New York City, Kenzie wasn't pathetic enough to pump her long-distance friend for information about a brother she rarely saw.

When she met Megan Carmichael—another friend from high school—at Diggers' for lunch on Wednesday, Kenzie was presented with yet another possible scenario.

"Did you hear the news?" Megan asked after Deanna, their usual waitress, had delivered their food.

"If you're referring to Spencer Channing's return, then yes—it seems to be all anyone is talking about this week," Kenzie noted.

"I mean *why* he's back," her friend clarified.

"Either he's home for Jason and Alyssa's wedding or he's been suspended from the circuit."

Megan nibbled on a french fry. "He wasn't suspended—he was injured."

Injured?

Kenzie's hand trembled as she lifted her glass of iced tea to her lips.

She knew that bull riding—Spencer's specialty—was both a physically demanding and dangerous sport, but she hadn't let herself think about the possibility that he might get hurt. Other cowboys, sure, but not Spencer, who'd always been so strong and fearless, seemingly invincible.

Of course he wasn't invincible, and the knowledge that he'd been hurt tied her stomach in painful knots.

Not that she should care. And she didn't really. Except that Spencer was her best friend's brother, and Brielle would be distressed to learn of any injury. Her own angst wasn't so easy to explain—or even acknowledge.

But maybe Megan was wrong. Maybe this was just another story generated by someone wanting to appear to be in the know about what was happening in town.

She sipped her soda, then managed to ask, "Where'd you hear about the injury?"

"Becky told Suzannah who told me," Megan said.

And since Becky worked in Margaret Channing's office at Blake Mining, Kenzie knew this rumor was most likely the right one. "What happened?"

"A bull named Desert Storm at a rodeo in Justice Creek," Megan responded.

Kenzie swallowed. "How bad is it?"

Her friend shrugged. "I figure it has to be pretty bad to get him to come home. Unless he's only coming home to reassure his mother that it's not too bad." Then she immediately shook her head. "No, the most convincing evidence of that would be to get back on the horse again—or bull, in this case." Megan smiled at her own joke.

Kenzie couldn't make her lips curve.

Instead, she picked up her buffalo chicken wrap and nibbled on a corner. She'd been starving when she sat down, but now, thinking about Spencer being tossed like salad by a vicious animal, she felt as if her appetite had been trampled to bits by angry hooves.

Because as much as she tried not to care, she couldn't deny that she did. Because when Spencer had left Haven seven years earlier, he'd taken a piece of her heart. No matter that he didn't want it, she'd given it to him and lost it forever.

"But I guess we'll have to wait and see to know for sure," Megan continued. "In the meantime—" she winked suggestively "—a girl can only hope he isn't completely out of commission."

"I thought you were dating Brett Tanner," Kenzie remarked.

"I am," her friend confirmed. "But until there's a ring on my finger, I'm keeping my options open...unless I'd be stepping on *your* toes."

"What? No!"

"Are you sure?" Megan asked. "I know you had a major crush on him in high school."

Kenzie could hardly deny it. Instead, she only said, "I got over that—and him—a lot of years ago."

"I had a crush on him, too," Megan confessed.

It was hardly a revelation. Most of the female contingent at Westmount High School had sighed when Spencer

Channing walked through the halls, his hands tucked in the pockets of his Wranglers.

"Of course, he never gave me the time of day," her friend continued.

"He was already a junior when we were freshmen—plus we were friends with his little sister," Kenzie reminded her.

"Which meant that we were never likely to get anything more than a brotherly nod of recognition," Megan noted.

It was true.

Mostly.

There had been the one time, the night before he was scheduled to leave town, that Spencer had looked at Kenzie as if he really saw her.

As if he really wanted her.

And maybe Kenzie had occasionally wondered if her life might have taken a different course if that night had ended differently. But she never dwelled on the what-ifs for too long. Because Spencer had been larger than life, with big dreams for his future, while she'd had much more modest plans.

In the end, they'd both got what they wanted.

Now he was a big-name rodeo star and she was a small-town massage therapist and, as decreed in the poem, "never the twain shall meet"—except maybe in her dreams.

And yeah, there were still times when she dreamed about him, because she had no control over the direction of her subconscious mind. And apparently her subconscious mind believed that sex with Spencer Channing would somehow be different—and better—than sex with any other guy she'd been intimate with.

"But I'm not just a friend of his little sister anymore," Megan continued, oblivious to Kenzie's meandering thoughts. "And he's going to want a date for his brother's wedding."

"The wedding's in Irvine," Kenzie reminded her friend.

"And I'd love to go to SoCal in December. Going with

Spencer Channing would just be delectable icing on the cake."

"Have you considered the possibility that he might not be all that anymore?" Kenzie wondered aloud.

"Have you not seen the June cover of *ProRider* magazine?" Megan countered.

"I saw it," she admitted.

Of course, she'd seen it. Because Spencer Channing was the closest thing to a celebrity to ever come out of Haven, Nevada, and as soon as the issue hit newsstands, all anyone could talk about was the local boy who'd made it big on the rodeo circuit. As if being able to stay on the back of an angry bull for eight seconds was some kind of accomplishment.

Okay, maybe it was. She'd watched some of his competitions on TV, and she'd held her breath and curled her hands into fists, as if doing so might somehow help him hold on. And maybe she'd been excited for and proud of him every time he'd beat the buzzer. But still, it wasn't as if he was changing the world. He was just playing at being a cowboy, as he'd always wanted to do, so that he didn't have to grow up and get a real job.

So yes, she'd seen the magazine. She even had a copy of it—and all the other magazines that had featured him on the cover or mentioned him in a footnote—in the bottom drawer of her desk.

"If you saw that cover, then you know the guy who was all that in high school is now all that *and* a whole lot more," Megan said.

"The whole lot more could be staging and airbrushing," Kenzie suggested.

Megan pushed her empty plate aside. "I'm a little surprised by your lack of interest," she admitted. "Of all the girls in our class, you had the biggest crush on him. If he ventured within ten feet of you, you'd get completely tongue-tied."

"It was embarrassing," Kenzie agreed. "It was also a long time ago."

"You really don't care that he's coming home?"

The only thing she cared about was that she might see him, and then have to face the memories and humiliation of the last time she'd seen him. When she'd thrown herself at him and practically begged him to take her virginity.

Not surprisingly, he'd rejected her offer.

She'd been both heartbroken and relieved when he left for UNLV the next day—and certain she couldn't ever face him again.

Over the years, he'd made regular if not frequent visits home, and Kenzie had always been careful to stay away from any and all of the places he might be.

If Megan was right about the reason for Spencer's return, and if he planned to stay in Haven for any significant period of time while his unknown injuries healed, it was inevitable that Kenzie would cross paths with him.

But she was confident that when that happened, he wouldn't detect any hint of the pathetic, lovestruck teenager she'd been inside the confident and capable woman she was now.

"Your two o'clock is waiting in treatment room four," Jillian, the clinic receptionist, told Kenzie when she got back after lunch.

She glanced at her watch. "Mrs. Ferris is early today."

"Mrs. Ferris canceled," Jillian informed her. "She wasn't feeling well."

Kenzie shook her head. "She complains that her treatment isn't working but refuses to take any responsibility for the fact that she only shows up for half her scheduled appointments."

"And complains when we bill her for the ones she misses last-minute," the receptionist added.

"So who's my two o'clock?" Kenzie asked.

"A new patient rehabbing a shoulder injury." Jillian sighed dreamily. "And, oh-my-god, does he have fabulous shoulders. And a smile that could melt any woman's panties from across the room."

Though Kenzie was accustomed to Jillian's outrageous and unapologetic objectification of their attractive male clients, the remark made her cringe—and glance around to ensure there were no other clients within earshot.

"Not *my* panties," she asserted confidently. Because only one man's smile had ever had the power to do that, and that had been a long time ago.

"I'm telling you, if you'd been five minutes later, I might have snuck into the treatment room to massage him myself," Jillian said, then immediately amended her claim. "No, I probably wouldn't have lasted more than three minutes."

Kenzie shook her head. "Does Mr. Panty-Melter have another name?"

"As a matter of fact, he does." The receptionist glanced down at her computer screen, where the scheduled appointments were displayed. "It's Spencer Channing."

Chapter Two

It couldn't be.

There was no way Spencer Channing was *here*. In Haven, yes. In her treatment room, no.

"I'm sorry," she said. "I didn't catch that."

Jillian touched the screen, where his name and number were noted in the two o'clock slot. "Spencer Channing," she said again.

Clearly. Unequivocally.

An injury, Megan had said.

Kenzie had immediately wondered what kind of injury and how bad it was. Somehow, she'd never considered that he might come to Back in the Game for treatment.

She made her way to room four, then paused with her hand on the knob to draw in a deep breath and will her heart to stop racing. *Confident and capable*, she reminded herself, then stepped into the room.

"So it's true," she said, by way of greeting.

Spencer's head turned toward the door, the widening of

his deep blue eyes suggesting that he was as surprised to see her as she'd been to hear Jillian speak his name.

Then his lips curved in a slow, sexy smile that confirmed the receptionist's assessment of its power.

That smile was lethal. But it was only one weapon in an arsenal that included mouthwatering good looks, a tautly-muscled physique, quick wit and effortless charm.

Yeah, Spencer Channing *was* all that and a whole lot more.

But it was her job to treat his injury, not lust after his body like a hormonal teenager.

"It's good to see you, Kenzie."

"I take it you didn't know your appointment was with me," she guessed.

"I didn't," he confirmed. "When I was told there'd been a cancellation, I just said I'd take it, without asking any questions."

She wondered if it would have mattered if he'd known, but she didn't voice the question.

"What brings you in?" she asked instead.

He tipped his head toward his right shoulder. "Glenohumeral dislocation."

She winced sympathetically, imagining the pain he must have endured. Of course, he showed no outward evidence of any discomfort now. Then again, Spencer had never let anyone see what was going on inside.

He handed her a large manila envelope. "Copies of the doctor's report and test results."

She opened the flap, slid out the sheaf of papers. "Have you had any therapy?"

He shook his head. "The doc said not before six weeks."

"How long has it been?" she asked.

"Six weeks and three days," he admitted.

"Not that you're impatient," she noted dryly.

He smiled again. "I don't believe in sitting around."

And because she refused to admit that his smile did

strange things to her, she took a jab at him instead. "But that's your job, isn't it? To sit on the back of a bull for eight seconds."

His smile didn't waver. If anything, it grew wider, and the twinkle in his eye suggested that he knew exactly what was going through her mind. "Most people wouldn't consider it sitting," he told her.

She shifted her attention back to the papers in her hand and began to scan the report.

"You look…different," he noted, when she flipped the page.

"I'm not sixteen anymore," she told him.

His gaze skimmed over her again, slowly, considering. "I can see that."

She returned her attention to the notes in her hands.

"You're not wearing a ring," he remarked.

"Rings get in the way when I'm working."

"Which suggests that you have a ring to wear."

She glanced up. "What do you really want to know, Spencer?"

"Are you married? Engaged?"

He had no right to ask those questions. Her personal life was none of his business. And yet, something stirred inside her in response to his inquiries, as if pleased that he was asking. As if the questions suggested that he cared about her status.

Or maybe he was just making conversation.

"Not anymore," she finally responded.

"Not married anymore? Or not engaged anymore?" he asked.

"Never married," she clarified. "Briefly engaged."

"Anyone I know?"

"Dale Shillington."

He made a face. "How briefly? Like you were really drunk one night and said yes, then sobered up and threw the ring back at him?"

"Not quite that briefly," she admitted.

"You can do a lot better than Shillington," he told her.

"Dale has a lot of good qualities," she said, wanting to defend not just the man but her acceptance of his proposal.

Yes, in hindsight she could acknowledge that it had been a mistake, but at the time, she'd thought he was a man who could give her everything she wanted. To belong with someone. To be loved. To have a family.

But no matter how hard she'd tried, she couldn't make herself love him—and she knew that a marriage without love wouldn't last. And she didn't want to end up like her own mother, abandoned by her husband and raising a child alone.

"If there aren't better options in this town, maybe you should leave Haven," Spencer suggested.

She shook her head. "That's not the answer for everyone."

"And apparently not for me, either," he said.

Before she could ask what he meant by that cryptic remark, he posed another question.

"Are you dating anyone now?"

"You've got an awful lot of questions for a guy who suddenly reappeared in town after seven years."

"It's not so sudden," he denied. "And it's hardly my first trip home."

She knew that, of course. He'd been home every year for Christmas, frequently for Mother's Day and on various other occasions, but never for his birthday, because there was always a major rodeo event somewhere on the Fourth of July.

"Why did you come back?" she wondered.

"Obviously I'm not in any condition to compete right now, and Haven seemed as good a place as any to rehab my injury," he said.

A reasonable explanation, but she sensed that it wasn't the whole reason. It was, however, the only reason that mattered right now because it was why he was sitting on her table.

"You're going to have to take your shirt off," she said, reaching into the cupboard for a sheet.

When she turned back again, the shirt was already gone, revealing his chest—wide and strong—and lots of bronzed skin stretched over rock-hard muscles.

She spent a lot of time focused on naked body parts in her job. She was familiar with soft bodies and toned bodies. She'd worked with varsity stars and armchair athletes.

She'd never reacted to seeing anyone else's body the way she reacted to seeing Spencer's naked chest.

Her heart pounded faster.

Her mouth went dry.

Her knees felt weak.

Because this wasn't any patient, this was *Spencer.*

Her first crush.

Her first kiss.

Her first heartbreak.

But that was a lot of years ago, and she was no longer a teenage girl infatuated with her best friend's brother. She was twenty-three years old now—a grown woman and a professional massage therapist. She'd had more than a few boyfriends since he'd left town. Even a few lovers. But her body still reacted to his nearness as if she was sixteen again and she would just die if he didn't love her, too.

She shoved all that old baggage aside and drew her professional demeanor around her like a cloak. "I guess you don't want a sheet," she said lightly.

"Do I need one?"

"No." She returned the folded flannel to the cupboard. "Some people prefer to be covered. The room can feel cold at times."

"It's warm enough in here," Spencer said.

Warm? Definitely.

Maybe even hot.

Certainly her body temperature seemed to have spiked.

She gave a passing thought to checking if Darren was back from lunch yet and asking Spencer if he'd be more comfortable having the other therapist work with him on his rehab.

Except that the question implied that *she* was uncomfortable with the situation. Which she was, but she wasn't eager to admit as much to the man who seemed completely unaffected by any memories of the last time they'd been together.

Of course, after seven years, it was entirely possible that he didn't even remember the events of that night.

"Do you want my pants off, too?" Spencer asked.

Yes.

"No!" she responded quickly.

And maybe a little too vehemently.

He quirked a brow.

She cleared her throat. "We'll just focus on the shoulder today—get everything loosened up and assess your recovery."

"Okay," he agreed.

"Lie down on the table," she instructed, determined to assert control of the situation.

"On my front or back?"

"Front." She could manipulate the muscles of his chest and back from either position, but if he was on his front, she wouldn't have to worry about him watching her with those deep blue eyes that had always seen too much of what she was thinking and feeling.

He stretched out on the table, his arms at his sides.

She breathed a quiet sigh of relief, because now she could pretend he was just a patient, like any other patient. No one special.

But the tingle that danced through her veins as her hands stroked over his skin said something very different.

* * *

As Kenzie gently probed the injured area with her fingers, Spencer acknowledged that this might have been a mistake.

It was true that he'd been so eager to start therapy he hadn't asked who would be treating him. He hadn't imagined it would matter, because he hadn't known that Kenzie worked at the clinic.

In fact, he knew very little about where she'd been or what she'd done over the past seven years, because he'd never asked anyone. Because asking would have suggested that he thought about her, and when he'd left Haven, he'd been determined to put all thoughts of his little sister's best friend out of his mind.

Still, he'd be lying if he said that he'd never thought about her. But the truth was, whenever he did, he remembered the girl she'd been. A kid with barely a hint of feminine curves and an obvious crush on him.

He hadn't been the least bit interested in any kind of a romantic relationship with her in high school, but he hadn't wanted to hurt her feelings, either. So he'd mostly tried to keep his distance from her, and he'd succeeded—until the night before he was scheduled to leave for UNLV.

He'd made plans to meet his current girlfriend in the barn at Crooked Creek Ranch that night. The meeting was Ashleigh's idea, so that they could say goodbye in private.

He knew what that meant. And when he climbed up to the hayloft, his body was already stirring in anticipation of what was going to happen. But he was a little wary, too, because Ashleigh had made no secret of the fact that she didn't want him to go—and that she'd do almost anything to make him stay.

But Spencer wouldn't let anything distract him from his goal of getting out of this one-horse town—especially not a girl he'd only been dating a few weeks. So despite her assurance that she was on the Pill, he had a condom in his pocket, unwilling to trust his future to anyone else's hands.

He sure as heck wasn't going to end up like his buddy, Mason, whose wedding was scheduled for the last week of September and whose baby was due the following April. And while Gina's pregnancy might not have been planned, at least Mason and Gina were in love.

Spencer wasn't in love with Ashleigh. But she was pretty and popular and willing to go all the way, and he was eager to use that condom in his pocket.

But when he got up to the hayloft, instead of Ashleigh, he'd found Kenzie waiting for him.

"What are you thinking about?"

Kenzie's softly spoken question forced him to put the brakes on his trip down memory lane.

"Nothing important," he said.

"Are you sure?" Her hands—so much stronger than he would have guessed—moved over his shoulder, probing and kneading.

She knew what she was doing, and he'd had enough massage therapy that ordinarily his muscles would respond to the skillful touch. But his brain couldn't seem to let go of the fact that this was *Kenzie's* touch, and it teased him with intimate memories of the last time she'd touched him—and let him touch her.

"I'm sure," he said.

"Because you're strung tight as a drum," she noted, her fingers sliding over his skin, pressing into the knotted muscle.

He was also hard as a rock.

Thankfully, his facedown position on the table allowed that to remain his own little (or not so little, he amended immodestly) secret.

"Some clients like to talk while they're on the table."

"I'm not fond of chitchat," he told her.

"Imagine that," she said. "And you used to be such a chatterbox."

The situation was awkward and uncomfortable—probably for both of them—but he felt his lips curve in response to her dry remark.

"And you never used to be a smartass," he added.

She chuckled softly before acknowledging, "Probably because I could barely put together a coherent sentence around you."

"I guess it's true that people do change," he noted.

And obviously she'd done so. The skinny, geeky teenager he'd remembered had grown into a confident and attractive woman.

A *very attractive* woman.

She didn't say anything else after that as she focused her attention on doing her job.

And while she continued to work on him, he couldn't seem to focus his attention on anything but how good it felt to have her hands on him. At least until he started to imagine how it might feel to have her hands stroking other parts of his body. And, of course, the harder he tried *not* to think about her touching those other parts, the harder he got.

Unfortunately, his life was already complicated enough without adding any extracurricular activities—or relationships—to the mix.

And that realization was admittedly a little bit disappointing.

The day before, when Spencer had passed the Welcome to Haven sign on the highway (if the seldom-used rural road could be called a highway), he'd experienced a sense of recognition and familiarity, but not much more than that.

There'd been no sense of homecoming. As far as he was concerned, Haven had ceased to be his home a long time ago. Now it was just the town where he'd grown up and where most of his family still lived. He didn't mind visiting on occasion, but he had no intention of putting down his own roots in the dry, hardpacked dirt.

His opinion hadn't changed when he arrived at his parents' house on Miners' Pass. Of course, that house had never been his home. Sure he'd stayed there on his infrequent visits, in the room his mother had designated as his and filled with his childhood trophies and buckles, but he'd never lived there.

In Spencer's opinion, the three-story stone-and-brick mansion was a ridiculous and ostentatious display of wealth and status. Which was undoubtedly why Ben and Margaret Channing had built it. With three of their four adult children living independently, they certainly didn't need six bedrooms, seven baths, a great room with a twelve-foot ceiling and a soaring river-rock fireplace, or three more fireplaces around the house.

On the other hand, if it made his parents happy, who was he to judge?

But now, as he turned off the highway and onto the access road that led to Crooked Creek Ranch, he felt a tug of something in his chest. Because as eager as he'd been to escape from Haven, he did have some good memories of the town—and almost all of them had happened at the ranch.

A lot of them involved some kind of chore, too, because Gramps didn't tolerate laziness. But Spencer didn't mind the work, and mucking out stalls, grooming horses and cleaning tack at least gave him something to do in a town that, at the time, offered little in the way of entertainment beyond the two screens at Mann's Theater. And when he did his chores well, Gramps would let him saddle up one of the horses and ride out with him to count the cows.

Because even after gold and silver had been discovered in the hills and the family had turned their attention away from ranching and toward mining, Gramps had continued to raise cattle. It was a small herd that he managed—nothing comparable to that of the Circle G—but it was his and he took pride in the routine of breeding, calving, culling, weaning. There were more lean years than profitable ones, but he didn't care. Of course, now that the family was making its fortune in gold and silver, his interest in the market price of beef was mostly academic.

Whenever Spencer returned to Haven, he tried to visit the ranch and ride out with Gramps. But today's visit had another purpose—to check on Copper Penny.

He didn't have a trailer hitch on his truck and, truthfully, he hadn't felt up to wrestling with a thousand-pound animal on the eight-hundred-mile journey, so he'd arranged to have the mare delivered. He'd received confirmation that she'd arrived that morning, and he was eager to ensure that she'd suffered no ill effects from the journey, which was why he'd headed to the ranch as soon as he'd completed his first therapy session with Kenzie.

He was on his way to the barn when he spotted her grazing in the nearest corral. The sun shone on her chestnut coat so that she gleamed as bright as her name, and her tail flicked leisurely back and forth. If she was at all distressed by the recent travel or the change in her environment, she gave no evidence of being anything but perfectly content.

"She's a beauty," Gramps remarked, joining him by the fence.

Spencer nodded his agreement. It had been the mare that caught his eye first, five years earlier at a barrel racing event in Cherokee, Iowa, before he'd noticed the pretty girl hunkered low over her back. As horse and rider raced the familiar cloverleaf pattern, he'd been impressed by their form and their speed. Afterward, the girl who'd introduced herself as Emily had proven that she was just as fast outside of the ring.

"Where'd you pick her up?"

He was taken aback by the question, until he realized that Gramps was asking about the horse.

"Denver," Spencer told him.

"Any particular reason you decided to buy a horse?"

"I didn't buy her," he said. "She was a gift."

His grandfather's pale gaze shifted to the horse again. "Heckuva gift," he remarked.

"Yeah. And that's not the half of it."

The old man's bushy white brows lifted. "I didn't figure you came home just to deliver the horse."

"I'm also rehabbing my shoulder, hoping to be ready for the National Finals."

"It's a good thing you can usually manage to stay on the back of a bull for eight seconds, because you'd never make any money at the card tables in Vegas," Gramps noted.

"What's that supposed to mean?"

"It means you can't bluff worth the stuff that comes out of the back end of those beasts you ride."

Spencer felt a smile tug at his lips. Though Gramps had never been one to mince words, his wife had disapproved of coarse language. Widowed now for more than three years, the old man still lived by her strict rules.

"We both know you could rehab that injury anywhere," Gramps said, calling his bluff.

"Maybe I wanted to do it at home."

"And maybe those cows out there are gonna sprout wings and fly away."

Spencer shifted his gaze to the far pasture, dotted with the thick bodies of his grandfather's cattle—no wings in sight.

"I decided to take some time to reevaluate my life and my priorities."

Gramps shifted the toothpick he held clenched in his jaw from one side to the other. "You knock up some girl?"

Though he was often amused by his grandfather's characteristic bluntness, this time, Spencer couldn't even fake a laugh.

His body was hurting, his mind was spinning and nothing about his current situation was the least bit amusing.

Chapter Three

Seven years was more than enough time for a girl to get over a silly crush. And when Kenzie had been at lunch with Megan earlier that day, she'd been confident that any feelings she'd had for Spencer Channing had been trampled into dust a long time ago. Of course, that was before she'd walked into her treatment room and found him waiting for her.

Well, not waiting for *her*. Waiting for a therapist to work on his injured shoulder, and she just happened to be that therapist. She'd studied hard and trained carefully so that she knew how all the muscles in the body worked, how they were affected by various types of injuries and how she could manipulate the tissue to release tension and ease pain.

She'd treated the same kind of shoulder trauma in other patients, but when Spencer had removed his shirt, all that experience had faded from her mind. She'd been mesmerized by the taut bronzed skin molded to hard, sinewy muscle. She'd wanted to press her lips to his shoulder, drop kisses across that broad, powerful chest, then slowly lick her way down those washboard abs.

She didn't entirely trust herself to continue to touch his body and maintain a professional distance, which meant that she should ask one of her coworkers to take over Spencer's treatments. Therapists traded patients all the time and for various reasons, but she had no intention of admitting that being near Spencer, touching the exquisitely sculpted body that her hormonally-driven teenage-self had lusted for with every fiber of her being, had reawakened long dormant feelings inside her and started the playback of memories in her mind.

She'd always liked hanging out at Crooked Creek Ranch, and she never missed an opportunity to go down to the barn and visit with the horses that were stabled there. Brielle's grandfather had taught her to ride, and she remembered how hard her heart had knocked against her ribs the first time she'd sat in the saddle astride the black gelding with white markings for which he'd been named Domino. She'd been equal parts excited and terrified, and she'd felt the same way waiting for Spencer to show up.

He'd been dating Ashleigh Singer for the past few weeks. Of course, he'd dated a lot of girls—and gone "all the way" with more than one, if the rumors were to be believed. According to the conversation Kenzie had overheard, Ashleigh was going to give Spencer a going-away present that just might change his mind about going away.

Kenzie hadn't been sure what that meant, so she was glad when Rebecca asked for an explanation—and heart-sick when Ashleigh told of her plan to meet Spencer at nine o'clock in the barn at the Crooked Creek Ranch and "knock boots" in the hayloft.

So Kenzie got to the barn first, and when Ashleigh showed up, she told the other girl that Spencer had asked her to meet him there. Ashleigh, furious at the thought of her boyfriend two-timing her with one of his little sister's friends, stormed off. And when Spencer showed up to meet with Ashleigh, he found Kenzie there instead.

"Where's Ashleigh?" He asked the question gruffly, without even saying hello.

Her heart was racing, her throat was dry, and she was grateful to be sitting on the edge of a hay bale, because her knees felt so wobbly she was certain they wouldn't hold her up. "She, uh, had to go."

"Where?" he demanded.

She shrugged, because she really didn't know, didn't care. All that mattered was that Spencer was here—with her.

"But I waited for you," she pointed out to him.

He looked wary. "Why?"

"Because Brie told me that you're leaving tomorrow."

"Did she tell you to meet me here, too?"

Kenzie felt her cheeks flush. "Of course not. She has no idea that I'm here."

And she'd probably be horrified if she knew what her friend had planned. But Kenzie wasn't worried that Brielle would find out, because Spencer's sister had snuck away from the house to meet someone, too.

"And I'm still waiting for you to tell me why you're here," *Spencer said impatiently.*

"I just wanted to, uh, say goodbye."

"Goodbye." *He turned away.*

"Wait!" *She leaped up.*

He sighed and turned back. "What do you want, Kenzie?"

"Are you, uh, ever gonna come back?"

"I'm only going to college," he said. "I'll be home for Christmas."

But Christmas was a long way away, and she couldn't wait that long. Besides, she was here now. And she was ready.

"It was my birthday last week," she said.

"Happy birthday," he replied, *with more than a touch of impatience.*

"I'm sixteen now," she told him, hoping he understood the significance of the revelation.

"Okay," he acknowledged cautiously.

The next words spilled out of her mouth in a rush: *"Sixteen's the legal age of consent in Nevada."*

His brows drew together and his mouth thinned. *"How do you know that?"*

"I looked it up," she admitted, her cheeks burning.

"Why?" he asked.

She lifted her chin to meet his gaze. *"Because I'm ready."*

"For what?"

"To do it." Her cheeks were hot and her armpits were damp, but she forged ahead determinedly. *"With you."*

He sighed. *"Kenzie, you're not ready to have sex if you can't even say the words."*

"I am ready," she insisted, with far more certainty than she felt. *"And I want you to be my first."*

He shook his head. *"That's not going to happen."*

"Why not? You were going to have sex with Ashleigh, weren't you?"

"I'm not going to talk to you about Ashleigh," he told her.

"But she left and I'm still here."

"You shouldn't be," he told her bluntly.

In the past, Kenzie had rarely managed to string a complete sentence together in his presence. But she was sixteen now, and she would not be dissuaded.

Instead of taking the hint, she took a step closer.

Then she lifted herself onto her toes and pressed her mouth to his.

He didn't respond at first, but she refused to give up. She refused to consider that this night might not end the way she'd planned. Then he muttered a shocking curse against her lips and finally gave in to the deep and abiding love she was certain he must feel for her.

She gasped a little when his tongue slid between her parted lips, but she didn't pull away. Not even when he pushed her back against the hay bales and pressed his body against hers—

The ring of her cell phone jolted Kenzie back to the present.

Seven years later, the memories of that night were still vivid enough to make her feel hot and shaky. Inwardly chiding herself for this reaction, she pressed cool hands to her heated cheeks and drew in a deep, steadying breath, then reached for her phone.

"Hey," Kenzie said, smiling as she answered the Face-Time request from Spencer's sister. "How are things in the Big Apple?"

"Everything's great here," Brielle said. "But there might be a bit of a tremor on its way to the Silver State."

Kenzie heard the worry underlying her friend's deliberately casual words and immediately suspected the reason for the call. "If you're talking about Spencer returning to Haven, your warning is too late."

"Who told you?"

"It would be a shorter list to mention the people who didn't tell me," Kenzie noted dryly.

But she was touched by her friend's concern. Although Brie didn't know all the details about what had happened— or *almost* happened—between Kenzie and Spencer before he went away to college, she knew about her friend's crush and that she'd been heartbroken when he left.

"That's only one of the many things I don't miss about living in a small town," Brielle muttered.

"But you miss your friends, don't you?"

"I miss *you*," Brie confirmed. "I've lost touch with almost everyone else from high school."

"They'd be happy to see you if you came home for a visit," Kenzie said.

"I will," Brielle responded, as she always did. And

though she always sounded as if she meant it, she'd only ever returned to Haven once since she'd moved to New York City for college and decided to stay—and that had been for her grandmother's funeral.

"In the meantime, I thought you should know that Spencer is on his way home."

"Your intel is a little out-of-date," Kenzie noted.

"Huh?"

"He's not on his way, he *is* home. In fact, he came into the clinic today."

"How bad is his shoulder?" Brielle asked.

"You know I can't share any details of a patient's treatment," she said. She probably shouldn't even have disclosed his appointment, but it was hardly a secret as anyone might have seen Spencer on his way into or out of the building.

"He's not a patient—he's my brother," Brie reminded her.

Kenzie relented enough to say, "And he's healing."

Brielle considered this for a moment before asking, "You don't think it's anything that would keep him away from the circuit, do you?"

Though she knew she was breaching the rules regarding patient confidentiality, she was eager to assuage the concern she heard in her friend's voice. "Numerous tests and physical examinations suggest a simple glenohumeral dislocation."

"Okay." Brie nodded. "That's good. I mean, I have no idea what a gle-no-whatever is, but the way you said it was reassuring."

Kenzie smiled at that. But her friend's earlier question made her ask, "Do you know something that you're not telling me?"

"No," Brie denied. "But when we talked last week… he seemed to suggest that he was thinking about making a career change…and I didn't get the impression that it was entirely willingly."

"Bull riding takes a toll on the body," Kenzie noted. "He's probably starting to feel his age."

"He's twenty-five."

"And he's been a professional bull rider for five years already, after competing in college and as an amateur for I-don't-know-how-many years before that."

"At least ten," Brielle admitted. "Because that's how old he was when he won his first buckle for steer riding."

"Maybe he's just ready for a change," Kenzie suggested.

And as she considered the possibility that Spencer might not just be home for a visit but forever, a tiny blossom of something that felt like joyful hope began to unfurl inside her heart. Then she remembered how eager he'd been to leave Haven, how determined he'd been to find fame and fortune away from "this backwards backwoods town," and that tiny blossom shriveled up again.

"Maybe," her friend echoed, though her tone was dubious.

"And speaking of change—rumor has it that the Mountainview kindergarten teacher put in for a transfer to Reno."

"Shelby Bradford's been making plans to leave Haven since long before I did," Brielle remarked. "She's not going anywhere."

"Well, she'll have to retire eventually," Kenzie pointed out.

Her friend laughed. "Don't hold your breath."

They chatted for a few more minutes, then Brie had to run to meet some friends for dinner, which prompted Kenzie to think about her own evening meal.

Not that she was really hungry, but anything was better than thinking about Spencer Channing—and the long-forgotten feelings that his return had stirred inside her.

If Spencer had asked around town, he might have learned that Kenzie rented an apartment above a law office on Main

Street, not too far from the clinic where she worked. Instead, he'd taken a more circuitous route to get there.

"Hey," he said, when Kenzie replied to the buzz of the intercom from the street level entrance behind the building.

"Spencer? What are you doing here?"

There was reservation along with surprise in her tone. He had no reason to assume that she'd want to see him, but he was counting on her long-term friendship with his sister to at least get him in the door. "Can I come up?" he asked. "Or are we going to have an entire conversation through this speaker?"

She hesitated. Or maybe he only thought she did, because the next sound he heard was the lock being released.

"Now are you going to tell me why you're here?" she asked after letting him into her apartment.

He took a moment to appreciate the fact that she'd changed out of the all-black she'd been wearing at the clinic and into a pair of slim-fitting jeans and a flowy kind of top in a patchwork print. She'd released her hair from its ponytail, too, so that the long tresses hung like a curtain of shiny silk around her face. Her driver's license probably described her hair as brown, but it was actually an intriguing mix of many shades, including hints of gold and copper.

"Spencer?" she prompted, when he didn't respond to her question.

"Sorry," he apologized, realizing he'd been staring. "I just—wow, Kenzie. You really look great."

"Thank you," she said, a little cautiously.

He couldn't blame her for being wary. Although she'd been best friends with his sister, he'd never been particularly close with Kenzie. Well, there was that *one* time… but it was probably best not to think about that night right now. Or ever.

Except that being back in Haven and seeing Kenzie again, he couldn't seem to stop thinking about that night.

And, seven years later, he still didn't know if he was relieved or disappointed that it hadn't ended differently.

Firmly pushing those memories to the back of his mind, he focused on the present—and his empty stomach. "I came by to see if you wanted to grab a bite to eat."

"Grab a bite?" she echoed the words as if he'd suggested a quick trip to the moon.

Okay, so she was surprised by the invitation. And obviously skeptical about his motivations for showing up at her door. But a buddy had once remarked that he could charm a nun out of her habit if he put his mind to it, so he didn't figure it should be too difficult to convince Kenzie to share a meal with him.

"Dinner," he clarified, his lips curving in an easy smile. "You know—when you sit down at a table, sometimes in a restaurant, and enjoy a meal."

"I'm vaguely familiar with the concept," she said dryly. "In fact, I've got soup heating on the stove for mine."

"Soup isn't a meal," he chided. "Even Diggers' menu lists it as a starter."

"Well, it's my meal tonight," she insisted, and turned her back on him.

Which afforded him a spectacular view of her nicely shaped derriere encased in snug denim.

He followed that sweetly curved butt to the kitchen, where she picked up a spoon from the counter and stirred the soup.

He averted his gaze so she wouldn't catch him staring again and looked around the ultramodern kitchen with dark walnut cupboards and stainless steel appliances. A granite-topped island separated the kitchen from the open-concept living area with a trio of tall windows that overlooked Main Street.

"Nice place," he remarked.

"I like it," she agreed.

"How long have you lived here?"

"Just over a year," she said. "Katelyn used to live up here and work downstairs, but then she married the new sheriff and they bought a house over on Sagebrush. As soon as I heard she was moving out, I asked if she'd rent the place to me."

"Katelyn…Gilmore?"

"It's Davidson now," she told him.

"I didn't know she'd married the sheriff." Then he frowned. "Or maybe I just don't pay much attention when my mother starts gossiping about local events." It was also possible that Margaret Channing hadn't said anything, preferring to pretend that the entire Gilmore family didn't exist.

"Not just married but a new mom now to the most adorable little girl," Kenzie told him.

Though she hadn't invited him to sit, he straddled a stool at the island and folded his arms on the counter. His stomach rumbled.

"You know, if you made sandwiches to go with that soup, you'd probably be able to feed two people," he told her.

"Is that your way of inviting yourself to stay for dinner?"

"Soup's not dinner," he said again. "But if you added a sandwich…"

She shook her head, but the smile that tugged at her lips confirmed that she was warming up to his presence. "Grilled cheese, okay?"

He grinned. "Grilled cheese is the best kind of sandwich with soup."

Kenzie turned the knob for another burner, set a frying pan on it, then retrieved the ingredients for the sandwiches.

"Can I help?" he offered, as she began to butter slices of bread.

She nodded to the pot on the stove. "Just keep an eye on the soup."

He picked up the wooden spoon she'd set down, so that he was armed and ready.

"If you haven't kept up with local events, how did you know that I was living here?" Kenzie asked him now.

"Your mother told me," he admitted.

The knife she'd taken out of the block to slice the cheese slipped from her grasp and clattered against the counter. "When did you talk to my mother?"

"When I stopped by the house on Whitechurch Road earlier."

"Well, that would explain the three voice-mail messages she left for me," Kenzie noted, picking up the knife again.

"Three messages and you didn't call her back?" he asked in feigned shock.

She shrugged and resumed slicing the cheese. "If it had been anything important, she would have said so."

He mimed thrusting a dagger in his heart. "Ouch."

She rolled her eyes.

"She was surprised to see me," he confided. "And reluctant to let me know where I could find you."

Butter sizzled as Kenzie set the sandwiches in the hot pan.

"She's always been…protective of me," she said.

"I knew that," he acknowledged. "I just never knew that she disliked me so much. Which was a surprise, because most women usually find me charming. Even moms."

"No doubt."

"And I never did anything to earn her disapproval." But they both knew that wasn't exactly true, so he clarified, "At least not anything that she knows about." He sent Kenzie a questioning glance. "Or does she?"

She dropped her gaze to the pan, as if turning the sandwiches required her complete focus. "There's nothing for her to know."

He nodded, relieved by her response. Glad to hear her confirm that what happened between them hadn't been a big deal to her, either.

Glad…and a little bit skeptical.

But he didn't express his doubt. He didn't want to have the awkward conversation they probably should have had seven years earlier. And he especially didn't want to dig up old feelings of guilt and regret—not hers or his own.

She reached into the cupboard over the sink for dishes, then pulled open a drawer for cutlery.

He rose from his seat at the island to help.

"I do appreciate this." He slid the sandwiches out of the pan and onto the plates while she poured the soup into the bowls. "You feeding me, I mean."

She smiled at that. "As if I had a choice."

"You always have a choice," he told her.

She sat down beside him. "So tell me why you showed up at my door instead of grabbing a bite with Gage or Brett or one of the other guys you used to hang out with," she suggested.

"Truthfully—" he dipped his spoon into his bowl "—I didn't keep in touch with anyone when I left Haven. Aside from you, I don't have many friends remaining in this town."

"I was your sister's friend," she said, as she tore off a piece of her sandwich and popped it into her mouth. "Not yours."

"Maybe we weren't friends," he acknowledged. And then, because he apparently *did* want to have the awkward conversation they'd skipped seven years earlier, he added, "But we were almost lovers."

She shook her head as she finished chewing. "A quick roll in the hay would not have made us lovers."

He touched a hand to her arm. "I treated you badly that night, and I'm sorry."

"It was a long time ago—and long forgotten," she told him.

But he didn't believe it.

Certainly he'd never forgotten.

"Then you're not still mad at me—about what happened that night?" he prompted.

"*Nothing* happened," she said again, tearing off another piece of her sandwich. "And I was never mad at you," she confided. "I was mad at myself. And...embarrassed."

"Why would *you* be embarrassed?" he wondered aloud.

She swirled her spoon in her soup. "Because I threw myself at you."

Apparently they had different recollections of that night. Because while there was no denying that she'd made the first move, he'd made a lot more after that. "As you said, it was a long time ago and nothing happened."

"Nothing of any significance," she agreed. "But not for lack of trying on my part."

It was true that she hadn't been shy about what she wanted. And he'd been unexpectedly and shockingly aroused by the bold actions of a girl he'd previously dismissed as just another friend of his little sister.

"Back then, you and me—" He shook his head. "It would have been a mistake."

She nodded. "I know."

"But now..." He deliberately let the words trail off and dramatically waggled his eyebrows.

She smiled, seemingly appreciative of his effort to lighten the mood, but immediately shot him down. "Now it would be an even bigger mistake."

She was probably right—for more reasons than even she knew—but he was curious about her rationale. "Why would you say that?"

"Because even if we weren't friends before, I get the impression you showed up at my door because you need a friend now."

"Or at least wanted to see a friendly face," he acknowledged, as he shoved the last bite of sandwich into his mouth before turning his attention back to the soup.

"What was going on at your parents' place tonight that you didn't want to eat there?" she asked.

"Celeste had a thing this afternoon—a baby shower?

Bridal shower? Some kind of shower, anyway. And I told her that I'd fend for myself so she didn't have to rush back."

"Fending for yourself meaning inviting yourself to share my dinner?" she queried dryly.

"I offered to take you out," he reminded her. "You could have had a thick, juicy steak at Diggers'—or anything else on the menu."

"Mmm… I do love their strip loin, but this is better," she told him.

He spooned up the last of his soup which, along with the sandwich, had sated his gnawing hunger but was, by no stretch of the imagination, better than steak. "Why?"

"Because if we'd walked into Diggers' together, the whole town would be buzzing about it before the meat hit the grill."

"And that would bother you?"

"I don't like being the subject of gossip and speculation," she said.

"You're not worried that people will remark on my truck being parked outside your apartment?"

"I wasn't—" she frowned as she stacked the empty bowls and plates "—until just now."

"I'm sure they have better things to talk about," he said, attempting to reassure her.

"You're the closest thing this town has to a celebrity," she reminded him, as she transferred the dishes and cutlery to the dishwasher. "Everything you do and say is major news."

"Then the gossips are going to throw a ticker tape parade when they find out about Dani."

She sent him a quizzical look. "Who's Dani?"

"My daughter."

Chapter Four

Kenzie stared at him, stunned. "You're serious? You have a child?"

Spencer nodded. "A little girl."

There were so many thoughts swirling through her mind, she didn't know where to begin.

"How old is she?" she asked, latching onto the most obvious question first.

"Three. Well, almost four."

"Are you…married?"

He shook his head. "No. Never. I mean, I would have married Emily, but she never told me that she was pregnant. In fact, it was only six weeks ago that I found out about Dani."

"I can't… I never…wow."

"Yeah, that about sums up my reaction, too," he admitted.

She took another minute to absorb the information he'd provided, but her brain was stuck on the fact that the wild child of the esteemed Channing family had a child of his own now. But maybe even more shocking was that the object of her adolescent adoration was sitting in her kitchen talking to her about it.

And while it had taken a concerted effort not to drool over his hotness as she sat beside him eating her dinner, this new information made her uneasy, because now she knew she hadn't been ogling—surreptitiously, of course—the hottest guy in school but a little girl's father.

Obviously her tired brain needed caffeine to process this.

She reached into the cupboard for a mug, then remembered the hot guy still in her kitchen. "Do you want coffee?"

"Sure," Spencer said.

She grabbed a second mug, then popped a pod into the single-serve brewer. "Cream? Sugar?"

"Black's good," he said.

She handed him the first mug then brewed a second, to which she added a splash of milk.

"So." She lifted her cup toward her lips, sipped. "An almost-four-year-old daughter."

He nodded.

"And you only found out about her six weeks ago?"

He nodded again.

Which jived with the timing of his shoulder injury, she realized. Probably not a coincidence. More likely, he'd been distracted by the revelation when he'd climbed onto the back of the bull for that fateful ride.

"Why did her mom track you down now?" Kenzie wondered.

"She didn't," he acknowledged, his tone grim. "Emily died in a motorcycle accident three months ago."

"Oh, Spencer." She set her mug on the counter and instinctively reached out to touch a hand to his arm. "I'm so sorry."

"Me, too," he said. "Mostly for Dani. But I'll admit to

being a little frustrated, too, because now I'll never know why she didn't tell me about my child."

"Then how did you find out?"

"Linda—Emily's mom and Dani's grandmother—tracked me down through the PRCA," he said, referring to the Professional Rodeo Cowboys Association.

"Just to stop by and tell you that you were a father?"

"No, to tell me that Emily put in her will that she wanted me to have Copper Penny—her horse—and custody of Dani."

"Wow," she said again.

"Can you picture it?" he asked her. "Me? With a kid?"

She lifted her mug to her lips again.

It was obvious what he thought her response would be, and her knee-jerk reaction was to give him the definitive "no" he expected. Because when she tried to picture the Spencer Channing she'd known in high school as a dad, the image refused to form. But when she looked at him now and took a moment to really consider his question, she realized that her instinctive reaction wasn't just unfair, it was wrong.

"Actually, I can—and it's not as hard as I would have imagined."

"Well, I can't," he told her. "I mean, what was she thinking? We met at a rodeo—she knows what my life is like."

But there was a hint of something in his voice that made Kenzie think he wished his situation was different—something that suggested he might want to be a father to his daughter but just didn't know how. "She was probably thinking that a child should be raised by a parent," she told him.

"Without even giving me a heads-up that I *was* a parent," he noted.

She could empathize with his frustration, but there was a bigger issue at the forefront of her mind. "Where's Dani now?"

"In Denver. With her grandmother." He unlocked his phone, then turned it toward Kenzie.

The wallpaper on his screen was a picture of a little girl with familiar Channing blue eyes, wispy blond hair and a sweet Cupid's-bow mouth curved in a tentative smile. "Oh, Spencer. She's beautiful."

"She is, isn't she?" he said, sounding pleased and proud—and more than a little overwhelmed.

"Are you going to honor her mother's wishes?"

He turned the phone around again and studied the picture for a long minute before responding to her question. "I'm going to try. Maybe I wonder about the wisdom of Emily's choices and worry that I'm going to screw up…but Dani's my daughter—and I want to be her father." He managed a wry smile. "And no one could be more surprised by that realization than me."

Obviously Kenzie's perceptions were colored by her own experiences. She'd grown up without a father because her own had abandoned his pregnant wife and, as a result, Spencer's quiet determination to do the right thing made him even more appealing to her.

Not that she would ever let him know it. Although he'd been flirting and teasing earlier, she had no intention of opening up her heart to him again. The revelations about his daughter only strengthened her resolve, because Dani's grieving heart was the only one that mattered.

"Do you have a plan?" she asked cautiously. "What's going to happen next?"

"Well, I'm still hopeful that I can compete at the National Finals."

Which she knew took place in December—barely six weeks away, and which confirmed her suspicion that his return to Haven was only temporary.

"I meant with Dani," she clarified.

"The caseworker thought she should stay with Linda until I had suitable accommodations."

"Caseworker?" she echoed, surprised.

He explained that Dani had been in the care of a teenage babysitter when Emily was killed. Apparently she'd promised to be home by ten o'clock, and when it got to be midnight and she still hadn't returned, the babysitter tried to reach her on her cell phone. Emily didn't answer, so the babysitter called her parents, who then contacted the police. They, of course, reached out to family services to take custody of the child until her next of kin could be contacted. At the time, that was her grandmother because nobody knew anything about Dani's father.

He recited the facts in a level tone, but his hands were holding on to the mug so tightly that his knuckles were white. And though Kenzie didn't want to add to his worry, she had to ask, "Is it possible that the grandmother might fight for custody?"

"No," he said confidently. "Linda made it clear that she'd already raised one daughter and this one was my responsibility."

"Charming," Kenzie remarked.

"I know she loves Dani," he said. "And she's been taking care of her since the accident, even moving into Emily's place so that Dani could stay in familiar surroundings."

"But only temporarily."

He shrugged. "Her boyfriend is some rich international banker who likes to jet-set around Europe and she wants to be free to see the world with him."

Maybe the grandmother did love Dani, but it seemed to Kenzie that she loved her boyfriend—or at least the lifestyle he could provide—more. And without even having met the little girl, Kenzie ached for the child who'd lost the only parent she'd ever known and who would soon be facing even more changes and challenges.

"Speaking of grandparents," she said. "How did your parents respond to the big news?"

Spencer sighed. "Well, it was awkward, that's for sure."

"You didn't tell us you were coming home tonight," his

mother said, but softened the admonishment with a kiss on his cheek.

"I wasn't sure myself," he told her.

"How's the shoulder?" his dad asked.

"It's coming along," he said, as if the words might lessen the current throbbing in the joint. "I'm hoping to start therapy this week."

"That's good news," Ben said.

"Speaking of news," Spencer said.

"Please tell me you're going to give up riding bulls and come home to work at Blake Mining," Margaret implored.

Since he couldn't confirm her request—because even if he didn't know how long he was going to stay in Haven, he did know that didn't ever want to work at Blake Mining— he decide to ignore it.

Instead, he took two chocolate cigars out of his pocket. They were wrapped in shiny pink foil with paper bands announcing, "It's a Girl." As he handed one to each of his parents, he said, "Congratulations, you have a grand-daughter."

His father's brows drew together; his mother's eyes went wide.

"Is this some kind of joke?" Ben wanted to know, obviously not amused.

"It's not a joke," he assured them. "It's happy news."

"For Christ's sake, Spencer." His father shook his head. "Of all the stupid, reckless—"

Margaret reached up to put her hand on her husband's arm, the gesture effectively halting his outburst. "Is it true... you have a baby?"

"Well, she's not actually a baby," he said. "Dani will be four in a few weeks."

"Then why in hell are we only learning about her now?" his father demanded.

"Because I only found out about her myself a few weeks ago," he admitted.

But he didn't share any of those details with Kenzie now, opting to summarize the hour-long confrontation by simply saying: "My dad yelled, my mom cried, and then, when they'd both had some time for the news to sink in, they said that they're looking forward to meeting Dani."

"I think I'm beginning to understand why there was so much tension in your body when you were on the table today," she remarked.

"Yeah, that's part of it," Spencer acknowledged.

"Well, and your injury, obviously."

"That, too," he agreed.

Spencer left a short while later, after thanking Kenzie again for dinner—and for listening to him. She still wasn't sure why he'd come to her. It might have been as simple as he'd claimed: that he hadn't kept in touch with any of his old friends and just wanted someone to talk to. Whatever the reason, she was glad he'd shown up at her door.

She was also admittedly a little disappointed that he was already planning his return to the rodeo. When she'd heard about his injury, she hadn't expected it would keep him sidelined for long. But finding out that he was a father—well, she would have thought that might have more of an impact.

Of course, the change in his circumstances was fairly recent, and it was entirely possible he was still processing what it meant to be a father and how that status would impact every aspect of his life.

But when I talked to him last week...he seemed to suggest that he was thinking about making a career change...

Brielle's words echoed in her mind, assuring her that Spencer was thinking about his future—and his daughter's, too.

And maybe, after some thinking, he would decide to stay.

Not that it should matter to her one way or the other. Sure, she'd love to meet his daughter. And maybe, if he stuck around, Kenzie and Spencer might become friends.

But she wasn't going to start spinning fairy tales in her head about some kind of happily-ever-after with a guy who'd broken her heart once before.

But listening to him talk about Dani, she'd been impressed by his commitment to doing the right thing for his child. Sure the little girl was grieving the loss of her mother, but at least she had a father who was willing to step in to fill the void in her life.

Unlike Kenzie's own.

She pushed that thought aside and set the empty mugs in the dishwasher.

Her phone rang as she was programming the wash cycle. She glanced at the display and immediately winced.

Three messages and you didn't call her back?

She braced herself for the fallout from that oversight and connected the call. "Hi, Mom."

"Spencer Channing's back in town," Cheryl Atkins said, apparently deciding this news took precedence over reprimanding her daughter for ignoring her prior calls—or even a basic greeting.

"Yeah, I heard something about that," Kenzie confirmed.

"He came here looking for you."

"Is that what you called to tell me earlier? Sorry I didn't get to the phone before it went to voice mail."

"And you didn't return my call," Cheryl said, now taking the bait Kenzie had dangled to avoid talking about Spencer.

"Sorry," she said again.

"I know you think I'm nosy and interfering," Cheryl said. "But I can't help worrying about you."

"I appreciate your concern," Kenzie told her. "But there's really no reason for you to worry."

"I won't worry if you promise to keep your distance from him."

She held back a sigh. "Spencer's not a bad guy, Mom."

"He broke your heart."

"My foolish, fragile teenage heart," she acknowledged.

And in a desperate effort to end the pointless conversation, she set her oven timer for thirty seconds. "Which was my fault more than his—and seven years ago."

"Still, first love is always the hardest to get over."

The fact that she'd had other boyfriends and even lovers since then was proof to Kenzie that she'd moved on. The fact that she'd secretly compared each of those other boyfriends and lovers to Spencer and never found one to measure up was proof she'd romanticized a relationship that had never really existed outside of her fantasies.

Her first sexual experience hadn't happened until she was away at college, and even then, she'd been apprehensive— her mother's warnings about unplanned pregnancy echoing loudly in the back of her mind whenever she was alone with a guy. And although she'd been on the patch, she'd made sure she had a condom at the ready, too, because "you can never be too careful."

She'd picked Brandon Ross to be her first because he was cute and smart. In fact, he'd aced anatomy class and could name all the bones in the human body from head (frontal) to toes (phalanges), or even alphabetically from calcaneus to zygomatic. Unfortunately, he didn't have the first clue about the location—or even the existence—of a woman's erogenous zones.

The experience had been less than memorable. And it had lasted less than three minutes. She knew because the radio was on and Katy Perry was singing when he tore open the condom packet. He was finished and almost asleep while "Wide Awake" continued in the background. But he was a good student, and she'd been optimistic that he'd study her body and learn what she liked. Unfortunately, the sex had never gotten any better, and she'd ended the relationship wondering if she would ever understand what all the fuss was about.

Apparently her subconscious believed that getting naked with Spencer Channing would assist her comprehension, because it was always him that she dreamed about at night. And maybe that belief wasn't completely unfounded, because she'd experienced more arousal and pleasure in the hayloft at Crooked Creek Ranch with her best friend's brother seven years earlier than with anyone else since then.

But she didn't confide any of that to her mother. Instead, she said again, "It was seven years ago. And I'm not going to let the memories of a high school crush interfere with a potential adult friendship."

"You've seen him then," Cheryl determined.

There was no point in denying it. If it wasn't already public knowledge that Spencer was going to Back in the Game for therapy, it soon would be, and confiding the truth now was simpler than explaining a deception later.

"As a matter of fact, he came in to the clinic today," she said, unwilling to admit that they'd also spent the last few hours together in her apartment—because that would lead to a lecture she did *not* want to hear tonight.

"To see you?"

"No. For therapy." Then, thirty seconds having finally elapsed, the buzzer sounded, giving Kenzie the excuse to say, "I've got to go now and get my muffins out of the oven."

"You're making muffins?"

"Banana nut—your favorite," she said. "I'll drop some off for you on my way to work in the morning."

"That would be nice," Cheryl said, her tone much more agreeable now.

"Bye, Mom. Love you."

"Love you, too."

Kenzie disconnected the call and began gathering the necessary ingredients to make her mother's favorite muffins.

The enormous house on Miners' Pass was dark when Spencer got home—save for a single light in the kitchen confirming that Celeste was back, likely planning the next day's menus or even doing some advance prep work. It was too early to think that his parents were home and settled in for the night. More likely they'd stayed late at the office, as was their habit.

He considered turning on the television in the family room and watching the game on the big screen—because there had to be some kind of game playing on one of the many sports channels. But he didn't feel like going another round with his parents when they got home.

He'd long ago accepted that he'd never live up to their expectations. Not if those expectations were for him to take a job at Blake Mining. And the absolute last thing he wanted was to put on a suit in the morning and spend most of every day trapped in an office. Not even if it was a corner office with windows all around.

Margaret Channing blamed her father for what she viewed as her youngest son's irrational affection for the land and the creatures that grazed upon it. Jesse Blake had been a child at Crooked Creek Ranch before gold and silver were discovered. He clearly remembered the lean times, his father's worries about grain prices and beef prices and droughts and floods, his mother's efforts to repair clothes they couldn't afford to replace and her ability to make two days' worth of food stretch over three.

The discovery of precious metals had been a boon to the struggling family. And although Crooked Creek was a ranch more in name than practice these days, Gramps continued to manage a modest herd that bore its brand. He'd sat his grandson on his first horse and taught him not just to ride but to tack and groom and even muck out stalls. And while Spencer understood why the focus had shifted from ranching to mining, he had no desire to be a cog in the machine that was Blake Mining.

His brother and youngest sister had made similar choices—Jay was now the CEO of Adventure Village, a family-friendly recreation park on the outskirts of town, and Brielle was a kindergarten teacher in New York City. Only Regan had opted to go into the family business, because she loved working with her family as much as numbers. Spencer didn't understand it, but he didn't judge her for it, either.

Still, he wasn't eager to hear again that his parents were shocked by his news and disappointed in him. He'd experienced all those same emotions when Linda appeared in Justice Creek to tell him that he had a child.

Those same emotions and more.

Most prominently: disbelief.

It wasn't possible. It couldn't be true. No way could Emily's little girl be *his* little girl. Okay, so maybe the timing of her birth fit. And there'd been that one slip—literally—with the condom. But still, he refused to believe it.

Didn't want to believe it.

Because that would mean he'd screwed up—Emily's life and now his own. And as Linda expected him to take the kid, chances were, he'd screw up her life, too.

That fear had driven him to confide in Kenzie. Not because she was his friend but because, as she'd pointed out, she wasn't. Because their history was such that she wouldn't feel obliged to spare his feelings or blunt any harsh truths. She didn't owe him anything, which was why he knew she'd be nothing less than honest.

But she'd surprised him—and maybe herself—when she'd responded to his question by saying yes, she could see him as a father. And her faith gave him at least a little bit of hope that it might be true.

That vote of confidence also helped lift some of the worry he'd been carrying since he'd learned about Dani's existence and Emily's hope that he would raise their daughter. He still had a wagonload of doubts about his ability to be a single parent to a little girl he barely knew, but he would try his darnedest to figure it out. He'd come home to Haven because he figured he'd have a better chance of doing that with the support of family and friends.

After enjoying the simple pleasures of sharing a meal and conversation with Kenzie, he thought maybe, someday, she might be one of those friends. And if he felt the stirring of an unexpected and unwelcome attraction in her presence, well, he could certainly put that aside.

Or so he believed until he dropped off to sleep and dreamed about her—about the night he'd found her waiting for him in the hayloft at Crooked Creek Ranch.

"I'm sixteen now." She made the announcement in a way that suggested the number meant something, but the significance was lost on him.

"Okay," he acknowledged cautiously.

"Sixteen's the legal age of consent in Nevada." The words spilled out of her mouth in a rush.

"How do you know that?" he wondered aloud.

"I looked it up," she admitted, her cheeks flushing with color.

"Why?" he asked, though he suspected he didn't want to hear the answer to his question.

She lifted her chin to meet his gaze, her soft gray eyes reflecting both uncertainty and determination. "Because I'm ready."

"For what?"

"To do it." The color in her cheeks deepened. "With you."

Ah, hell.

"Kenzie, you're not ready to have sex if you can't even say the words," he told her.

"I am *ready," she insisted. "And I want you to be my first."*

He shook his head. "That's not going to happen."

But Kenzie would not be dissuaded. Instead of taking the hint, she took a step closer. Then she lifted herself onto her toes and pressed her mouth to his.

He held himself still. He couldn't think of a better way to communicate his disinterest than to refuse to kiss her back.

But he hadn't counted on her lips being so soft. Soft and sweet and seductive. And as her mouth moved tentatively against his, he began to respond.

She gasped a little when his tongue slid between her parted lips, but she didn't pull away. And when he pushed her back against the hay bales and pressed his body against hers, she didn't protest. Even when he rubbed against her, so that she could feel the press of his erection—because he was a guy with a willing girl in his arms and, at eighteen, that was all it took to make him hard—she offered no resistance.

Not that he was going to get naked with his little sister's best friend. No way. No matter that she thought she was ready, or even that she'd told him she wanted him to be the first, he wasn't that much of an ass.

But he was enough of an ass to want to teach her a lesson. To make her understand that, if she was going to offer herself to guys in dark, shadowy corners of barns, she was going to get herself into trouble. So he yanked her shirt out of her jeans and slid his hands beneath the fabric. His palms moved over her skin, from her narrow waist to her ribs, then higher.

He was only going to touch her through her bra—confident that action would be enough for her to realize things were moving too fast and push him away. But when his hands found the gentle swell of her breasts, he belatedly realized she wasn't wearing a bra.

Her unrestrained nipples pebbled against his palms, attesting to her excitement. Innocent, sixteen-year-old Kenzie Atkins was aroused. He gently pinched the rigid peaks, causing her to moan and arch against him.

The instinctive movement pressed her pelvis against his, and damn if the moaning and rubbing didn't stoke the fire rushing through his veins, throbbing in his groin.

"Kenzie," he said.

"Yes," she whispered.

He hadn't intended to go this far; he knew he should stop. But his body and his brain were locked in a battle between what he wanted and what he knew was right.

I want you to be the first.

And why shouldn't he be?

Because she's barely sixteen years old.

Because she's your sister's best friend.

Because she obviously thinks she's in love with you and you're going to break her heart when you leave tomorrow.

Even as he silently cursed the nagging voice of his conscience, he knew he that he had to end this. Now.

Then she reached down and palmed him through his jeans. He suspected the boldness of her touch was more a product of curiosity than confidence, but the effect was the same...

He woke with his breathing labored and his body aroused.

Well, at least he'd held it together in his bed—which was more than he'd managed to do in the barn seven years earlier.

Shoving back the covers, he headed for the shower. The last thing he needed right now was an inconvenient attraction to his little sister's best friend, but with so much heat coursing through his veins, he couldn't deny it was there.

Thankfully, the town wasn't currently under any water restrictions because he could see a lot of cold showers in his future.

Chapter Five

She should have accepted Megan's invitation to go to a movie.

Instead, at eight o'clock on Friday night, Kenzie was already in her pajamas, sitting cross-legged on her sofa, television remote in hand, flipping between a home reno program, a low-budget rom-com and the Game Show Network. None of which succeeded in holding her attention for long because her thoughts were preoccupied with Spencer—as they'd been since she'd heard the first rumors of his return.

She'd been apprehensive about seeing him again, worried that she might not be as completely over her teenage crush as she wanted to believe and that she'd somehow make a complete fool of herself. *Again.*

But Kenzie was confident she'd handled that first meeting with professionalism and poise. Well, mostly. And if sexual awareness had hummed quietly in her veins, that was hardly cause for concern. After all, he was a good-looking guy and she was a red-blooded female who had obviously been celibate far too long.

Which was another reason she should have gone out with Megan tonight—to at least preserve the illusion that she was willing to meet new people and potentially change that status. But the truth was, since ending her engagement eight months earlier, she'd started to lose faith that she was ever going to find her own happy-ever-after.

She had no regrets about breaking up with Dale, because marrying a man she didn't love would have been the wrong thing for both of them. And while her former fiancé had claimed to be heartbroken when she gave him back the ring, he'd started dating someone else only a few weeks later.

She was glad that he'd moved on—she only wished she could do the same. It had taken less than five minutes with Spencer Channing for her to realize he was the real reason she hadn't been able to fall in love with Dale—or anyone else over the years.

Still, there was no harm in seeing a movie simply for the purposes of entertainment. But she knew that conversation with Megan would eventually come around to Spencer again, and Kenzie didn't want to have to deflect her friend's questions.

By now everyone in town knew that Spencer was going to Back in the Game for therapy on his injured shoulder, but there was still speculation about the severity of the injury, how long he was likely to stay and whether he'd give up riding bulls. Kenzie didn't let herself get drawn into those conversations, but she did wonder—especially about his future plans. Especially now that she understood how much was at stake.

He'd said nothing more about his daughter when he'd been half-naked on her table again that morning. Not that she'd expected him to. But as her hands moved over his body, she'd found herself wondering how much of the tightness and tension was a consequence of the injury and how much was caused by worry and uncertainty about being a father. He'd told her that Dani's grandmother was planning to bring her to Haven the following weekend, which didn't give him much time to get ready for her arrival.

Vanna White was revealing the contestant's selected letters for the bonus round when the intercom buzzed. Kenzie uncrossed her legs and went to the speaker box, suspecting that Megan had changed her mind about the movie and decided to stop by instead.

"Hello?"

"Can you buzz me up?" It wasn't Megan's voice.

"Spencer?"

"Yeah."

She glanced down at her microfleece pants and the well-worn Henley that did nothing to hide her braless status. "I'm, uh, not really dressed for company," she told him.

There was a momentary pause before he said, "Are you naked?"

"Of course I'm not naked," she immediately replied, shocked that he would even ask such a question.

"Damn," he muttered, shocking her again.

Then, when she made no response to that, he said, "I don't care what you're wearing. I have to tell you something, so just buzz me up."

Something in his voice suggested that *he* was a little buzzed, and though she knew she might be making a mistake, she released the lock on the exterior door. While he made his way up the stairs, she raced to her bedroom and grabbed her robe.

He was knocking before she'd succeeded in knotting the belt at her waist. With her flannel coat of armor finally secure, she pulled open the door.

His blue gaze swept over her in a leisurely perusal, then he shook his head. "You're not even naked under that robe."

She eyed him cautiously. "Have you been drinking?"

"Yeah," he admitted. "But apparently not enough."

"Why don't you come in?" she invited. "It'll just take me a minute to make coffee."

"I don't want coffee." He caught the two ends of her belt in his hands. "I want you."

Her heart stuttered. Because even if she was completely over her teenage infatuation, it was gratifying and exciting, and—Lord help her—more than a little tempting to hear those words from the object of her one-time crush.

"You *are* drunk," she decided.

But he pinned her with a surprisingly clear-eyed gaze. "You're on my mind, Kenzie. And I've got too many things messing up my head already without adding an unwanted attraction to the mix."

She was simultaneously flattered and insulted by the remark. "I'm sorry—who knocked on whose door?"

One side of his mouth turned up in a half smile that did crazy things to her insides. "You're right. I shouldn't be here."

"Okay, then," she said, and started to close the door.

He stuck the toe of his boot into the opening. "You invited me to come in," he reminded her.

"For coffee," she said firmly, before stepping back to allow him entry.

"I'd rather have a beer," he told her.

She didn't ask how many he'd had already, because he was a grown man and it was none of her business. But she felt compelled to caution, "You shouldn't mix alcohol with your pain meds."

"I'm not taking any pain meds."

Though she'd personally never dislocated her shoulder, she knew it was an uncomfortable injury and recovery, and that management of the pain helped a patient attain the mobility necessary to rehab. "Why not?"

"They make my head feel fuzzy."

"And the alcohol doesn't?"

He smiled. "Touché."

She put a coffee pod in her machine, set a mug under the spout and gestured for him to take a seat at the island.

"What kind of muffins are those?" he asked, reaching for the bag on the counter.

She snatched it out of his grasp. "The kind that are for Mrs. Powell."

She'd delivered the first batch to her mother, as promised, the previous morning. Then she'd made a second batch as an excuse to stop by and visit her widowed friend on the weekend.

But Spencer looked so sincerely disappointed by her response, she opened the bag and removed one of the muffins, setting it on a plate for him.

"You said you had something to tell me," she reminded him, as his coffee finished brewing.

He nodded, his mouth full of muffin. Then, after he'd swallowed, he said, "Yeah, we should talk about that first."

"Talk about *what* first?" she prompted.

"I asked for another therapist to take over my treatments."

"What?" She was stunned. "Why?"

"Because instead of loosening up my shoulder, my whole body tightens up when you touch me."

She carefully set the mug of coffee beside his plate, resisting the urge to chuck it at him, as conflicting emotions warred inside her. She was hurt that he'd take such a step without talking to her first, relieved that she wouldn't have to deal with the temptation of his half-naked body on her table—and the undoubtedly unprofessional thoughts that filled her head while her hands were on him—and angry, because the implication was that she wasn't meeting his needs—professionally speaking, of course.

"Well," she said, "I hope you explained my incompetency in clear terms to my office manager. It will undoubtedly be very helpful at my next performance review."

He eyed her warily as he drew the mug closer. "I didn't say you were incompetent. I told her that we had some personal history that might interfere with the success of my treatment."

"Personal history?" she scoffed, her pride still stinging. "I was your sister's best friend—nothing more."

"I tried to think of you as my sister's best friend." He sipped his coffee, then shook his head. "No, the truth is, because you were my sister's best friend, I tried *not* to think about you at all."

"I'm good at my job," she told him. "In the fifteen months I've been working at the clinic, I've never had any complaints about my techniques or my results."

"I'm sure that's true," he said.

"Now my hopes of getting full-time when Eva goes off on mat leave are pretty much out the window," she said, refusing to be placated. "And all because we shared a few kisses seven years ago?"

He pushed away from the island. "Not just because of that."

"Then what?" she demanded to know.

"Because I want to kiss you again. Now. And I don't want to stop there."

Before Kenzie could decide how to respond to his unexpected confession, Spencer *was* kissing her.

And…*wow.*

It was everything she remembered kissing him had been, but somehow more. Because it wasn't just a memory, it was happening *now*.

His mouth was hot and hungry, demanding a response from her. She willingly—eagerly—gave him what he wanted.

What *she* wanted.

This. Here. Now.

He deepened the kiss, and her lips parted. Her tongue dallied and danced with his in a sensual rhythm that made her knees weak. Thankfully, he had those strong, broad shoulders that she could hold on to, and she did.

She was so caught up in the seduction of his talented mouth that she didn't realize he'd unbelted her robe until his hands were inside it, under her pajama top. His rough, callused palms sliding over the soft skin of her torso, making her shiver and want.

Oh, how she wanted.

You wanted him once before, and look how that turned out.

She couldn't ignore the warning that echoed in the back of her mind, because it was true. She'd been down this path before, and when he'd gone away, she'd been left trying to put together the pieces of her broken heart.

That same heart hammered against her ribs now, as if to reassure her that it wasn't just healed but fully functioning.

And hey, hadn't she been thinking—just before he showed up—that she should have gone out with Megan tonight? Hadn't she decided that she'd been celibate for too long and resolved to change that status? So really, it was kind of convenient that he'd stopped by and seemed favorably inclined toward helping her rectify that problem.

It was also incredibly arousing the way his strong palms gently cradled her breasts, his thumbs tracing and teasing her nipples.

But don't you deserve more than just a quick roll in the hay?

Because although they weren't actually in the hayloft this time, she knew that whatever happened between them tonight wouldn't mean anything more to him than that.

And maybe it wouldn't mean anything more to her, either, but she didn't trust herself not to fall for him again. That was a risk she wasn't willing to take.

She finally turned her head away, breaking the kiss.

"We can't do this." But even to her own ears, she sounded more uncertain than firm as his lips trailed along her jaw.

"I promise you, we can," he said, nibbling on her ear.

She shook her head, determined to resist, though the rasp

of his stubble against tender skin as he nuzzled her throat had every other part of her shaking with desire.

"Let me show you all the things we can do," he urged.

But Kenzie lifted her hands to his chest and pushed him away. Then, in case that wasn't clear enough, she took a step back, putting more space between them.

"Sorry to disappoint you, but I'm no longer the infatuated teenage girl you knew seven years ago."

Spencer took a minute to draw in a breath and attempt to get his raging hormones under control. Not an easy task when Kenzie's lips were still swollen from his kiss and her nipples were almost poking holes through the thin cotton top.

He forced his eyes back to her face. "I noticed," he assured her. "And I'm not at all disappointed."

She pulled her robe together again, covering her chest. As if that was going to make him forget the image of those perky breasts, the feel of them in his hands.

Kenzie had been something of a late bloomer. The girl he remembered from high school had cruelly been called Ken by some of the guys, because her body had fewer curves than that of Barbie's plastic boyfriend. But when she'd finally bloomed, she'd done so very nicely.

For most of the past seven years, he'd managed to relegate his memories of her to the back of his mind. After all, she hadn't been anything to him—she was Brielle's friend. And it had been easy to dismiss her as a kid with a crush—until she kissed him.

Despite the absence of any technique in that first kiss, her lips had been temptingly soft and sweet. What she'd lacked in experience, she'd more than made up for with enthusiasm. And when he'd taken the lead, she'd been eager to follow.

There was little evidence of that girl in the woman before him now. This new Kenzie was confident, strong, sexy.

And smart enough to push him away.

She cleared her throat. "And didn't we agree, just the other night, that this—you and me—is a bad idea?"

"I've had a change of heart on that."

"I don't think it's your heart calling the shots," she remarked dryly.

He chose to ignore the not-so-subtle gibe, instead asking, "Do you want me to apologize for kissing you?"

"No," she said, a little primly. "I just want your assurance that it won't happen again."

His brows lifted. "You want me to promise not to kiss you again?"

"Yes."

"I don't think I can."

She frowned. "Why not?"

"Because it seems that lately, I can't seem to think about anything but how much I want you."

"You're looking for a distraction."

"What?"

"I can only imagine how difficult these past few weeks have been—finding out that you have a child, dealing with your injury, coming home."

"None of that has anything to do with us," he told her.

"Not you and me specifically," she agreed. "But all of it has added to your stress, which you want to alleviate with sex."

He blinked, not sure whether he should be insulted or amused by her clinical assessment.

"You really have changed," he mused. "The last time we kissed, you couldn't say the word *sex* without stammering and turning a dozen shades of red."

"I'm not a sixteen-year-old virgin anymore."

"Thank goodness for that," he agreed.

"I'm also not going to fall into bed with you just because you think it's what you want."

"I *know* it's what I want," he said. "And I think it's what you want, too."

She shook her head. "It's not going to happen."

"But you didn't deny that you want me," he noted.

"I want a lot of things that aren't good for me."

"I'll be good for you—I promise."

She shook her head again, even as a smile tugged at her lips. "Good night, Spencer."

He sighed. "I guess that's my cue to leave."

"Wow," she said. "Not just handsome but quick, too."

"So…you think I'm handsome?"

She shoved him toward the door.

He didn't resist; he had no intention of overstaying his welcome. But before he walked out the door, he dipped his head for one last brief kiss. Just to be contrary.

She closed the door in his face, but not before he saw the tip of her tongue touch her top lip, as if she was savoring the taste of him.

He was grinning as he descended the stairs and whistling as he made his way across the parking lot to his truck.

Sharing a few kisses with a pretty girl wasn't going to fix everything that was wrong in his world, but for the first time in a long time, things were starting to look up.

While Kenzie was growing up, Helen and Harold Powell had resided in the house beside the little bungalow on Whitechurch Road where she lived with her mother. If Cheryl had to work late at her job cleaning rooms at the Dusty Boots Motel, as she frequently did, Kenzie would go to the Powell house after school.

Mrs. Powell would offer her a snack and supervise her homework or, if she was lucky enough not to have any homework, they'd play cards or board games. But only until four-thirty, when *The Light of Dawn* came on TV. Helen was addicted to "her story," as she referred to the soap, and nothing else happened in her house during the half hour it was on Monday through Friday.

Helen had a particular fondness for the character of

Brock Lawrie, played by Peter Ross, and Kenzie still remembered the tension that had filled the half hour during a five-week period of prolonged contract negotiations between the studio and its star, during which Brock languished in a coma. Harold had confided to Kenzie that he'd been just as relieved as Helen when the character finally emerged from the deep sleep to declare his love for Lorelei, because he'd been certain his wife would have gone into a real period of mourning if the show had killed off Brock.

When Kenzie went away to college, she missed the Powells as much as she missed her mother. Then Harold died and Helen decided she didn't want to stay in the house that had been their home for forty years together. Six months later, she'd moved to a ground-floor apartment in a three-story triplex now owned by Spencer's brother, Jason.

It was a pleasure for Kenzie to squeeze out time to spend with Helen, as she did that Saturday morning. She arrived armed with the second batch of muffins—minus the one she'd given to Spencer the night before—and two tall vanilla lattes from The Daily Grind.

"I heard Spencer Channing is back in town," Helen remarked, as they sipped their coffee and nibbled on the muffins.

"Obviously there's nothing wrong with your hearing," Kenzie teased.

"Or my eyes. And—" Helen boldly winked one of those clear green eyes "—in my opinion, the boy is even better looking now than when he left."

"He's hardly a boy anymore," Kenzie remarked.

"You've seen him, too, then," her former neighbor guessed.

She nodded, although she hadn't only seen him, she'd touched him, lusted for him and even kissed him. And the memory of that kiss had kept her awake—and yearning—late into the night.

"Was it awkward?" her friend asked.

She blinked. "What?"

"Seeing him again," Helen prompted gently.

"Not as awkward as I thought it might be," she said. "And still, more awkward than I'd like to admit when he started taking his clothes off."

Helen rubbed her hands together gleefully. "Oh, this sounds almost as good as what happened on *The Light of Dawn* yesterday."

Kenzie had to laugh. "I'm sure it's not."

"Let me be the judge of that," her friend suggested. "You just tell me what happened—and don't skimp on any of the juicy details."

"It was a Wednesday afternoon in Haven," she began, setting the stage for the story. "When our unsuspecting heroine, relaxed after lunch with a friend, walks into her office to find the hero there, waiting for her. After seven long years apart, they can deny their love for one another no longer and come together in a passionate embrace."

Helen sighed dreamily—then narrowed her gaze on the storyteller. "How much of that is actually true?"

"Well, it *was* Wednesday," Kenzie said. "And I did have lunch with Megan on Wednesday."

"And the part about him taking off his clothes—that was in your treatment room, right?" her friend guessed.

Kenzie nodded.

"So no declarations of love? No passionate embrace?"

Of course, Helen already knew the answers to those questions and shook her head, so obviously disappointed that Kenzie felt a little guilty about teasing her.

"I'm sorry we're not Brock and Lorelei," she said.

Her friend waved a hand. "Believe me, you don't want to be Brock and Lorelei. The things those two have been through—well, of course, it's just a story. But the way they always come back to one another is a testament to the power of love."

Or good writing, Kenzie mused, though she knew better than to say so aloud.

"But one thing I can tell you—in strict confidence," she warned, "is that Spencer Channing has a body to rival that of Brock Lawrie in his prime."

The revelation made Helen sigh happily again. "And you got to run your hands all over those tight muscles."

"Not *all* over," Kenzie pointed out. "And strictly for professional reasons."

"I understand." Her friend nodded. "Strictly professional," she agreed, tongue firmly in cheek. "I'm sure you didn't enjoy it all."

"Well, maybe just a little," she allowed.

Of course, the opportunity for stolen moments of guilty pleasure was officially closed to her now that Spencer had asked for a new therapist. And she was grateful that he'd taken the step she'd only contemplated, sparing them both the awkwardness—and temptation—of being behind closed doors together.

"You know, too many people underestimate the value of physical attraction," Helen said now. "Sexual compatibility is an important component of any relationship."

"So I've heard," Kenzie noted.

"If you're going on the basis of hearsay, it's a good thing you gave back Dale's ring," her friend remarked. "Of course, it would have been even better if you'd never accepted it in the first place."

"I thought you liked Dale."

"Sure, but I never believed he was the right man for you." Then she shrugged. "But I've also never believed that a woman needs a man to make her happy."

Kenzie lifted her almost empty latte cup in a toasting gesture. "I'll drink to that."

"For really great sex when you're out of C batteries, yes," Helen continued, causing her guest to choke on her coffee. "For happiness, no."

When Kenzie stopped coughing, she started to laugh. "I'll keep that in mind," she promised. "But right now, I need to get over to The Trading Post to pick up some groceries or I'll be having muffins for dinner tonight."

Helen rose with her and wrapped Kenzie in a White Shoulders–scented embrace. "I'm so glad you stopped by."

"Me, too," Kenzie said sincerely.

Her comment about the barren state of her pantry had not been much of an exaggeration, and she was mentally reviewing her grocery list when she closed the door and nearly bumped into Spencer Channing—and a teary-eyed little girl who could only be his daughter.

Chapter Six

Finding himself face-to-face with Kenzie wasn't the first surprise of Spencer's day. And it definitely wasn't the biggest one. It was, at least, a pleasant one. But his happiness at seeing a familiar and friendly face barely lasted long enough to register before Dani pulled her hand out of his and threw herself at Kenzie, wrapping her little arms around Kenzie's legs and crying, "Wanna go home with Nana."

Kenzie lifted a brow; he lifted his shoulders.

"If only her caseworker could see us now," he said dryly.

She stroked a hand over Dani's silky blond hair, instinctively attempting to soothe the distressed child. He'd tried to soothe her, too, but Dani had resisted his efforts, apparently blaming him for all of the recent upheaval in her life.

"Did I lose a week somewhere?" Kenzie asked, obviously remembering that his daughter was expected to arrive the following weekend.

"Change of plans."

"Apparently." She loosened Dani's arms and crouched down to the child's eye level. "You must be Dani."

His daughter sniffled and nodded.

"Your daddy told me all about you," Kenzie said. "And I know he's really happy that you're here in Haven."

Dani sneaked a glance at him, then looked quickly away again. "Wanna go home," she insisted stubbornly.

"I know change can be scary," Kenzie said. "It's just going to take some time for this to feel like home."

She shifted her attention to Spencer to ask, "But what are you doing here?" Then, as a thought occurred to her, "Visiting your brother?"

He shook his head and gestured with his thumb to the door marked 1A. "I'm subletting Alyssa's apartment," he said. "What are *you* doing here?"

She nodded her head in the other direction, toward Unit 1B. "I was visiting Mrs. Powell."

"Of Mrs. Powell's muffins," he remembered.

She smiled at that. "The same," she confirmed.

"Muffin?" Dani echoed, looking at Kenzie with teary eyes.

"Are you hungry?" Kenzie asked her.

The little blond head nodded.

"She had breakfast," he said, not wanting Kenzie to think that he'd let his daughter go without food. "At the Sunny-side Diner with her g-r-a-n-d-m-o-t-h-e-r," he said, spelling the word in the hope that Dani wouldn't know who he was talking about and start crying all over again. "But then she was so upset about…the situation, she threw up her pancakes all over the floor."

"Nothing like easing you into the whole parenthood thing, huh?" Kenzie mused.

"Tell me about it."

She turned her attention back to his daughter again. "What kind of muffins do you like, Dani?"

"Choc'ate chip?"

"They're my favorite, too," Kenzie said.

Dani rewarded this confession with a tentative smile.

"And there's a little coffee shop not too far from here that makes these *ginormous* chocolate chip muffins," she continued. "Maybe you and your daddy could walk over there for a snack."

"You an' me walk," Dani said to Kenzie.

Kenzie glanced at him, confusion and apology in her gaze.

"Wendy, the caseworker, warned me that Dani hasn't had much interaction with men and might take some time to warm up to me."

And he was trying really hard not to take it personally, but when his daughter chose the arms of a stranger for comfort over those of her father, it was even harder.

On the other hand, he couldn't blame her when he'd found comfort in Kenzie's arms, too—although not nearly as much as he'd wanted to.

"I guess that makes sense," Kenzie agreed, straightening to her full height again.

"So…will you come with us?" he asked her.

"To The Daily Grind?" She immediately shook her head.

"Why not?"

"I know you've been gone a long time," she said, "but surely you haven't forgotten that gossip is the only thing hotter than the coffee at The Daily Grind."

He looked at Dani, who was wrapped around Kenzie's legs again.

"Please," he said.

"I have a better idea," she said. "Why don't me and Dani wait here while you go pick up some muffins?"

Spencer knelt down next to his child. "Is that okay with you, Dani? Do you want to stay with Kenzie while I go get you a muffin?"

She nodded.

Of course, she did. Because anything was better than being with the big, scary man who claimed to be her daddy.

Shaking off the frustration, he stood up again and unlocked the door of his apartment.

"Do you want anything?" he asked Kenzie.

"A vanilla latte would be appreciated."

Spencer vowed to open a tab to cover Kenzie's vanilla lattes for a whole year—it was the least he could do.

When he got back to the apartment with the muffins and coffee—and milk for Dani, he found Kenzie and Dani sitting on the sofa, snuggled close together, looking at something on an iPad.

Kenzie glanced over when he walked in and offered him a smile as she closed the cover on her device and set it aside.

"She was even more tired than hungry," she said quietly.

That was when he realized the little girl was sleeping, with a blanket clutched in one fist and the thumb of her other hand resting against her bottom lip, as if she'd fallen asleep sucking on it. According to Linda, Dani had stopped sucking her thumb when she was two, but Wendy explained that it wasn't unusual for kids' behaviors to regress after a traumatic event and suggested that Spencer not make a big deal about it.

Kenzie carefully eased herself away from the sleeping child, gently shifting her so that her head was cushioned on the arm of the sofa. Dani didn't stir.

He set the tray of drinks and muffins on the table and shrugged out of his jacket, draping it over the back of the chair.

"Thanks." Kenzie accepted the cup he offered and, after sitting down across from him, pried off the lid. "So when did you find out about the change of plans?"

He glanced at his watch. "About three hours ago."

"You're kidding."

He shook his head. "I was planning a trip to the hardware store to get paint and painting supplies to do Dani's room when Linda called to tell me that she wouldn't be able to bring her to Haven next weekend as scheduled. And—" he stared at the murky dark liquid in his own cup "—I'm ashamed to admit that my first reaction was relief."

"That's not surprising," Kenzie said. "You haven't really had much time to adjust to the realization that you're a father—I can understand why you might be grateful for a reprieve."

"Well, I was," he admitted. "Not that I expected having another week or two to prepare for her arrival would somehow transform me from completely clueless to father-of-the-year, but I figured it couldn't make me any more clueless."

She smiled at that.

"And then I remembered what you'd said—about the possibility that Linda might change her mind and decide to file for custody of Dani, and I panicked, imagining that I was going to lose the daughter I never even had a chance to know."

She reached across the table and touched a hand to his arm. "And that's why I know you're going to be a great dad."

"Right now, I'd be happy if the thought of staying here with me didn't make Dani burst into tears," he told her. "Anyway, before I could offer to make the trip to Denver next weekend to pick up Dani, she suggested that she bring her this weekend. As in today, because—by the way—they were already in Haven."

Kenzie's brows lifted. "What if you'd said no? What if you hadn't been here?"

"I'm not sure she ever considered either of those possibilities," he said. "And, half an hour later, she dropped Dani off along with one big suitcase, a few boxes and her car seat.

"And Dani just stood there, looking bewildered, until Nana gave her a hug and said, 'Be a good girl for Daddy,' then got in her car again and drove away."

"I can't imagine," Kenzie said.

"It took her a few minutes to understand that Nana had gone—and that she'd been left behind. And then…she was inconsolable." It wasn't until hot coffee spilled onto his hand that he realized he was squeezing the cup. He pulled his hands away and wiped them on his jeans. "I wanted to show her around, show her the room that was going to be hers, but she wrapped both hands around the doorknob, desperately trying to turn it, to make her escape so that she could 'go home with Nana,' as she repeated over and over while tears streamed down her face."

"I hope I never meet that woman," Kenzie said, tears of empathy shimmering in her eyes.

Spencer knew how she felt. When Dani's heart-wrenching sobs had finally been reduced to shuddery hiccups and quiet whimpers and he was mopping up the remnants of her breakfast from the tiled floor, he'd felt like crying right along with her.

He'd suggested a walk to the park instead. She hadn't seemed thrilled about the idea, but she hadn't resisted, either. And when they'd left the apartment, they'd run into Kenzie.

"Did she offer any kind of explanation for dumping her granddaughter on your doorstep ahead of schedule?"

"Oh, yes. It turns out the boyfriend has to go to Montpellier on business, and he invited her to go with him."

"All of this upheaval to a little girl's life so that she could go to France?"

"So it would seem," he agreed.

"I think I'm beginning to see why Emily didn't choose her mother as Dani's guardian."

"Oh, there's more," Spencer told her. "When I was on my way to The Daily Grind, Wendy called."

"The caseworker?"

He nodded.

"She had a meeting scheduled with Dani today, to prepare her for the upcoming move, and she didn't want me to panic, but she thought I should know that Dani and Linda weren't there."

"How did she react when you told her that Dani was here?" Kenzie prompted.

"I'd say she was relieved that she hadn't lost a child under her supervision, worried about Dani's response to the transition and furious with Linda for taking it upon herself to change the plans."

"All of which will work in favor of your custody application," Kenzie noted.

He managed a smile. "You're one of those people who always sees the glass as half-full, aren't you?"

"I try to be," she admitted. "Although Dani and I did some poking around the apartment while you were out, and it seems that her bedroom is completely empty."

"I ordered a bedroom set for her," he said. "Bed, dresser, night table—it's all being delivered on Wednesday, which I figured would give me the time I needed to paint her room and have it ready for her arrival next weekend."

"So what's your Plan B?" Kenzie asked him.

Spencer shrugged, as if unconcerned, but the casual movement was at odds with the desperate helplessness in his eyes.

And though she knew that Dani was *his* daughter and this was *his* situation to figure out, and the best thing—the smartest thing—that she could do was to back away, Kenzie couldn't help but respond to that desperation.

Or maybe it was the memory of how his little girl had clung to her, as if Kenzie was a buoy and she was being tossed around by a stormy sea, that compelled her to stick around. Regardless of the reason, she heard herself say, "I have an idea that I think might help Dani want to be here."

"I'm listening," he assured her.

"Let her help you turn the spare bedroom into *her* bedroom."

He looked at her blankly. "Huh?"

"Take her to the hardware store, let her pick the color of paint she wants for the walls. You could even let her help you paint."

"She's not yet four," he reminded her.

"I'm not suggesting you hand her a roller and put her on top of a ladder," Kenzie said dryly. "But I don't think there's any harm in giving her a brush and letting her paint the inside of the closet. Then, when she looks around the room, she'll have pride of ownership in the space, because she helped make it hers."

He looked skeptical.

"You could also let her pick out her own comforter and curtains."

"There are curtains on the window already," he pointed out.

"And I'm sure the geometric print coordinated nicely with everything else in Alyssa's spare room," she said. "But it doesn't really work for a little girl's room."

"I'll have to defer to your expertise on that," he said.

"Were you ever in her room at Emily's place?"

He nodded.

"What was it like?"

He sipped his coffee, then shook his head. "I don't...purple," he suddenly remembered. "There was a lot of purple. Everywhere. The walls, the bed cover, even the fluffy rug was purple.

"And there were colorful little horses on the shelf under her window."

"Pocket Ponies," she told him.

"What?"

She smiled. "It was a Saturday morning cartoon when I was a kid. And, of course, a whole series of toys. I didn't realize they were still around until Dani and I were looking at bedding on my iPad—before she fell asleep—and she pointed out a comforter that she liked and it had Pocket Ponies all over it."

"Was it purple?"

"No. Well, the background was white, but some of the ponies have bodies or manes and tails in shades of purple," she acknowledged. "And there were matching curtains available."

"Fine, if that's what she wants, I'll give you my credit card and—"

"Mommy?" Dani's plaintive call cut off his words.

Glancing over, Kenzie saw that she was sitting up now, hugging her blanket to her chest, her sleepy eyes showing confusion.

When there was no immediate response to her call, the little girl tried again. "Mommy?"

Spencer winced, as if empathizing with his daughter's pain, but his voice was cheerful when he said, "I'm here, Dani. And I've got the chocolate chip muffin you wanted."

"Want Mommy," she said.

"You and me both," he muttered, his voice pitched low enough that only Kenzie could hear.

"Does she know what happened to her mom?" she whispered back.

He nodded. "But apparently preschoolers have trouble grasping the finality of death. I think she still thinks that Emily might walk through the door at any minute."

Then, in a brighter voice again, he said, "Did you have a good nap, Dani?"

She didn't reply to that.

"Are you hungry?" Kenzie chimed in to ask.

Dani waited a beat, then nodded.

"Daddy got your chocolate chip muffin."

The little girl reached out her hand.

Spencer started to get up, as if to deliver it to her, but Kenzie put a hand on his arm to stop him. "Do you really want muffin crumbs and chocolate all over your sofa?"

"I really want her not to hate me," he said.

The dejected tone tugged at Kenzie's heart, but she only

said, "She doesn't hate you—she just doesn't know you."
And then she said to Dani, "Come on up to the table to
have your snack."

Dani pulled her outstretched hand back to her blanket.

Spencer looked at Kenzie.

"If she's really hungry, she'll come to the table," she said.

The words were barely out of her mouth before the little
girl was wiggling toward the edge of the sofa and stretching her feet toward the ground.

Spencer nudged the nearest chair away from the table,
a wordless invitation. She took a few tentative steps, then
stopped. He opened the carton of milk and stuck the straw
in it, then removed a muffin from the bag and set it beside
the milk on the table.

Her hunger finally overcame her reticence, because she
climbed up onto the chair and immediately bit into the muffin.

She took a few more bites, then a sip of her milk.

"Is it good?" he asked.

Dani nodded, then lifted her head to look at the man
seated beside her. Her tentative gaze immediately shifted
away again, but she ventured a cautious, "Thank you."

They were two little words, so quietly spoken they were
almost inaudible, but Kenzie saw that they meant the world
to Spencer.

He cleared his throat. "So, other than chocolate chip muffins, what do you like to eat?"

"Ice cweam?"

"Well, who doesn't love ice cream? But that's more of a
dessert—what you eat after you've eaten something else,"
he pointed out to her.

She nibbled on another bite of muffin. "S'ghetti?"

"That's good," he said, nodding. "Because that's actually
something I know how to make. Anything else?"

Her little brow furrowed as she sipped her milk. "Nug-
gets."

"How about pizza?" he asked.

She responded to that with an immediate and enthusiastic nod.

"Okay, I think I can work with those options," Spencer decided.

Dani pushed her muffin away, indicating that she'd had enough.

Kenzie collected the empty coffee cups and remnants of Dani's snack to toss them in the garbage. "Thanks for the latte, but I'm going to head out now—"

"No," Spencer interjected quickly, and maybe a little desperately. "Not yet. Please."

She felt herself wavering, because it felt good to be wanted. But whenever she'd dreamed of Spencer Channing wanting her—as she'd admittedly done in the past—it hadn't been to act as a buffer between him and his child, and that was all he wanted from her now.

"I have to do my grocery shopping—"

"I need groceries, too," he interrupted her again. "Why don't we all go together?"

"You were going to take Dani to the hardware store to pick out paint for her bedroom," she reminded him.

"We can do that, too." And then, as if remembering her concern about being caught up in the inevitable gossip that would follow his appearance in town with his child, he said, "We could take a road trip to Battle Mountain and get everything we need there."

"I think Dani probably spent enough time in the car yesterday," Kenzie pointed out.

"Battle Mountain isn't very far," he noted, then turned to his daughter. "What do you say, Dani? Do you want Kenzie to come with us to pick out some stuff for your new room?"

Kenzie narrowed her gaze to let him know she was aware of his deliberate manipulation of the question, but when

Dani nodded her head, there was no way she could refuse the request.

And truthfully, she didn't want to.

Chapter Seven

Four hours later, Spencer was starting to think he might actually survive Day One of parenthood—but only because Kenzie hadn't ventured too far from his side. She seemed to have instincts that he lacked, somehow anticipating Dani's ever-changing moods and shifting her focus any time the little girl started to feel melancholy or sad.

When they finally got back to Haven, his truck was filled with paint, painting supplies, bedding and curtains, a half dozen bags of groceries and another two bags of what Kenzie insisted were "essentials." Because apparently Dani needed kid-friendly shampoo and body wash and toothpaste, and he didn't know if any of that stuff was in the boxes Linda had dropped off.

Obviously he was going to have to make more than one trip back to the truck to unload. For now, he grabbed as many grocery bags as he could carry. Kenzie took the paint in one hand and Dani's hand in the other.

It was only when they got to the door that he realized

he'd tucked his keys in his pocket, as he was in the habit of doing, but he didn't have a free hand to retrieve them.

"Do you need help with something?" Kenzie asked, as he ineffectually juggled bags.

"Yeah," he said. "Can you reach into my right front pocket and grab my keys?"

She set the paint can on the ground and her hand moved toward his pocket, then her gaze narrowed suspiciously and she drew her arm back to take a couple of grocery bags instead. "Reach into your own pocket."

"Spoilsport," he grumbled good-naturedly, as he used his now-free hand to retrieve the keys and unlock the door.

She nudged Dani inside; he picked up the paint and followed.

"We'll start putting the groceries away while you get the rest of the stuff," she suggested. "Okay, Dani?"

The little girl nodded and happily followed Kenzie into the kitchen.

When he brought in the last load from the truck, they were discussing dinner options. He heard Kenzie suggest spaghetti and Dani counter with a request for "p'za."

"What's your vote?" Kenzie asked him.

"Gotta side with my girl," he said, winking at Dani. "And vote for pizza."

"Fine," Kenzie relented. "Then you can go pick it up."

"Are you going to stay and eat with us?" he asked hopefully.

"I'm definitely staying for pizza," Kenzie said. "Because I was so focused on your shopping at the grocery store that I forgot to do my own."

He couldn't resist teasing, "You probably have some soup at home."

"Probably," she agreed. "But soup isn't really much of a meal."

He grinned at that. "So what do you like on your pizza?"

"Anything except A and Z," she said.

"A and Z?" he queried.

"Anchovies and zucchini."

"I don't have a problem skipping both of those," he assured Kenzie. Then he turned to his daughter, "What do you like, Dani?"

"P'za," she said.

He smiled. "Yeah, I got that. What do you like on your pizza?"

"Cheese?"

"Get half with just cheese and half with whatever else you want," Kenzie suggested.

So Spencer headed out again, this time to Jo's for pizza.

After he'd placed his order, his attention was snagged by a wave from a table by the front window. Recognizing a couple of friends from high school, he raised a hand in response, then made his way over to their table.

"Join us for a drink?" Brett offered, lifting a half-empty pitcher of beer from the middle of the table.

Since he had twenty-five to thirty minutes until his order would be ready, he decided "Why not?"

Gage snagged an empty chair from a neighboring table for him, and Ellis handed an empty glass to Brett to fill.

Spencer settled in to catch up with his buddies. It didn't take him long to realize that his friends didn't want to talk about their lives but preferred to interrogate him about his.

"It must be exciting, traveling around the country and seeing the sights," Brett commented.

"I don't usually get to see much outside of the arenas," he said.

"Arenas filled with pretty ladies wanting to hook up with cowboys?" Ellis guessed.

"There are lots of pretty ladies," he confirmed. "Often with their husbands and kids."

"Speaking of kids," Gage said, pouncing on the opening Spencer had given him. "Rumor has it you've got one of those now."

He wasn't surprised to learn that his friends had already heard about Dani. Though he'd only told his family and Kenzie, he hadn't asked anyone to keep the news quiet. Partly because he'd known that such a request would be ignored (his sister Regan couldn't keep a secret to save her life), but mostly because he didn't want to give anyone—least of all his daughter—the impression that he was ashamed of her. No doubt the news that he had a child had made the rounds long before she arrived in town.

"A little girl," he confirmed.

"Heard about her mom passing away, too," Brett said. "That's a tough break."

Spencer nodded. "Yeah, it is."

"She living with you now?" Ellis asked.

He nodded again.

"So where is she?" his friend demanded.

"At home, waiting for her pizza," he said.

Brett scowled. "You left your kid at home while you came out to get pizza?"

"She's almost four—she knows not to answer the door or turn on the stove," Spencer said, and lifted his glass to his lips.

His friend's scowl deepened.

"He's kidding," Gage said. Then, to Spencer, "You're kidding, right?"

He swallowed a mouthful of beer, nodded. "Of course I'm kidding," he confirmed. "Kenzie Atkins is babysitting."

"So you strolled back into town and picked up right where you left off, huh?" Ellis said.

"What are you talking about?"

"You and Kenzie."

"There was never a 'me and Kenzie,'" he denied.

"Ha!" Gage said. "I told you I wasn't breaking the code."

Ellis shrugged. "I guess I was wrong."

As Spencer's gaze shifted from Ellis to Gage and back again, the pieces slowly clicked into place.

"*You* and Kenzie?" he asked, the idea settling like a lead weight into the pit of his belly.

"Well, it wasn't really all that," Gage told him.

"*What* wasn't all that?" he demanded.

"We just went out a few times," his friend said. "Very casual."

Spencer scowled. He knew from personal experience that "casual" didn't necessarily mean "platonic."

"But that shouldn't bother you," Brett remarked. "Since there was no *you and Kenzie.*"

"It doesn't bother me," he lied.

"Because you obviously had lots of other women rockin' your world," Ellis noted.

"The rodeo isn't an orgy," Spencer said dryly.

But his friend apparently didn't believe him. "I mean, who knows how many other little Channings are running around in the world?"

"Zero," Spencer said firmly.

Because he was always careful when he was with a woman.

But he'd been careful with Emily, too, and still there was Dani.

Ellis poured the last of the beer into his glass, then abruptly stood up with the pitcher in hand. "I'm gonna get a refill on this."

As their other friend made his way to the counter, Gage explained, "He's still touchy because Pam lied about her baby being his."

"Pam Morgan?"

"That's the one," Brett confirmed. "When she told Ellis she was pregnant, he immediately put a ring on her finger. But it turned out that she'd been sleeping with Todd Sherwin, too, and the paternity test revealed that Todd was the father of her baby."

"I'm guessing Ellis wasn't relieved by the news?"

Gage shook his head. "He really thought he was in love with her."

"I wasn't in love with Emily," Spencer admitted. "But I would have done the right thing."

"She didn't want to get married?"

"She didn't even tell me about the baby," he confided.

"When did you find out?"

"Seven weeks ago."

"You got the results of the paternity test seven weeks ago?" Brett asked, seeking clarification.

Spencer shook his head. "There wasn't a paternity test."

His friends exchanged a look.

"Why not?" Gage demanded.

"I didn't think it was necessary."

"Not necessary?" Brett's tone was incredulous. "You've gotta be kidding."

"Emily put my name on the birth certificate when Dani was born."

"Well, then, I guess that's that," Gage said sardonically.

Brett shook his head. "You can't just take her word for it that you're the one who knocked her up."

"Emily wouldn't lie about something like that," he said, certain it was true.

"We're not saying that she *lied*," Brett allowed. "Just that it might have been a guess more than a certainty."

"She also didn't sleep around," Spencer said, because she'd told him—when she took him back to her hotel room—that she didn't usually do that kind of thing. He'd believed her because he had no reason not to and because, truthfully, he'd just cared that he was going to get laid.

Of course, when Linda first told him that Emily had given him guardianship of her child, he'd been adamant that Dani wasn't—*couldn't be*—his child. And then she'd shown him a picture, and those big blue eyes had winded him like a sucker punch to the gut.

"Dani is my daughter," he told his friends. "I have no doubts about that."

"If that's true, then a paternity test will only confirm what you already know," Brett said reasonably.

The topic was abandoned when Ellis returned with another pitcher of beer. A short while later, Spencer's pizza was ready, so he said goodbye to his friends and headed home.

When he walked through the door, he saw Kenzie and Dani were kneeling on opposite sides of the coffee table with some kind of board game between them.

"I told you that you Daddy would be home before we got to Lollipop Woods," Kenzie said to her playing partner. Then she looked over her shoulder at Spencer and added, "Of course, I didn't realize it would be on our *fifth turn around the board*."

"What are Lollipop Woods and why are you going there?" he asked.

"'Cuz they're on the way to Candy Castle," Dani said.

It was the most words she'd spoken to him in one sentence and the first time she'd answered one of his questions without additional prompting.

"We found some books and games in one of Dani's boxes," Kenzie explained. "Apparently Candy Land is a favorite."

"Well, I hope all that candy hasn't spoiled your appetite," he said. "Because I've got pizza."

"I'll get the plates," Kenzie said.

"C'mon, Dani," Spencer urged.

She tipped her head back to look up—way up—at him. At six feet, he wasn't overly tall, but to a little girl who was about half that height, he probably seemed like a giant. A scary giant.

He started to offer his free hand, then dropped it back

at his side again, unwilling to risk his overture being re-buffed. Again.

Dani stood up and took a couple of steps toward him, then she reached up and put her tiny hand into his—and somehow squeezed his heart.

She let him lead her to the table, and even lift her up into her booster seat. Yeah, he knew they were baby steps, but they felt pretty huge to him. And maybe to Kenzie, too, because when he looked over, he noticed that her eyes were shiny.

But Dani's eyes were focused on the flat box he'd set in the middle of the table. He lifted the lid to reveal the pizza, and she gave him a shy smile that squeezed his heart again.

He cleared his throat. "We've got half with just cheese and half with cheese and pepperoni. Do you like pepper-oni?"

She looked uncertain.

Kenzie, settled into a chair across from Dani, put a slice with cheese and pepperoni on her plate, then peeled off a circular piece of meat and offered it to the little girl.

Dani cautiously nibbled on the edge.

"Is it good?" Kenzie asked.

She nodded, then nibbled again and shook her head.

"Cheese it is," Spencer said.

He transferred a slice to her plate, earning another shy smile that gave him hope they were starting to bridge the gap between them.

After everyone had eaten their fill, they wrapped up the leftovers and Kenzie again tried to make her exit so that Spencer could bathe Dani and get her ready for bed. But both father and daughter protested her efforts to leave, so she agreed to stay a little while longer.

She helped Spencer muddle through the bath routine, which Dani resisted because of the lack of bubbles in the tub.

"Daddy will get you some bubbles tomorrow—and bathtub toys," Kenzie said, with an apologetic glance for Spencer. "But you still need to have a bath tonight."

The little girl wasn't swayed by her promises. "No bath."

She tried another tact. "The shampoo will make bubbles in your hair."

"Lotsa bubbles?" Dani asked hopefully.

"Yes, we can make lots of bubbles in your hair."

The child finally moved closer to the tub, and she even held on to her daddy's arm for balance as she climbed over the edge.

Of course, once she was in the tub, Dani was in no hurry to get out again. When she was finally clean and dry and dressed in a pair of too-small pj's that she'd picked out of her suitcase, insisting they were her favorite, Spencer let her choose which one of the toothbrushes she wanted from the two-pack he'd purchased. She opted for the pink handle with butterflies and dutifully pushed it back and forth over all her teeth.

"Now into bed with you," Spencer said, pointing to his bed, having resigned himself to sleeping on the sofa for the next few nights until Dani's new bedroom set was delivered.

In the meantime, Kenzie noticed that he'd put Dani's new comforter on his bed for his daughter. Of course, it was too small to cover the queen-sized mattress, but plenty big enough to cover the little girl who would be snuggled beneath it.

Dani climbed up onto the bed and settled back against the pillow. But her eyes stayed wide open.

Since Spencer didn't seem to know what to do next, Kenzie led the way. "Night night," she said, and bent down to kiss Dani's forehead.

The little girl shook her head. "No night night. Sto-wee time."

"Story time?" he looked at Kenzie blankly.

"There were some books in the box we unpacked," she remembered. "I'll go get them."

She returned to the bedroom with a pile of books.

Dani immediately found the one she wanted, appropriately titled *The Going to Bed Book.*

She pulled it out of the pile and handed it to Kenzie, designating her the story reader. Then she patted the side of the bed, where she wanted her to sit.

"Don't worry," Spencer teased, sensing her hesitation. "No one aside from the three of us has to know that you were in my bed."

Kenzie rolled her eyes at that but eased a hip onto the mattress, leaning back against the headboard and opening the cover of the book.

But Dani wasn't looking at the book—she was looking at Spencer, and then she patted the bed on her other side. He didn't hesitate to accept the invitation.

Kenzie began to read: "The sun has set…"

By the time she got to the last page, the little girl was struggling to keep her eyes open. She finished the story, closed the cover and said, "Night night."

This time, Dani replied with "Night night."

Kenzie kissed her forehead again, smiling as she breathed in the scent of her baby shampoo.

"Night night," Spencer echoed. Then he stood up and straightened Dani's covers and, after a moment, bent to kiss her, too.

The gesture wasn't easy or natural, but it was more proof to Kenzie that he was trying hard to be the daddy that his little girl needed.

"Now can I go home?" Kenzie asked, only half joking, when Spencer followed her out of the bedroom.

"I'd prefer if you stayed," he told her.

"For how much longer?" she wondered, thinking that he wanted to ensure there weren't any other crises to deal with before Dani fell asleep.

"Until she's ready for kindergarten?"

She laughed softly. "Nice try."

"Okay, just tonight then," he said.

"You're serious?"

"I know I have no right to ask you for anything—especially when you've already done so much. I'm just afraid that, if she wakes up in the night and I'm the only one here, she might freak out."

"She might," Kenzie acknowledged, then smiled just a bit. "Or *you* might. But she needs time to get to know you, to trust you."

"There's a spare toothbrush in the bathroom," he told her. "It's got a rainbow on the yellow handle, but it's yours if you want it."

She shook her head. "You're going to be just fine, Spencer."

"But what if I'm not?" he challenged, moving down the hall away from the bedroom. "It's obvious I don't have a clue about being a parent. Aside from providing the basic requirements of shelter, food and clothing, I don't know how to be a dad. And I hate to think that Dani is going to suffer because of my ineptitude. She's got enough to deal with as it is, grieving for her mother."

"You're not inept," she denied. "You just need some time to get to know one another. Sure, there are going to be some bumps in the road, but you'll figure things out as you go along."

"I don't know." He dropped onto the sofa, obviously weary. "Maybe this wasn't such a good idea."

The warmth that had filled her heart as she watched Spencer with his daughter immediately chilled. "You don't think it was a good idea to take responsibility for the child you fathered?"

"That's not what I meant," he said.

Kenzie folded her arms across her chest. "Then what did you mean?"

"I was referring to the apartment and trying to do this on my own."

"Oh," she said, duly chastened by his response.

"I would have taken responsibility from day one if I'd known Emily was pregnant," Spencer assured her.

"I'm sorry," she said. "I guess it's just a sensitive subject for me, because I grew up without a dad." And then, not wanting to delve any deeper into that topic, she asked, "So why did you decide to move in here?"

"I figured it would be easier to convince Dani's caseworker that I was a capable parent if I wasn't living with my own parents," he said. "That and I didn't really want to live with my parents."

"You've sacrificed a lot for your daughter," she noted. "And someday, when she's old enough to understand, it's going to mean the world to her."

"But today, she was clearly unimpressed."

"You've made more progress than you realize," Kenzie said confidently.

"With your help," he told her.

"It was my pleasure." She leaned down to kiss his forehead, as she'd done to his daughter, and said, "Good night, Spencer."

Then she let herself out of his apartment and headed back to her own, where she wouldn't be tempted to imagine that she could help father and daughter become a real family.

Or become part of that family herself, which was an even more dangerous thought.

Chapter Eight

After the kiss they'd shared Friday night, Kenzie had decided it would be smart to keep her distance from Spencer. Sure, she empathized with his situation, but it was *his* situation—it had absolutely nothing to do with her. Her resolve had lasted less than twelve hours, completely melting away when she saw him with his daughter and realized how much he was struggling to find some common ground with the little girl.

Now, less than twenty-four hours later, she was back at his apartment again—this time dressed in old leggings and an already paint-splattered T-shirt, with her hair tied back in a ponytail, ready to help paint his daughter's bedroom.

"As happy as I am to see you, Dani's going to be even more so," he said, when he greeted her at the door. "She's been asking about you since she woke up."

"She has?" Kenzie was both surprised and pleased by his revelation.

"Apparently she wants to be with anyone but me," he noted grimly.

"I'm sure that's not true," she said, stepping inside his apartment.

"She woke up crying for 'Mommy' again this morning," he admitted.

She winced sympathetically.

"And then, after I had to remind her that Mommy was gone, she wanted Nana. So I got to break her heart again by telling her that Nana had to go away on a trip, and she immediately asked for 'Ke'zie.' I tried to explain that you don't live here, but she apparently didn't believe me because she went from room to room looking for you."

"Maybe I spent too much time with both of you yesterday," she said.

He immediately shook his head. "Are you kidding? I'm not sure we would have made it through the day without you."

"Well, you know you'll be on your own tomorrow, right? I do have an actual job to go to."

"I know," he agreed. "And I'm sure we'll manage—at least until you finish at the clinic."

"I'm not stopping by on my way home," she told him.

He waved a hand dismissively. "We'll figure out the details later."

"There are no details to figure out," she said. "You and Dani need to—"

"Ke'zie!"

The little girl's happy exclamation cut off the rest of Kenzie's protest. And really, who could protest being greeted by a child's warm and enthusiastic hug?

She tugged gently on one of Dani's pigtails, smiling as she imagined Spencer's big hands trying to secure the little elastics around his daughter's fine hair—his struggles evident in the lopsided results.

"It looks like you're ready to paint," she said, noting the old T-shirt—likely belonging to Spencer—that covered Dani's clothes, with a knot tied at the back so it didn't completely fall off her much smaller frame.

Dani nodded. "I like to paint."

"Then I guess we should get started," Kenzie said.

Spencer had already taped off the trim to protect it from wayward brushes and rollers and spread drop cloths over the carpet. Dani was given a plastic cup of paint and let loose inside the closet. Conscious of Spencer's shoulder injury, Kenzie suggested that he stand on the ladder to do the edging, while she followed behind with the roller.

They worked in tandem for a while, making quick work of the first three walls while Dani contentedly dabbed away with her brush in her assigned space. They'd just started the final wall when Spencer's phone rang in the other room, and when he finally got down from the ladder to check the display, he saw that he'd missed a call from his agent. They'd been playing phone tag for nearly a week, so Spencer called him back right away.

There was a tiny bit of a mishap while he was out of the room on the phone. Dani tripped on the track of the closet door and, when she reached out to break her fall, her hand landed in the tray of paint. Then she put her hand on the door for support to stand up again, leaving a painted handprint on the surface.

And that gave Kenzie an idea.

When Spencer finally ended his call, Kenzie and Dani were in the bathroom washing up.

"You can't be finished already," he said.

"You were on the phone quite a while," Kenzie said.

"Talk, talk, talk," Dani chimed in, echoing what Kenzie had told her when the little girl asked what he was doing.

Spencer's brows lifted and Kenzie felt her cheeks flush.

"You didn't run out of paint?"

"No. Why?"

"Because you seem to be wearing quite a bit of it—" he

lifted a hand to trail a finger along her jaw "—here and—" his gaze skimmed over the rest of her "—everywhere."

"Painting can be messy work," she acknowledged.

But now that she'd managed to scrub most of the paint off his daughter, she started to use the cloth on herself.

"Dani, why don't you take Daddy into your bedroom and show him what we did?"

Spencer didn't expect that Dani would actually follow Kenzie's suggestion. Although she seemed less fearful of him today than she'd been yesterday, he knew she still wasn't completely comfortable around him, preferring to stick close to Kenzie. So he was surprised when she willingly took his hand to lead him back to her bedroom.

"Wow," he said, stepping inside the doorway and looking around the room. "It really looks good." He'd been a little concerned when Dani had chosen purple, but Kenzie had cleverly warned the little girl that the color she'd selected on the palette would probably be a little lighter once it was actually on the walls—and then she'd pointed to a color that was several shades lighter when she gave the paint to the guy at the hardware store to tint.

But Dani moved further into the room, tugging on his hand to draw him along with her. Then she turned to face the closet, and when he did the same, he saw the child-size handprints that decorated the lower-third of the doors. He took a couple of steps for a closer examination, then looked at Dani again.

"Did you do that?"

She nodded.

Kenzie, having scrubbed most of the paint off herself now, stepped into the room. "What do you think?"

"I think it looks great," he said sincerely.

"The first one was an accident," she confessed. "I was going to wash it off, but then I decided that adding more would make a nice accent."

"Did you have fun making painted handprints?" he asked Dani.

She nodded again and held up her hand—the one not holding his—and splayed her fingers, as if to demonstrate her technique.

"Since we all worked hard this morning—"

"Some of us harder than others," Kenzie interjected.

He inclined his head to acknowledge her point. "I think we all deserve a treat," he said. "How does ice cream sound?"

"Yummy!" Dani said, and dropped his hand now to race off toward the kitchen.

"It sounds like bribery to me," Kenzie muttered.

He grinned, unrepentant, and moved toward the doorway. "Do you want ice cream or not?" he asked over his shoulder.

"Of course, I want ice cream," she said in a tone that suggested her answer was never in doubt. "But while you're dishing it up, would you mind if I put Dani's clothes in your short dresser so that she isn't living out of a suitcase until Wednesday?"

He stopped then and turned back to face her. "How do you know I'm not using that dresser?"

"Because I checked," she admitted. "And you've barely used the top three drawers in the tall dresser."

"You were poking around in my drawers?"

"I only looked to see what space you were using," she assured him.

"Not to satisfy your curiosity about whether I'm a boxers or briefs type of guy?" he teased.

"I have no curiosity about your underwear," she denied, but the spots of color high on her cheeks suggested that she was thinking about them now.

He nudged her playfully with his elbow. "I'll show you mine if you show me yours."

"Not interested," she said firmly.

He was tempted to remind her that she hadn't kissed him like a woman who wasn't interested. But as much as he enjoyed teasing her, he didn't want to make her mad—especially when she'd come through for him in such a big way both yesterday and today.

"Not even in the ice cream?"

"*Only* in the ice cream," she assured him.

He chuckled as he turned toward the kitchen. "Go ahead and start unpacking Dani's stuff, if you want. I'll let you know when your ice cream is ready."

Kenzie spent the rest of the afternoon with Spencer and Dani, until it was time to head over to her mother's house.

Their Sunday night dinners had become a ritual when Kenzie moved into her own apartment in town. At first, she'd balked at the idea of every Sunday night, because she'd wanted to do her own thing on her own schedule. But Cheryl had made a lot of sacrifices to provide Kenzie with opportunities while she was growing up, and she couldn't help feeling a little bit guilty about moving out—as if she was abandoning the one person who'd always stood by her.

Brielle had assured Kenzie that she didn't have to apologize for living her own life, but Kenzie didn't think it was a big deal to share a meal with her mother one night a week. And usually it wasn't. But every once in a while, Cheryl seemed to forget that her adult daughter was capable of making her own decisions—most often when those decisions concerned the male species.

Kenzie understood that her mother wanted to spare her making the same mistakes that Cheryl had made, but she sometimes resented that her mother's experiences had colored her own expectations of personal relationships.

Growing up, she'd heard the story of her father's abandonment so many times that she didn't trust any man she cared about to stick around. When she'd fallen for Spencer in high school, she'd wondered if she'd chosen him because he'd never made any secret of his plan to leave Haven. And when he did, it was a self-fulfilling prophecy. It didn't matter that their relationship had existed mostly in her mind—she'd loved him and he'd abandoned her, which was exactly what she'd expected him to do.

She knew that Spencer's return was a trigger for her mother's concern, and Kenzie was prepared for an uncomfortable atmosphere around the dinner table. But Cheryl had recently been promoted from housekeeping supervisor and part-time evening desk clerk at the Dusty Boots Motel to full-time daytime clerk, making the new job the focus of her mother's attention. As a result, she asked only cursory questions about Kenzie's weekend and made no mention of Spencer at all.

The next day, when Kenzie finished her shift at the clinic, she had three voice messages and twice as many texts on her phone—all from Spencer. All requesting that she stop by his apartment "just to say hi to Dani" on her way home from work. She called him back as she made her way to the car.

"I have to stop at The Trading Post to get the groceries that I never got around to getting on the weekend," she told him, explaining why she couldn't take the time to detour to his apartment—and not admitting, even to herself, how much she wanted to do just that.

"Or you could come here to have homemade lasagna with me and Dani," he suggested.

"Homemade?" she said dubiously. "Who made it?"

"You didn't pause, for even two seconds, to consider that I might have layered the noodles and meat and cheese," he noted.

"When would you have had the time to do all that?"

He chuckled softly. "Yeah, because that's the only reason for your doubts."

"So who made it?" she asked again.

"My brother," he admitted.

"Jason cooks?"

"Apparently his fiancée has been teaching him."

"I'll bet that's more of a challenge than her senior math classes," Kenzie remarked.

"I'd be a fool to take that bet," he said. "And you'd be a fool to turn down homemade lasagna."

"No one ever wants to be called a fool," she assured him.

So she postponed her grocery shopping once again to share another meal with Spencer and Dani.

And so it went throughout the week, with Spencer—or Kenzie—finding a reason for her to stop by almost every day. Wednesday was a particularly exciting day, because Dani's bed and other furniture were finally delivered.

Apparently Spencer had also been persuaded by the sales clerk to pick up some extra items that coordinated with the bedding and curtains—decorative throw pillows, wall art, a bedside lamp, bookends and even a wastebasket. All the little touches truly transformed the room, and Dani—surrounded now by Pocket Ponies—absolutely loved it.

And Kenzie was loving the time she spent with Spencer and his daughter—and especially seeing the little girl warm up to her daddy. Though Dani had yet to actually call him "Daddy," she no longer hesitated to take his hand or snuggle close to him on the sofa, and her shy, sweet smiles came more easily and frequently as the week progressed.

Kenzie enjoyed hanging out with both of them, and their adventures including a quick stop at The Daily Grind Saturday morning. Of course, their paths crossed with several people who knew Kenzie or Spencer—or both—and she suspected that the news she was keeping company with the cowboy would soon make its way to her mother.

It happened even sooner than she'd anticipated. In fact, Kenzie was pouring gravy on her mashed potatoes the following Sunday night when Cheryl looked across the table and said, "So what's going on with you and Spencer Channing this time?"

Yes, she'd anticipated the interrogation, but she hadn't expected it to start before she'd even picked up her fork. "Nothing's going on," she said, because aside from the kisses they'd shared before Dani came to Haven, it was true.

"You've been spending an awful lot of time together." Her mother stabbed at a piece of meat with her fork. "And I'm concerned that you're going to get caught up in his... situation."

"What situation is that?" Kenzie asked.

"The man has an illegitimate child."

"Yes, a little girl whose whole world was recently upended by the tragic death of her mother."

"I didn't know she'd lost her mother," Cheryl said, in a quieter tone. "The poor thing."

Her mother's instinctive and sincere sympathy tempered Kenzie's annoyance.

Cheryl had always been—in Kenzie's opinion—overprotective, overbearing and overly strict. Which, of course, led to her daughter balking at the rules and constraints. But though their relationship had sometimes been contentious, Kenzie had never had cause to doubt that her mother loved her. And she couldn't imagine what she would have done—how her entire life might have changed—if something had happened to take her mother away from her.

Cheryl scooped up some mashed potatoes, then looked across the table, her expression worried. "I suspect you've spent even more time with Spencer than I realized."

"He's living in one of the units in that building his brother owns, across the hall from Mrs. Powell, in fact, and I ran into him—and his daughter—when I stopped by to see her last week," Kenzie confided.

"You've always been soft on him," her mother noted.

"I had a crush on him when I was a teenager," she allowed. "I'm not a teenager anymore, Mom."

"I know. I'm just…concerned that he might exploit those old feelings for selfish reasons."

"Translation, please," Kenzie said in response to her mother's uncharacteristically cryptic remark.

Cheryl pushed some peas around on her plate. "It's not easy raising a child alone."

Which was the same tune Kenzie had heard her sing plenty of times before, so she sat silently and chewed on her roast beef.

"Plenty of women do it," her mother continued. "But single fathers are a rarer breed. And I don't think it will be too long before he's looking for a mother for his little girl."

"He doesn't even have legal custody yet," Kenzie told her.

"Maybe I'm jumping the gun a little," Cheryl acknowledged. "I just want you to consider that he might have had ulterior motives for seeking you out."

"Even if Spencer is looking for a mother for his daughter, why do you think he'd choose me?"

As soon as the words were out of her mouth, Kenzie wished she could take them back. Because if she wanted someone to reassure her that she was a smart, beautiful woman and that, of course, any man would want to build a life and a family with her, that someone wouldn't be her mother. Cheryl had never been one to tiptoe around hard truths or shield her daughter's feelings, insisting that it was better to have a bruised heart now than a broken one later.

A philosophy that she proved once again when she said, "Because your history makes your heart ripe for the picking."

"Well." Kenzie blew out a breath, not sure how else to respond to that.

But Cheryl didn't expect a response, because she hadn't finished making her own point. "And you can bet that, when he has you wrapped up in his life again, willing to take on the burden of his responsibilities, he'll hightail it out of town again, just like he did seven years ago."

Kenzie had thought the same thing when Spencer first returned to Haven—that this was only a temporary stop. A place to recuperate and rehab his injury until he was ready to ride bulls again. But then he'd told her about Dani, and she'd witnessed firsthand the efforts he was making to be there for his daughter, and her opinion had changed.

"Spencer wouldn't do that," Kenzie said to her mother now. "He wouldn't leave his daughter."

"Are you sure about that?"

Kenzie wanted to respond affirmatively, but the truth was, she wasn't sure about anything. She didn't really know what his plans were—and it was entirely possible that her mother was right.

Dani's caseworker had spent a lot of time with Spencer at their first meeting in Denver, answering his endless questions and providing suggestions and strategies to help Dani adjust to all the changes in her life. She'd also suggested that Spencer should take some time to get to know her himself before introducing her to a lot of new people.

He'd hoped to rely on that sage advice as his justification for turning down his mother's invitation to Sunday dinner. But as Kenzie pointed out to him, Margaret and Ben weren't "a lot of new people," they were Dani's grandparents, and she was their first grandchild. So while Kenzie was having dinner with her mother, he took his daughter to his parents' house.

"Dani, I'd like you to meet your grandmother and grandfather," Spencer said to her. Then, to his parents: "Grandma and Grandpa, this is Dani."

"Hello, Danielle," Margaret said formally.

Spencer shook his head. "Her name is Dani."

"Isn't Dani short for Danielle?"

"No," he said. "It's actually short for Daniel."

His father frowned. "But Daniel is a b—"

"—great name," he interjected loudly.

"Dani *is* a lovely name," his mother acknowledged with a forced a smile. "If a bit…untraditional."

"Says the woman who named her daughters Regan and Brielle," he noted wryly.

Margaret turned her attention back to her granddaughter. "Are you hungry, Dani?"

The little girl gave a hesitant nod.

Though she'd started to open up to Spencer and seemed totally at ease with Kenzie, he could tell that she was a little uncomfortable in the big house filled with lots of shiny and breakable things.

"What's your favorite thing to eat?" Margaret asked.

"Ice cweam?" she suggested hopefully.

Spencer couldn't help but chuckle, pleased by this evidence of both her spirit and optimism. "Nice try, kiddo, but I don't think you're going to get ice cream for dinner."

"We'll see if Celeste has any in the freezer for dessert," his mother promised. "But for dinner, we're having mushroom-stuffed quail with a truffle wine sauce and seasonal root vegetables."

Dani looked worriedly at Spencer, clearly at a loss to understand the words that might as well have been spoken in a different language.

"That means you're probably going to be really hungry when you finally get your ice cream," he told his daughter. Then, to his mother, "You couldn't have gone for something simple, like burgers or pasta?"

"I wanted a special meal to welcome your daughter to the family. But I was only teasing. I didn't expect that Danielle— Dani—" she quickly corrected herself "—would find quail appealing."

"So we're not having quail?"

"Of course *we* are," Margaret said. "But Celeste is making chicken fingers and macaroni and cheese for Dani."

"Who are you and what have you done with my mother?" Spencer asked her.

She sniffed, clearly insulted by the question. "Do you really think I'm so out of touch?"

"Do you really want me to answer that?"

"Okay, so the chicken fingers were Celeste's idea," she admitted.

"My vote was for steak," Ben chimed in, and winked at Dani. "For all of us."

"There's nothing special about steak when you live in Nevada," his wife protested.

"At least it's a substantial meal."

"The quail sounds great," Spencer injected, noting that the bickering between his parents—although mostly light-hearted and familiar to him—caused Dani's grip on his hand to tighten.

"I remembered it was one of your favorites," Margaret told him.

Spencer didn't remember any such thing but kept that thought to himself. Instead he only asked, "When do we eat?"

Chapter Nine

They ate in the dining room, of course. At the ten-foot table set with pressed linen napkins, gleaming crystal, gold-rimmed china and polished silverware. And one plate and cup that he recognized from his own childhood.

Once upon a time, the face of the plate had been printed with a graphic of a cow jumping over the moon and the side of the cup with a cat and a fiddle. Over the years, they'd been used and washed so many times that the images had almost completely faded. But they'd never been used in the dining room before—his mother would never have allowed it.

Apparently she had mellowed over the years. Or maybe she hadn't noticed that Dani's place setting was different than the others around the table.

Dinner wasn't served until Regan got home. Despite it being a Sunday, his sister had gone into the office for a few hours—and lost track of time. Though his mother had grumbled that the quail would be overcooked, there wasn't much heat in her words. Probably because, of all her children, her eldest daughter was most like her—at least in so far as her commitment to Blake Mining. The rest of Regan's siblings knew that made her the perennial favorite.

While they were eating, he noticed that Dani seemed intrigued by the little birds everyone else was eating, so he pulled some of the meat off his and set it on the edge of her plate.

"It's a little bit like chicken, if you want to try it," he said.

She looked dubious, and nibbled on some more macaroni before deciding to stab a piece of the meat with her fork and lift it to her mouth.

Her grandmother smiled, obviously pleased by the girl's willingness to try something new.

Dani chewed, then decided she didn't like the quail and spit it out on her plate. Margaret's smile turned to a grimace.

In a stage whisper from the other side of the table, Regan said, "Believe me—I would have opted for chicken fingers, too, if I'd been given a choice."

Dani responded with a shy smile.

"Maybe next time we'll all have chicken fingers," Margaret suggested, a little testily. "Or maybe we'll go for something truly gourmet and head to the Elko Golden Arches."

"The quail was delicious, Mother," Spencer interjected.

"I'm glad you, at least, enjoyed it," Margaret said.

"Because it's all about me, right?" he said, and grinned at his sister.

"The prodigal son," Regan muttered. But then, because it was her nature to play peacemaker, she attempted to appease their mother. "Dad obviously liked it, too. He practically licked his plate clean."

"That's because your father's still a caveman in some ways," Margaret said, though with an affectionate glance at her husband.

"Now, Maggie—" her husband sent her a playful wink "—the kids don't need to know about our role-playing."

"Don't need to know," Regan said firmly. "And don't *want* to know."

"Your sister's still perturbed because she walked in on us when we forgot to the lock the door a few weeks back."

"Aside from the fact that this is an inappropriate conversation to have with a child at the table," Spencer noted. "Why would you walk into their bedroom?"

Regan shook her head. "Oh, no. It wasn't their bedroom—it was the boardroom."

"It was late," Ben pointed out in defense of their activities. "We thought everyone else had left the office."

"Believe me, I wish I'd left with everyone else," Regan said.

"Speaking of leaving, maybe it's time for me and Dani to go," Spencer suggested.

"But she hasn't had her ice cream," Margaret protested.

"We can stop for ice cream on the way home," he decided.

"You will have dessert here," his mother said firmly. "And we'll agree to pretend that each of our four children was delivered by a stork, conveniently ignoring the ten hours of labor I suffered through with you, Regan, and fourteen for you, Spencer."

"Did somebody say something about ice cream?" Regan asked, desperate to change the subject.

As if on cue, Celeste appeared to clear away the dinner plates and offer dessert. She had prepared a white chocolate mousse with cherries but confirmed that there was also ice cream in the freezer for anyone who preferred it.

"What kind of ice cream do you like?" she asked Dani.

"'Nilla?" she suggested.

"Plain or with chocolate sauce and sprinkles?"

Dani's eyes lit up and her lips curved. "Choc'ate sauce an' spwinkles."

"Do you want to help me dish it up?" Celeste invited.

The little girl looked at Spencer, as if for permission, and he nodded.

She slid off her chair to follow the housekeeper into the kitchen.

"She's a quiet thing, isn't she?" his father remarked.

"Her caseworker said she has a pretty extensive vocabulary for her age," Spencer said. "But she is very shy."

"She needs a mother," Margaret abruptly decided.

"She recently lost her mother," he reminded his own.

"And it's your job to find another one for her."

"Despite scanning all the street corners on the drive over here, I didn't see any obvious candidates."

Across the table, Regan hid her smile behind her wine-glass.

His mother huffed out a breath. "Must you always resort to sarcasm?"

"I apologize for mocking your ridiculous question," he said.

"Your mother was expressing a sincere concern about our granddaughter," Ben said.

"Well, 'mother' isn't a job opening—like a lab tech—that can be filled by any qualified college graduate," he pointed out to them.

"A little girl needs a mother," his own insisted.

"Luckily, she has a concerned and loving grandmother."

"You should think about Kenzie," Margaret continued.

He *had* been thinking about Kenzie—more than he wanted to admit, a fact that he had no intention of confiding to his mother.

"What about Kenzie?" he asked instead.

"I know you've been spending time with her," Margaret told him.

Of course she knew, because there were no secrets in Haven. "Where are you going with this?"

"Well, it's no secret that she used to have a crush on you," Margaret noted.

So maybe she wasn't as oblivious to the details of her children's lives as they'd always believed, but he still didn't see the relevance of the remark. "When she was sixteen," he noted dryly.

"Sometimes old feelings can be rekindled," his mother said.

"Right now, I'm focusing on my daughter."

"You should give some thought to your future, too," his father suggested.

"I have," he agreed. "But I'm still trying to figure some things out."

"You can't go back on the circuit," Margaret said.

He'd pretty much decided the same thing himself, but her implacable tone urged him to challenge the assertion. "Why not?"

"Because it's dangerous."

"Crossing the street can be dangerous," he pointed out to her.

"You didn't dislocate your shoulder crossing the street. You didn't crack three ribs last spring crossing the street. You didn't get either of your two concussions crossing the street."

"Okay, Mom. You've made your point," he said, grateful that she only knew about half the injuries he'd sustained riding bulls.

"Not to mention that living out of a suitcase, moving from one motel to the next, might be okay for a single man, but it's no life for a child."

She was right about that, too, but it wasn't in his nature to give in easily—especially when giving in meant giving up everything familiar to him. "I could get an RV," he suggested impulsively. "Dani might think it's fun to live in a house on wheels."

"She might enjoy ice cream for breakfast, too," his mother noted. "That doesn't mean it's good for her."

"Speaking of ice cream," he began, "I better go see what's taking so long with dessert."

And he escaped the rest of the parental interrogation by following the path his daughter had taken to the kitchen.

"That wasn't so bad, was it?" Spencer asked, as he unbuckled the harness of Dani's car seat, when they were finally home again.

"Bad," she said, and wagged a finger, clearly imitating something she'd seen and heard before.

He chuckled softly. "I meant 'not bad.' Good."

"Okay," she agreed.

"Of course, the best part is that we're home now," he said, as he lifted her out of her seat. "And it's time for your bath, then pajamas and bed."

"Bubbles?" she asked.

"As many bubbles as you want," he promised.

That earned him a small smile.

Then she put her arms around his neck and dropped her head to his shoulder.

It was probably an indication of her exhaustion more than anything else, but Spencer was happy to take it as a sign of her growing comfort with him.

Of course, it helped that he was with her almost twenty-four seven. Aside from his massage therapy appointments, before which he would drop Dani across the hall to hang out with Mrs. Powell, he was rarely apart from his daughter.

How was it possible that he hadn't even known this child existed a couple of months earlier? Already he couldn't imagine his life without her.

He was grateful that Emily had put his name on Dani's birth certificate, but he was still angry with her, too. Angry that she'd never made any effort to tell him that she was going to have his baby, that she'd never given him the chance to be there for her or their child.

Had she assumed that he wouldn't want to know?

Did she think he'd abandon her to raise their child alone?

And if she thought so little of him, why would she name him as Dani's guardian?

Of course, the most likely answer to that question was that she didn't imagine he'd ever have to step up and be a father. After all, there was no way she could have known that her life would be cut short by a tragic accident, leaving her young daughter to grow up without a mother.

And while he grieved for Emily, and especially for Dani, he also mourned the loss of the first years of his daughter's life. Maybe he hadn't been ready to be a father four years ago. Truthfully, he wasn't sure he was ready now, but he didn't have a choice. Dani needed him. He was the only parent she had left, and he was determined to step up for her.

"Sto-wee time?" Dani asked, after her bath.

She could barely keep her eyes open, but he'd already learned that she fought sleep to the bitter end. And although it was later than her usual bedtime, he'd read somewhere that routines were important to kids, and a story before bed was one of Dani's routines.

"Go pick a book," he told her.

She skipped over to the shelf under the window, immediately locating a familiar and favorite book.

He tucked her under the covers, then sat on the edge of the bed and began to read *The Going to Bed Book*.

As he'd suspected, Dani was asleep before the story-book characters had "brushed and brushed and brushed their teeth." He finished the story anyway, then set the book aside, kissed her soft cheek and turned out the light.

Conscious of her mother's warning, Kenzie kept herself busy through the week so that she didn't make excuses to stop by Spencer's place. But her efforts were for naught, because he called or at least texted her every day with a question or a request for a favor.

She wasn't blind to the fact that he was using her as a

buffer with his daughter. More troubling to Kenzie was the realization that she was willing to let him—and happy for any and every excuse to spend time with Spencer and Dani.

Which was how she found herself agreeing to meet them in Battle Mountain on Thursday afternoon.

Spencer knew that she didn't work at Back in the Game on Tuesdays or Thursdays. What he didn't know, until he invited her to go shopping with him and Dani, was that she worked at another clinic in Battle Mountain on both of those days, although she finished at one o'clock on Thursdays.

So they arranged to meet at 2:00 p.m. outside of Baby Cakes—a store specializing in infant and children's clothing.

"I really appreciate this," Spencer said to Kenzie, as they walked into the store, each holding one of Dani's hands—almost as if they were a family. "I wouldn't know where to begin if I tried to tackle this on my own."

"I'm sure you would have figured it out—or conned someone else into helping you," she added.

He lifted his daughter into the seat of a shopping cart. "Do you feel as if you've been conned?"

"Maybe not conned," she allowed. "But certainly manipulated."

"How did I manipulate you?" he wanted to know.

"You suggested this shopping expedition in front of Dani."

"Because it's for Dani. And you're the one who pointed out that most of her clothes are too small for her."

"Only because you didn't seem to notice that her leggings and T-shirts were more like capri pants and crop tops."

"Don't girls wear capri pants and crop tops?"

She shook her head despairingly. "Not in northern Nevada in the fall."

"And that's why I need your help to do this," he told her.

"And that's why I'm here," she confirmed, guiding him

past the infant and toddler sections to an area labeled Pre-school.

"I guess it won't be too long before she's a schooler rather than a preschooler," Spencer noted.

"Less than a year," Kenzie confirmed.

He seemed surprised by her response. "That soon?"

"Some parents start their kids in preschool even earlier."

He shook his head. "How is it possible? It seems like it was only a couple of months ago that I learned I was a father…oh, right—that's because it *was* only a couple of months ago."

"It's understandable that you'd be angry about missing the first years of your daughter's life," Kenzie acknowledged.

"Angry's one word," he agreed. Then he looked at his daughter, who wasn't saying anything but clearly taking in every word of the adult conversation, and he made a conscious effort to shake off his mood. "But now, we're happy," he said, in a deliberately upbeat tone. "Because we're shopping."

Kenzie felt a smile tug at her lips. "If only your high school buddies could see you now."

"Are you thinking about any one of my high school buddies in particular?"

"What?" She sounded baffled by the question, then her gaze narrowed. "Someone told you about me and Gage."

"Was there something to tell?" he asked innocently.

"Not even a little bit," she assured him.

Which admittedly made him feel a lot better than it probably should.

"Okay," he said, turning his attention to his daughter now. "What do you need?"

She thought about it for a minute. "Ice cweam?"

He chuckled. "Let's take care of your wardrobe first and then we'll see."

Kenzie pulled a long-sleeved T-shirt off the rack. It was

a soft pink color with a silhouette of a ballerina on the front and a ruffle at the hem.

"That's cute," Spencer said. Then, to Dani, "What do you think? Do you like it?"

She nodded.

But Kenzie shook her head and put it back on the rack. "She'll wear it once then decide the tulle is scratchy."

He retrieved the hanger to test the ruffle.

"Pwetty," Dani said.

So Spencer put it in the basket.

"I thought you wanted my help," Kenzie reminded him.

"You are helping," he assured her.

She gestured to the rack, inviting him to take the lead. He selected a bright blue microfleece top with delicate snowflakes embroidered on it.

Dani nodded again, and the shirt went into the basket.

Then there was a purple one with a unicorn, and an orange one with fuchsia and lime flowers, and a dark pink one with a sparkly rainbow.

Kenzie stood back as he randomly selected an item, looked to Dani for her approval, then dropped it into the basket or returned it to the bar. The little girl seemed to enjoy the game, occasionally shaking her head rather than nodding, as if to keep him guessing. When they finished the rack of tops, they went through the same routine with bottoms until Kenzie finally put a hand on Spencer's arm and gently but firmly told him, "Stop."

"What?" he asked.

"How many shirts do you think she needs?" she asked.

"I don't know," he admitted.

"Not sixteen," she assured him.

He scoffed at that. "I didn't put sixteen in the cart."

"Do you want me to count them?"

He looked at the pile of clothes and silently acknowledged that her guess might not be too far off the actual number.

"She also doesn't need leggings in every color of the rainbow," Kenzie told him.

"Why not?"

"Because she'll outgrow them before she has a chance to wear them all."

"Then I'll buy her new ones again," he decided.

"I have no doubt that you would," she said. "But I think you need to look at what you're really doing here."

"Buying the new clothes my daughter needs."

"Or trying to compensate for the fact that you missed most of the first four years of your daughter's life," she suggested gently.

"That wasn't my choice," he reminded her.

"I know," she acknowledged. "But you still feel guilty, don't you?"

He straightened the bow tied around one of Dani's lopsided pigtails. "Wouldn't you?"

"Probably," she admitted. "But buying out the store isn't going to alleviate the guilt—it's just going to cut into her college fund."

Then she lifted the pile of shirts from the cart and laid them out, so that Dani could see them all side-by-side. And damn, she was right—there *were* sixteen.

But aside from a pointed look over her shoulder, Kenzie didn't say anything to him. Instead, she said to Dani, "You get to pick five." And she held up her hand, counting on her fingers and thumb from one to five for the little girl. "Which ones do you like best?"

Dani pointed to the purple T-shirt with the unicorn.

"That's one," Kenzie said, and held up one finger.

Next Dani chose the dark pink shirt with the sparkly rainbow. And so it went until she'd chosen her top five. After the T-shirts, she selected two hoodies, three pairs of leggings and two pairs of jeans. Kenzie added socks and underwear, and then they moved to the footwear department where Dani picked out new running shoes. She was walking up and down the aisle, testing the comfort and fit, when she spotted a pair of pink cowboy boots on display.

"Look! Just like Daddy's."

He was so stunned to hear the word "Daddy" come out of her mouth that it took a minute for the rest of her comment to register.

When it finally did, he looked at the battered brown boots on his own feet, then at the pink ones that had caught her attention. He didn't think they were similar at all, but she seemed excited by the idea of having boots like Daddy, and that made him feel pretty good, so he bought those for her, too.

And then, because of course Dani hadn't forgotten his promise, they went for ice cream—wearing their "matching" cowboy boots.

Spencer hadn't planned to have kids.

Not that he'd consciously decided to never be a father—he just hadn't given the matter much thought. The truth was, he'd wasted no time contemplating the subjects of marriage and children because he'd been having too much fun living in the moment.

At twenty-five years of age, he was still a kid himself in many ways. And if anyone had asked, he would have insisted that he wasn't ready to take on the responsibility of a child.

Thankfully, no one had asked.

Instead, he'd been given the gift of this beautiful daughter. And then he'd panicked, because he knew he wasn't equipped with the necessary know-how to be a parent.

Certainly his own parents hadn't been ideal role models. Ben and Margaret Channing had ensured their children didn't want for anything, but they weren't overly affectionate—or even involved—with their offspring. Instead, it had been Celeste who offered warm beverages when he came in after school or applied cool compresses to heated skin when he was home with a fever. It had been Celeste who bandaged his scrapes, monitored his homework, cautioned him about the dangers of alcohol—and then picked him up when he'd proven that he wasn't smart enough to heed her advice but was at least smart enough not to drink and drive.

And it had been Celeste again who watched from the audience when Spencer graduated from high school because his parents were in Europe celebrating their twenty-fifth wedding anniversary. Not that he could complain, because they'd given him their gift—a brand-new truck—before they left.

He'd never been particularly bothered by their absence—not so much that he would admit, anyway. But now that he had a child of his own, he wondered if they ever regretted—or even thought about—all the events and milestones they'd missed. Every day with Dani, he was painfully aware that he'd come into the fatherhood game late. So much had happened in her life before he even knew of her existence, and he bitterly resented missing so many key moments: her first smile, her first steps, her first birthday.

He wanted to be mad at Emily—and he was. Then he felt guilty for being mad, because she was going to miss out on so much more. And his heart ached for his little girl, who would live the rest of her life without her mother.

Thankfully, she had a lot of other women in her life who would be role models for her, including Kenzie. His sister's best friend was already important to his daughter—and to him.

He knew Kenzie was bothered by Linda's willingness to relinquish care of her granddaughter, but Spencer was grateful that Emily's mom had acceded to her daughter's wishes to award him guardianship. Because he knew that if Linda had applied to the court for custody, he would not have opposed her. Certainly not two months earlier, when the idea of being a father had scared him a lot more than going nose to nose with the meanest, maddest bulls on the circuit. In fact, he would have been relieved, grateful. Because of course Linda was more suited to care for Dani than a man who'd never even met the child.

But now, after only three weeks, he had no more doubts that Dani was where she belonged—with her daddy.

And yet, he couldn't seem to forget the conversation he'd had with his friends at Jo's. Once the seed had been planted, the idea began to grow—like a toxic weed, its roots digging into his mind and wrapping around his heart:

What if he wasn't her father?

What if the DNA test came back negative?

As he tried to banish those questions from his mind, he regretted ever having the test done. But Brett's speculation had spurred him to impulsive action—not because he believed Emily had lied but because he didn't know for certain that she was certain. And if he wasn't Dani's father, then her real father was out there somewhere, missing out on everything it meant to be a dad to the little girl.

But now, if the results of the test were negative, he didn't know what he'd do. The only thing he knew for certain was that he couldn't imagine ever giving her up.

Chapter Ten

"Moving can be a stressful experience for anyone, but I think your decision to bring Dani to Haven was a wise one," Wendy said, as she scribbled some notes on her tablet. "A support network is invaluable to any new parent as they attempt to find some kind of rhythm in their new role. And although Dani's not a baby, the father-daughter relationship is new to both of you."

"I think we're making some good progress," Spencer said, anxious to ensure she didn't assume otherwise.

"I can see that," Wendy agreed. "After only three weeks, Dani seems very comfortable with you and in her new home. By the way—love the handprints on her closet doors."

"Me, too. In fact, I've already decided that I'm going to have to take those doors when we move."

The caseworker glanced up. "Are you planning to move already?"

"Not anytime in the near future," he hastened to assure her. "But eventually it would be nice to have a real place of our own."

She made some more notes. "It would be helpful if you were honest with me instead of giving me the answers you think I want to hear."

"I honestly want what's best for my daughter."

"That's what we all want," Wendy said, scrolling back in her notes. "How's your shoulder?"

"It's good." He rolled the joint to demonstrate, ignoring the slight twinge of discomfort.

"Any thoughts on your career plans?"

"Lots of thoughts, no decisions." He still had his eye on Vegas in December, hoping to end his career with a bang rather than a whimper, but he kept that information to himself for now.

"Okay." Wendy closed the cover of her tablet. "I think that covers everything for today, except to tell you that this is likely my first and last visit here."

"You're not coming back?"

"Sending a caseworker eight hundred miles away from her office isn't the best use of company resources," she told him.

"So this is finished?" he asked hopefully.

"Not just yet," she cautioned, with a smile and a shake of her head. "I've got a friend who works for Elko Family Services. I'll send her a copy of my preliminary report and she'll do the follow-up visits. But at this point, I don't anticipate any difficulties getting your custody application approved by the court."

She stood up then and offered her hand. "Good luck, Mr. Channing."

After Wendy had gone, Spencer immediately picked up the phone and dialed Kenzie's number. Because he agreed with the caseworker about the importance of a support network, and over the past three weeks, Kenzie had proven to be a major part of his.

Maybe they hadn't been friends in the past, but they were friends now. And, unless he was completely wrong about the chemistry between them, there was the potential for them to be a lot more. But he was keeping a tight lid on his growing attraction, because Dani really liked Kenzie, too, and he wasn't going to do anything to jeopardize that connection.

He didn't have a lot of experience with relationships. One-night stands and weekend encounters, sure, but his life as a rodeo cowboy hadn't lent itself to anything more. And that was okay, because he hadn't wanted anything more. Until Kenzie had given him a glimpse of the benefits and pleasures he would enjoy sharing his life with someone. *With her.*

Just the sound of her voice made him smile, and after summarizing the meeting with the caseworker, he got around to the other reason for his call.

"I need a favor," he told her. "Jay wants me to go to Battle Mountain with him and Carter and Kevin tomorrow afternoon to be fitted for our tuxes for the wedding."

"And you don't want to drag Dani along with you?" she guessed.

"I'm happy to drag her, but I don't think she'd be happy to be dragged."

"What time were you planning to head out?" Kenzie asked.

"Two o'clock."

"Sure, I can hang out with Dani for a few hours," she agreed. "But I have to be home by six."

"Curfew?" he teased.

"No." She hesitated, as if reluctant to say more, then finally admitted, "I've got a date."

"A date." His brows drew together. "Are you serious?"

"Is that so hard to believe?"

Of course, it wasn't. He just didn't want to think of Kenzie dating—unless it was him. And since they weren't going there, he didn't want her going there with anyone else.

"With who?" he demanded to know.

"How is that any of your business?"

"It's probably not, but—"

"*Probably* not?" she echoed.

"Okay, it's not," he relented. "I just didn't think, after the way you kissed me a few weeks back, that you were dating anyone else."

"It was one kiss—"

"Two," he interjected.

"And the only way I could be dating 'anyone else' would be if we were dating, and we're not," she pointed out.

"So who is this guy you *are* dating?"

"You're not my big brother, so don't start acting like you are."

"I'd say it's lucky for both of us that I'm not," he noted.

"I'll see you at two o'clock tomorrow," she said.

After she'd disconnected the call, Spencer sat staring at the phone for a long minute, an uneasy feeling churning in his gut.

It never occurred to Kenzie to say "no" when Spencer asked for a favor—especially if that favor involved his daughter. She absolutely adored the little girl and loved spending time with her. As Dani began to emerge from her shell, she showed glimpses of sass and spirit that Kenzie couldn't help but admire. And as the bond between father and daughter, tentative and fragile at first, grew surer and stronger, Kenzie was overjoyed for both of them—and perhaps just the tiniest bit envious.

She knew there were a lot of kids who grew up in single-parent homes, and she was grateful to her mother for everything she'd done to give her a good life. For as long as Kenzie could remember, Cheryl had worked as a housekeeper at Dusty Boots Motel. There weren't a lot of jobs available to a woman with only a high school diploma and, as she'd explained to her daughter, she had to do something to pay the bills and put food on the table.

She called it "hard but honest work" and prided herself

on being capable and reliable. Her work ethic was rewarded by her employer, who allowed Cheryl to rearrange her work schedule whenever necessary to ensure that she was able to attend school meetings, chaperone class trips or participate in other events with Kenzie—to be both a mother *and* a father to her daughter as much as possible.

And sometimes, when there was a day off school, Cheryl would implement a take-your-child-to-work day, sharing her tip money if Kenzie didn't grumble too much about helping to empty wastebaskets and strip beds at the motel. In fact, Kenzie remembered one time when she was eleven years old and had been diligently saving her every penny for…her mind blanked, forcing her to acknowledge that whatever it was her tween self had been absolutely certain she couldn't live without was, twelve years later, completely insignificant. What she did remember was that she'd worked really hard that weekend, and Cheryl had rewarded her efforts by giving her all of the tips they'd earned.

But while Kenzie was undeniably grateful to her mother for everything she'd done for her, the absence of a father was still a huge void—like one of those character-shaped holes that resulted when someone ran through a wall in a cartoon—that nothing else seemed to fill. Or maybe it was Cheryl's adamant refusal to talk about the man who'd fathered her child that ensured the emptiness remained. It wasn't just that Kenzie didn't know her dad—she knew *nothing* about him. It was as though he'd never really existed.

So she was glad for Dani that Spencer had stepped up to at least try to fill the hole created by the loss of her mother. And happier still that he didn't shy away from talking to Dani about Emily. Although, as he'd confided to Kenzie, he hadn't known Emily particularly well or for very long, he was happy to share what he knew to answer his daughter's questions.

The little girl was napping when Kenzie arrived at

Spencer's apartment Saturday afternoon, having crashed—he informed her—about half an hour earlier. But he tiptoed into her room to check on her before he left and bent down to brush a soft kiss to her cheek. It was an easy and natural gesture, as if he'd already done the same thing a thousand times, and Kenzie thought the complete lack of self-consciousness said a lot about the genuineness of his affection for the daughter he'd only known a short while.

"Do you want a goodbye kiss, too?" he teased, when he saw that she was watching from the doorway.

More than she wanted to breathe.

But she'd learned the hard way that wanting anything from Spencer was only an invitation to heartbreak.

She shook her head. "I want you to go—and I don't want you to be late getting back because I need time to make myself irresistible for my date."

He paused on his way to the door to give her a critical once-over. "You know, I can probably do this another day."

The implication, of course, being that she would need every minute left in the day to make herself appealing.

She pointed to the door. "Get out."

He was grinning as he reached for the handle.

Then he paused again. "Oh, one more thing."

She narrowed her gaze. "What?"

His teasing smile faded as he lifted a hand to stroke a finger along the line of her jaw. "You're already a knockout, Kenzie Atkins, and any guy who can't see that isn't worth your time."

And then he was gone, leaving her cursing his effortless ability to stir her up and make her want something she knew she couldn't have.

Since he had some time but he didn't have a supper plan and couldn't remember what was in his fridge, Spencer stopped at The Trading Post to pick up a few groceries on his way home.

"Sorry I'm late," he said, setting the grocery bags on the counter. "I ran into Beverly Clayton at the grocery store and had to ooh and ahh over all the babies before I could make an escape."

"Macy's triplets?"

He nodded.

"I heard she had the babies, but I haven't seen them yet," Kenzie admitted, obviously disappointed that he'd done so first.

"According to the proud grandma, today was their first outing—aside from check-ups with their pediatrician." He started to unpack his groceries. "So how was your afternoon?"

"We had a great time," Kenzie said. "We walked over to the park so Dani could play on the climber and the swings. There were a few other kids of a similar age there, too— kids she'd go to school with...if you're still here when it's time for her to go to school."

He flashed her a quick smile as he retrieved a big pot from the cupboard and filled it with water, then set it on the back burner of the stove. "You should bait your hook if you wanna go fishing."

"I'm not fishing," she denied, though they both knew she'd been doing exactly that. And since he wasn't taking the bait— "Did you know that Ashleigh has a daughter just a few months older than Dani?"

"Who?" he asked, feigning ignorance.

Kenzie rolled her eyes. "You're kidding, right?"

He washed his hands, then opened the package of ground beef and dumped it into a bowl.

"Ashleigh Singer was one of your many high school girl-friends. Beautiful, blonde, built."

The girlfriend he'd planned to meet in the hayloft the night Kenzie had been there instead.

Of course, she didn't say that aloud, but the flush in her cheeks confirmed that she was remembering the same thing.

"Oh, you mean Easy Ashleigh."

"Easy Peasy," Dani chimed in.

Spencer choked on a laugh.

"Of course, she goes by Hutchinson now," Kenzie told him.

He added a dash of salt and pepper, a handful of onion flakes and a few shakes of Italian seasoning, then mixed it all together. "She didn't marry Matt Hutchinson?" he asked, referring to the man who was a good friend and business partner of his brother.

"No, Matt's brother, Chance—the firefighter."

Dani moved closer, to see what he was doing. "Whatcha makin'?"

"Meatballs," Spencer told her.

Her eyes lit up. "For s'ghetti?"

He nodded.

"Yay!" She clapped her hands together. "S'ghetti an' meatballs!"

"Anyway, I gave Ashleigh your number so that she could call you to set up a playdate," Kenzie interjected.

He lifted his brows.

"For Dani and Paris," Kenzie clarified. "And before you get any ideas about anything else, try to remember that your ex-girlfriend is married to a man who knows how to wield an ax."

"I have no interest in anything else," he promised. Then he winked. "At least, not with Ashleigh."

"And on that note." Kenzie picked up her handbag from the counter, obviously intending to head out.

"Wait—aren't you going to stay and have pasta with us?"

"You know I can't."

"Oh, right," he said, as if he'd forgotten about her plans. "You have a date with...what was his name again?"

"None of your business."

"Right." He nodded. "Is 'None' his first name and 'Business' his last?"

"Good night, Spencer." She bent down to kiss the top of Dani's head. "Good night, Dani."

The little girl tipped her chin up and looked pleadingly at Kenzie. "Ke'zie, stay an' have s'ghetti."

She shook her head, though she at least looked tempted by his daughter's request—certainly more so than his own.

"I can't tonight, but I'll see you soon."

Dani pouted, obviously disappointed to be abandoned. Spencer knew just how she felt.

Her date's name was Jack Caldwell. He was a pediatrician who lived and worked in Battle Mountain, and a cousin of Jillian, the receptionist at Back in the Game, who'd set up the date.

Since he'd driven in from out of town, it made sense to eat in Haven, which meant eating at Diggers'. There were other options—Jo's for pizza or the Sunnyside Diner for all-day breakfast—but the grill side of Diggers' Bar & Grill was the most popular destination for couples on date night and, despite the casual décor, many of the residents would dress up as if they were going out to enjoy fine dining. Sure, the restaurant had a hostess rather than a maître d' and the wine list consisted of six lines on the back of the menu, but Kenzie was happy to eat there, confident that the food was always good.

She had high hopes for the evening when her date held her chair for her to be seated. He was handsome and well-mannered—and not just a doctor but one who specialized in caring for kids. She wondered how it was that he was still single.

Before she could find the words to ask him that question, she felt a vibration in the outside pocket of the handbag she'd hung over the back of her chair. As she laid her napkin in her lap, she surreptitiously slid her phone out of the bag and unlocked the screen to find a message from Spencer.

There's leftover pasta if your date is a bust.

She tucked the phone under her napkin.

"Can I get you started with something to drink?" Deanna asked.

Jack gestured to Kenzie.

"I'll have a glass of the merlot."

"The same," Jack decided.

The server nodded and slipped away to get their drinks.

"Do you eat here very often?" he asked Kenzie.

"At least once a week," she admitted.

"I should have taken you somewhere else," he said.

Her phone vibrated against her thigh. "No, this is fine."

"I just wasn't sure I'd feel up to driving here to pick you up, then somewhere else to eat, then back again," he said. "Especially after a day packed with sick kids battling some kind of virus that's going around the local elementary schools."

"This is fine," she said again, peeking at her phone.

But no ice cream. Dani ate it. ALL of it ☹

She felt a smile tug at her lips, because she knew how much the little girl loved ice cream. However, she wouldn't let herself be amused by the interruption. Spencer knew she was on a date and was obviously trying to sabotage her plans for a romantic evening.

But her fingers moved on the screen, as if of their own volition:

With sprinkles?

"This is my first ever blind date," Kenzie confessed, as she waited for her wine—and Spencer's response.

"Mine, too."

"Well, I know why I agreed to do this—Jillian couldn't say enough about her handsome and single cousin."

She stole another glance at her phone:

Lots of sprinkles.

"Technically, I'm not single... I'm divorced."

She blew out a relieved breath. "For a second, when you said you weren't single, I thought you were married."

"No, not married," he assured her. "My second divorce was finalized almost a year ago."

"*Second* divorce?"

Her phone silently signaled another message:

She wants Ke'zie to give her a bath.

"Yeah," he admitted. "Is that a problem for you?"

"No," she said, because she suspected it was the answer he wanted to hear, though not one that sounded very convincing. And then another thought occurred to her. "Any kids?"

He nodded. "An eight-year-old son with my first wife and a four-year-old daughter with my second."

Of course, his mention of a four-year-old daughter made her think of Dani. Was she really objecting to bath time? Even if she was, Kenzie had no doubt that Spencer would lure her into the tub with bubbles.

"Do you see them very often?" she asked.

"As often as I can," he told her.

Which somehow managed to sound both noble and vague.

"So where are your kids tonight?" she wondered.

Got her in the tub but she says she won't go to sleep until Ke'zie reads her a story.

"JJ, that's Jack Junior, has a youth group thing at the church this weekend. His mother—" he made air quotes with his fingers "—'found religion,' supposedly after we split up, and married the pastor six months later."

"And your daughter?" she prompted cautiously.

"Lexi has swimming lessons every Saturday night because her mom, who receives generous support so that she can be a stay-at-home mom to our daughter, always schedules extracurricular activities for the days that I'm supposed to be with Lexi."

"That must be difficult," Kenzie said sympathetically. Sure, he sounded a little bitter, but maybe he had reasons for dumping on his exes.

She picked The Going to Bed Book—again.

"Yeah," he agreed. "You'd think my ex-wives would understand that being a doctor means that emergencies sometimes interfere with my plans. Instead, they punish me for the rare occasions when I have to disappoint my kids because another child is sick or injured."

Kenzie was grateful to see the waitress returning with their drinks.

"Are you ready to order?" Deanna asked pleasantly.

"I haven't even had a chance to look at the menu," Jack confided. "I was in the mood for steak, but I'm not sure a place like this would offer the choicest cuts."

To her credit, Deanna's smile never faded.

"Our special tonight is the bison meat loaf, which has received favorable reviews," she told him. "It's served with a garlic potato mash and grilled asparagus."

"Meat loaf?" he said dubiously.

"It's very good," Kenzie said.

"All right then," he said. "I'll go with that."

"And for you?" Deanna asked her.

"The strip loin with whiskey-peppercorn sauce, medium, with the twice-baked potato and a house salad, please."

"I'll put your order in right away," the waitress promised.

She's cuddling the book and her blanket, waiting.

The mental image tugged at Kenzie's heart, making her wish that *she* was snuggled up with Dani now, instead of making conversation with a man she already knew would never be the father of her children. But Dani wasn't her child, either, and she couldn't let the little girl—or her daddy—manipulate her for their own purposes.

So resolved, she sent a quick response:

I'm a little busy right now.

"So…how about you?" Jack asked her now. "You ever been married?"

"No."

"Any kids?"

She shook her head. "No again."

"So who keeps texting you that you're stealing glances at your phone under the table?"

She felt her cheeks flush. "Just a friend. I'm sorry."

"Maybe you could tell your friend that you're on a date," he suggested.

"I can. I mean, I did," she said. "But he just had a question about something."

"Just one question?"

"Well, you know how sometimes an answer leads to more questions," she said.

"So you and this guy…" he let the thought trail off.

Kenzie shook her head. "No. Just a friend."

"A friend who keeps interrupting though he knows you're on a date," Jack pointed out.

"This is the last time," she promised, tapping a quick reply that said:

Unless there is blood or fire, I don't want to hear from you before tomorrow!

Then she set her phone on the table, so that Jack could see her turn it off, and so that even if there was blood or fire, Spencer would have to deal with it on his own.

Not that she was really worried about a major disaster. She had faith in Spencer's ability to keep his daughter safe and not burn down his apartment. But even as she chatted with her date and enjoyed her meal, she nevertheless found her mind wandering.

Spencer had taken to fatherhood with an aptitude that surprised her—and made her yearn. Yes, even at twenty-three, she knew that she wanted a family of her own some-day. Maybe because she'd never felt as if she had one growing up. Now that she was older, she could appreciate everything Cheryl had done to provide for her, but she'd always been aware of that empty space that should have been filled by a father.

Spending time with Spencer and Dani, she couldn't help but admire his dedication to his daughter. And that was what she wanted. Not Spencer, specifically—because she wasn't foolish enough to give her heart again to the man who had broken it once before—but a man like Spencer. A man devoted to his family.

Unfortunately, she didn't think Jack was that man. Maybe it wasn't fair to make snap judgments, but she didn't want to marry a man who'd already broken marriage vows—twice.

But even disregarding his two ex-wives and children, there really wasn't any chemistry between them. And considering how long it had been since she'd had sex, that was disappointing. Unless it was her unplanned but extended period of celibacy that was the reason for her lack of interest.

Maybe she just needed to be warmed up, like the modeling clay Dani liked to play with that became easier to shape the more it was manipulated.

And was she really comparing herself to a cold lump of clay? Suggesting that a man just needed to warm her up to mold her into an amenable sex partner? The absurdity of the comparison made her smile and, giving her head a mental shake, she refocused her attention on her dinner companion.

"Dessert?" Jack nudged the menu toward her.

"Oh. No, thanks."

"Coffee or tea?" Deanna asked.

She shook her head.

"Just the check then," he told the server, who nodded and hurried off to do his bidding. Then to Kenzie, "Maybe we could head back to my place tonight? I've got early rounds in the morning, so it would be more convenient to spend the night close to the hospital."

It took Kenzie, whose attention was still split between the man seated across from her and the little girl who might or might not be sleeping across town, a minute to realize what he was suggesting. And when she did, she was taken aback by his audacity. "Look, Jack, I don't know what Jillian told you about me, but I'm not the type of girl who goes home with a guy after a first date."

"She didn't tell me that you were." He punctuated the assurance with a smile that had undoubtedly persuaded a lot of other women to do just that. "I'm just an eternal optimist."

"I did have a good time tonight," she told him, because he was Jillian's cousin and she didn't want to create any tension with her colleague by completely blowing him off.

"So maybe we can do it again sometime?" The illegible signature he scrawled on the credit card slip attested to his occupation.

"Maybe." She offered the noncommittal response as he helped her on with her coat. And though she mentally awarded him bonus points for that, they weren't enough to make up for the fact that he'd insulted the food before even tasting it.

She wanted to be attracted to him. He was a good-looking man, nicely built, obviously intelligent and successful. And Cheryl had been thrilled to hear that her daughter was going on a date with a doctor—a tantalizing tidbit that Kenzie had thrown into their recent conversation when her mother started to get on her case about spending too much time with Spencer and his little girl. But despite Jack's numerous and impressive attributes, there was just no sizzle between them.

"Thanks for dinner," she said, when he walked her to her door. "And my apologies, again, for all the interruptions."

"Is your phone still off?" he asked.

She nodded.

"Good," he said, then leaned in to kiss her.

Though she didn't think she'd given him any signs that this was a direction she wanted to go, she decided to test her theory. She let her eyes drift shut and hoped that kissing Jack would be the catalyst to start the sparks flying.

His lips were firm and confident as they moved over hers, and while it was a pleasant enough kiss, it wasn't anything more than that. Then his hands slid down her back and over the curve of her butt, his fingers kneading her flesh. And with the modeling clay analogy still in her head, she wanted to giggle.

Thankfully, she managed to stifle the instinct and settled for pulling away. "Good night, Jack."

"You're not going to invite me in?" He sounded surprised.

"Didn't we have this conversation at the restaurant?"

He shrugged, smiled. "Eternal optimist."

"Good night," she said again.

"Good night."

She unlocked the exterior door, then stood inside the foyer and watched him walk back to his car.

After three hours in a body-hugging dress and killer

heels, she was only one flight of stairs away from the comfort of her favorite pj's and bare feet.

Instead of climbing those stairs, she stayed where she was until Jack's Mercedes had driven away. Then she stepped outside again and got into her own vehicle.

As she pulled out of the parking lot, she acknowledged that she was probably making a big mistake—but she couldn't seem to help herself where Spencer Channing was concerned.

Chapter Eleven

Spencer was scrolling through the channel guide on TV when his phone beeped with a new text message from Kenzie.

Is Dani still awake?

No, he immediately replied. She finally crashed about half an hour ago.

Then he asked, Are you home from your date?

No.

Then why are you texting me?

Because I'm standing outside your apartment.

His only reply to that was to open the door.

She unbuttoned her coat as she stepped over the threshold, then shrugged it off and tossed it over the arm of the sofa.

His eyes nearly popped out of his head and his jaw hit the floor.

She was wearing a dress the color of ripe eggplant, with long sleeves and a very short skirt. In between, the fabric hugged her curves like a lover's hands, and below the hem of that short skirt—*wow*.

How had he never noticed that she had such great legs?

Maybe because he couldn't ever remember seeing her in a dress before. And it irked him to know that she'd put on that dress to go out for dinner with another man.

His irritation was slightly tempered by the realization that she wasn't with any other man now. Instead, she was here with him—and with fury and frustration rolling off her in waves.

"Are you here to yell at me in person?" he asked, a little warily.

She shook her head, and the big, loose curls she'd put in her hair swayed with the motion. Her soft gray eyes were enhanced by smoky shadow on the lids and mascara on her lashes. Her lips were naturally pink, sweet and tempting.

He scowled. Fancy hair. Fancy dress. Fancy shoes that added enough inches to her height that her mouth was almost level with his own. Which was probably something he shouldn't be thinking about now, because she hadn't gone to all this effort for him. No, she'd done it for some guy whose name she wouldn't even tell him. Apparently someone who really mattered to her.

He felt a slight twinge of guilt, considering that he might have spoiled her evening with his playful text messages. But only a slight twinge, because if she really hadn't wanted to be disturbed, she could have silenced her phone and ignored the messages.

And then even that twinge was gone, as he acknowledged that even if he had messed up her night, he wasn't sorry.

Because he didn't want her hooking up with some guy—unless that guy was him.

But he probably did owe her an apology of sorts. Or at least an explanation.

"I can understand why you might be upset," he began, "but—"

"Just shut up for a minute."

Not only angry, he realized, but frustrated and…something else he couldn't quite pinpoint.

"I'm trying to expl—"

Since he apparently wouldn't obey her instructions, she shut him up by pressing her mouth to his.

He'd spent a fair amount of time perfecting his moves over the years—and he knew that he had some pretty good ones. He also liked to be the one to make the moves and considered pushy women to be a major turnoff.

Until now.

Until Kenzie moved in, tipped her chin up and settled her soft, sweet lips against his.

Definitely *not* a turnoff.

She lifted her arms to his shoulders, her fingers sliding into his hair, nails gently scraping his scalp.

Her tongue swept along the seam of his lips, a silent request. He welcomed the deepening of the kiss, wrapping his arms around her, anchoring her body against his. Breasts to chest, thigh to thigh and other good stuff in between.

When she finally eased her lips from his, they were both breathless.

As oxygen slowly made its way to his brain, he had a vague thought that he should maybe let her go.

But he didn't want to.

"That was…um…"

She looked at him, her eyes wide with awareness and arousal, her lips moist and swollen from their kiss, and his mind went blank.

At a loss for words, he decided the only appropriate response was to kiss her again.

He'd been keeping a tight leash on his desire for weeks, for a lot of reasons. Of course, Dani was the biggest one. He was no longer a freewheeling bachelor—he was a dad now. Taking on the responsibilities of a child had required some major lifestyle changes. Changes he'd happily made for his daughter. He had responsibilities to Dani, not the least of which was to be a good example.

And he thought he was doing a decent job as a parent. Sure they'd hit some bumps in the road, but so far, they'd negotiated the journey without any major mishaps. Keeping up with his daughter usually kept him busy from morning till night. But there were a lot of long, empty hours after Dani was tucked into bed that he found himself thinking about various and interesting ways he might fill that time. Most of those ways involved sex.

He missed sex. Not just the physical act of coupling but everything that went along with it. The initial attraction, the rise of anticipation, the slow dance of seduction and finally the culmination of a woman's warm, naked body entwined with his own.

Yeah, he *definitely* missed sex. But the bigger dilemma was that lately he hadn't been thinking about sex in the abstract but sex with Kenzie. Since his return to Haven, she was the only woman he wanted.

And the way she was kissing him back right now, he was pretty sure she wanted him, too.

But then, just when he'd located the pull of the zipper at the back of her dress, she tore her lips from his and pushed at his chest with both hands.

"Damn you, Spencer Channing."

He took a minute to drag air into his lungs—and try to figure out what he'd done wrong that had caused her to shift from hot to cold in the blink of an eye. But if there was a man who understood the workings of a woman's mind, it sure as hell wasn't him. So he gave up trying and simply asked, "Why are you mad now?"

"Because I didn't want to feel anything when you kissed me."

Now he was truly baffled. "Huh?"

She huffed out a frustrated breath. "I was hoping it was just me," she continued her nonsensical explanation. "That I was tired and cranky and not in the mood to feel anything."

"I'm starting to see the cranky part," he said, trying to tease a smile out of her.

It worked. Kind of.

Her lips curved a little, then her expression grew somber again and she sighed. "It was probably a mistake from the beginning. I never should have agreed to go out with him."

"This is about Mr. None-of-My-Business," he realized.

"Actually, it's *Dr.* None-of-Your-Business."

"Ah, so that's why you agreed to go out with him."

"It is not," she denied.

He lifted his brows, conveying his skepticism.

"I went out with him because—" she began, then shook her head. "It doesn't matter. The point is, I was only going through the motions. And when Jack kissed me—"

He held up his hands to stop her. "I really don't want the details."

"It was…nice," she told him anyway.

"Nice?" he echoed, trying to decipher what she was saying.

"Not unpleasant, but nothing that would melt a girl's panties. Or at least not mine."

"Well, that's good then," he said gruffly, finding a measure of satisfaction in the fact that she'd left the other man to come to him.

"No, it's *not* good," she denied. "I want heat and passion. I want to be overcome by lustful thoughts and feelings.

"Of course, I want a guy that I can have a conversation with, too," she allowed. "But when we've finished talking, when he leans in and makes his move, I want his kiss to make my toes curl and my nether regions tingle."

Nether regions?

Though his brows lifted at her use of the euphemistic term, he didn't comment, because he was happy to listen to her lament the lack of chemistry she'd shared with her dinner companion.

"Is that too much to ask?" she demanded.

"Of course it's not too much to ask," he said magnanimously, smug in the knowledge that the chemistry between him and Kenzie was off-the-charts sizzling.

Her sigh was filled with weariness and frustration. "I just want a man who can make me feel the way I feel when I'm with you."

"Um…hello?" he said, gesturing to himself.

"No. You and me—" she shook her head "—not a good idea."

"Why not?" he demanded. "Obviously we've got the heat and passion thing covered."

"Because I want more than heat and passion," she told him.

And they both knew he wasn't in a position to offer anything more than that right now—and that he wouldn't likely offer more even if he could.

But he stared at the back of the door after she'd gone and found himself wishing, perhaps for the first time, that maybe he could.

The following Saturday morning, after another visit with Helen Powell that included an update on all the latest plot twists and romantic escapades of *The Light of Dawn*, a text came through as Kenzie was on her way out.

Instead of replying to Spencer's message, she crossed the hall and knocked on his door.

It was the first time she'd been to his apartment since the night she'd driven across town for the sole purpose of planting her lips on his. More than a week later, the memory of that kiss still made her lips tingle.

So while she'd continued to spend time with Spencer and Dani—meeting them at the library or hanging out at the park—she'd avoided returning to the scene of the crime, such as it was. But she was no longer worried about a relapse, because sufficient time had passed that she was able to look back with some perspective. It had been late that night, and she'd been feeling lonely after a promising date turned out to be a dud, and none of those factors existed now.

Not to mention that she could always count on Dani to serve as a buffer to the sexual attraction that simmered between the adults in the room. There was nothing like the presence of a curious child to keep wayward hormones in check.

"You were visiting Mrs. Powell," he guessed, when he opened the door in response to her knock.

"I was," she confirmed.

He grinned. "Did she share her theory about Lorelei's affair with Stefano?"

"Don't tell me she's got you hooked on *The Light of Dawn* now," she chided.

"She watches Dani for me when I have therapy, and we sometimes chat about the plotlines afterward."

"Is the therapy working?"

He nodded. "I'm not nearly as stiff as I used to be," he said, then he grinned again. "Not in my shoulder, anyway."

She rolled her eyes at the innuendo.

"So do you think it was Lorelei or her evil twin in Stefano's bed?" he asked her. "Because I think it was both."

Kenzie laughed. "Of course you do. That's every man's fantasy, isn't it?"

"I don't know," he said. "Lately my fantasies have centered on only one woman."

"Yeah, not going there," she reminded him.

"Okay, how about going to Crooked Creek instead?"

She was surprised—and maybe the teensiest bit disappointed—that he dropped the subject of his fantasies so readily. Yes, she was the one who'd put on the brakes. And she was grateful that he'd respected her wishes. But it might have been nice if he'd at least faked disappointment at being shut down.

"Was this Dani's idea?" she asked, aware that since Spencer's grandfather had started giving the little girl riding lessons, she asked to go out to the ranch every five minutes.

"Actually, Dani's not here," he admitted.

"Where is she?"

"With Linda."

"The jet-setting Nana is back?"

He chuckled at the nickname. "Yeah. She and her new husband returned from Europe a few days ago and wanted to spend the weekend with Dani."

The "husband" revelation didn't factor into Kenzie's response—her only thoughts were of the little girl. "They took her for the whole weekend?"

"Well, they picked her up early this morning and are bringing her back tomorrow afternoon."

"And now you've got all kinds of free time on your hands and no idea how to fill it," she realized.

"I do have an idea," he reminded her. "I'm going to head over to Crooked Creek Ranch and saddle up a horse."

"That does sound like fun," she agreed.

"It would be even more fun if you came with me."

"I haven't been to the ranch in…five years," she realized.

"Since Brie left?" he guessed.

She nodded.

"So what do you say?" he prompted. "We'll take a picnic lunch and go for a nice long ride."

"I just told you that I haven't been on a horse in five years. I'm not sure a long ride would be nice—or advisable."

"Just a ride then," he said.

She was tempted, but, "Didn't the forecast warn of a storm this afternoon?"

"Does that look like a stormy sky?" he asked, gesturing to the expanse of cloudless blue visible through the window.

No, it didn't. In fact, it looked like an incredible day. The type of day that inspired one to get out and breathe in the brisk autumn air.

"Domino could use a good workout," he cajoled, playing a trump card with the mention of Brielle's gelding.

Kenzie felt herself weakening. "Has anyone ever told you that you don't play fair?"

"I play to win," he told her.

"And that's why I don't play games with you," she said.

Not to mention that Spencer Channing was way out of her league. Maybe it wasn't as painfully obvious now as it had been when she was sixteen, but it was still true.

"Okay, forget the games," he suggested. "And come for the ride."

She wanted to say yes. She wanted to spend the afternoon out at the ranch with him. But being around Spencer wasn't just stirring up old feelings again—it was creating new ones. Deeper and more dangerous feelings.

At sixteen, she'd believed herself in love with him. But she'd hardly known him back then—certainly not well enough to really love him. And the truth was, if she'd known him better, she'd have recognized that he was spoiled, selfish and self-centered, and she probably wouldn't even have *liked* him.

He'd changed a lot in the time that he'd been away. Or maybe since he'd come back to Haven. He'd be the first to admit that discovering he was a dad had changed him in all the very best ways. The one thing that hadn't changed? He was still the sexiest man she'd ever laid eyes on.

Watching that strong, sexy man with his adorable daughter, being witness to the patience and gentleness and affection he displayed in his interactions with the little girl, only made him more appealing. And the more time she spent with Spencer and Dani, the more she realized that she didn't want to be an observer of the family they were building together—she wanted to be a part of it.

But that was a dangerous desire. Personal experience had taught her that relationships were fragile and that counting on others was a shortcut to heartache.

It was a lesson she'd learned when Spencer left town seven years earlier—and a lesson that had been reinforced by her short-lived romance with Brandon and her ill-advised engagement to Dale and a few other dalliances in between. Not that she'd been devastated or traumatized by any such involvement, but she'd been abandoned by her father before she was even born, and each subsequent experience had added to her distrust.

But Spencer was proposing a horseback ride not a relationship, so she pushed her worries aside and said, "Okay, but if I end up with a bruised butt—"

"I'll kiss it better for you," he promised.

"Are you seriously offering to kiss my ass?"

"I'll kiss anything you'll let me kiss," he assured her.

"Then you'll be kissing nothing," she said firmly.

He just grinned.

She decided it would be wise to refocus the conversation on his proposed outing. "Can you give me half an hour to run home and change?" She glanced at her watch. "I'll meet you back here at noon."

"I'll give you twenty minutes and pick you up on the way."

Spencer had called ahead to the ranch and asked his grandfather to saddle up Domino and Copper Penny, and the horses were both tacked and ready when they arrived.

"Who's this pretty lady?" Kenzie asked, stroking the long nose of the chestnut mare that had trotted over to the fence upon their arrival.

"That's Copper Penny," he told her. "She belonged to Dani's mom."

"And now to Dani?" she guessed.

"Technically," he agreed. "But she's a lot of horse for a little girl, so Gramps borrowed a little Welsh Mountain pony named Daisy from a friend so that she can learn on a mount more suitable to her size. I don't know if she'd been on the back of a horse before Gramps put her in the saddle, but he insists that she's a natural."

"That's not surprising," Kenzie said. "Considering her mom was a successful barrel racer and her dad a champion bull rider, it's probably coded in her DNA."

"It might be," Spencer agreed.

Though he kept his tone light, the casual reference to genetics weighed heavily on his heart. Because only a few days after he'd crossed paths with Brett and Gage at Jo's, Dani had complained of an earache. Hating to see her in any kind of distress, he'd immediately whisked her off to the doctor to have it checked out. While there, Spencer had impulsively inquired about paternity testing. After a few more questions had been asked and answered, the doctor had swabbed both his and Dani's cheeks.

The procedure had been quick and painless; the waiting for results anything but. The doctor had cautioned that it might take several weeks for the lab report to come back, so Spencer had put the test out of his mind. Mostly.

The more time he spent with Dani, the deeper his conviction that she was his daughter. Now he wished he'd never let his friends bait him into thinking he needed to have the test done—and he felt ashamed that he'd done it.

"Hey, there, Domino." Kenzie turned as her friend's gelding, with the glossy black coat and white star and socks, came over to the fence to nudge her shoulder. "Do you remember me?"

The horse rubbed his cheek against hers, as if in response to her question, and she laughed. "It's been a long time, hasn't it?"

"Too long," a gruff voice said from behind them. "Thought you'd forgotten how to get here."

She turned to face Spencer's grandfather. "It's good to see you, Mr. Blake."

He nodded an acknowledgment of her greeting before turning to Spencer to warn, "It's gonna storm."

"There's barely a cloud in the sky," he protested.

Because in the time it had taken them to drive to the ranch, a few clouds had formed, but they were fluffy and white and completely innocuous-looking.

"Forget the sky—I can feel it in my bones," Gramps said.

"We'll keep an eye on the weather," Spencer promised.

"See that you do."

And then, with a tip of his hat to Kenzie, his grandfather wandered back into the barn.

"You ready to do this?" Spencer asked.

"Why not?" Kenzie agreed.

He gave her a leg up, and she settled into the saddle to guide Domino around the corral, getting accustomed to the feel of the horse beneath her. He kept an eye on her progress as he tied the saddle bags onto Copper Penny, pleased to note that Domino easily followed Kenzie's commands, smoothly accelerating from a walk to a trot to a canter.

Satisfied with her control of the animal—or at least Domino's manners and self-restraint—he mounted Copper Penny and started away from the barn. They rode across open fields toward the mountains that speared up in the distance, following the creek for which the ranch was named.

After a rainfall, the water would gurgle and bubble as it rushed over the rocks. But this was the desert and there hadn't been rain in a while, so the banks were dry, the creek now not much more than a trickle.

The chill in the air warned of winter just around the corner, but the sun was shining as they made their way toward the valley that Spencer had decided would be the ideal place to break for lunch.

"What's on the menu?" Kenzie asked, as she spread the blanket over the grass.

"Ham-and-cheese sandwiches, apple slices and chocolate chip cookies," he identified each of the items as he unpacked them from the saddlebags.

"Sounds yummy."

"And wine," he added, pulling a bottle of merlot from the bottom of the bag.

"Good choice."

"I asked Alyssa what you usually drink when you're at the bar," he admitted.

"A question that seems to imply I spend a lot of time 'at the bar,'" she remarked.

He chuckled. "Well, in Haven, it's really the only place to go."

He piled the food in the center of the blanket, before stretching out on it himself. He folded his hands behind his head and looked up at the blue sky dotted now with a few more clouds.

"This was a good idea," Kenzie told him.

"I have them on occasion," he said.

"Another good idea would have been a corkscrew," she teased.

He took the bottle from her hand, looked at the seal and swore.

"You're not usually a wine drinker, are you?"

"Not usually," he admitted.

But he also wasn't a man to admit defeat.

He sat up and rummaged through his bag until he came up with a Swiss Army knife. It wasn't a fancy one with all the bells and whistles—or a corkscrew—but it had a decent blade that worked well enough to score the foil so he could peel it away, then he stabbed it into the cork so that he had some leverage to turn and twist and pry. The cork was halfway out of the bottle when it broke.

"Don't worry about it," Kenzie said. "I'm not very thirsty anyway."

But having tasted a modicum of success, he couldn't give up.

"I've got this," he promised, yanking the broken cork from the blade before resuming his attack on the piece that remained stuck in the bottle. This time, the blade pushed right through the cork.

Kenzie opened the bag of fruit and munched on an apple slice while she watched him struggle. It was tedious work—the cork would wiggle a little, then the blade would start to slip. So he'd push it in again, twisting a little to gain traction, and wiggle the cork some more.

"Ta-da!" he said, as he finally managed to pull what was left of the cork free.

Her eyes twinkled mischievously as she took the bottle he offered, then slayed his sense of accomplishment with a single word: "Glasses?"

Chapter Twelve

Spencer huffed out a breath. "Isn't it just like a woman to never be satisfied?"

"Is that a frequent problem for you?" Kenzie asked, with wide-eyed innocence and feigned sympathy. "Not being able to satisfy a woman?"

His eyes locked on hers then, and there was so much heat in his gaze, she felt singed.

"Not in the bedroom," he assured her. "Or pretty much anywhere else with a horizontal surface." Then he tapped his finger to his chin, as if thinking. "Actually, I've never had any complaints about my vertical performance, either."

Of course, now her brain was imagining all those various scenarios, making her blood rush hot and fast in her veins. Obviously it had been a mistake to start the teasing, because he was way out of her league.

"So I guess I misspoke," he continued now. "Because the only grumbling I've ever heard was about the fact that I forgot to pack glasses."

"And a corkscrew," she felt compelled to remind him.

"I got the cork out of the bottle, didn't I?" he asked, tossing a sandwich into her lap.

Kenzie peered into the bottle, where tiny bits floated on top of the wine. "Mostly."

But she lifted the bottle to her lips, sipped.

Spencer, having already devoured half his sandwich, reached for the bottle. But he held it for a moment, his thoughts appearing to be a thousand miles away.

"You know, it's okay to admit that you're worried."

"I'm not worried." He swigged a mouthful of wine. "A little bit of cork never killed anyone."

She nibbled on her sandwich. "I mean about Dani."

"Why would I be worried about Dani?"

"C'mon," she said. "It must have crossed your mind when Linda came home from her trip and immediately wanted to spend the weekend with her granddaughter that she'd missed Dani and might have changed her mind about not fighting for custody."

"Maybe it did," he acknowledged. "But Emily chose me as Dani's guardian, and I think Linda—and the courts— will respect that."

"You're really not worried?"

He sighed. "I'm more worried that Emily might have chosen wrong. That maybe Dani would be better off with her grandmother."

"The woman who chose her boyfriend over her grieving grandchild?" she asked dryly.

"Well, when you put it like that."

Kenzie gave his arm a reassuring squeeze. "Emily made the right decision—Dani should be with her father."

"But what if…" Spencer began.

"What if what?" Kenzie prompted.

"What if she—" He shook his head. "What if *I* can't do this on my own?"

"You don't have to. You've got family and friends to lend a hand when you need it."

"What if I want to keep riding bulls?" He threw the idea out there like a header tossing a lasso at a steer.

She chewed another bite of sandwich. "Do you?"

He shrugged. "I always figured I'd do it until I was at least thirty. By then, I might have been ready to think about settling down with a wife and starting a family."

"Life doesn't always work out the way we planned," she said philosophically.

"You're telling me."

"So revise your plan," she suggested.

"Haven't I done that already?"

"I don't know if you have or if this is only a temporary detour while you figure out how to get your life back on track again."

"How's your butt?" he asked, in a not-at-all-subtle effort to shift the topic of conversation.

She rubbed a hand over her bottom, as if to check. "Right now, it's a little numb," she admitted. "But not too bad, considering."

"I knew your riding skills would come back to you."

"I guess I did remember most of the basics," she agreed. "But I was even more surprised that Domino seemed to remember me."

"Of course, he remembered you," Spencer said. "You're not a woman anyone—man or beast—could easily forget."

She scoffed at that as she finished her sandwich.

"You don't think I thought about you when I was gone?" he asked.

"I hope not," she said. "Or, if you did, I hope it wasn't about the last time you saw me."

"You mean when you offered your virginity up as a going-away present?"

Seven years later, the memories of that night still made her cheeks burn. She averted her face, looking toward the nearby tree where the horses were tethered, so he wouldn't see her shame.

Spencer gently nudged his shoulder against hers. "I'm sorry—that was crude and unnecessary."

"But not untrue," she acknowledged ruefully. "I would have given you anything and everything you wanted that night."

"It's probably a good thing I didn't know that then," he told her.

"I'm sure you knew. *Everyone* knew I had a desperate crush on you."

He didn't deny it. "Well, I'm glad, for your sake, that I didn't take everything you were offering."

"And I'm glad you were kind in your rejection," she told him.

"I don't recall being particularly kind," he admitted. "In fact, the way I remember it, I was kind of cruel."

"You weren't," she denied. "You tolerated my sloppy kisses and clumsy groping, even though it was obvious you didn't want me."

He seemed taken aback by that statement. "You think I didn't want you?"

"I *know* you didn't want me," she admitted.

"How could you possibly know something like that?" he challenged.

"It was obvious in the way you pushed me away."

He shook his head. "You really were an innocent, weren't you?"

"You know I was."

"Tell me, was it obvious in the way I kissed you that I didn't want you? Was it obvious when my hands were under your shirt and I was grinding against you?"

"I think I'd be happy to skip this trip down memory lane." Although now she was wondering if maybe her recollection of that night was perhaps a little faulty.

"I'd be happier to refresh your memory," he offered.

"Why don't we take a few steps back in this conversation and talk about this detour you're on?" she suggested instead.

He was silent for a moment, considering the request, before he finally responded. "Well, the original plan was to retire at age thirty—or when I was a ten-time PBR champion."

"You'd have to earn eight more championships in five years to retire at thirty," she noted.

He quirked a brow. "Someone's been following my career."

"Not on purpose," she said. "But you know how it is in town, the former Rookie of the Year wins a title and it's all anyone can talk about."

He smiled at that, then his expression turned serious. "I have a real chance for one more," he told her.

"I know."

"Might be my last chance."

She nodded.

"You don't think I should go to Vegas, do you?"

"It doesn't matter what *I* think," she told him.

"It matters to me," he said, and realized it was true.

She shook her head. "It's your call to make—no one else's."

"That doesn't stop everyone else from having an opinion," he noted.

"I'm sure it doesn't."

"My mom thinks riding bulls is dangerous and foolish."

"I wouldn't argue with the dangerous part."

"And my dad says I need to grow up and act like the father that I am."

"So…when do you leave?"

He chuckled softly. "Do you really think I'm so contrary?"

"I think it's normal to chafe against parental expectations," she told him.

"Did you chafe against yours?"

"My situation was a lot different than yours, because it

was always just me and my mom. I sometimes balked at her rules and restrictions, but I was more subtle about it."

"Give me an example of something you did that you know your mother wouldn't approve of."

"I smoked a cigarette once."

He gasped, as if horrified. "A whole cigarette?"

"No," she admitted, with a small smile. "Only a few puffs were enough to convince me I wasn't a smoker."

"I'm shocked."

"I also got drunk at my senior prom and told my mother it was because someone spiked the punch."

"Every year, someone spikes the punch at prom," he noted.

"But that year, the someone was me."

"No kidding? *You* spiked the punch?"

"No kidding," she confirmed.

"Anything else?"

"For the most part, I toed the line," she admitted. "And the only thing she really got on my case about were boys. I think I was twelve when Eric Vacca called to ask a question about an English assignment. Seriously, that was the only reason for the call, but after three minutes on the phone, I got a thirty-minute lecture about the debauched morals and lustful desires of the entire male species."

He chuckled.

"Sure, *you* can laugh. I went to school the next day and told Eric to never ever call me again."

"Did he?" Spencer wondered.

"Not until several years later, when I finally had a cell phone and my mother wasn't able to monitor all my calls and text messages."

"What would she say if she knew you were here with me now?"

"I don't know that she'd say anything, because she's said it all so many times before, she knows I just tune it out. But her mouth would thin with disapproval and her eyes would cloud over with all those unspoken worries and warnings."

"Maybe you should heed those warnings," he suggested, shifting closer on the blanket to brush his lips along her jaw.

The casual caress sent a sensual shiver down her spine, but she kept her tone light as she replied, "Because you just want to get into my pants?"

"It isn't *all* I want, but it's definitely on the list of my top ten desires." He nuzzled her throat—one of her top ten erogenous zones. "Top three."

"If you invited me to come out here today so that you could seduce me, you're going to be disappointed," she told him.

"How about a make-out session with some heavy petting?" he suggested.

She wondered how it was that he could make her want to laugh even while her body yearned for him desperately. "No."

"Just the making out?" He nibbled teasingly on her bottom lip. "I really love the taste of your mouth."

There were a thousand reasons that this was a bad idea. She was almost certain of it. But right now, with Spencer's mouth dawdling and dallying with hers, she couldn't seem to remember a single one.

And really, how bad could it be when it felt so good?

"Okay," she relented. "Maybe a little making out."

"Just a little," he agreed.

Then he covered her mouth with his own.

It was more than a kiss—it was an assault on all her senses, and Kenzie nearly whimpered in response to Spencer's complete and masterful seduction of her mouth. Or maybe she did, because he immediately took the kiss deeper.

His tongue skimmed over her lips, and dipped inside when they parted. She met it with her own, following his lead in a slow and sensual dance. Without knowing how it happened, she was suddenly beneath him on the blanket, his lean, hard body levered over hers as his mouth continued to tease and taste. Gradually the tenor of the kiss changed. It got hotter and hungrier, and maybe a little desperate— exactly how she felt for him.

She'd nixed the petting idea in their conversation, but she didn't protest when his hand slid from her hip, under the hem of her shirt, his callused palm creating delicious friction against her skin as it skimmed up her torso to her breast. And when his thumb brushed over the turgid peak through the delicate lace of her bra, she felt the rush of blood through her veins like molten lava, melting her bones, and she sighed with pleasure.

"Maybe a little petting," she allowed.

He chuckled softly against her lips as his thumb circled around her nipple.

Yes. Please. More.

Her hips instinctively lifted.

His unshaven jaw scraped against her tender skin as he kissed her throat.

He found the center clasp at the front of her bra and released it, then pushed back the cups, baring her breasts to his gaze, his hands, his mouth.

His hot, wet and oh-so-talented mouth.

She knew that her breasts were on the smallish side of average. As a result, they didn't get a lot of attention, even in intimate situations. Spencer was certainly remedying that now. His exploration was leisurely and thorough, and shifted from one aching peak to the other and back again. He nipped and nibbled, licked and suckled, until she was almost unbearably aroused.

She drew up her knees to bracket his hips and tilted her pelvis, wordlessly urging him closer.

He stilled, then lifted his head. "Was that—"

"What?"

The answer came in the form of a fat drop that hit her forehead and slid down her temple to disappear in her hair.

"—rain?" he finished.

But there was no longer any question that it was.

He swore and rolled off her, beginning to gather up the remnants of their picnic while she refastened her bra and tugged her shirt back into place.

What had started as sporadic drops quickly changed to a steady fall. By the time they were packed up and mounted on their horses again, it was a driving rain.

A *frigid* driving rain.

As if Mother Nature had decided they both needed a cold shower, and Kenzie shivered as water slid past the collar of her jacket and down the back of her shirt.

She instinctively turned her mount back in the direction from which they'd come, but Spencer caught her reins in one hand and gestured to the hills with his other. "The hunting cabin is just over that ridge."

She nodded and followed his lead, grateful not to undertake a thirty-minute ride back to barn in these conditions.

The cabin was less than five minutes away, but in only half that time, the icy rain had soaked through her denim jacket and jeans, chilling her to the bone.

Spencer told Kenzie where to find the key near the front door, then waited until she'd unlocked the cabin and ducked inside before leading the horses to their nearby shelter.

Though it was only midafternoon, the sky had gone dark. She looked around for a light switch, but found none. Apparently the cabin wasn't just rustic but primitive. She did, however, find a kerosene lamp on the counter by the sink—which suggested running water, at least—and a box of wooden matches. She picked up the box of matches, then decided that Spencer wouldn't be happy to come in and find she'd set the cabin on fire, and set it down again.

At least her eyes had started to adjust to the dimness of the interior, so she looked around for supplies—specifically towels and blankets. The offerings were scarce: a couple of clean but threadbare towels from under the sink in the tiny bathroom, a woolen blanket laid across the foot of the solitary cot tucked into the corner of the main room and another tossed over the back of an ancient sofa.

She removed her cross-body bag and her jacket, setting them both over the back of one of the mismatched chairs around a scarred wooden table. Her shirt was wet, too, and she was contemplating how to get dry without taking off her clothes when Spencer finally came in. Water poured off his hat when he hung it on a hook by the door. Then he dumped the saddlebags on the table and shrugged out of his coat.

Moving to the fireplace next, he opened the damper then selected logs from the stockpile, assembling them in the grate with an easy confidence that assured Kenzie he'd done this once or twice before. He topped off the stack of wood with paper and twigs and struck a match. In no time at all, the kindling was fully engaged, flames crackling and dancing.

"That should warm this place up in short order," he told her.

"I h-hope so."

His brows drew together. "You should get out of those wet clothes."

She nodded.

He yanked his boots off his feet, then quickly stripped out of his shirt and jeans, leaving him clad in only a pair of knit boxer briefs and wool socks. He should have looked ridiculous. To Kenzie, those long, muscled legs, taut abs, broad shoulders and strong arms were ridiculously tempting.

He scooped up the wet garments and laid them out on another one of the chairs that he moved closer to the fire to speed up the drying process. She quickly averted her gaze so that he wouldn't catch her staring.

He pulled the blanket off the back of the sofa and draped it over her shoulders. "Clothes off," he instructed firmly.

She might have made some joke about expecting a guy to buy her dinner before she got naked with him, but her teeth were clenched together to prevent them from chattering, so she only nodded.

He moved away—perhaps to give her some privacy—and busied himself tending to the fire. Not that it needed tending, judging by the tongues of flame that eagerly licked the dry wood. But her fingers were too cold to work the buttons of her shirt. When he turned around again, she'd only managed to release the first two.

Realizing it wasn't reticence but numbness that slowed her progress, he brushed her hands away and made quick work of the remaining buttons. He set another chair by the fire and draped her shirt over the back of it. She pulled the sides of the blanket together, to cover her pink lace bra.

"Jeans, too," Spencer told her.

She managed the snap and the zipper but struggled to get the damp denim over her hips. A task made even more difficult because she was pushing at her pants with only one hand while holding on to the blanket with the other.

He took pity on her again, working the fabric down her legs. Of course, he couldn't get the pants off with her boots on, and he gently nudged her down onto the sofa and knelt on the floor in front of her to relieve her of her footwear and then the jeans. His movements were brisk and efficient, but she was aware of the intimacy of their position and their near-nakedness, and a fire started to flicker low in her belly to rival the heat from the hearth.

He looked up at her. Though his face was mostly in shadow, their gazes met and held for a long moment. Then he abruptly stood up and turned away, busying himself by setting her clothes out alongside his own.

She pulled the blanket tighter around her body, but the coarse fabric felt scratchy against her bare skin and abraded her chilled nipples even through the lace of her bra.

He took her hand and drew her to her feet again, urging her closer to the fire. As the warmth of the flames began to penetrate the chill that enveloped her, she sighed in blissful relief.

He rubbed his hands up and down her arms, through the blanket, to increase the circulation of her blood and speed up the warming process. "Better?" he asked.

She nodded. "Much. Thanks."

"Well, that's the last time I'm going to disregard a weather warning from Gramps," he assured her.

"I didn't believe it, either," she said. "Until the sky got really dark really fast."

"I haven't been out here in so long, I almost forgot about the cabin," he admitted. "But I'm not surprised Gramps keeps it stocked for emergencies. There's enough wood to keep the fire going for days, a cupboard full of canned goods and a couple of jugs of water."

"Right now, I'd gladly trade a can of beans for a hair dryer," she told him.

"A hair dryer's pretty useless without electricity," he pointed out.

"True," she acknowledged, wrapping the towel around her braid so that she could squeeze some of the water out.

"Come here," he said.

She moved a tentative step closer. He uncurled her fingers from the towel and pulled it away from her hair. Then he tugged the elastic fastener from the end and began to separate the wet strands. His touch was gentle, and somehow intimate, as he worked his way toward her scalp, his fingers patiently combing through her hair to remove any tangles. When the braid was completely undone, he picked up the towel again and rubbed it over her head.

"Thanks."

"My pleasure," he said gruffly.

They were silent for a moment, each huddled in their respective blankets, watching the fire.

"Are you starting to thaw out yet?" he asked.

"I think so."

In fact, she was starting to feel very warm.

And unexpectedly bold.

For weeks now, the attraction had been simmering quietly in the background while they focused on other things—his daughter being the most obvious and important one. But now, there were no other things. No distractions. They were isolated here, a man and woman alone—and more than halfway to naked.

Maybe there were a thousand reasons she should huddle inside her blanket until the storm passed and their clothes were dry. But there was at least one compelling reason not to play it safe: she wanted him. And she suspected that if she wasted this opportunity, she'd spend another seven years wondering "what if?"

"There's probably whiskey in the cupboard," he said. "If you want something to help warm you from the inside."

"Let's try this instead," she suggested, and leaned closer to touch her mouth to his.

Just like that night in the hayloft, she made the first move. Unlike that night, this was a woman who knew what she wanted—and she wasn't shy about communicating it to him.

She let the blanket fall open, so that she could press herself against him. She wasn't quite naked, but the scraps of lace that covered her breasts and bottom were more seduction than substance, and Spencer was unable to prevent his body's instinctive response to her and—in his current state of undress—helpless to hide it. She pressed closer and rubbed playfully against him, leaving him in no doubt that she was aware of his arousal—and thrilled in it.

She parted his lips with her tongue, stroked the inside of his mouth with tantalizing little licks. At sixteen, she'd been shy about French kissing. She wasn't shy anymore. She was bold and hot and she completely stole his breath.

She continued to kiss him as she reached a hand between their bodies and stroked the hard length of him through his briefs, murmuring a low sound of approval as she traced his shape and size, from base to tip.

His eyes crossed with lust. "What are you doing, Kenzie?"

"You're a smart guy—I'm sure you can figure it out."

"I'm trying to figure out what's gotten into you," he admitted.

"I'm hoping—" she nipped playfully at his bottom lip "—it's going to be you."

His fingers encircled her wrist to remove her hand, because there was no way he could be expected to concentrate on conversation when she was touching him like that. "How much of that wine did you drink? Are you drunk?"

Her throaty laugh hit low in his belly. "No, Spencer, I'm not drunk." She nibbled the underside of his jaw, then drew the lobe of his ear into her mouth. "I just figured that, since we're both mostly naked anyway, we might as well take advantage of the situation."

"You said you didn't want this," he reminded her.

Reminded himself.

Because he'd always respected the word *no* and she'd said it loud and clear. Of course, she'd pretty much nullified that directive by sliding her tongue into his mouth, but still.

"I lied," she said, unapologetically.

"Why?" he cursed himself for asking the question.

Did it matter why?

Did anything matter except that she obviously wanted him as much as he wanted her?

"Because I didn't want to want it," she confided. "Because I should have stopped wanting you a long time ago. But I think I've wanted you, wanted this, since I saw you sitting on my massage table that first day."

He'd fought against wanting her. Wanting this. And it had been a losing battle from the start.

Still, he made one last-ditch effort to do the right thing.

"You also said that you wanted more than heat and passion," he recalled.

"I've decided that, for right now, heat and passion are enough."

It was all he'd ever wanted before. But he'd never been with a woman that he cared about as much as he cared about Kenzie, and he suspected the no-strings sex she was advocating wouldn't be enough—for either of them.

"So what do you say we agree to enjoy some fun and games together until it's time for you to ride off into the sunset again?" she suggested.

And then, in case the words weren't incentive enough, she dropped the blanket.

Chapter Thirteen

"I guess you're not cold anymore," he remarked inanely.

"I'm so cold I'm numb," she said, stepping closer so that her body brushed against his. "But I'm trusting you can warm me up."

"I'll do my best," he promised.

He held her gaze as he spread the blanket on the floor, close enough to absorb heat from the fire but not so close as to be in danger from any wayward sparks, then he slowly eased her down onto it.

Maybe he hadn't been waiting for this for seven years, but he wanted it now. Wanted her with an unexpected and intense hunger that might have worried him if he'd given it too much thought. But right now, he was more focused on doing than thinking.

He took his time removing her sexy underwear, exploring her body with his hands and his mouth, discovering her curves, savoring her sweetness. Her breasts were small and firm; her nipples rosy and erect. Irresistible. He lowered his head and took one of those nipples between his lips, drew it into his mouth and swirled his tongue around it. She sighed and moaned, telling him without words what she liked... and what she *really* liked.

Then she took his hand and guided it to where she wanted it—between her thighs. He would have made his way there eventually, but she was in a hurry. Demanding.

And damn but her impatience was incredibly arousing.

He parted the soft curls, the slick folds of skin. She was already wet, more than ready. His mouth shifted to her other breast as he continued his intimate exploration, circling the sensitive nub with his thumb as he dipped a finger inside. He suckled her nipple, groaned as she flooded his hand.

So much for taking it slow. Her eager response snapped the last restraint on his desire, and he slid lower, kissing and licking his way down her body, his own wants fueled by the soft, sexy sounds she was making. He tasted her wetness, her sweetness, his tongue lapping up her juices, drinking in the heady flavor of her arousal.

"Spencer...please."

It pleased him to please her, to watch and witness her undoing as she came apart in his arms. Passionately. Completely.

He started to shed his briefs, eager—almost desperate— to bury himself deep in the welcoming haven between her thighs. He just needed to reach into the nightstand—

He swore.

She blinked, confused by his sudden withdrawal. "What...where are you going? Don't you want to..."

"I want to," he assured her. "More than you can possibly imagine. But I don't have—" he huffed out a frustrated breath. "I didn't prepare for this to happen."

"Oh." She exhaled, sounding relieved. "If that's all...inside pocket of my bag."

He found her bag—and the promised condom. Actually, there was more than one little square packet in there, assuring him that they wouldn't get bored if the rain continued through the rest of the afternoon.

When he returned to the blanket, she rose up onto her knees to take the condom from his hand, carefully tearing it open and unrolling it over his rigid length.

Just like when he was eighteen, her touch nearly undid him.

Thankfully, he had more experience and stamina now, and he gritted his teeth and held on to the slippery thread of control.

Then she leaned back on the blanket and drew him down with her, her knees bracketing his hips, her mouth seeking and finding his.

"Now," she whispered against his lips.

He didn't make her wait any longer for what they both wanted.

In one smooth stroke, he was buried deep. He captured her mouth again, swallowing her blissful sigh, and began to move. Her arms wrapped around him, holding him close, holding on, as their bodies merged and mated, seeking and finding a rhythm that drove them both inexorably toward the pinnacle of pleasure.

His hands fisted in the blanket as he teetered on the brink, fighting for control. But she was already off-balance, starting to fall. And the rippling waves of her climax washed him over the edge right after her.

When he'd caught his breath and regained some strength, he gathered her close and rolled over, so that she was on top now, draped over him like a blanket. She tucked her head against his shoulder and exhaled another blissful sigh.

"Now that's what I call riding out a storm," Kenzie murmured, when her heart rate had slowed to something approximating normal.

Spencer chuckled softly, then touched his lips to hers in a kiss that was unexpectedly tender. "Are you okay?"

"Mmm," she agreed, because more words were too much

of an effort in her current state of complete and total relaxation.

"The floor's kind of hard, and I wasn't very gentle."

"I'm okay," she assured him. Truthfully, she felt better than okay, but she didn't figure his ego needed the boost of knowing how thoroughly and completely he'd rocked her world—especially since he'd been there every step of the way.

"Wanna do it again?" he asked.

The hopeful tone made her smile.

Again and again.

But she reminded herself to tread carefully. To remember that this wasn't a relationship and she shouldn't start envisioning happy-ever-after just because she'd experienced mind-blowing sex.

"It sounds like the rain's stopped," she noted. "Don't you think we should head back?"

Without disturbing her prone position, he reached his hand up to check the jeans hanging over the back of the chair by the fire. "Our clothes are still wet."

"Oh, well, in that case..."

He gave her that naughty smile that made the muscles in her thighs quiver.

A panty-melting smile, Jillian had called it.

Kenzie decided her coworker didn't know the half of it. But her panties had been discarded a long time ago, and she decided to take advantage of that fact.

Kenzie woke up early, snug and warm in Spencer's arms, in his bed.

She never would have guessed that he was a cuddler. Oh sure, most guys talked the talk and would willingly hold a girl for a few minutes after sex, but then they were all about wanting their space. And that was okay, because she'd never thought she was a cuddler, either.

And yet, she'd spent the entire night in Spencer's embrace.

Fun and games, she reminded herself. And only for the three weeks that remained of his stay in Haven.

No cuddling required or even desired.

With that thought in mind, she carefully disengaged herself from his hold and tiptoed to the bathroom.

Her body ached in places she hadn't even known existed. She might have been able to explain away some of the twinges as a consequence of the horseback ride, but she knew that many others were the sweet aches that resulted from a much more intimate form of exercise.

She had absolutely no regrets about anything that had happened between them, but now it was time to go back to her own place. Her own life. Reality.

It was only when she was dressed and ready to slip out the door that she remembered Spencer had picked her up on the way to Crooked Creek yesterday. Without her own transportation, she had two choices: doing a three-mile walk of shame or waking Spencer and asking him for a ride.

She decided to wake him. If she snuck out, he might think that she couldn't face him. But if she greeted him with an easy smile on her face, maybe she could assure him that last night hadn't meant anything more than the fun and games she'd promised both of them.

Of course, Spencer didn't seem to be in any hurry to take her home. He insisted on making breakfast first, to replenish all the calories they'd burned off the night before. While they fueled up with coffee, eggs and toast, Kenzie was surprised at how easy he made the morning after seem—no doubt because he had a lot of experience with mornings after. But she was still glad she hadn't snuck out.

Then somehow, while they were tidying up the kitchen, he presented his case in favor of morning sex, arguing that it was different than any other kind of sex. Kenzie didn't try to hide her skepticism, especially when he offered to give her a demonstration. It was an obvious ploy to get her back into his bed and she was smarter than that.

Then he kissed her, and she discovered that the knowledge in her brain was no match for the desires of her body. Ten minutes later, she was naked again, enjoying his patient and thorough demonstration. After that, there was a discussion about shower sex, followed by another demonstration.

"Tell me about your engagement," he suggested, when they were finally on their way to her apartment.

"Really?" she said skeptically. "You want to know about my relationship with Dale?"

He shrugged. "I'm curious about why you agreed to marry him—and why you changed your mind."

"How do you know *he* didn't end the engagement?"

"Did he?"

"No," she admitted.

"So what happened?"

"My mom and I went to look at bridal gowns and I realized that I was more excited about planning a wedding than the marriage that would come after."

"You don't want to get married?"

"I *do* want to get married," she confided. "But only if it's for the right reasons—and saying yes just to avoid hurting the feelings of the guy who asked didn't seem like the right reason."

"You weren't in love with Dale," he realized.

"I wanted to be, but—" She shook her head. "No, I wasn't in love with Dale."

"Then you're not still nursing a broken heart?"

"Definitely not." She turned her head to look at him. "How about you?"

"I can assure you that Dale didn't break my heart, either."

She smiled at that, but she wasn't willing to let him off the hook so easily. "Have you ever been in love?"

He shook his head. "I haven't stayed in one place long enough to get attached to any one person."

"It doesn't take long to fall in love with the right person," she told him, as he pulled into the parking lot behind her building.

"How would you know?" he challenged.

"Touché," she murmured, unbuckling her seatbelt.

Of course, Spencer insisted on seeing her up to her apartment. Then kissing her goodbye. And she'd barely closed the door behind him when a FaceTime request came through.

"Where were you yesterday?" Brielle asked, after they'd exchanged the usual pleasantries.

"Spencer invited me to go riding at Crooked Creek Ranch," she admitted.

Her friend sighed wistfully. "One of the things I miss most living in New York."

"For what it's worth, I think Domino misses you, too," Kenzie told her.

"I'm glad you got to spend some time with him."

"And he's got a couple of new friends to keep him company. Copper Penny, a former barrel racer, and Daisy, a pony your grandfather brought in for Dani's riding lessons."

"So how was the ride?" Brie asked.

"Great," she said. "Until we got caught in a storm and had to take shelter in the hunting cabin."

"That must have been a scary experience for Dani."

"Oh. Well, actually, she wasn't with us," Kenzie admitted.

Her friend was silent for a beat before asking, "It was just you and Spencer?"

"Uh-huh." She kept her tone casual and easy.

Move along, folks. Nothing to see here.

Unfortunately, Brie knew her better than that. "What else aren't you telling me?"

And because Kenzie didn't want to hold anything back

from her best friend, she confided, "I couldn't FaceTime when you called because I was mostly naked."

"You were at the hunting cabin—*mostly naked*—with my brother?"

"It was a torrential downpour and our clothes were soaked, so we were drying them by the fire," she explained meekly.

"This would be a good time to tell me that nothing happened, because my thoughts are moving in a very different direction."

"If that direction is naked bodies tangled together in front of the fire...it wouldn't be wrong," she confided.

"You had sex with my brother?"

Kenzie nodded. "And it was the most amaz—"

"No!" Brielle said. "There are some things that even a best friend doesn't need to know, especially when those things involve the best friend's brother."

"Sorry," Kenzie said, "but that's why I needed to tell you. I need some advice."

"Well, if you'd asked me before yesterday, my advice would have been to *not* sleep with my brother," Brie told her.

"And today?"

Her friend sighed. "Today, I guess all I can say is don't give him your heart—unless that warning's already too late, too."

"It's not," she promised.

Thankfully, Brielle seemed willing to believe her, and they chatted for a while longer about other things.

But when the call finally ended, Kenzie wondered if she'd been honest with her friend—or if she was lying even to herself.

When Spencer came back to Haven, she'd been certain that her teenage crush was a thing of the past. Maybe, when she first saw him, there had been a flutter of something, but she'd disregarded that something as purely physical attraction. She hadn't worried about her heart, because how could she have real feelings for a man she didn't even know anymore?

But spending time with Spencer and Dani had given her the opportunity to know him, and to realize that the man who'd returned bore little resemblance to the cocky cowboy who'd left Haven to find fame and fortune seven years earlier.

As a result, what she felt now was so much deeper and more real than anything she'd ever felt before. And she realized that any promises she'd made to herself to hold back her heart had already been broken. She'd fallen for his little girl—and was well on her way toward tumbling head over heels for Spencer again, too.

Brielle wasn't the only person to express concern when she learned that Kenzie had spent the previous day at Crooked Creek Ranch with Spencer.

"I warned you not to get involved with him again," her mother said grimly, as she tore the lettuce for a salad later Sunday afternoon.

"You warned me about every boy or man I ever showed any interest in," Kenzie pointed out.

"With good reason," Cheryl told her. "And Spencer already has one child born out of wedlock."

She bit her tongue, because she knew that coming to Spencer's defense would only convince her mother that she was halfway in love with him again. And maybe she was, and maybe it was a mistake, but she didn't need a lecture right now.

"He probably didn't even think about possible repercussions from his actions," Cheryl continued. "And didn't stick around long enough to find out."

Kenzie shook her head, unable to bite her tongue a minute longer. "You don't know anything about Spencer's relationship with Dani's mom."

"It's an all-too common story," Cheryl insisted bitterly.

"A handsome cowboy sweet-talks a lonely girl into his bed and then disappears when he can't handle the consequences."

The bitterness fairly dripped from her words, leading Kenzie to suspect that her mother's deep resentment toward Spencer might be about more than his relationship with Kenzie. In fact, it might not be about Spencer at all.

Growing up without a father, Kenzie had been full of questions that, for the most part, remained unanswered. But she was twenty-three years old now, and she figured she was entitled to the truth.

"Is that what happened to you?" she asked. "Was my father a rodeo cowboy?"

Her mother seemed startled by the question—or maybe she was just surprised that her daughter had dared to ask it. Over the years, Kenzie had mostly given up asking the questions her mother refused to answer. But this time, she didn't back down.

"Was my father a rodeo cowboy?" she asked again.

Cheryl pressed her lips together in a tight line. "You never had a father."

She nodded, acknowledging that it was true. But at the same time, she needed to know what had happened between her parents, why her father had left before she was even born. Why he'd never wanted her.

"You're right," she said. "But I need to know why."

Her mother shook her head. "I can't talk to you about this."

"Why not?"

"Because it hurts too much," Cheryl admitted, her voice quivering.

With anger? With sadness? How could Kenzie know when her mother always shut down her emotions? Especially when it came to anything about her father.

And she was tired of the secrecy and emptiness inside

her. "Can't you see how much the not knowing hurts me?" she implored.

Cheryl lifted her chin. "You know everything you need to know."

Kenzie disagreed—but she was tired of fighting for answers she obviously wasn't going to get.

"You know what hurts the most?" she asked her mother. "Remembering all the times over the years when you insisted that I could come to you, talk to you, about anything. Because every time I try to talk to you about this, you shut me down."

So instead of saying anything else, she walked out the door.

"Ke'zie! Ke'zie!"

Dani abandoned the Pocket Ponies she was playing with and ran over as soon as Spencer opened the door, wrapping her arms around Kenzie's legs and squeezing tight. He might have been envious of the enthusiastic greeting, but she'd been just as excited to see him when Linda dropped her off a few hours earlier.

"We're gonna have ice cweam," Dani told her. "You wanna have ice cweam with us?"

"I'd love some ice cream," Kenzie told her.

"With choc'ate sauce an' spwinkles?"

"Of course," she agreed.

"I didn't think I was going to see you today," Spencer remarked. And then, as if to remind her that she'd woken up in his bed that morning, he smiled and said, "Or should I say 'again today'?"

"I didn't think so, either," she said. "And I wasn't planning on it, but I had an argument with Cheryl and…somehow I found myself here."

He appreciated that she referred to her mother by her given name within earshot of Dani, having learned that any mention of "mom" or even "mother" could send his daughter into tears.

Spencer's brows lifted in silent question.

Kenzie just shook her head. "Long story."

"You look like you could maybe use a glass of wine instead of ice cream," he noted.

"Can I have a glass of wine with my ice cream?"

He rubbed her shoulders. "You can have whatever you want."

So she had wine and ice cream, but she suspected it was the comfort of being with Spencer and Dani that took most of the weight of the anger and frustration from her shoulders.

While Spencer was giving Dani her bath, Kenzie offered to unpack the boxes that Linda had brought over when she dropped off her granddaughter.

"Find anything interesting?" Spencer asked, after he deposited his pajama-clad daughter into her bed and tucked the covers around her.

"Actually, yes," Kenzie said. "Along with a lot of clothes that Dani probably outgrew a year ago, there was a box of keepsakes. Her ID bracelet from the hospital, a copy of her birth certificate, a lock of hair from her first haircut. And these."

"These" were envelopes—at least a dozen of them. They were bound together by a fat rubber band and addressed, in a distinctly feminine script, to:

Spencer Channing
c/o Crooked Creek Ranch
Haven, NV

"Maybe one of us will get some answers today," she said.

It was the only hint Kenzie had given him about the nature of her fight with her mother, and though he hoped she would open up and talk to him about it, he was admittedly distracted by the letters she'd given to him.

He thumbed through the stack of envelopes—eighteen of them, all addressed the same way but none ever sent. None even stamped.

The answers he'd been seeking might be in the pages. And if he didn't like the answers—well, at least he would know.

"Sto-wee, Daddy," Dani said impatiently.

Since the day they'd gone shopping, she'd started calling him "Daddy" much more easily and frequently—proof that she'd finally accepted his role in her life—and he never got tired of hearing it.

But Kenzie came to his rescue now, plucking Dani's favorite book from the shelf and asking, "Would it be okay if I read your story tonight?"

Dani's head bobbed up and down. "Ke'zie wead."

"Thanks." He brushed a light kiss on Kenzie's lips, then another on Dani's forehead, and carried the letters out to the living room.

He started with the one of top, confident it was the first one as the date corresponded with Dani's birthday.

Dear Spencer,

You're probably wondering why I'm reaching out to you now. It's been eight months since I last saw you and so much has changed in my life since we decided to go our separate ways. Even though I'm writing this letter to tell you some things you need to know, I can't promise that I'll actually find the courage to mail it. I hope I will. I hope I can be strong enough to tell you about our beautiful, perfect daughter who was born only a few hours ago.

I named her Daniel, after my dad, but I'm going to call her Dani...

He could almost hear Emily's voice as he read the words she'd written detailing the birth of their child. The second letter was dated a month later, the third another month after that and so on, with a new letter written each month throughout the first year of Dani's life. She recounted the highlights and milestones of their child's growth and development, her love for Dani evident in every word. But while they were interesting to read, he didn't get a sense of why she'd kept their daughter's existence a secret from him for so long.

By the time he opened the last envelope, he was torn between gratitude for the memories she'd shared with him and frustration that so many questions remained unanswered. When he unfolded the final pages, he was startled to note the date on the last letter, only a couple of days before Emily was killed.

Dear Spencer,

I registered Dani for preschool today. It was a shock to me, to accept that my baby isn't a baby anymore but a preschooler. As I filled out the paperwork, I realized that I may very well have made the biggest mistake of my life by not telling you about our daughter, by not giving her the opportunity to know her father. I hope and pray that it's not too late to rectify that mistake.

So on Monday, I'm going to bundle up all the letters I've written over the past three-and-a-half years, take them down to the post office and put them in the mail. And cross my fingers that Crooked Creek Ranch in Haven, Nevada, still belongs to your family.

If you want to meet your daughter after you've read these letters—and I hope you will—I know she would be thrilled. I also know that you'll probably have a thousand questions and just as many reasons to be furious with me. I'm going to try to answer some of those questions for you now.

I don't know if you're going to be angry or relieved that I granted you a reprieve from fatherhood. When I saw the plus sign on the pregnancy test, I wanted to call you. I definitely didn't want to make any decisions on my own—not about something so huge. Because—ohmygod—we were going to have a baby! And maybe I didn't know you well, but I knew you'd stand by me, whatever I wanted to do.

I wanted our baby, but I didn't ever want you to feel trapped by *my* choices…so I chose not to tell you. And not a single day has gone by since that I haven't wondered if it was the wrong choice and wished I could have given her not just all the love in my heart but a real family.

Having Dani changed everything for me, and I can't help but wonder if knowing you were a father— if knowing *her*—would have done the same for you. But I guess we'll find out soon enough.

I hope you can forgive me. More important, I hope you can be the father our little girl deserves.
Emily

Of course, she'd never put any of the letters in the mail, because she was killed before she'd had a chance to do so.

As Spencer refolded the pages and slid them back into the envelope, he silently promised Emily that he would do his best to honor her wishes.

Chapter Fourteen

While Spencer was reading Emily's letters, Kenzie stretched out beside Dani to read the little girl's favorite bedtime story. Usually by the time she got to "rock and rock and rock to sleep," Dani's eyes were closed. But not tonight.

"I think somebody had too much chocolate sauce on her ice cream."

"I like choc'ate sauce," Dani said.

Kenzie smiled and brushed the little girl's hair away from her face. "I know you do—almost as much as you like sprinkles."

Dani grinned and nodded.

"And all that sugar is keeping you awake."

"Can you wead the sto-wee again?"

"I've already read it twice."

"Thwee times!"

"Okay," Kenzie relented. "But only if you promise to close your eyes when I get to the part where they turn off the light."

The little girl patted her pillow, beside her head. "You cuddle with me?"

So Kenzie put her head down beside Dani's and opened the book again.

When she got to the part where the lights were turned out, Dani immediately squeezed her eyes shut. Smiling, Kenzie finished the story and set the book aside, then pulled the chain to turn off the bedside lamp.

"I love you, Ke'zie." The words were a quiet whisper in the darkness.

It was hard to speak when her throat was clogged with emotion, but she managed to whisper back, "I love you, too, Dani."

Because as much as she'd tried to fortify the walls around her heart to keep Spencer on the outside, she had no defenses against his little girl.

In the dim light that spilled into the room from the hall, she saw Dani's lips curve. A few minutes later, Kenzie suspected the child was finally asleep, but she decided to stay where she was for a little while longer, until she was certain.

Spencer stood in the doorway of his daughter's bedroom, a feeling of warm contentment spreading through him. Though Dani was tucked under the covers and Kenzie was reclined on top, they were snuggled close—two females who, in the course of only a few weeks, had managed to completely steal his heart. He wasn't entirely sure when or how it had happened, he only knew that it was true and he couldn't imagine his life without either of them.

They could be a family. Kenzie and him and Dani. He could give his little girl the family that her mother had only dreamed of for her—the family he was only beginning to realize that he wanted just as much.

He kissed Dani's forehead, then went around to the other side of the bed to lift Kenzie into his arms so that he could carry her to *his* bed, where she belonged.

But the woman wasn't as deeply asleep as the child, and her eyes immediately popped open.

"What—oh…Spencer."

"You were expecting someone else?"

"I expect you to put me down," she said, keeping her voice pitched low so as not to wake Dani.

"I'm not going to drop you," he assured her.

"I'm more worried that you're going to strain your shoulder."

"My shoulder is fine."

She finally relaxed against it. "Did you get your answers?"

"Yeah."

"I'm glad," she said.

He kicked his bedroom door closed, then sank down onto the mattress with her. In the darkness of the night, mouths met, clothes were shed and finally…bodies tangled together.

Afterward, he started to drift off to sleep with Kenzie in his arms, confident in the knowledge that he was exactly where he was supposed to be.

Kenzie had to go.

The longer she stayed, the more she gave of her heart, and she couldn't risk giving it all to Spencer again.

She shifted toward the edge of the mattress and started to gather her clothes.

"Stay," he said. "Please."

She shook her head. "That's not a good idea."

"Why not?"

"Because it would be confusing for Dani if she woke up in the middle of the night and found me in your bed," she said, and tugged on her panties.

"Aside from the fact that she'd love to have you here all day every day, she's not yet four," he pointed out. "I don't think she'd give it enough thought to register confusion."

"And Mrs. Powell would know if my car was parked outside all night."

"And would undoubtedly ask for all the juicy details the next day."

Yeah, Kenzie thought as she wiggled into her jeans, unable to deny that was a likely scenario there.

"Of course, anyone else could see my car there, too, and then word would inevitably get back to my mother," she said instead.

"And you could point out that her disapproval has only made me more appealing to you," he teased.

"Maybe she was the catalyst for this," she acknowledged, looking for her bra.

"The catalyst for what?" he asked, a hint of worry creeping into the question.

"The realization that I need some space."

"What are you talking about?" he demanded. "Space for what?"

"I've gotten too wrapped up in your life." She gave up on finding her bra and tugged her shirt over her head without it.

"That's ridiculous."

She shook her head. "I was upset about an argument I had with my mother, and what did I do?"

He looked blank.

"I raced over here," she told him. "And you immediately knew something was wrong. You even offered me a glass of wine and asked me if I wanted to talk."

"Still not seeing the problem."

"That's not us," she protested.

"Did you suddenly start speaking a different language? Because none of this is making any sense to me."

"We're supposed to be having a good time until you ride off into the sunset again," she reminded him. Because she'd counted the days on the calendar from his first day back in Haven to the start of the National Finals, and she'd been reassured by the six week timeline—certain she could maintain the barriers around her heart for that brief period.

"Is that what this is about?" he asked. "You're afraid that I'm going to pack up and leave again?"

Yes.

She shook her head. "No."

She needed him to pack up and leave again, before he broke her heart.

"Because I do want to go to Vegas for the Finals, but that will be my last competition," he assured her.

"It's not about Vegas," she said. "It's simply about your dreams and mine being incompatible."

"I don't think that's true."

"I'm a small-town girl with traditional ideas and simple plans." She spotted her bra, peeking out from under the bed, picked it up and stuffed it in her pocket.

"You want to get married and have a family," he guessed.

"Yes, I do," she said, refusing to apologize for the fact. "Not necessarily right now, but someday."

"So let's do it."

She blinked at him. "What?"

"Let's get married."

If only she could believe that he was asking for the right reasons. But no, even if he declared undying love, it wouldn't change her mind.

She needed distance.

She needed to protect her heart.

"Are you insane?" she asked him. "You don't respond to someone's request for space with an impromptu marriage proposal."

"Why not?" he challenged.

"Because exchanging vows is kind of the opposite of taking a step back," she pointed out.

"I don't believe you really want to take a step back," he said. "I think you're running scared, that this sudden desire for space is just an attempt to protect your heart because you offered it to me once before and I was stupid and careless with it."

Was he really that attuned to her thoughts and feelings or was he just taking a shot in the dark? Either way, his comment hit the bull's-eye. Which was only further proof that her heart was in serious danger and she needed to stick to her original plan.

"I care about you, Spencer, but I'm not going to fall in love with you again."

He shook his head, but there was a glint of amusement—and determination—in his eyes. "Honey, you can take all the steps back that you want, but you have to know I'm going to interpret that kind of statement as a challenge."

And, as he'd told her before, he never backed away from a challenge.

"It wasn't a challenge," she assured him.

"Too late to take it back now," he said.

"So what—you're going to make me fall in love with you so that you can add another tally to your 'win' column?"

He shook his head. "Do you really think I would toy with your emotions just to get a win?"

No, she didn't. Which begged the question: "Then what was that all about?"

"My only motivation for wanting you to fall in love with me is so that we can make plans for our future together."

What? Was he suggesting—

No. She cut off that thought before it had completely formed, before hope could bloom in her heart. Because there was no way he was saying—

"I love you, Kenzie. And I really hope that the next time I ask you to marry me, you'll say yes."

Spencer was optimistic that Kenzie would come around. She just needed some time to think about his proposal—to realize that she loved him as much as he loved her.

When two days went by with no word from her, he decided he couldn't just sit back and wait any longer. Familiar with her schedule, he decided to track her down at the clinic. But when he showed up at noon on Wednesday, Jillian confided that she'd had a cancellation and went for an early lunch.

Since lunch most likely meant Diggers', he headed to the Bar & Grill. She was seated alone in a booth, although the two menus on the table indicated that she was waiting for someone to join her.

He slid into the empty bench across from her.

"That seat is taken," she told him.

"And as soon as Megan gets here, I'll let her have it."

"How do you know I'm waiting for Megan?"

"Jillian told me," he admitted.

"You weren't on the schedule today."

"No, I stopped by to ask for your help with something," he told her.

"What?" she asked warily.

"Planning a birthday party for Dani."

"You know I'd do anything for Dani," she admitted—and which he'd been counting on. "But I really don't know anything about birthday parties for little girls."

"You have to know more than me," he said.

"Why?" she challenged.

"Because I know less than nothing," he admitted.

"Then ask your mom. Or your sister. Or Celeste," she said, throwing out alternatives for him to choose.

He shook his head. "I'm asking you, Kenzie."

"Why?" she asked again.

"Because this needing-some-space thing isn't working for me."

Kenzie couldn't deny that it wasn't working for her, either. It certainly wasn't helping her gain the emotional distance or even objectivity she wanted to attain. In fact, being away from Spencer and Dani only made her miss them more.

On the other hand, it had only been three days and she wasn't ready to throw in the towel just yet. Tempted—yes. In fact, she was tempted to not just throw in the towel but throw herself in his arms and lick him all over like a lollipop. Thankfully, she had a little more self-respect and self-restraint than that. She hoped.

"If I agree to do this—plan Dani's birthday party," she immediately clarified, "it's going to be on my terms."

"Anything you want," he promised.

"Okay. You give me the guest list and a budget and leave the details to me."

"I can do that," he agreed. "Why don't you stop by after work today and—"

"I'm sure you can email me the names and numbers."

"Well, of course, I can," he agreed. "But Dani would really love to see you."

So she stopped by on her way home from work, because she really wanted to see Dani, too. Then she ended up staying for dinner, because when she decided it was time to go, Spencer was taking Shake 'n Bake chicken out of the oven and there was more than enough to share. From there it was easy—maybe too easy—to fall into the familiar routines of eating and tidying up together, then getting Dani ready for bed.

While the little girl was being tucked in, Kenzie gathered her jacket and handbag. She grabbed the strap of her bag and pulled it toward her, causing several pieces of mail to spill onto the floor. Silently chastising herself for her clumsiness, she bent to retrieve the envelopes and flyers.

And paused when she saw the Genetix logo in the corner of one of the envelopes.

She got all kinds of junk mail attempting to solicit interest in various products and services, and she knew it could be something like that—one of those "type your DNA and determine your ancestry" sort of things. But when she moved that envelope to the top of the pile, she saw that it wasn't addressed to an unidentified occupant but specifically to "Spencer Channing—Personal & Confidential."

"Dani wants a glass of water," he said, returning to the kitchen. "This is part of her new routine—how many hoops can we make Daddy jump through before finally falling asleep?"

He reached into the cupboard for a cup, set it under the tap.

Kenzie stood silent, shocked by the implications of what was in her hand.

He shut off the tap. "Is something wrong?"

She turned the envelope so that he could see the logo. "Did you have a paternity test done?"

He was silent for a moment, as if considering his response.

Would he deny it?

Would she believe him if he did?

But then he nodded. "Yes, I did."

She knew it had nothing to do with her. Not really. And yet—she could barely swallow around the tightness in her throat.

"You disapprove," he guessed.

"I just...why?"

"For the obvious and usual reasons," he said cautiously.

She shook her head, not just disappointed but devastated by this confirmation. "Over the past few weeks...all the time I've spent with you and Dani... I actually thought you were stepping up to be the father she needs."

"I did. *I am.*"

"Unless and until the DNA results let you off the hook?" she challenged.

"That's not fair, Kenzie."

"What's not fair is letting her get attached to you if—"

"The attachment goes both ways," he interrupted to assure her.

"Then why the test?" she asked again.

"I just wanted to know for sure that I *am* her father."

"And if this paper says you're not?" she challenged.

It was a question he'd been asking himself since the doctor had swabbed the inside of his cheek.

He'd told himself he was seeking formal confirmation of paternity, so that no one could ever dispute his legal right to custody of Dani. But there had admittedly been a part of him that wondered "what if?"

He didn't want the life he'd had before Dani. He didn't want to go back to living out of a suitcase on the rodeo circuit.

He had no regrets about the way he'd lived the last five years of his life. It was what he'd wanted to do. He'd loved the excitement, the glory, the adulation. But even while he'd been basking in the sound of the crowd chanting his name, he'd known he couldn't live like that forever.

Still, he'd never thought he'd want to come home. He'd been so happy to ride out of town and yet, when his life had gone to hell, he'd felt drawn back here, as if pulled by invisible strings.

Or maybe the draw wasn't the town. Maybe it was—and had always been—Kenzie. Lord knows, of all the women he'd been with through the years, she was the one he'd never been able to get out of his mind.

Of course, he'd never actually been with Kenzie before he left Haven. The brief interlude in the hayloft when she was only sixteen had not ended the way either of them had intended—for which he could only be grateful. He could imagine the fallout if he'd actually taken the innocence of his little sister's best friend. Maybe she hadn't been untouched when he left, but she'd still been a virgin.

She wasn't that anymore. She was the woman he loved, the one he wanted to spend his life and share his family with.

"I don't give a damn what the report says." He took the

envelope from her and tore it in half, then the halves into quarters, to prove it.

Kenzie watched, not saying a word, as he tossed the four pieces into the wastebasket under the sink.

"When I decided to have the test done, I had some doubts," he confided. "And I wanted to be certain."

"And now?" she prompted.

"Now I know the results don't matter."

She didn't look convinced.

And her skepticism was both frustrating and infuriating. Hadn't he proven that he'd changed? How long was she going to make him pay for the mistakes of his past? Mistakes that weren't even his own. Because he sensed it was her personal history that was as much to blame for her distrust as anything he'd ever done.

"Dani *is* my daughter," he said to her now.

"Do you really believe that? Or are you just saying that because you think it's what I want you to say?"

"It's what I know, in my heart," he said. "Maybe, when Brett first suggested that I have the test done, I was still reeling from the news that I was a father. And maybe there was a part of me that wondered if it was true—and even hoped that it wasn't. Because I didn't know the first thing about raising a child and I was terrified that I would screw up and hey, wouldn't it be so much easier if it turned out that I wasn't her father then I could walk away and let someone else worry about screwing it up?

"But Emily chose me to raise Dani. No matter what that piece of paper says, she is my daughter. Over the past few weeks, I've realized that blood isn't everything. It's not even the most important thing. Linda's willingness to give up her granddaughter proves that.

"It's love that makes a family," he said, imploring her to understand. "It's love that matters. And even if that paper said I wasn't her father, I'd fight to keep her with me. Because I love her and she's mine in every way that matters.

"I'd fight to keep her," he said again. "And I'm going to fight to keep you, too."

Then he picked up the cup of water and took it to his daughter.

Kenzie suspected that she might have overreacted.

By the next morning, when the shock had worn off and the sense of betrayal had faded, she could acknowledge that Spencer's actions hadn't been unreasonable. But even if he hadn't done anything wrong, he hadn't been honest with her, and there were too many secrets in her life for her to readily forgive his deception.

But she wasn't going to let her anger and frustration get in the way of planning Dani's birthday celebration, and she was researching party games on the internet the following afternoon when her mother stopped by.

"Mom—what are you doing here?"

"I brought you a vanilla latte." Cheryl held up two cups bearing The Daily Grind logo.

Though Kenzie hadn't completely forgiven her mother for her determined silence on the issue of her father, she stepped away from the door to allow her entry. After twenty-three years, she felt that she was entitled to some answers, but she could hardly force Cheryl to give them.

"I thought you were working tonight," she said.

"Jacqui agreed to cover my shift."

"Why?" she wondered aloud.

"Because I thought we should talk." Cheryl perched on the edge of the sofa, her cup cradled in her hands. "Actually, Spencer called me this morning and suggested we talk."

Kenzie peeled back the lid on her latte. "I'd really rather not talk about Spencer."

"Okay," her mother agreed. "Then let's talk about your father."

Chapter Fifteen

"He wasn't a rodeo cowboy—he was a rancher," Cheryl began her story. "Actually, his father owned a ranch in Wyoming on which my dad—your grandfather—was the foreman."

Kenzie realized then that as tight-lipped as her mother had been on the subject of her daughter's father, she'd been just as silent on the topic of her own family—until now.

"We might have been friends growing up, except that his parents disapproved of us spending time together," Cheryl continued. "Of course, as we got older, Cody was less willing to abide by their wishes."

"Cody," Kenzie echoed, testing the sound. "That's his name?"

Her mother's eyes were filled with tears and regrets when she looked at Kenzie now. "I never even gave you that much, did I?"

She shook her head. "You never wanted to talk about him at all. And I understand that he broke your heart when he walked out on you—abandoning his pregnant wife to have and raise their child on her own."

"His name was Cody Dunham, and he did break my heart," Cheryl confirmed. "But the truth is…we were never married." She lifted her cup to her lips while she let Kenzie absorb that revelation. "It probably seems silly to you now, but twenty-four years ago, having a baby out of wedlock was a much bigger deal.

"A pregnant woman without a ring on her finger would be talked about, judged," her mother explained. "An expectant wife abandoned by her husband would be talked about, too, but in a different way. She would more likely be the subject of sympathy than scandalous gossip."

"So you lied about being married—even to me?"

"I didn't intend—" Cheryl shook her head, cutting off her own explanation. "No, I'm done making excuses. And yes, I lied to you. I lied to everyone.

"Cody did offer to marry me," she continued. "When I told him I was pregnant, he immediately suggested that we get married. And I immediately said yes, not just because I was pregnant but because I loved him.

"It wasn't until we went together to tell his parents about our plans that I found out he was already engaged."

"Oh, Mom." Kenzie didn't know what else to say.

"I was such a fool," Cheryl admitted softly. "I thought we were sneaking around because his parents disapproved of our relationship. I had no idea that we were sneaking around because he was planning to marry someone else.

"And when he told his parents that he'd proposed to me… they were furious and accused me of getting pregnant on purpose to trap their son into a marriage that, they assured me, they would never allow to happen.

"Cody tried to stand up to them. He pointed out that we were both over eighteen and didn't need their permission or approval. His defiance surprised them, and they immediately backtracked—suggesting that they would support our plans to be together if we promised to keep the news of my pregnancy quiet for a while longer, until they figured out the best way to end his engagement."

"Why do I get the feeling they weren't nearly as supportive as they pretended to be?" Kenzie wondered aloud.

Her mom managed a smile. "Because you're a lot smarter than I was."

"So what happened next?"

"Mrs. Dunham came to have a private chat with me," Cheryl confided. "And she promised that if I followed through on my plan to ruin her son's future, she'd see that my father was fired and my entire family evicted from their home."

"That's a lot to put on the shoulders of a teenager," Kenzie acknowledged.

"She obviously felt that she had a lot at stake—and she offered me a deal."

"What kind of deal?" Kenzie asked uneasily.

"They would provide a home for me and my baby if I agreed to leave Wyoming before anyone knew—and without even telling my parents—that I was pregnant."

"Is that how you ended up in Nevada?"

Cheryl nodded. "I didn't immediately agree to her terms, though. I didn't want to leave my family, so I promised I would never identify the father of my baby if I could stay. But my proposal was rejected out-of-hand, probably because they were worried my child might bear some family resemblance, and then how would they deny the truth?"

"Do I...look anything like...him?" Kenzie asked.

Her mother shook her head. "You're almost a carbon copy of your maternal grandmother when she was your age."

The grandmother she'd never known, because her father's mother had taken that option away from her.

"I'm so sorry, Mom," she said, her throat thick with tears.

"Don't," Cheryl said firmly. "You have absolutely nothing to apologize for."

"But...you gave up your family for me."

Her mother touched a hand to her arm. "You are my family."

Kenzie set her forgotten latte aside to put her arms around her mother. "I love you, Mom. Always and forever."

"I love you, too," Cheryl said. "Because you are, always and forever, the best thing that ever happened to me."

Spencer had conscripted Kenzie to help with Dani's birthday party because he figured it would ensure ongoing contact leading up to the big day. His plan was thwarted by her determination to take over the planning—and by his own secrets. So he decided to give her some of the space she said she wanted, in the hope that she would miss him... and maybe eventually forgive him, too.

He was surprised when she called early on the morning of Dani's party and asked him to stop by Crooked Creek, where she was setting up for the party. She was filling pink balloons with helium when he walked in.

"I'm not sure if I should tell you to butt out of my life or say thank you," she said in lieu of a greeting.

"Then how can I know if I should say 'not likely' or 'you're welcome'?"

She pulled the balloon off the nozzle and handed it to him to tie. "My mother finally told me about my father."

"Ah." He looped ribbon onto the knotted end of the balloon, to secure it to the weight.

She continued to fill balloons while she summarized her mother's revelations—probably a lot more balloons than were needed, but he sensed it was easier for Kenzie to talk while her hands were busy.

"So my mother cut herself off from her entire family because she believed it was the only way she could give me a decent life."

"What about your father?" he asked. "You'd think he would wonder why she suddenly disappeared."

She nodded. "About a year later, he tracked her down. He'd been married for several months already by then and had just discovered that his wife was pregnant. Apparently that got him thinking about the other girl he'd knocked up, and he decided to find her, to tell her how sorry he was that she'd miscarried their baby."

"What?"

"Yeah, he was surprised, too, when he discovered a six-month-old crawling around on the floor and realized his parents had lied to him."

"You know this story has more plot twists than *The Light of Dawn*," he noted.

She managed a smile. "I thought the same thing when my mom was telling it to me."

"So what happened when he realized you were his daughter?" he prompted gently.

"Cheryl said he cried and he apologized and he begged her to forgive him. But, of course, he didn't offer to leave his now-pregnant wife to marry my mother, so she firmly but politely asked him to leave.

"Six months later, on my first birthday, he showed up again and confided that his wife had miscarried. So Cheryl invited him to come in for a piece of cake." She abandoned her task for a moment to retrieve a photo from her handbag.

He studied the image of the little girl sitting on a man's knee, then he looked at Kenzie, and back at the photo again. "You don't look anything like him."

She smiled. "I know. Apparently I'm a carbon copy of my maternal grandmother."

"And after your birthday…did you ever see him again?"

She shook her head. "But surprisingly, his parents honored the terms of the agreement they'd made with my mother, and on my eighteenth birthday, they sent the deed to the house. The next day, she went to the bank to mortgage the property so that I could go to college."

He tied up the last balloon. "How do you feel about all of this?"

"I honestly don't know," she confided. "Everything just seems to be a tangle of emotions. I'm glad I know, of course. Maybe the answers aren't what I'd hoped for, but at least I know.

"And that's my life story."

"That's only part of your history," he told her. "Your life story is still being written, and I have some pretty good ideas for the next chapter."

"What kind of ideas?" Having emptied the tank of helium, she started to group the balloons into clusters.

"Well, I was thinking the heroine might enjoy a sizzling hot romance with a sexy bull rider."

"She probably would," Kenzie agreed. "But I think she pretty much blew her chance at that." She looked at him, all the emotion she refused to acknowledge shining in her eyes. "Didn't she?"

He shook his head. "You didn't blow anything, Kenzie."

"I came down on you pretty hard about the paternity test," she acknowledged.

"You were disappointed in me," he noted. "Probably because, from the beginning, you've been my biggest cheerleader with respect to my relationship with Dani. You had faith in me even when I didn't have faith in myself. And I should have trusted you enough to share my doubts and fears with you."

"I had faith in you because it was obvious to me, right from the beginning, how much she means to you," Kenzie said. "Because you stepped up for her, to be the father that she needed."

"Because I love her," he said simply.

"I know."

"So you believe that I love Dani?"

"Of course, I believe it," she said, eager to reassure him.

"Your feelings would be obvious to anyone who sees you with her."

He nodded slowly. "Then I guess the question is—if you can believe that I love Dani, why can't you believe that I love you, too?"

Spencer decided that if Kenzie ever wanted to make a career change, she had a promising future as a party planner. Dani was absolutely thrilled with every part of the celebration at Crooked Creek, where the birthday girl and her young guests could enjoy pony rides in the corral in addition to games and crafts in the house.

He hadn't been sure Gramps would accede to the request to hold the party at the ranch—and especially inside the house that he'd moved out of three years earlier, after his wife's passing. But the old man had surprised Spencer, saying the house had been too quiet for too long, and maybe it was time for some new life around the place.

Kenzie had transformed the main floor living room into party central. In addition to the balloons, there were streamers and Happy Birthday banners, party hats and noisy horns, lots of snacks and drinks and an enormous cake—with layers of chocolate and vanilla and sprinkles on top. In addition to taking care of all those details, Kenzie had supplemented the guest list he'd provided so that Dani was able to celebrate her special day with kids her own age—including her new BFF, Paris.

But those weren't the only unexpected guests in attendance.

"You were surprised to see us," his mother commented, stealing him away from the party for a private word in the den.

"A little," he admitted.

"Because your father and me were never at any of your birthday parties?"

And because, for that reason, he hadn't even put their

names on the guest list. Obviously Kenzie had corrected that oversight. Without telling him.

"I'm glad you're here," he said, and realized he meant it. "But…a pony? Don't you think that's a little over the top?"

He hadn't known about their extravagant gift until Gramps brought Daisy out of the barn for the pony rides and the animal was adorned with a big pink bow around her neck and an oversized tag that read, To Dani—Love Grandma & Grandpa. It had taken some explaining to make Dani understand that it meant that Daisy was actually her pony now and would stay at Crooked Creek Ranch forever.

"It didn't seem like so much," Margaret said, "considering all the birthdays and Christmases we've missed."

And then he got it. "Sixteen T-shirts."

His mother looked understandably baffled by his remark. "I'm sorry?"

"It was something that Kenzie once pointed out to me," he told her.

"So…you and Kenzie?" she prompted.

"I'm working on it."

"I know it's a little late in the game to be offering any kind of motherly advice," she told him. "But whatever it takes—do it."

"Not overly helpful, but I'll keep it in mind."

"And remember, nothing worthwhile is ever easy."

He nodded. "The last few weeks with Dani have certainly taught me that."

She smiled, a little wistfully. "You're already a much better parent to her than I ever was to you."

"I think I had a pretty good life growing up," he said, unable to directly dispute her claim.

"No thanks to me," Margaret said. "I was a horrible mother."

"I wouldn't say horrible," Spencer teased, attempting to inject some levity into their conversation.

His mother rewarded the effort with a small smile, but

then her expression turned serious again. "I thought parenting would come naturally, but it didn't. Not to me. I know you think I preferred to be at work rather than at home—and maybe that was true, but only because I knew what I was doing there. At the office, I was competent and capable. At home, I was completely inept."

"I'm sure that's not true," he said, wondering what had caused his mother's sudden introspection and self-flagellation.

"It *is* true," she insisted. "Honestly, I don't know what I would have done if Celeste hadn't been there. She had the maternal instincts I lacked. And while I was, of course, desperately grateful to her for stepping in to help, the ease with which she did the simplest tasks only made me more aware of my own inadequacies. The result was that I started to spend more and more time at the office and less and less at home."

"Why are you telling me this now?" he wondered.

"I'm trying to help you see that the rodeo is your office. It's where you feel competent and capable."

"So that's what this is about," he realized. "You're trying to convince me not to go back on the road." And while he was starting to think that the National Finals would be the end of his bull-riding career, he hadn't yet confided that possibility to his family—mostly because he didn't know what he'd do next.

"I have my own selfish reasons for wanting you to stay in Haven," she acknowledged. "But disregarding those for the moment, what kind of life would it be for a child?"

It was a question he'd been wrestling with since he'd learned of his daughter's existence.

"And what happens when it's time for her to go to school? Obviously Dani would be welcome to stay with us," Margaret continued, without giving him a chance to respond. "But then you'd only see her three or four times a year, and I don't think that would make either of you happy."

She was right about that. Competing on the circuit meant

being away from home for weeks—sometimes months—at a time. And after missing most of the first four years of her life, there was no way he could be away from Dani for so long.

But if he wasn't a bull rider, what was he?

"Daddy?"

He realized, when he heard his daughter's quiet voice in conjunction with a gentle tug on his shirt, the answer was just that simple.

He was her daddy—and that was the most important job in the world.

He scooped her into his arms. "What's up, birthday girl?"

"I wanna 'nother piece of cake."

"Hmm…what did Kenzie say?" he asked, suspecting she'd tried that route first.

"She said ask Daddy."

He chuckled. "Okay. Let me finish talking to Grandma, then we'll get you another piece of cake."

He set her back down again and she raced off.

"Watching you with Dani, I've been given a tiny glimpse of everything I missed out on while you and your brother and sisters were growing up," Margaret confided. "The first time I met her, I thought of you at the same age. And I realized then that I always thought I'd have time to make it up to you, to be a better parent. But that window of opportunity closed a long time ago. You're not my little boy anymore—you're a grown man now with a child of your own."

"There are times when that still surprises me, too," he acknowledged.

She opened the desk drawer to retrieve a legal-sized envelope that she'd obviously tucked away earlier.

"What's that?"

"It's a gift for you in honor of your daughter's birthday."

Spencer lifted the flap and pulled out a single page, his gaze immediately drawn to the bold letters in the middle of the page: *NEVADA QUIT CLAIM DEED*.

His brows drew together as he scanned the rest of the page. He saw his name and the legal description of what he guessed was a parcel of land. "I don't understand."

"You keep saying that riding bulls is all you know how to do. Your grandfather thinks you just need a chance to try something different.

"That's the deed for this house and the land it sits on, plus a few more acres. This could be the opportunity of a lifetime to give a good life to your daughter. The only question is—do you want it?"

While Spencer was in the den with his mother, Kenzie was in the kitchen, tidying up, when she heard footsteps behind her.

"I thought I'd find you in here," Helen said. "Women always seem to gravitate toward the kitchen at social events."

As Dani's occasional babysitter and Kenzie's long-time friend, she'd been pleased by the invitation to the little girl's party and thrilled to attend.

"I'm just wrapping up the leftover cake," Kenzie told her.

"Individual slices?"

"For the guests to take home," she explained.

"Well, then, let me give you a hand."

"I've got it. You should go back to the party—and flirting with Mr. Blake."

"There's something wrong with a woman if she can't enjoy a little flirtation with a handsome cowboy," Helen said. "I mean, Jesse Blake's no Brock Lawrie, but he's got a nice smile beneath that bristly moustache."

"So go on back out there and make him smile," Kenzie urged.

"I will," Helen promised. "As soon as you tell me why you're hiding out from Jesse's grandson."

"I'm not," she denied.

"I've known you a lot of years, Kenzie Atkins, and as

far as I know, you've never told me an outright lie—until right now."

"I'm wrapping cake," she insisted.

"The cake is nothing more than a convenient ruse."

"Okay, fine, the cake is a ruse."

"Now we're getting somewhere," Helen said.

"And I'm hiding in the kitchen because being out there—with Spencer and Dani...it hurts."

Her friend seemed surprised by this admission. "It hurts to be with them?"

She sighed wistfully. "No, it hurts because I want so much to be part of their family."

"And Spencer told you that's not going to happen?" Helen suggested, when Kenzie didn't elaborate on her response.

"No," she said again. "He's letting me believe that I can have everything I ever wanted."

"Well, that's just cruel, isn't it?"

Kenzie managed to smile through her tears. "You think I'm being ridiculous."

"Maybe. A little." Helen slid an arm across her shoulders. "It's okay to be scared," she assured her. "It's not okay to let your fear hold you back from going after what you want."

She was thinking about those words when Spencer found her in the kitchen a short while later.

"All the guests are gone and Dani is in a sugar coma on the sofa in the living room," he told her.

"You're the one who said yes to the second piece of cake," she pointed out.

"I did," he confirmed. "I'm getting better at saying no, but...well, it's her birthday."

Kenzie nodded, understanding.

"And I don't think it's one she'll ever forget—thanks to you."

"I didn't do so much."

"You did everything," he said. "And every time I tried

to steal a minute with you today, you were running here or there."

"Well, you managed to corner me now," she said lightly.

"Then I'll say thank you now, for everything you did."

"You're welcome."

He framed her face in his hands and kissed her gently. "I love you, Kenzie."

She closed her eyes, so that he wouldn't see her tears. So that he wouldn't see the truth of her own feelings.

"Is it the words or my feelings that make you uncomfortable?" he asked gently.

"I just...this isn't the time or the place."

"To tell you that I love you? Or for you to finally admit that you love me, too?"

"We're supposed to be taking a step back," she reminded him.

"That was never my idea."

"You need to think about this as much as I do," she argued.

"The only thing I need is you."

Her heart stuttered. She told herself to remain strong. "You don't need me, Spencer. And if you took some time to think about it, you'd probably realize you don't love me, either."

"Kenzie," he said, speaking in the same deliberate and patient tone he used to explain a difficult concept to his daughter. "I'm not the kind of guy who casually throws those words around. In fact, I've never said them to another woman, because I've never felt about anyone else the way I feel about you."

"I've never felt this way about anyone else, either," she admitted.

He smiled then. "Say that you'll marry me, Kenzie. Give us another reason to celebrate today."

"I want to say yes," she told him. "More than I've ever wanted anything."

"Then say yes," he urged.

"I guess I just need to know, if I do say yes…then what?"

"Then I put the ring on your finger and we set a date for our wedding." And he pulled a stunning diamond solitaire out of his pocket.

Her breath caught in her throat. She wanted to jump up and down and say "Yes! Please!" but there were more important issues to be decided than rings and dates. "That all sounds wonderful," she agreed. "But then what?"

"I don't actually have the next five years of our lives planned out," he told her, evidently not understanding the source of her concern.

"Let's start with the next year," she suggested. "Will you go back on the circuit?"

"No," he answered without hesitation. "After the National Finals Rodeo in Vegas, I'm done."

"What if you change your mind?"

"Kenzie, I asked you to marry me because I want to be with you. Putting a ring on your finger and then spending the better part of the year traveling around the country would take me away from you. You and Dani."

"We could come with you," she suggested.

"Why would you offer to do that?" he wondered.

"Because I don't want you to give up your dream."

"My dreams are different now," he told her. "I'm ready to be done with that life. I want a home, a family. You, me and Dani, together forever."

"You're not going the miss the adrenaline rush, the roar of the crowds, the adulation of hordes of fans?"

"I'm hoping I'll get plenty of adulation from my wife and our daughter."

As if his proposal hadn't already choked her up, the idea of becoming not just his wife but Dani's stepmother had the tears that filled her eyes spilling over. "I don't know about adulation," she said. "But I can promise that we'll love you."

"Even better," he said, and kissed her. Then he drew back. "But I'm still waiting for you to say yes."

She lifted her arms to link them behind his head. "Yes," she finally said in response to his question as she drew his mouth down to hers. "Definitely yes."

Epilogue

Several months later

The renovated barn marked with the stylized logo of Channing Horse Trainers was only one of the many changes that had taken place at Crooked Creek Ranch since Spencer had finally decided on a plan for his future and officially opened for business. He'd shamelessly traded on his pseudo-celebrity status to draw clients to his door, but it was proven results that kept them coming back.

The old farmhouse that had originally belonged to his great-grandparents showed signs of new life, too. Curtains fluttered in the breeze of the open windows, flowers bloomed in the pots lined up on the porch and a bright pink bike with a basket on the front and training wheels on the back was abandoned by the steps. Other toys were scattered here and there—a soccer ball, a half-finished puzzle, countless Pocket Ponies. Because no matter how many times he told his now four-and-a-half-year-old daughter to put her stuff away, she rarely remembered to do so.

Kenzie had assured him that Dani wasn't being defiant, that leaving her stuff scattered around was a sign that Dani felt comfortable and settled in what was now their home. He wasn't entirely convinced of the reasoning, but he couldn't deny that his daughter was thriving at Crooked Creek Ranch. Since her arrival in Haven eight months earlier, she'd grown in so many wonderful ways, absolutely basking in the attention of her doting aunts and uncles and grandparents. She continued to enjoy visits with her maternal grandmother when Nana wasn't traveling with her husband, and she'd taken to calling Kenzie's mom "Nana Too."

Because while Cheryl Atkins might have taken some time to warm up to Spencer, the same could not be said about her relationship with Dani. In fact, Kenzie's mother and his daughter had immediately become members of a mutual admiration society.

An even bigger surprise was the recent peace between Kenzie's mom and her dad. With Spencer's support and encouragement, Kenzie had finally reached out to her biological father, who'd been thrilled by the contact. Kenzie still had some reservations and resentments—justifiable, in Spencer's opinion—but they were slowly getting to know one another.

There was no doubt that coming home was the best thing Spencer could have done for his daughter, but it had worked out pretty well for him, too. He was enjoying the company of his family and friends, the challenges of his new business and the numerous and pleasurable benefits that went along with the platinum band on the third finger of his left hand.

At the wedding, Jay, as best man, had commended the bride for catching her cowboy in only six weeks. Then Brielle, as maid of honor, stood up to clarify that it was actually "seven years and six weeks." Of course, everyone had laughed at that. And maybe it was true that Kenzie had fallen in love with him first, but Spencer knew it wasn't possible that she loved him more.

And yet, there were occasional moments when he couldn't help but think about the life he'd left behind. Such as when he'd stopped by The Trading Post and spotted a flyer that advertised The Silver State Stampede pinned to the community board. Or when he'd been scrolling through the channels on TV and caught a broadcast of the Xtreme Bulls Tour. In those moments, he could almost hear the approving roar of the crowd in his ears and feel the unrestrained power of the beast beneath him. And he wondered if he might someday regret hanging up his spurs at the peak of his career.

Today, it had been a phone call from a long-time friend and fellow competitor who was on his way to an event in Reno. But the wondering only lasted for about half a minute, until Spencer walked into the kitchen and saw his sexy wife helping their adorable daughter measure and mix the various ingredients scattered over the butcher-block table.

Because in that moment, his heart filled with so much happiness and love there wasn't room for anything else.

"We're makin' muffins!" Dani announced happily.

Her enthusiasm made him smile. Apparently it was another testament to how well she'd adjusted to her new surroundings, that his shy, quiet child had turned into an exuberant whirlwind who did everything at maximum speed and full volume.

"What kind of muffins?" he asked.

"B'nana nut, cuz they're Nana Too's fav'rite—and mine, too."

"I thought you liked chocolate chip best."

She nodded, the blond pigtails on either side of her head bobbing up and down. "We're puttin' choc'ate chips in the b'nana nut."

"The best of both worlds," he mused.

Kenzie sent him a smile as she handed Dani an egg to crack.

"How's Duchess?" she asked, referring to the pregnant mare he'd gone out to the barn to check.

"Definitely in labor," he said.

She was immediately concerned. "Shouldn't you be with her?"

"Nah, Gramps is keeping an eye on her." His grandfather continued to live in the old bunkhouse and manage his small herd of cattle, but he also enjoyed helping Spencer with the horses now and again.

"I hope you aren't so quick to abdicate responsibilities when your wife is in labor," Kenzie said.

"Wild horses wouldn't be able to drag me away," he promised.

"We'll see," she mused.

The sparkle that lit her beautiful gray eyes told him more than the words, but he tried to keep a rein on his emotions—just in case he was misinterpreting her remark.

"When will we see?" he asked cautiously.

Her lips curved. "My guess would be about seven and a half months."

Joy filled his heart—so much that he felt as if it might burst out of his chest. He took the mixing spoon out of her hand and gave it to Dani, then he pulled Kenzie into his arms. "You're sure?"

She nodded. "I took a test this morning."

"Are you feeling okay? Maybe you should be sitting down."

She chuckled softly. "I think maybe *you* need to be sitting down—you look a little dazed."

"I feel a little dazed."

He thought fleetingly about Griff's call again and realized he didn't envy his friend at all. Because there wasn't a buckle shiny enough or purse big enough that could compare to everything he had in this room right now—or any of the adventures he knew were yet to come.

"And a lot like I just won the National Finals Rodeo for the tenth time."

"Then you can retire happily now?" Kenzie teased, obviously remembering that ten titles had been his original career goal.

"I'm already retired." He brushed his lips over hers in a lingering kiss. "And you already made me the happiest man in the world."

* * * * *

MILLS & BOON

Coming next month

CINDERELLA'S NEW YORK CHRISTMAS
Scarlet Wilson

Leo finished the call. New York. He'd wanted to go back there for days. But somehow he knew when he got there, the chances of getting a flight back to Mont Coeur to spend Christmas with his new family would get slimmer and slimmer.

Here, he'd had the benefit of a little time. Everything in New York was generally about work, even down to the Christmas charity ball he was obligated to attend. As soon as he returned to the States…

His stomach clenched. The Christmas ball. The place he always took a date.

For the first time, the prospect of consulting his little black book suddenly didn't seem so appealing.

'Nearly done.' Anissa smiled as he approached.

'I have to go back to New York.'

Her face fell. 'What?'

She was upset. He hated that. He hated that fleeting look of hurt in her eyes.

'It's business. A particularly tricky deal.'

Anissa pressed her lips tight together and nodded automatically.

The seed of an idea that had partially formed outside burst into full bloom in his head. He hated that flicker of pain he'd seen in her eyes when she'd talked about being in Mont Coeur and being permanently reminded of what she'd lost.

Maybe, just maybe he could change things for her. Put a little sparkle and hope back into her eyes. Something that he ached to feel in his life too.

'Come with me.' The words flew out of his mouth.

Her eyes widened. 'What?'

He nodded, as it all started to make sense in his head. 'You said you've never really had a proper holiday. Come with me. Come and see New York. You'll love it in winter. I can take you sightseeing.'

Anissa's mouth was open. 'But...my job. I have lessons booked. I have chalets to clean.'

He moved closer to her. 'Leave them. See if someone can cover. I have a Christmas ball to attend and I'd love it if you could come with me.' His hands ached to reach for her, but he held himself back. 'I called you Ice Princess before, how do you feel about being Cinderella?'

He could see her hesitation. See her worries.

But her pale blue eyes met his. There was still a little sparkle there. Still a little hope for him.

Her lips turned upwards. 'Okay,' she whispered back as he bent to kiss her.

Continue reading
CINDERELLA'S NEW YORK CHRISTMAS
Scarlet Wilson

Available next month
www.millsandboon.co.uk

Copyright ©2018 Susan Wilson

COMING SOON!

We really hope you enjoyed reading this book. If you're looking for more romance, be sure to head to the shops when new books are available on

Thursday
6th September

To see which titles are coming soon, please visit
millsandboon.co.uk

MILLS & BOON

LET'S TALK
Romance

For exclusive extracts, competitions
and special offers, find us online:

f facebook.com/millsandboon

⊙ @millsandboonuk

🐦 @millsandboon

Or get in touch on 0844 844 1351*

For all the latest titles coming soon, visit
millsandboon.co.uk/nextmonth

*Calls cost 7p per minute plus your phone company's price per minute access char

Want even more
ROMANCE?

Join our bookclub today!

'Mills & Boon books, the perfect way to escape for an hour or so.'

Miss W. Dyer

'Excellent service, promptly delivered and very good subscription choices.'

Miss A. Pearson

'You get fantastic special offers and the chance to get books before they hit the shops'

Mrs V. Hall

**Visit millsandbook.co.uk/Bookclub
and save on brand new books.**

MILLS & BOON